DAMENGIN

JENNY WELLINGTON

Published in Australia by Sid Harta Books & Print Pty Ltd,
ABN: 34632585293
23 Stirling Crescent, Glen Waverley, Victoria 3150 Australia
Telephone: +61 3 9560 9920, Facsimile: +61 3 9545 1742
E-mail: author@sidharta.com.au

First published in Australia 2022
This edition published 2022
Copyright © Jenny Wellington 2022
Cover design, typesetting: WorkingType (www.workingtype.com.au)

Jenny Wellington
Damengin
ISBN: 978-1-925707-85-4
pp392

ABOUT THE AUTHOR

A former journalist, Jenny Wellington lives on a farm near Kenilworth in Queensland with her husband Peter where they breed Angus and Droughtmaster cattle. She negotiates the paddocks in her trusty old Landrover assisted by a menagerie of dogs, including three kelpies and two Jack Russells.

During her years spent working as a country reporter, Jenny gained firsthand knowledge of the ups and downs, as well as the "goings on" in small country towns. She also met dozens of hilarious and lovable characters, all of which form the foundation of *Damengin*, her first book.

CONTENTS

CHARACTERS

Paddy Murphy	Owner of Damengin's only pub who is bankrolling most of the shire
Mary Murphy	His sister an alcoholic nun
Billy Murphy	His son home from mustering up north
Bomber Reed	Damengin's Mayor a former Wallaby and owner of Redlands Station
Teddy Reed	His selfish playboy son
Annabel Grey	Bomber's sister married to shire clerk Shifty Grey
Huw Hawtrey	A corrupt Bank Manager
Audrey Hawtrey	His wife a social butterfly and dreadful snob
Timmy Hawtrey	Their son a frustrated ballet dancer
Deidre (Dee) Hawtrey	Their horse- mad out of control daughter

Claude Hewlett	Dee's godfather and chairman of Australia's Provincial Bank
Ben Bangor	Owner of Abington Station who shoots Roos to keep the banks at bay
Felicity 'Fee' Fluke	His Greenie neighbour whose mission is to save the kangaroos
Sid Luxton	Wizened old bloke who lets Fee Fluke live in his old shearing quarters
Angus Wilton-Smith	Drop-dead gorgeous owner of the district's biggest property
Millicent Wilton-Smith	His stuck-up mum
Nurse Phoebe Taylor	Hectare hunter looking for a rich husband
Sam Spink	Alcoholic editor of the Damengin Star
Maggie Spink	His sister, the Hospital Matron, adored by everyone
Masie Mattens	Hardworking owner of the town's IGA
Chloe Mattens	Her teenage daughter with raging hormones who drives her crazy

Dickie Davis	The town's only doctor a ditherer who can't make a decision
Geoffrey (shifty) Grey	Shire Clerk a crook married to Bomber Reed's sister Annabel.
Dolly McIntyre	His oversexed and underqualified secretary
Simon (Scrooge) McKay	Council Treasurer so crooked he couldn't lie straight in bed
Micky Dixon	Devious property developer, chair of council's planning committee
Cyril Rowe	Dodgy Council Works Foreman
Phil Martin	His partner in crime shire engineer
Scorcher	Head of a notorious bikie gang
Percy Plod	Local copper who spends his days watching soapies

CHAPTER 1

CIVIC MATTERS

Damengin Pub owner Paddy Murphy doused his head under the water tap in the yard and grabbed a towel. Hot and dusty, he had just returned from dropping feed off to what was left of his sheep at his property Paddylea, to go to a special meeting of the Damengin Shire Council. The entire district was staggering with the effects of the worst drought in living memory. Paddocks had turned to dust, everywhere the carcasses of sheep and cattle rotted in the burning heat, dams were dust bowls and trees blackened and died. Properties were being abandoned and banks were like vultures hovering and waiting. The only help lay in gaining drought relief from the government but despite numerous applications, there had been nothing forthcoming.

'It's not bloody good enough,' Paddy said running a comb through his wet hair and dragging on a clean shirt.

He pulled on his still dusty boots and headed down the

street to the town's council chambers where all hell had broken out. Around the large oval table people were shouting and yelling and the town's mayor, Bomber Reed was on his feet and red in the face. He banged his hammer on the table.

'For Christ's sake will you bloody well shut up, let's get some order. Now, where the hell is Paddy?' he asked.

'Right here old mate,' Paddy yelled striding into the room. Nodding to Bomber, he threw his battered hat on the hook behind the door and sat down at the large oval table.

Following Paddy through the door was editor and owner of the *Damengin Star*, Sam Spink who wandered over to the rickety old Press table and sat down dragging out his notebook and pencil.

'Morning, Bomber,' he called out, 'you're making a lot of noise.'

Bomber's large red face cracked into a grin.

'Good to see you, Sam,' he said. 'Should be some interesting stuff this morning if I can get this rabble to shut it.'

Putting on his glasses, he looked around the table.

'Right now,' he said banging his hammer on the gavel, 'let's have less noise. Councillor Fluke and you, Councillor Dixon, shut up or I'll throw you through the bloody door.'

Councillor Fee Fluke jumped to her feet, her skinny frame shaking with rage. 'How dare you speak to me like that?' she hissed. 'Apologise at once.'

'Oh, for God's sake,' Bomber said shaking his head sadly. 'Councillor Fluke, I apologise, now will you please sit down and keep quiet.'

'I declare this special meeting of the Damengin Shire Council open. Shire Clerk, please read the minutes of the last meeting,' he said sitting down and wiping the sweat from his face with a large spotted handkerchief.

Shire Clerk Geoffrey Grey, or Shifty as he was called behind his back, stood up and opened a huge file. Setting his glasses on the end of his long thin nose, he coughed importantly and began to read the previous month's minutes in a flat expressionless voice.

Around the table councillors sighed with boredom and began cracking jokes and scribbling on their pads. On and on he droned until finally Bomber could stand it no more.

'How much more of this bureaucratic drivel do we have to listen to?' he said.

Shifty looked at him blankly. 'I don't understand,' he said in a pained voice.

'The mayor's right, it's absolute garbage and you know it,' Paddy said almost drowned out with everyone yelling in agreement.

Bomber stood up. 'I second what Councillor Murphy said. Now cut out the crap and tell us when the drought relief is coming.'

Shifty looked round the table and realising the game was up, he closed his file and moved that the minutes be accepted as read.

'Right, I second the move,' Bomber said quickly. 'Thank you Shire Clerk, now let's get down to work and sort out what's going on with the bloody Feds.'

Bomber had been Mayor of Damengin for twenty of his sixty-two years. A former Wallaby fullback, he was a huge bloke with massive shoulders and a thick bull neck. His once blond hair had receded backwards but his large face, reddened by years of hard work in the hot sun and which featured a nose broken one too many times was still attractive.

Like almost all the district's graziers, Bomber's sheep station Redlands was suffering the ravages of drought and he was battling on with no help from his playboy son Teddy who was swanning around Brisbane spending the trust money left to him by his mum.

Councillor Dickey Davis, the town's only doctor, glared at Bomber as he sat down rustling his agenda.

'In future I insist the mayor refrains from using profanities,' he said. 'I find it offensive.'

Dithering Dickey as he was known because he could never make a decision and was almost always late, hated Bomber with a passion. Thin and stooped from peering down throats and into ears, he wore horn-rimmed glasses and had a long pointy nose and thin mouth. He had worn the same pinstriped suit for as long as anyone remembered and was looked after by his housekeeper Annie Smith who kept him clean and fed. His former wife Susie had fled for greener pastures years ago.

The only person to pay any attention to him apart from Annie, who knew which side of her bread was buttered and who paid her wages, was Matron Maggie Spink, who had a kind heart and felt sorry for him. Dickey spent most of his leisure hours devouring the classics and had Maggie on a pedestal so high that no earthly being including himself, could ever attain her.

Bomber banged his gavel. 'My dear Councillor Davis,' he said sneering, 'please accept my humble apologies for offending your delicate disposition. Now let's get on with it, Councillor Matten, the Finance Report, please.'

Councillor Maisie Matten or 'Loose Lips' as she was known, smoothed her skin-tight skirt seductively over her hips, shook her blond curls before smiling at Bomber and giving him a wink.

Bomber blushed and tried to concentrate as Maisie began reading the report of the council's finances; like most of the town, he adored her even if she was a habitual gossip. Tell Maisie and you tell the world but who could resist her pretty face and those gorgeous blue eyes that twinkled with fun but welled with tears for a hard luck story.

She owned the town's only grocery shop, which, since the drought, was buckling under the weight of unpaid bills. Fifteen years ago, her husband, a drop kick from down south, had bolted leaving behind his gambling debts, a massive overdraft and a tiny baby. After years of hard work Maisie had brought the business into the black but now was barely surviving and the baby was a teenager called Chloe who drove her nuts.

As Chair of Finance, Maisie didn't have a clue about the complicated financial reports presented to her by Shire Treasurer Simon 'Scrooge' Mackay. But he flattered her so outrageously and plied her with food and drink that she trusted him. Sometimes when Chloe was hopefully visiting a girlfriend, the couple retired to explore more interesting subjects in Maisie's cosy bedroom above the shop.

Breathing a sigh of relief Maisie beamed happily at the mayor. 'That's the full report,' she said passing the folder over to Bomber and sitting down on her disgracefully short skirt while exposing rather lovely legs.

Bomber glanced at her legs and blushing, threw the report on the table. 'Can't make head nor tail of the bloody thing,' he said.

Councillor Sid Luxton nodded in agreement. 'You can't make sense of it, well join the club mate, neither can the rest of us.'

Sid was Chair of Engineering and had been a councillor for forty years. Over seventy, he was a wizened little bloke with bandy legs and false teeth that slipped when he talked and were likely to fly across the floor should he happen to sneeze. He owned a small property on the edge of town which had been so badly affected by drought he had shot most of his flock and sent a few of his remaining breeders to a mate's property down south. Fiery when pushed, he was fed up with the inaction of the Canberra politicians and furious with the government's indifference.

'I, like the rest of the district, am fed up to blazes and move a motion that we send a delegation to Canberra to find out what the hell's going on with our drought assistance money. We paid bloody taxes and we want our bloody share. Every other bloody shire's got some and we are far worse than most of them.'

Councillor Felicity 'Fee' Fluke stood up. 'I agree with Councillor Luxton and further,' she said referring to her copious notes, 'move that the Shire Clerk, Shire Treasurer, Shire Chairman, Deputy-Shire Chairman and I go to Canberra and seek clarification on our eligibility for drought relief and the hold up.

'I want to be sure that any relief comes with the proviso that funding be allocated to feed the kangaroos and other wildlife. They need help too.'

Paddy stood up and roared. 'What a load of bloody codswallop, the bloody roos are outnumbering the bloody flies, she should be locked up, the woman's nuts.'

Fee burst into tears. 'You are a murderer with no heart,' she sobbed.

Councillor Syd Luxton leant over and patted her heaving shoulders. 'Leave her alone Paddy, she doesn't understand,' he said.

Fee wiped her eyes on Syd's rather scruffy hanky. Tall and skinny with bones sticking out at her shoulders, ribs and hips, Fee was devoted to Syd and lived in his old shearing quarters surviving on lentils and vegetables that she grew and shared with the wildlife.

A passionate greenie with long flowing black frizzy hair on her head, under her arms and on her legs, she wore long hippie-style clothes and Jesus sandals. Fee had a university degree in something rather important but no one knew what it was. She was elected to council when Councillor Barney Long, who was ninety-five, dropped dead and no one else could be bothered to nominate. Her stated mission was to save the kangaroos that were in plague proportions eating up whatever pasture was left and leaving the remaining sheep to starve. In this she was in direct opposition to her neighbour Ben Bangor who lived 5 km down the road from her and kept the bank at bay by culling kangaroos.

Bomber stood up. 'Councillor Fluke, there is no way in this world that we will allocate funding to feed the roos, they're already wiping out any bit of pasture we've got left. If they keep breeding we might as well all pack up and leave. Grow some sense and for God's sake have a feed of meat. If you get any thinner you'll disappear.'

'How dare you,' Councillor Fluke said crossing her arms in front of her skinny boobs. 'Well I'm not supporting the motion.'

Bomber shrugged, 'Right,' he said. 'Now I am speaking to Councillor Luxton's motion which is the big issue of drought relief or lack of it. We all know things are bloody crook and if those bastards in Canberra don't come good with the money we'll all go to the wall. Every other bloody shire has had funding and we're in a far worse state than any of them. I like Councillor Luxton's idea that we go down and front the buggars.'

Paddy stood up. 'I agree with the mayor, I second the motion, the only solution is to go to Canberra.'

Bomber glanced around the table. 'I have a motion and a seconder, let's have a show of hands.

'Those in favour, Councillors Luxton, Matten, Murphy,

against Dixon, Dickie and Fluke. Three for and three against, and my casting vote gives us a motion carried.'

Chairman of Town Planning Councillor Micky Dixon, owner of the town's only real estate agency, property developer and auctioneer stood up.

'Mayor, I think we're being a bit hasty with this. Let's see what the Shire Clerk comes up with first.'

A close friend of the Shire Clerk, Micky was a genius at double-dealing and had a develop and be damned attitude. As Town Planning Chairman, he was in a perfect position to ensure his deals had a smooth ride to approval. And he gave the Shire Clerk and engineer generous kickbacks so that most of his applications were pushed through without a council airing. A divorcee with three ex-wives and numerous children dotted around the state to support, he was interested only in making money and pity help anyone who tried to stop him.

As far as the drought relief was concerned, he was damned if he wanted it. He was waiting for property prices to reach rock bottom before moving in for the kill. The sooner the town went broke the happier he would be. And he loathed all greenies, especially Fee Fluke who blocked every deal he put up. 'If I had my way,' he was fond of telling everyone, 'I'd shoot the lot of them with her first in line.'

Bomber stared at him. 'Councillor Dixon' he said angrily, 'let me reiterate for you, the motion was moved, seconded and carried. Now butt out,' he said banging his hammer on the table. 'I call the meeting to order,' he said loudly.

'Shire Clerk, you are directed to make an appointment for a deputation to meet with the relevant minister to find out what the hell has happened to our drought relief money.'

Shire Clerk Shifty Grey stood up and turning to Bomber shook his head sadly. Keeping his eyes fixed on the file in front of him he said quietly, 'Mayor, I implore you to give it more time.'

Bomber glared at him. 'Shire Clerk, your time has run out. You have been given a direction from this council, now get on with it,' he shouted rising to his feet and knocking his chair over. 'It's no use you procrastinating, Shire Clerk, we want action now. Things are crook and if those bastards in Canberra don't come good with the money, we'll all go to the wall.'

Shifty pulled himself together and stood up. 'Mayor, I am at a loss,' he said shaking his head and looking miserable. 'We have heard nothing from the government despite sending numerous letters and dozens of phone calls.' He waved a sheaf of correspondence in the air. 'I will personally go to Canberra and meet with the minister.'

'Like bloody hell, you will,' Bomber shouted his face red with anger. 'You've had your bloody chance, now it's our turn. This time we'll all go make it official and then they might take some notice.'

Shifty stood up and started to protest but Bomber towered over him and poked him in the chest. 'Sit down, it's no use you arguing, I have a motion on the books and you'll bloody do as we say. Let's understand who's in charge here.'

A stricken Shifty leaned forward his nose almost touching Bomber's shirt front. 'Mr Mayor I cannot allow it,' he said. 'It is absolutely out of order. You must leave it to the experts. I will arrange to go immediately.'

Paddy glared at him. 'Didn't you hear what the mayor said you useless shit? Let me repeat what he said so you can get it in your thick head. The deal is, we the elected representatives as against you lot, our employees, are going to Canberra as soon as we can organise things. Now, book the bloody tickets.'

Bomber raised his hammer and banged it on the table. 'I declare this meeting of the Damengin Shire Council finished. I'm off to the pub. You coming Paddy?'

CHAPTER 2

CROOKS AND SCAMS

Back in his office at the rear of the chambers, Shire Clerk Shifty produced a large white handkerchief from his pants and removing his thick glasses blew his nose. *Christ,* he thought, *things were tricky,* trickier than they had been for many years, in fact trickier that they had been since he had fled his home in New Zealand twenty-five years ago.

He had landed in Brisbane working as a stoker on a slow-moving cargo ship with the arse out of his pants and nothing but a few dollars and his passport in his pockets. Slapping his money on a rank outsider in the last race at Eagle Farm Racecourse, he got lucky and won a bundle. Rushing to the bookie to collect his winnings, he sent a good-looking woman coming the other way flying.

He helped her up and, feeling generous after his big win, invited her for a drink at the bar where they celebrated, knocking off several bottles of wine. The next thing he remembered was waking up beside her nursing a massive hangover in a posh hotel. But, his luck held. It turned out his drinking mate was Annabel Reed who, though well past her prime, lived on a large sheep station in western Queensland and was, she confided in him, the recipient of a hefty trust fund.

On the money trail, Shifty invested the rest of his winnings on a major charm offensive. He wined and dined her, bought her expensive presents and made passionate and expert love to her morning, noon and night. He also told her outrageous lies about his 'wealthy family' back home, failing to mention they had chucked him out years ago or that the Kiwi coppers were waiting to throw him in the slammer should he ever decide to cross the Tasman.

Annabel, whose biological clock was sitting at a minute to midnight and was desperate to land a mate was sated with sex and overwhelmed with his lavish attention. When Shifty begged her on bended knee to make him the happiest man in the world and offered her his 'darling Grannie's engagement ring' (bought from an outer city hock shop the day before) what could she do?

They were married by special license and honeymooned extravagantly on the Gold Coast until their pooled resources ran out. Returning to the family property Redlands, Shifty was horrified to discover that his new brother-in-law Bomber was the keeper of Annabel's trust fund.

But Bomber was a kind-hearted fellow who loved his little sister and was relieved to see her finally married. At first, he made them welcome but soon tired of Shifty loafing around the property sponging off him.

'He's driving me crazy,' he told his mate Paddy over a beer one night. 'Wants to do the accounts, tells me how to run the place, wants me to build them a new house, want, want, want and does bloody nothing all day, can't even ride a bloody horse. Can you find the bastard a job, get him out of my hair?'

Paddy had a soft spot for Annabel having spent several steamy sessions with her over the years. And he was a bit miffed she had gone off and married such a loser but he couldn't stand by and see his mate Bomber in a fix so he persuaded old Duke Edwards, the Shire Clerk who was pushing ninety-six, to retire so Shifty could take his place.

Bomber was so delighted to get rid of his brother-in-law he released Annabel's trust fund and the couple, armed with bucket loads of cash, went on a spending spree buying a large home on the edge of town with a tennis court and swimming pool. Shifty, an undischarged bankrupt — (the bailiffs were still looking for him) put everything in Annabel's name so he couldn't lose the lot.

The new job was a gift from heaven for Shifty. It gave him complete control of council's finances and within weeks he'd formed a syndicate with a couple of crooks, council works' foreman Cyril Rowe and shire engineer Phil Martin, siphoning off thousands of dollars of council funds.

They had also invested a good lump of the shire's rate revenue in a tax scam growing early tomatoes in the Ord River region. Sadly for the shire's budget bottom line, the tomatoes were never early enough for the market but the tax savings they made were a grower's delight for them.

Using state and federal road infrastructure funding they had leased millions of dollars' worth of road maintenance machinery including dozers, graders and trucks and then auctioned them off to shady developers. Result was no major roadwork or repairs had been done in the shire for years and potholes were so deep in some areas that one smart arse had put up a sign on the outskirts of town that said: 'Beware deep holes, novice drivers, unlucky tourists have disappeared without trace.'

Two years ago, the trio had pocketed the drought relief funds that the district desperately needed with help from Damengin Bank Manager Huw Hawtrey. Another bright idea of Shifty's was to buy six tattoo parlours in Sydney which acted as fronts for his money laundering scheme.

Hawtrey also concocted a scheme to send large amounts of cash to offshore tax havens using their unsuspecting wives, Audrey and Annabel. They had a fabulous time jetting off to the Cayman Islands travelling Qantas first class dropping off small packages for their respective husbands.

Now it seemed, Shifty's dreams were shattered, his luck had turned sour and it would take all his considerable skills to wriggle out of the mess he was in. The syndicate needed to meet urgently but Cyril wasn't due back until Monday. He and council secretary Dolly McIntyre had gone on a Sister City Fact Finding trip to Hawaii where the only fact Dolly discovered was that Cyril's dick was bigger than Shifty's.

The phone rang and he picked it up. 'Shire Clerk here,' he said.

There was a pause and a deep guttural voice said, 'You're late with the bread mate — ten grand or we bake.'

Shifty gasped. 'Who is this,' he croaked.

'Ten grand, usual place or we start cooking.'

'You can't do that, we agreed five, no more,' he groaned.

The phone went dead and Shifty started shaking. For months he had been paying Scorcher, the head of a notorious bikie gang, five thousand dollars a month to prevent his tattoo parlours on the Gold Coast that were a front for money laundering from being torched. Now he was demanding ten thousand or else.

'Greedy bastard,' Shifty raved pacing the floor. 'How the hell does he think I can find that in a hurry? I'll have to pay or they'll burn them. What a bloody mess,' he sighed.

Everything was tied up in Annabel's name. She was worth millions but without the parlours there was no cash flow and no way to pay the bikies. Council coffers were empty and all the ready cash was locked away in the Caymans.

Pulling a large white handkerchief from his pants and removing his thick glasses he blew his nose and considered his options. *What if someone talked?* he thought. No, they were all in it up to their necks, especially Cyril married with two kids and madly in lust with Dolly. *No worries there, I've enough on him to drop him right in it.*

He picked up the Shire Treasurer Simon 'Scrooge' McKay's file from in front of him. 'Not a problem,' he said out loud. 'That bastard's involved in so many rorts it makes my eyes water.'

There was a knock on his door and Micky Dixon, the town's only real estate agent, who was so crooked he couldn't lie straight in bed, walked in.

Shifty sighed with relief. 'Sit down Micky, have a drink mate?'

'Thanks,' he said taking the almost full glass of whisky and sitting down opposite him.

'Well we're up shit creek,' Shifty said miserably. 'If they go to Canberra, we could all end up in the slammer.'

Micky downed his drink in one gulp and put his glass down in front of him. Wiping his thin moustache with the back of his hand he fixed his small beady eyes on Shifty.

'Don't get your knickers in a knot mate, there's ways and means. This is what we do, we get some funds together, I'll tip in a few grand, say $10 000, and if you and the others put up the same, we can come up with say $50 000. Right, we put it in the council's finance account, McKay can fudge the figures and then we tell them we've received part-payment of the drought relief money from Canberra. That should keep them quiet for a while.'

Shifty groaned and waved his hand. 'Can't do it mate, money's tight and I've staked a heap on those mining leases you talked me into. Annabel's not getting anything from the property and let's get real, fifty grand's just a drop in the ocean, it's not going to go anywhere, be like a band aid on a flood.'

Micky leaned over and grabbed his shoulder. 'Those mining leases are a bloody certainty, it's just a matter of time. Now pull yourself together, sell something, just get some money because it's your only chance of slithering out of this.'

Shifty spluttered, 'What do you mean my chance? You're in this up to your neck and if I go matey, we all go.'

Micky shrugged and got up. 'Whatever you say Shifty but my advice is to call a special meeting and bloody quick. Tell the bastards you've got some of the money and it'll buy you time. And, by the way,' he said softly, 'you've got nothing on me mate, I'm not worried in the slightest.'

Shifty glared at him. 'It's alright for you, you're not married to the big fella's sister. If he twigs to what's going on, he'll bloody kill me.'

Micky frowned and said in a vicious whisper, 'Pull yourself together or I'll beat him to it. Now take my advice. I'm off.'

Micky wandered over to the pub to clear his head. As far as the drought relief was concerned he really couldn't give a damn what happened, just a slight hiccup. If the shit hit the fan, he'd head north, maybe one of the islands, still plenty of opportunities up there. This wasn't the first town he'd left in a hurry and he had plenty of cash planted in bogus accounts around the state.

That reminds me, he said to himself, *have to have a word with Huw at the bank, wise him up about things.*

After Micky left Shifty poured himself a drink with trembling hands. Where the hell would he find ten grand in a hurry? He couldn't ask Annabel or she might tell Bomber.

He picked up the phone and started dialling. There was a knock on the door and Shire Engineer Phil Martin burst in.

'Christ Shifty I just heard the news about the Canberra trip, what the hell are we going to do now?' he asked slumping into a chair by the window.

Shifty glared at him. 'Close the bloody door you fool and let me think. There's nothing for it,' he said miserably, 'we'll have to stall for time and you'll have to go down next week and bring some cash back from the parlours.'

Phil looked at him in horror. 'Shit mate, give me a break, that place is full of crims.'

Shifty shrugged. 'Take Dolly with you, she'll smooth talk the thugs.'

Phil's eyes lit up. 'Can we have a stopover in the Hyatt Casino?' he asked.

'No you bloody can't, you can get the bloody money and hot-foot it back.'

When he'd gone Shifty picked up the phone and rang Huw Hawtrey on his private line.

'Shifty here,' he whispered, 'get your arse over here now, we need to talk.'

On the other end of the line, Huw shuddered. 'Christ all bloody mighty, what now?'

CHAPTER 3

BOMBER AND MATLOCK

After the council meeting, Bomber followed Paddy over to the pub where most of the councillors were gathered including the town's only doctor Councillor Dickie Davis, who was sitting at the bar nursing an empty glass.

'Another beer, Dickie?' Paddy called to him, signalling to Annie the barmaid.

Wiping his long thin nose on a crumpled hanky Dickie adjusted his glasses and looked up hopefully at Paddy but then spotted Bomber walking in behind him and shook his head.

'Not for me thank you Paddy,' he replied sanctimoniously. 'Unlike some,' he said, nodding at Bomber, 'I have work to do.'

Dickie hated Bomber who he saw as a rival for the love of Maggie Spink, Matron of Damengin Base Hospital. When his wife Susie ran off with a house painter saying she'd rather watch paint dry than live with him, Maggie had wiped his tears and fed him endless cups of tea and her special crunchy biscuits while he poured out his heart to her. Unfortunately, Dickie mistook her kindness for something else and had made a complete ass of himself at that year's Damengin Show Ball.

Poor Dickie, who had been dreaming about Maggie for months, had been looking forward to the ball as a chance to get her on her own and was all dolled up in his best blue pin-striped suit. Before he left, he cheekily told the housekeeper to change the sheets and intended to ask Maggie to dance and invite her home to listen to his latest recording of Wagner's 'The Ring'. He went bright red thinking about what it could lead to.

It was a hot night and after downing several large glasses of fruit punch (spiked with three bottles of vodka by Bomber) he went outside desperate for a pee and spotted Maggie who greeted him with a peck on the cheek.

'How are you, Dickie? Don't forget to save me a dance,' she said, smiling at him.

Overwhelmed with adoration and sloshed from the punch, he took hold of her arm intending to ask her for a dance but tripped over his feet and fell over peeing himself in the process. Bomber, who had walked outside looking for Maggie, saw the whole thing and laughed until the tears ran down his face.

Maggie tried to help him up but Dickie was so shocked he pushed her away and dashed blindly inside where he bumped into the substantial form of Alice Broomhall and came to an abrupt halt.

Alice, the shire's librarian, had been on the shelf so long

she felt like one of the first editions, saw her chance and grabbed him by his arm.

'Dickie, what's the matter?' she said holding him to her in a grip of iron, 'let me help you.'

But Dickie was hysterical and shook her off.

He escaped through the front door, fell into his car and roared home so fast he missed the turn into his garage and slammed into the front verandah almost wiping out his ancient cat Tiddles who was sleeping on the steps. Tiddles, who was second only to Maggie in his affections, got such a fright the vet had to put her on tranquilisers.

From that day even the sight of Bomber filled him with pure hatred. Finishing the dregs of his beer, he stood up and walked haughtily out of the bar.

Bomber, happily ignorant of Dickie's loathing downed his beer in one swallow, wiped his mouth with a massive fist and waved to Billy, Paddy's son who was serving behind the bar.

'Another one here Billy,' he called offering up his glass.

Bill poured him a beer from the tap. 'There you are Bomber, have one on me.'

Bomber raised his glass. 'Thanks Bill. Good to see you back, pity my fella doesn't have your attachment to the place. Do him good to put in a day's work.'

Bomber downed his beer and decided he was becoming bloody miserable. *Must be the drought getting to me* he comforted himself. He handed his empty glass to Annie the barmaid and was just about to leave when Maisie Matten called to him from across the room.

'Bomber, wait on a minute,' she said, tottering over on her treacherously high heels and staring up at him. 'You were a bit hard on the shire treasurer today; he's doing the best he can in these difficult times you know.'

Maisie was fond of Shire Treasurer Simon 'Scrooge' McKay, who always flattered her indecently. And, although she was street smart, she didn't have a hope of understanding the complicated financial reports he placed in front of her.

Bomber liked Maisie, she worked hard to keep her business alive and support her daughter Chloe who, at seventeen with raging hormones, was driving her crazy. He patted the stool next to him and called out to Annie, 'Get Maisie a beer will you love and another for me.'

Turning to Maisie he said, 'You know that man's a crook, Maisie, and we've got to sort this mess out.'

Maisie leaned over and took her beer from Annie. 'Thanks Bomber,' she said, 'I've known Simon for years and he's okay, what have you got against him?'

'Nothing concrete but he's a creep,' Bomber said.

Sid Luxton leaned over from his seat next to Bomber and said angrily, 'Bomber's right, he's a bloody wanker, either incompetent or a crook — take your choice. Now look here Maisie, we're all stuffed and nothing's being done. Every other bloody shire in this state has had a hand up from the government and we've had zilch. Look what we're going through. You don't see any of the bloody council staff doing without so their stock can have a feed and look at you, you're doing okay.'

'Just a minute there Sid,' Maisie said angrily, 'you've got to be kidding, my takings are awful. My credit list is so long I go blind looking at it. That was uncalled for.'

'Sorry Maisie, but you need to know how things stand and the sort of bloke you're associating with,' he said, slamming down his glass and moving to the other end of the bar.

He knew he had been angry and Maisie was a decent bird but hell, she needed to understand the mess they were in. There was no water left for his stock, his windmills had pumped dry and he had sent what remained of his breeders to an old mate down south. He was also worried about Fee Fluke living alone at his place. How the hell she survived giving everything she had and more to the local wildlife he had no idea.

Fee had told him her mission was to save the kangaroos. Problem was the silly woman didn't understand that they were out of control, in plague proportions eating up whatever pasture was left, while the poor bloody sheep, what was left of them, were left to starve. And, his generosity to Fee had backfired. She had attacked his friend and neighbour Ben Bangor who was struggling to feed his surviving stock with the money he made from kangaroo culling.

Bill walked up to him and leaned over the bar. 'What's up Sid, haven't seen you let off steam like that before,' he said. 'Here mate, have a beer on me, I'll have one with you.'

Sid's wrinkled old face lit up. 'Thanks Bill, I think we're all getting a bit rattled.'

Bill poured two beers and handed one to Sid. 'How's your

place standing up to the drought?'

Sid took a sip of his beer and wiped the froth off his mouth. 'Not good, sent me breeders to a mate and I've got a lodger in the shearers quarters that's giving me nothing but heartache. She's the oddest person I've ever met.'

'I heard something about her from Ben. How did you come to let her stay?'

Sid grunted, 'It's a difficult one, truth be told I felt sorry for her. Thanks for the beer. I'm off to bed.'

Sid had been living at the pub since the drought had wiped out his stock. He'd told Paddy that he'd hurt his back but the truth was he couldn't face the misery of seeing his property reduced to dust.

Maisie sipped her beer thoughtfully. Sid's outburst had annoyed her and he was just plain wrong criticising her. The shop takings were down, half the district owed her money and her overdraft was sky high. If things didn't improve soon she would have to close down. The only reliable income she had was her appearance fee as a councillor and the way things were looking that would soon come to an end.

'Silly old buggar going off about our treasurer like that,' she said to Bomber. 'I know he's upset but I still don't think Simon is at fault.'

'I have to agree with Sid, Maisie love, I have no confidence in either him or our shire clerk. Anyway, I'm off home.'

Bomber drove home thinking what a rotten council meeting it had been. He was sick of the rows and fed up with trying to get anyone to do anything. Most of all, he was fed up with living by himself on Redlands, a sheep station that had been in his family for generations. His once blond hair had turned white and retreated to the back of his head, his nose had been broken once too often but he was still a fine figure of a man.

He lost his wife Caroline twenty years ago when she'd fallen overboard in a drunken stupor while cruising aboard the *Queen Mary* with her girlfriend Susie. Their only child Teddy, who had inherited a fortune from her estate, had given him nothing but heartache.

Bomber sat down on the verandah steps with his dog Tessa resting her head against his knees and thought about Caroline.

In his prime, he had been a football hero. He had scored a magnificent match winning try for the Wallabies against the All Blacks and was celebrating at a Brisbane pub when a group of rugby fans including the vivacious Caroline Smyth joined them. She was blonde, buxom and bloody gorgeous, he remembered.

The couple were instantly attracted to one another and after a night of partying they merged into a mixture of thrashing arms and legs as they bonked the night away in his hotel room. Even Bomber's incredible fitness and stamina was hard put to stay the distance with the insatiable Caroline and totally besotted he took her with him when the team toured New Zealand.

Bomber scored on and off the oval and when they finally returned to Brisbane sated with sex and success, he proposed.

Madly in lust, they were married a few weeks later just before the bump that was Teddy was glaringly obvious.

The couple settled on his property, Redlands, and for the first five years were deliriously happy. Then Caroline became bored and missed the bright lights and excitement of the city. She moaned to Bomber that watching flies copulating on the ceiling was the only highlight of her day and, leaving Teddy in the care of their housekeeper Joyce and Charlie the cook, went off on that fateful cruise.

Bomber was so shattered when she died and that he allowed her staggeringly wealthy parents open slather with Teddy, who became outrageously spoilt. They had doted on Caroline who was their only child and transferred their devotion to Teddy by pandering to his every whim.

Not a scholar, his main achievements at school were on the sports fields. He starred at rugby and on the cricket field and could easily have worn the baggy green if he had practised instead of partying.

When he finished school, Bomber was keen for him to return to the farm but he decided to become a professional cricketer. Then his mum's trust fund kicked in and with shit loads of money at his disposal, he ditched cricket and focused on fast cars and faster women.

The last contact Bomber had was a drunken phone call from England where Teddy was celebrating the Aussies winning the Ashes.

Leaning against the verandah rail Bomber rubbed his chin and stroking Tessa's head asked, 'What's a bloke to do?' Tessa looked up at him, cocked her head on the side and whined sympathetically.

'You're a good old girl,' he said fondly stroking her soft head. She gazed at him adoringly with her orange flecked eyes and put her paw on his knee.

'There's only you and me old girl,' he said softly. 'What would I do without you?'

Tessa yawned and settled back down at his feet. She understood his every word and loved him with every breath in her body.

Bomber gazed out over the verandah at paddocks cracked from a searing heat and the stark skeleton forms of dying gum trees.

'This drought will be the death of all of us,' he moaned.

With his massive shoulders and powerful frame he had fought and won many battles but they were no help against the worst drought in living memory.

'Bloody drought and hopeless bloody Teddy,' he sighed to no one in particular.

At the crack of dawn the next day he loaded up his ute with fodder for the breeders in the far paddock and put in a bale of hay for the bull. 'Poor sod doing it tough since the cows have all gone,' he muttered to Tessa, who jumped in beside him.

He drove out to the far windmill to scatter feed for what was left of his prize merino sheep. Tessa jumped down and the skinny ewes stumbled feebly to their feet as she slowly, recognising their miserable state, herded them towards where Bomber was filling the food trough.

Tears coursed down Bomber's dusty lined face as he looked at the pathetic mob, the last of the famous Redlands flock.

'Look at the poor sods,' he said, his heart breaking. 'Come Tessa let's go.'

They left the sheep and drove back to the bull paddock next to the cattle yards that had stood empty since the cows had been sent to the meat works last year. All that was left was Matlock, the huge Brahman stud bull that Bomber had paid $50 000 for in the good times.

Since the departure of his beloved herd, Matlock had been forcibly celibate and his testosterone levels had skyrocketed to boiling point. He regarded Bomber as the architect of his agony, the enforcer of his celibacy and when he saw him coming through the gate something exploded in his brain and he charged, hitting him full on.

Bomber flew up in the air and hit the ground heavily falling on his left arm. Tessa, barking furiously, tore to his rescue dancing round and round the enraged bull until he was in a tight circle drawing him away from Bomber across the yards where she baled him against the rails. Tearing back and forth in front of the bull that was stamping and snorting with rage, she kept him pinned against the rails until Bomber, realising her tactics, managed to drag himself through the still open gate and kick it shut behind him.

He was lying outside barely conscious and in agony when Tessa raced up and started licking his face and whimpering.

'It's alright girl,' he said touching her gently with his good arm. But it wasn't alright and when he tried to sit up the pain in his ribs took his breath away and there was no way he could move his arm.

It was no use yelling out for help, there was no one for miles around. He lay back on the ground and closed his eyes to think.

'Tessa,' he called, 'go get Ben.'

Tessa put her head on the side and looked at him.

'Tess, get Ben, go, go,' Bomber said pushing her away.

Tessa walked away and then turned round.

'Tess, get Ben,' Bomber roared. 'Go now.'

Tess stood still for a moment before walking away with her tail down and her head turned in his direction. She ran back and stood looking at him whining, her ears flat against her head.

'Tessa get Ben, go, go, go now, 'Bomber yelled angrily. 'Get Ben.'

She put her head on the side and looked at him.

Summoning all his strength, Bomber lifted his good arm and pointed to the west.

Tessa looked to where he was pointing and with a sharp bark raced off over the paddocks.

It was over 5 km across country to Ben Bangor's place and even if he was home, Bomber knew that there was no telling if he would understand what the dog meant.

He decided the only thing was to try and reach the homestead himself. Unable to stand because of the agony in his chest, he started dragging himself along the ground with his good arm. It was past midday before he saw the welcome sight of Ben Bangor's ute coming down the track.

Before the engine had stopped Tessa jumped out of the back and was at his side licking his face. 'Good girl,' Bomber said his voice breaking as he fondled her ears. 'Good old girl.'

Ben strode over to Bomber and knelt beside him. 'What the hell happened mate?'

'Had a buster with Matlock, Tessa saved me and thank God she got you or I'd still be here in the morning. Took a hit in the ribs and the left arm's gone. Think you can get me into the hospital?'

Ben dragged a mattress from a bed and managed to lift Bomber into the back of the ute. After an agonising trip he was put onto a hospital trolley and mercifully passed out.

He vaguely remembered bright lights and people talking but he didn't become fully conscious until the next day when he opened his eyes and found himself looking into the kindly face of Matron Maggie Spink.

'Well my lad, you've had some fun and games. What happened to you?' she asked, tidying his bedclothes.

Bomber's face cracked into a lopsided grin. 'Came off second best with the bull. How much damage did he do Maggie?'

'Broke your arm in two places, fractured your pelvis and cracked a couple of ribs, nothing too serious but enough to keep you in here for a few weeks.'

Bomber looked horrified. 'Few weeks, I have to get back to the property, can't stay. What about Tessa, is she alright?'

Maggie pushed him back on his pillows. 'Ben Bangor dropped you off and took Tessa back with him. Some dog you've got there, deserves a medal.'

Bomber nodded, smiling. 'She's the best.'

Maggie tucked in his sheets and offered him a glass of water. 'Dr Davis has put a pin in your arm and taped the ribs — you were a fraction away from piercing your lungs. We've contacted Teddy and he's on his way. Now stop fretting and close your eyes.'

He turned slightly and groaned with pain. It had been a rotten day. Now he was laid up in hospital and who would look after things at Redlands? The property had been in his family for three generations and it looked like this was the last.

'If Teddy comes home he doesn't know the arse from the head of a sheep,' he muttered.

'What are you moaning about now,' Maggie said as she adjusted his pillows. 'You blokes are always whingeing about something.'

Bomber went bright red, he hadn't known she was listening. 'Things are not good.'

Maggie gave him a smile. 'Nothing is as bad as it seems. What happened to that fighting spirit?'

Bomber shrugged. 'Easy to fight when there's something to tackle, not so easy when it's the weather.'

Maggie looked at him fondly. He was a lovable fellow and still attractive.

'It's Teddy,' he moaned. 'Still arsing around in spending what's left of his mother's money. Couldn't care less what happened here.'

Maggie smoothed his bedcover. 'Well maybe if you buried your pride, sat him down and spelled it out to him it might make a difference. He's not a bad lad, he just needs some responsibility.'

'Harrumph', said Bomber, 'doesn't know what the word means.'

Maggie plumped up his pillows. 'Open your mouth and swallow these tablets. You can have a sleep until Teddy arrives.'

Bomber stared at her departing back. There was no messing with Maggie, a big girl with an even bigger heart. She ran the tiny country hospital with a rod of iron but everyone loved her. *Including me, Bomber said to himself. Having her looking after me is almost worth the pain.*

Drowsy from the tablets, he fell asleep dreaming of Maggie, Matlock and Tessa.

Several hours later his son Teddy gunned his late model BMW and screamed to a halt at the front of the hospital terrifying Alfie the wardsman and the old lady he was pushing around the path in a wheelchair.

Jumping out of the car, Teddy took the front steps two at a time. 'Anyone here?' he called, ringing the bell.

Nurse Phoebe Taylor wandered out, took one look at Teddy and another at his gleaming car outside and put on her most seductive smile.

'How can I help you?' she said flashing her beautiful blue eyes at him.

'Teddy Reed, here to see my dad Bomber.'

Phoebe smiled. 'He's in Room 2 A — I think he's sleeping, matron gave him some tablets a while ago. Do you want to see him or wait until he's awake?'

'How is he?' Teddy asked.

'He's got a few broken bones but he'll recover. I'll take you to him and if he's asleep you can come back later.'

Teddy followed the trim figure in the starched uniform along the corridor to a small room where Bomber was snoring loudly.

'Thank you nurse,' Teddy said sitting down on a chair beside the bed. 'I'll just sit here until he wakes up.'

'Certainly, Mr Reed, would you like a cup of tea?'

'My name's Teddy, and no thanks I prefer to get something stronger later.'

Nurse Phoebe Taylor walked back to reception thinking about the visitor. Her sole purpose in coming to the country was to find a rich husband with a large property. Teddy appeared to be rich and while he didn't have the other prerequisite, a large property, his dad did and that counted for something.

CHAPTER 4

BEN BANGOR

After dropping Bomber at Damengin Hospital Ben took Tessa, the now famous red kelpie, back to his property Abington Station, loaded his battered old ute and drove out to feed what was left of his stock.

Five years ago, Abington Station had produced some of the finest merino wool in the country. Now it was a desert devoid of vegetation where survival for even the hardiest of creatures was a test of endurance.

Ben pulled up at the first water trough where a small mob of bone-thin sheep were gathered. Vanes on the lone windmill struggled to catch the small puffs of wind vital for lifting life-saving water from the Great Artesian Basin. This pitiful mob were almost all he had left of his breeding stock and he was fighting hard to save them.

As he cleaned the muddy residue out of the water trough and poured grain into the feeders, ravenous crows hovered overhead cawing loudly. 'Buggar off you bastards,' he shouted. 'Go somewhere else for a feed.'

Driving west along the fence he came to the next windmill where a group of ewes lay prone, too weak to lift their heads. During the night several had lambed and the tiny blobs of white struggled to get a drink from withered and dry teats.

He quickly dispatched them throwing the carcasses in the back of the ute and after distributing the rest of the grain, he called his dogs and headed back to the homestead.

There had been droughts before. He remembered the drought hit in the 60s when he was a lad of twelve and the wool market crashed. Many producers switched to cattle, but his family had held on refusing to abandon their flocks. Then after years of poor returns, they finally clinched a lucrative deal with the Italian fashion trade and prospered. Fifteen years ago Ben had finished his stint at Agriculture College and taken over the reins of the 50,000 hectare property. Wool returns were excellent and his parents had retired to spend more time with his married sister Ann and her children in Brisbane. Fired with enthusiasm, Ben had invested heavily in top rams to further improve his blood lines and the future looked rosy. Then five years ago, the drought to end all droughts hit. Pastures parched from lack of rain died and stock died with them, returns plummeted and now the property was drowning in debt.

Ben drove trucks by day for Paddy Murphy at the pub and culled kangaroos at night selling their carcasses to an abattoir. He was just managing to keep his prize rams and a handful of breeders alive and meet his overdraft payments. But the bank was getting impatient and bank manager Huw Hawtrey kept hassling him.

Back at the homestead he unloaded the carcasses of baby lambs and was putting them into a large pit when a horn blared and Billy Murphy, Paddy's son drove up.

'Where the hell did you come from,' Ben asked walking over and pumping Billy's outstretched hand. 'Heard you were mustering up the top end. How long have you been back?'

'Good to see ya mate. Got back yesterday, great to be home but hell the place looks awful.'

'Is this a social visit or do you want to see how the other half lives?'

Bill punched Ben's arm. 'I've spent six months mustering up north, it's bloody desperate up there. Cows hardly able to stand were dropping calves and we had no choice but to shoot them, bloody awful job. We took a mob of 12,000 to the abattoir and it was mercy killing, they were skin and bone. I never want to see conditions like that again. A lot of stations were buggared, and a couple of top blokes suicided. Awful mess,' he said shaking his head. 'Tell you what Ben, I was bloody glad when the work ran out and I could come home.'

'Well, it's not much better here, I've had to shoot 80 per cent of the flock and now some of the remainder have died lambing, had to shoot their orphaned lambs. Keeping only a few breeders and my best rams but I don't know how much longer I can keep going.'

Billy shook his head and gazed around. 'Bloody drought, it's got to rain sometime.'

Ben sighed. 'Sheep are dying and wouldn't you know, wool prices are their highest level in years. A man can't win a bloody argument. Bloody crows are the only buggars getting a feed, them and the dingoes. Come to the homestead and we'll sink a few beers.'

They walked out onto the wide shady homestead verandah and Ben dragged two beers from the fridge. He took a long pull from his stubby and leaned back in the old cane chair.

'Things are bad mate,' he said, 'bloody bad. If it wasn't for the few dollars I make roo shooting and driving trucks, the banks would own the lot. Then there's another bloody nightmare, the neighbour from hell.'

Bill looked up from his beer. 'What's that all about. What neighbour from hell?'

'Councillor Fee bloody Fluke, the bird that's living in Sid Luxton's place, she's mad, absolutely raving mad. I went roo shooting last night, had my sights on a big one and that bloody woman appeared in a white shift thing screaming and waving a bloody lantern. Gave me the fright of my life. I very near shot her.'

Bill burst out laughing. 'Christ mate, pity you didn't, what's her problem?'

'She's the problem, a raving bloody greenie. I could kill Sid for letting her live there. It's alright for him, he's been living at the pub with your dad since he hurt his back. Sent his breeders off to a property down south and let her have the run of the place. She arrived here out of the blue looking for someplace to live. Wanted to 'commune with nature' or some bloody silly thing.'

Ben downed the rest of his beer and got up. 'Thing is Bill, she met Sid at the pub and the silly old buggar felt sorry for her and told her she could stay at his place. Now I've got to put up with her. She'll end up dead if she's not careful and serve her bloody right.'

Bill took a swig of his beer. 'Why don't you confront her, tell her what you're doing, explain it to her?'

Ben stared at him. 'You've got to be joking, you can't talk to her, and she's a loony. Last time I went over there she started accusing me of murder and threatened to bring in a mob of her greenie mates, that's all we need, more of the bastards.'

'You know Bill, I don't want to kill roos, but if it's a choice between them and losing this place, I've got no option. I've still got to look after the folks in Brisbane, I haven't been able to send them any money for years and God knows what they are living on.'

Billy leaned over to pat Lucy, a beautiful black and white kelpie with the softest eyes who was resting her head on his knees. 'Well for God's sake Ben, go and tell her, if you lay it on the line she'll probably back off.'

'I've got more to do than mess around with that woman. I'm going to see the cops and get her locked up, she's a menace. I'll get us some more beer,' he said walking back into the house.

Bill finished his beer and put the empty stubby on the floor. He felt sorry for his mate and hated to see him so upset.

'What about the drought assistance Ben,' he called out, 'would that make any difference?'

Ben returned with two more stubbies and handed one to Bill, 'Course it would but where the hell is it? We've been waiting years and still no sign,' he said sitting down.

'Well, they held a special council meeting and they've decided to go to Canberra and front the government. Dad says every other shire has got relief except us.'

'Drought funds would make a hell of a difference, it would keep the banks at bay and buy some feed. But what we need is rain and more bloody rain.'

Billy nodded. 'Gotta come sometime, been five years and you know what they say, cycles and all that. Change of subject Teddy Reed's on his way. Maggie contacted him told him Bomber was in dire straits and worried sick about the property and he needed him.'

Ben leaned back in his chair and sipped his beer. 'Poor Bomber, be good to catch up with Teddy, haven't seen him for yonks. He inherited a heap of money from his mum's estate, some warehouses in Brisbane and plenty of shares. Seemed to turn him into a bloody playboy.'

'Shit, what a waste, he was set to be a great cricketer, when he wasn't chasing skirts,' Bill said laughing. 'Is that a car?'

The dogs leapt from the verandah and were going ballistic when Sam Spink, owner and editor of the *Damengin Star* drove into the yard in a swirl of dust. He parked his car in the shade of the shed and walked over to the verandah.

'Gidday Sam,' Ben said standing up. 'I'll grab you a beer.'

'Thanks mate,' Sam said gratefully as he walked onto the verandah and sat down on the proffered chair. 'Ben, I called in to tell you I was speaking to Damengin's Shire Clerk Shifty Grey earlier and he was acting very cagey about the drought relief. Told me he couldn't or wouldn't release any correspondence with Canberra. Any rate I told him I'd get it through Freedom of Information, and that really put the wind up him. Christ he almost threw me out.'

Ben handed him a beer. 'Yeh sneaky little shit of a bloke. You're doing some checking?'

'Sure am. I tell you what I thought,' Sam said downing his stubby in one huge draft. 'I'll get a picture of you with some skinny ewes and send it off to the major dallies to let the mob in the city know what's going on. Might stir something up and get some action from the bloody politicians in Canberra. What do you reckon?'

Ben finished his beer and wiped his mouth. 'Those pen pushing bastards sit on their arses and wouldn't know what was happening in the real world. But I'll do anything to get some action.'

Sam unpacked his camera. 'Right, which way are we heading?' he asked.

Ben got up and put his hat on. 'Come with us Bill, you can be part of this, it's just as bad at your place. We'll start with those dead sheep on the way to the trough and take one of you and me feeding out.'

Driving along the rutted path, Ben spotted crows swirling over an ewe lying prone on the ground and pulled over.

'She's barely alive, give us a hand to lift her in the back mate,' he said to Bill. 'We'll take her over to the water trough, give her a drink, and she'll either live or die,' he said shrugging his shoulders.

They drove to the next windmill; its sails waving slowly in the heat pumping a slow stream of brown water into the trough. Around it were gathered a hundred or so skeletal sheep waiting for a feed.

Opening the back of the ute, the two men heaved the ewe they had rescued onto the ground and, plunging his hat into the water trough, Ben offered her a drink. The ewe lifted her head slightly and then fell backwards, too weak to care.

Ben looked at her and sighed, 'Poor sod, she's had it.' He went to his ute and got the gun. The ewe shuddered slightly at the impact of the bullet.

Stashing his gun, Ben walked over to the sheep. 'That's the last of it,' he said waving his hand. 'I've been cutting scrub trees for this lot's fodder but there's buggar all left now.'

His mouth was set in a grim line as he poured grain into a feeder and watched as the sheep crowded round.

A shocked Sam stopped filming and stared at him. 'Mate, is this all you have left of thousands?'

'Yep, that's it, the remains of the Babington fine merino herd,' Ben said throwing the feeding can in the back of the ute. 'Right,' he said slamming the tail gate, 'it's too bloody miserable here. Let's go back and drown our sorrows.'

Sam had taken dozens of photos of dead and dying sheep and a picture of a handful of pathetically skinny ewes gathered around the water trough with several tiny lambs too weak to stand.

After several beers, he returned home. It had been a long time since he had felt so motivated and after feeding his smelly old dog Otto a tin of his favourite dog food, he sat at his desk and began to type. Several hours later he realised with surprise that apart from the beer at Ben's he hadn't had a drink since the morning.

It had been a long time since he'd written anything newsworthy. But with pictures of dying sheep and a story that tugged at the heart strings he knew he was on a winner. Next morning, he sent the story and pics off to a dozen of his old mates in Brisbane and Sydney and hoped for the best.

CHAPTER 5

BANK FORECLOSES

Huw Hawtrey, Manager of the Damengin Provincial Bank sat hunched over his desk staring at the thick blue folder open in front of him. Ten years ago he had been the high flying chief of the Australian Provincial Bank's International Department until a damning auditor's report discovered evidence of insider trading. Hauled in front of the bank's board, he was saved from prison by the intervention of the bank's Chairman Claude Hewlett who luckily was his wife Audrey's uncle and godfather to his daughter Deidre.

But while Huw escaped jail, he didn't escape the humiliation of being sent to the bank's furthermost enclave, the one-horse town of Damengin which was about as far west as the crow flew.

His wife Audrey, a social butterfly and dreadful snob, was at that time president of Australia's Banker's Wives Association and was devastated when she heard the news.

So was his son Timmy who adored the city life and simply couldn't bear to quit his ballet class, but his horse mad daughter Deidre was overjoyed to be heading west where horses ruled.

When the family arrived in Damengin they were made very welcome by the locals. Although Huw had been drastically de-promoted and his staff reduced from 239 to just three, he was still a 'bank manager' and as such a VIP in the town's pecking order.

The first to offer the dazed couple the hand of friendship were Damengin Shire Clerk Shifty Grey and his wife Annabel. They were invited to dine with them at their magnificent home on the edge of town and lavished with gourmet food and lashings of excellent wine.

Later when he was sitting comfortably with Shifty on the spacious verandah knocking back a few glasses of vintage port while the ladies chatted in the sitting room, a well lubricated Huw raged on and on about the bank consigning him to 'this God-forsaken hole'.

Shifty, who had suffered a similar fate himself was hugely sympathetic and, sensing Huw could be seriously useful to his devious schemes, made him a very tempting offer. And Huw, realising that he had less than no chance of leaving this hell hole of a backwater before retirement enthusiastically accepted and became an integral part of Shifty's syndicate.

The evening was also a huge success for his wife Audrey who, wrapped in a haze of self-pity over her changed circumstances, had perked up when she met Annabel, who she discovered was the sister of the town's mayor Bomber Reed and one of the district's landed gentry.

Annabel was Show Society Vice President, organiser of the coming Damengin Show Ball, the town's social event of the year and just about every other organisation in the district. A great delegator, she was always scouting for people she could lumber with the 'hands on' stuff and instantly persuaded Audrey to take on the Society's most hated job, that of secretary. Audrey was thrilled, this was the vital first rung that would enable her to scale the heights of the region's social ladder.

Now ten years later Audrey had taken over and was running most of the district's clubs and associations including the Country Women's Association, Royal Flying Doctor and Flying Art School.

But the one thing she desperately wanted and still hadn't got was inclusion in the squattocracy. This she knew could only be achieved by owning a sheep or cattle property and she constantly nagged Huw to buy one despite him moaning he couldn't tell a cow from a sheep. She also insisted on sending their son Timmy, a frustrated ballet dancer who hated the land, to the state's finest agriculture college so he could run the place she was determined Huw would buy.

Audrey also told Huw that buying a property would solve the problem of their madcap, out-of-control daughter Deidre. Dee spent her time roaming the district on her horse Knacker and had been chucked out of her expensive boarding school, the only one that would take her and her horse.

Audrey had insisted Huw dish out a fortune to send Deidre

to the same Swiss finishing school the very wealthy Wilton-Smiths were sending their daughter to.

When Deidre was 'finished', Audrey dreamed she might have a chance with Angus Wilton-Smith, the son and heir. Would she wear soft mauve or perhaps a cream lace as Mother of the Bride? It was all so difficult.

Huw was in a quandary. Audrey had upped the pressure and was driving him nuts about buying a property, Timmy was due home from Agricultural College next month and Deidre was so out of control she was impossible.

ɡ

Much worse was that he was still waiting for the bottom to fall out of property prices before he moved in to buy, and now Shifty Grey had just told him a deputation led by Mayor Bomber Reed was going to Canberra to lobby the government for drought relief.

Shifty said, 'If they get the drought relief, prices will stabilise and that'll be the end of it. And if they find out what really happened to the drought relief money, we're all up the spout.'

The Government funds had been received and spent long ago and Huw's share was sitting in a bank account in Audrey's name (to avoid tax) waiting for the kill.

When the drought really kicked in most local graziers had borrowed heavily from the bank and were battling to keep up their payments. Using past valuations, Huw had his eye on

Abington, one of the finest properties in the district with a magnificent homestead and a reputation for fine micron wool.

It was owned by Ben Bangor who was battling to service his overdraft and make his mortgage payment. But Huw knew that when the drought ended, the property had excellent prospects.

'It's now or never,' he said to himself.

Huw took a deep breath and stood up. 'Time is right, buggar ringing Shifty back. Whatever he wants can wait,' he said, putting the file under his arm and marching through the door.

9

Out at Babington, Ben Bangor was about to feed out the last of his grain and walked over to the shed, filled the buckets and dumped them as well as a couple of hay bales, in the back of his old ute. Whistling his dogs Lucy and Pippa, he was driving through the gate when he saw a car pulling in. He recognised it as belonging to Huw Hawtrey, the self-important manager of the Damengin Bank.

'Now we've got problems,' he muttered reversing the ute backwards and pulling up.

Huw Hawtrey got out of the car and carefully locked the door.

'Morning Huw,' Ben said walking over to him and offering his hand. 'When is it going to rain?'

Huw Hawtrey took his hand and gave it a limp shake.

'Morning Ben, you tell me and we'll both know.'

'Come on up,' Ben said walking onto the verandah and pulling up a couple of chairs.

'Sit down Huw, might as well say what you've got to say here, it's cooler than inside. Want a drink?'

Huw wiped the sweat off his red face with a big white handkerchief and with shaking hands opened his briefcase.

'Ben, this isn't a social call,' he said nervously. 'I've got some bad news. Unless you can pay something substantial off your mortgage, the bank is going to foreclose.'

Ben drew in his breath. 'Come off it Huw, you know I haven't a hope of paying anything more with this drought. Any money I earn goes to buying food for the stock.'

Huw cleared his throat. 'Ben, your overdraft is out of control, you are mortgaged to the hilt and the bank can no longer carry you. Unless you pay something off, the bank is forced to foreclose.'

Ben stood up and began pacing the verandah in shock. He had mortgaged the farm five years ago to buy micro fine breeding rams to upgrade the flock but the drought had trashed that idea and he'd been forced to sell thousands of dollars' worth of stud rams and ewes to the meat market before they starved to death.

He stopped pacing and stood in front of Huw. 'Right. Let's have it. How much and how long have I got to find the money?'

Huw took a deep breath and stood up facing him. 'I'm afraid it's not that simple, Ben — time's up, we have already started foreclosure proceedings.'

Ben's face went bright red with rage and he leaned over him and poked him in the chest. 'Now listen here you little shit, I've been making regular payments and you'll take this farm over my dead body. It's been in my family for generations and I have worked my arse off here since I was a kid. There is no way in this bloody world that you are going to take it off me, no bloody way.'

Huw was shaking and hastily began stuffing papers back into his briefcase.

'There's no need to get upset and use that language,' he said nervously. 'I'm only doing my job and informing you that you have been given notice and have to be off this property before the end of the month or you will be evicted. I'm warning you Ben, this property now belongs to the bank,' he said, turning and stumbling in his haste to get away.

'Wait right there you little shit,' Ben yelled after him and jumping down the verandah, he grabbed him by the shirt.

'Don't you bloody dare warn me about anything. If you think you can take this place off me you're dreaming. Now get the hell out of here before I really get mad, go on get out of here before I shoot you, you rotten bastard.'

Huw stumbled and fell over in his haste to get to his car and just as he got his keys in the door, there was a loud bang and a bullet ricocheted off the dirt in front of him.

Huw screamed, 'You maniac, you almost shot me. I'm reporting you to the police.'

'You mangy little creep, if I'd have wanted to hit you I would have. Now buggar off and if you step foot on my place again, it'll be the last thing you do.'

Falling into the driver's seat Huw roared off nearly missing the side of the car shed in his haste to reach the road.

❡

Still shaking with rage, Ben went inside and took a bottle of rum down from the cupboard. 'Take my farm — no way, I'll kill the bastards first,' he said pouring a large amount of rum into his glass. He drained it in a gulp and almost fell into his old chair by the fireplace.

'Bloody bastards, waiting like vultures for the kill.' He bent down and poured another drink. This was his home, his father's and grandfather's. There had been bad times, droughts and the wool glut but nothing like this. He'd had no decent income for five years. Everything he could sell was gone, all his stud breeding stock, the lambs too weak to stand he'd shot and all that was left were a few hundred breeders.

Where could he find some money? Ben racked his brain — his tractor was ancient, his truck falling apart, he owed money at the Produce store and had been living on mutton for months. He'd used the money he earned driving trucks to buy fodder and his parents who relied on him for an income were living on the age pension and owned nothing but their Brisbane home. There was no way he was going to ask them to sell that.

He poured another drink and thought about the last few years. The worst day was when he had to sell off his rams.

Tears poured down his face as he poured the dregs of the rum into his glass.

'Life was hard, bloody hard,' he choked brokenly and finishing off his drink he passed out. Hours later the dogs furious barking woke him and then he heard a wailing siren.

'Bloody hell,' he said holding his cracking head as he walked onto the verandah. 'Who's there?'

A police car with flashing lights pulled up in the yard and Damengin's only police officer Sergeant Percy Plod eased his enormous gut out of the door.

'Ben,' he shouted waddling towards the house, 'get your arse out here, you're under arrest.'

Feeling like death Ben stared blankly at him. 'What are you talking about you silly fat sod, what for?'

'Well,' he said, hitching up his pants, 'according to our Huw Hawtrey you tried to kill him. He's even signed an official complaint and is gunning for your hide, so get down here and into the car, I'm taking you in.'

'Look Perc, I'm as sick as a dog and there's no way I'm getting in that car. What about my sheep and the dogs?'

'Ben, old mate, get this clear. You are under arrest — if you don't come, I'll have to force you. Give a man a break,' he pleaded, 'don't make this harder than it is, just get in the car. We'll sort it all out down at the station.'

Ben let Percy take his arm and put him in the car. He felt so ill, he hardly remembered the trip into town or Percy putting him into the lockup until he woke next morning suffering from the worst hangover of his life.

Using the cell wall for support, he stood up and his pants fell to the floor. 'What the,' he said. Then he remembered Percy had removed his belt and because he had lost so much weight worrying over the last few months he had nothing to keep his pants up.

'You right there mate,' Percy called. 'I'm coming with your brekky, bacon and eggs and a lump of steak,' he said unlocking the cell door.

Ben was holding his pants up when he put the tray on the floor.

'Geez mate, lost your daks?' he laughed.

Ben frowned. 'Not funny, give me my belt so I can be decent. And you can take that food away, I'm too crook to eat anything. How long you going to keep me here?'

'How the hell do I know? Look I'll give you your belt if you eat the grub. Cooked it myself you ungrateful buggar.'

Percy was worried, Ben was a good mate and he knew his family, who were decent hardworking people.

'Look mate,' he said handing Ben his belt, 'Hawtrey has made a serious charge against you, what the hell possessed you to pull a gun on him?'

Ben stared at his hands. 'I only did it to scare him. If I'd wanted to hit him I would have.'

Percy sighed. 'Well mate, I reckon you'll need to come before the magistrate but with Paddy on the bench you might get off with a fine. I'll give him a call and ask him to get down here.'

He came back and found Ben staring gloomily out of the bars of the cell.

'Got some bad news,' he said. 'Paddy's away so you'll have to rest your heels here until he gets back.'

'Come on Percy, give a man a break, I've got stock to feed,' he said imploringly.

'Sorry mate can't do it, worth my job. Look I'll give Sid a ring, see if he can go out and see to your stock.'

Ben sat down and put his head in his hands. This was all he needed.

Over at the pub Sid was finishing off his breakfast with Bill when Rosie told him Percy Plod wanted him. Putting down his knife and fork he wandered into the lobby and picked up the phone.

'Sid here — what's the problem, Sergeant?'

'Got Ben Bangor in the slammer, he pulled a gun on Hawtrey yesterday and Paddy's not here to hear the case and bail him. He's worried about things at his farm and I said I'd give you a ring.'

'Thanks, Percy I'll come down and see the poor buggar.' Sid walked back in the kitchen and grabbed his hat from the chair.

'I'm off down the police station. You won't believe what's happened. Ben Bangor lost his cool yesterday and pulled a gun on that conniving creep Huw Hawtrey.'

'I'm coming with you,' Bill said getting up.

g

Sid led the way to his car and the pair drove through town to the Police Station and fronted the counter.

'You there Percy,' Sid called.

'Coming, morning Sid, morning Bill, Ben's out the back worrying himself to death,' Percy said waddling his bulk to the counter. Having Ben in the slammer was a ray of sunshine in his boring existence which he generally spent watching soapies on the television.

Ben's face lit up when he saw them. 'Thanks for coming. That bloody swine Hawtrey threatened to sell me up and I fired a shot to give him hurry up, now he wants to charge me.'

Sid wiped a gnarled hand across his face and sat down on the bunk. 'Jesus Ben, I wish you'd keep that temper of yours under control.'

'No wonder he lost it, 'Bill said. 'He's working night and day to keep the place and the bank steps in and says game over, farm's ours. What would you do?'

'I know, it's bloody hard and I don't know what I'd do,' Sid said turning to Ben. 'Look mate I'll go out and take care of the place. You just cool your heels here until Paddy gets back.'

Bill got up. 'Ben, I'm going to let Sam Spink know what's going on. He can write something to tell people what the banks are doing to the farmers.'

Ben nodded. 'Thanks Billy, they'll take Abington over my dead body.'

CHAPTER 6

DEIDRE HAWTREY

Over at Damengin's only bank, its three staff members — the accountant, teller and ledger clerk — huddled together, ears jammed against the dividing door that led to the bank's residence, sniggering as they listened to their boss Huw Hawtrey, his wife Audrey and their daughter Deidre screaming at each other. The noise was so loud, a small crowd had gathered on the footpath outside to listen.

Huw was still reeling from being shot at by Ben Bangor when he threatened to sell him up and now, after dishing out mega bucks because Audrey insisted that Deidre go to a Swiss finishing school, she was standing in front of him, her arms crossed, dirty, defiant and definitely not finished. He was furious to hear she had cashed in her Qantas first class ticket and bought the clapped-out red ute sitting out front.

'This is your last chance' he yelled, 'you either go back and get on the next plane to Switzerland or you can get out.'

'How could you after all we've done for you,' Audrey shrieked collapsing on the sofa. 'You are a disgrace, you should be ashamed of the way you go around, and you look like a tramp.'

'Better than looking like an overdressed tart,' Deidre yelled back.

'How dare you? Who are you calling a tart?'

'Well Mum, if the cap fits ...'

'Deidre,' Huw shouted, 'that's enough, apologise to your mother right now.'

'I don't want an apology from her, she is an apology,' Audrey said burying herself in a cushion. 'She has no respect for anyone, my poor mother was disgusted with the way she spoke to her.'

'That old cow,' Deidre yelled scornfully. 'This is all her fault; every time she comes here she causes trouble.'

'Don't you dare speak about my mother like that,' Audrey hissed. 'Huw speak to her, this is just too much.'

Deidre clenched her fists and glared. 'You know what, I'm sick of the bloody lot of you. All you care about is Timmy, you don't give two hoots about me. You didn't listen to me when I begged to go to ag college, no you send bloody Timmy who couldn't give a shit about farming. You're always on at Dad to buy Tim a sheep station just so you can have a bloody ego trip and lord it over your snooty friends. Let's face it Mum, all Timmy wants is to get the hell out of here. Why don't you send him to the bloody finishing school?'

'Deidre, I have spent thousands on you and not one word

of gratitude, you are an absolute disgrace,' Huw said, shaking his head wearily and running his hands over what remained of his hair.

'Look, how many times do I have to tell you, I want to work on the land. Buy me a bloody sheep station and you might get a return on your money.'

'Huh, I'm not spending another cent on you, you've had your last chance with me,' Huw said, walking away.

Deidre stood up and glared at them. 'Listen to me, I will not go to a bloody finishing school and I'm not going to stay where I am not welcome. So fuck you and fuck bloody Grannie for stuffing up my life,' she yelled to the delight of the listening bank staff and the crowd on the footpath.

Marching into her bedroom Dee flung herself on the bed.

'What don't they understand, it's all Grannie's fault,' she moaned to herself punching a pillow.

Audrey's mum, Edith, a social climbing snob with a talent for name dropping had arrived for her annual visit and been shocked when Deidre arrived home disgustingly filthy and smelling of sheep. And she had almost fainted when Deidre told her she'd been castrating lambs.

'It's like this Gran, you grab hold of their testicles with your teeth and bite. Delicious,' Deidre said, grinning wickedly.

That had propelled her grannie into ganging up with her mum to persuade Huw to send her off to a posh finishing school in Switzerland. And caused Deidre to cash in her tickets and buy a red ute.

'Just listen to her,' Audrey wailed. 'She is always like this, using foul language, rude and disrespectful, does nothing to help me, she's never home and when she does grace us with her presence she arrives filthy with that flea-bitten dog. Then she eats everything in sight, clears off and we don't hear from her for days. Just look at that dog, the disgusting mongrel sneaks in and sleeps on her bed and she'd bring her horse in too if she could.'

Deidre sighed to herself, now the shit had hit the fan and there was nothing for it but to go. Throwing some clothes in a bag, she whistled Rusty her faithful old cattle dog who had been shivering behind the hall cupboard since the shouting started and marched through the house ignoring her parents who were huddled together.

'Right, I'm off and you can both go to hell,' she shouted slamming the back door so hard it shattered the lock.

Throwing her swag into the back of her ute she hitched up the horse float and drove over to the council cattle yards where her horse Knacker was standing in the shade of an ancient fig tree. He whinnied with joy to see her and was even more excited when she loaded him into his float. Patting Rusty on the seat next to her, she turned the radio on full blast and drove west as fast as the old rattle trap could take her.

A couple of hours later she stopped to buy fuel and some food at the Woppa Road petrol station and was given a hoy by a mob of blokes eating pies at the outside tables.

'Where you off to then?' one of them called out.

Deidre strolled over to them. 'Nowhere in particular, looking for work, heard of anything?'

'Can ya cook?' a big fellow with a pot belly and bright red face asked.

'Sure,' she replied crossing her fingers behind her back. 'Done plenty of cooking.'

'Well,' said the big fellow, 'shearing boss Harry Hoffer has just fired the last cook after his three-gun shearers went down with food poisoning, here's his number.'

Harry almost cried with relief when Deidre stood in his office and told him with a completely straight face that she was a 'great' cook. Yeah, he reasoned to himself, she looked capable and anyway, a female was a better option than the last bloke who was roaring drunk most of the time.

'Right, you can sign on with us, we've got a shed out at Rangoon, the Wilton-Smith's place, you know?'

'Sure,' Deidre said. 'I was at school with their daughter Angela. I'll follow you out.'

Deidre's idea of cooking consisted of grilling chops or steaks over a campfire and throwing together some flour and water for damper. Food to her was fuel and she hadn't the slightest interest in how it was prepared.

'Cooking for a gang of shearers would be a piece of cake,' she smiled to herself. 'Only thing is, I'll have to work out how to bake the bloody cake and scones for smoko.'

In great spirits, Deidre followed the shearers out to Rangoon Station and shrugged off an offer to bunk down with them in the shearer's quarters. She parked her ute round the back of the cookhouse and threw an old tarp over the back for shade and shelter.

After settling Knacker in the horse paddock she wandered over to the kitchen where Harry was waiting for her.

The kitchen was a large, long room separated from the quarters by a covered breezeway. It had a wide-open verandah across the front which was dotted with an assortment of tables and chairs. Inside, a long pine table dominated the centre of the room and in the centre of the back wall was a massive wood burning stove. Under the left side window was a large sink with draining boards and plenty of storage cupboards for crockery and pots and pans.

'This is a great old stove love,' Harry said patting the huge wood burning stove lovingly. 'Cooks beaut roasts.'

Dee frowned. The stove was wood burning and had two large ovens and six hot plates.

'I'll get one of the blokes to chop some more wood but there's a bit in the box to get you started,' Harry said. 'Better get things going, it'll take a while for those ovens to heat up.

'You'll find plenty of tucker in the storeroom and I brought some chops for tonight. I put them in the fridge but we'll knock off a killer for the rest of the week.

'By the way,' he said turning to her, 'the men like something nice for sweets, but a couple of tins of fruit will do for tonight until you get into it. Don't forget to get the bread ready for tomorrow, there's eggs there and you can fry a few chops to go with them.'

'Right there Dee, 'he said smiling, 'I'll leave you to it.'

Dee felt sick as she watched him walk away. 'He's got to be kidding, bread, smoko, pudding, buggar me.

'At least I know how to get the stove going,' she told Rusty who was slumped in the doorway. She crumpled paper set the kindling and pine in the fire box opened the flue and watched as the fire roared to life.

'See,' she said to Rusty, 'not too hard.'

Dee went into the storeroom and found sacks of potatoes, onions, bags of flour, tins of peas, beans and fruit, syrup, canned milk, powdered milk and a large container of tea.

Filling the kettle at the kitchen sink, Dee put it on the back of the stove, threw a bucketful of potatoes in a large pot of water and set it at the back of the stove to boil. She found a couple of frypans gave them a rinse under the tap and put them on the rack above the stove to dry.

Pouring herself a cup of tea, she looked out of the window and saw the sun sinking in the west sending a golden glow over the beautiful old Rangoon homestead. 'Magnificent,' she sighed. 'One day I'll get a place like that.'

Draining her tea Dee set the frypans on the front of the stove and threw the chops in to cook. Suddenly there were screams and howls outside and she dashed outside to find Rusty attacking a pack of dogs. Grabbing her stock whip, she cracked it over their heads and dragged Rusty off. But by the time she had tied him up to the ute and gone back to the kitchen the chops were on fire.

'Bloody hell,' she cried throwing the pans on the bench. Frantically she searched the fridge for more chops but there weren't any. 'Gravy, I'll cover them with gravy. No one will give a damn,' she said, mixing flour, water and throwing in half a packet of gravy mix. She threw the chops in a baking pan, covered them with the lumpy mess and shoved them in the oven.

She had just opened a can of peas when the dinner bell rang and the shearers started pouring into the kitchen cracking jokes and drinking cans of cold beer.

'What's for tea love?' Harry called.

'Won't be a minute Harry,' Dee called, 'just got to mash the spuds.'

But the 'spuds' were hard and solid and wouldn't mash no matter how she tried so she cut them into pieces, threw them in a bowl and put it on the table with the peas. Then she pulled the dish of chops from the oven and put it next to them.

Plates clattered as the shearers helped themselves.

'What the, this is bloody awful,' Harry yelled pulling a piece of burnt chop from his teeth and throwing down his knife and fork. 'I thought you said you could cook. You should be shot for serving shit like this.'

He got up and grabbed her arm. 'The chops are burnt to buggary, the spuds are raw and even the peas are cold. What's the big idea telling us you can cook, you're not a bloody cook's arsehole.'

Howls of outrage followed and the mob began swearing abuse and hurling chops at her.

Deidre was terrified and tried to run but her escape was blocked by Harry.

'Oh no you don't,' he said grabbing her arm.

Only the split-second arrival of the boss's son Angus

Wilton-Smith saved her from the angry mob.

'What the hell is going on here?' Angus said, pushing Harry aside and removing his hand from Dee's arm.

'Said she could cook and she's a bloody liar,' Harry said. 'Anyway, she's sacked.'

Angus pulled Dee behind him and turned to Harry. 'Look here, that's no way to treat a woman. I'll send some food over from the house and you can have our cook for the shearing. Come on,' he said taking hold of Dee's arm, 'better get out of here before they lynch you.'

He took the still shaking Dee back to the homestead and gave her a brandy.

'What on earth are you doing working as a shearer's cook? I thought you were off to Switzerland with Angela?' he said, looking at her in amazement.

Dee shook her head. 'There is no way I want to go to a bloody school, and I packed up and left.'

Angus laughed. 'No doubt about you Dee, you've got guts. What will your parents say when they find out you're out here?'

'Who cares, they couldn't give a damn about me and it's my life and I'll spend it my way.'

Angus shook his head. 'Surely you haven't been sleeping in the shearers' quarters?'

'No, I wouldn't bed down with that lot. I've got my swag in the back of the ute, Rusty and I will camp in there.'

'Well grab your things and you can move into the homestead, there's heaps of room. Mum's gone on a cruise and you know where Angela is,' he said grinning.

'Dad was pissed off too so he packed a bag and his golf clubs and flew to the Gold Coast. He won't be back, he hates the place so there's just me and Mrs Hooper. Bring your stuff in and Rusty can come too.'

When they sat down for tea that night, Dee told him about the fight with her parents and how she left in anger.

Angus felt sorry for her. He had been battling along on his own since he graduated from agriculture college. Before his return, Rangoon had been left with a work-shy manager who had run it into the ground and when the drought hit, there was little left in the kitty to carry them through. His selfish parents, who were absolutely sick to death of the drought, escaped to their pad at the Gold Coast and left him to it.

And although they had plenty of assets and blue-chip shares, they refused to put any more cash into the place. Angus had made hard decisions to de-stock and told his parents to stop spending and cut back.

But nothing could stop his mum whose latest splurges, Angela's Swiss finishing school and her cruise, gave him nightmares thinking about them.

Rangoon was his love and he was too busy trying to get it on a level plain to think of much else but he admired Dee for standing up to her parents and doing what she wanted to.

'Poor Audrey,' he had overheard his mother say to his sister Angela. 'Where on earth did she get Deidre from? She's simply out of control and quite dreadful.' *Not dreadful at all,* he thought to himself.

'Look you can stay here and help in the shed for the shearing but stay away from the kitchen,' Angus said.

Angus took Dee over to the shed the next day and gave her the job of tar boy which had her dashing here and there dabbing tar from her can on sheep nicked by careless shears.

She enjoyed working in the classic old shed which had been built at the turn of the century in solid iron bark timber. It was a magnificent building that had stood the test of time and invasion by white ants. Lanolin from the thousands of sheep that had passed through had put a shine on the wooden floor and the huge poles as thick as a big man's girth reared 60 ft and supported massive roof trusses that bore the corrugated roofing iron affording protection from the burning sun and drenching rain.

When the fleece were removed, they were thrown to Nigel the wool classer who graded them on a large table that ran the full length of the shed. He was a top operator and an alcoholic.

A few days into the shearing a drunken sot left a half-full flagon of rum in the outside loo. Stopping for a pee, Nigel noticed the rum, downed the lot and headed down the track to the nearest pub. Angus took over and called on Dee to help.

'Right Dee, here's your chance,' Angus said. 'You can help me.'

Picking up a fleece from the floor of the wool shed, he tossed it so that it fell perfectly flat on the wool classing table and using his index finger and thumb he rubbed the greasy wool to determine its quality and strength before throwing it to the back of the table to be packed.

The pair worked easily together sorting the fleece while outside in the holding yards sheep bleated noisily as they waited to be chased up the chutes to the shearers who dragged them backwards to the stands and relieved them of their filthy wool.

Despite the heat, noise and flies, Deidre was incredibly happy although she dreaded the end of the shed. To break the gruelling monotony of the backbreaking work, a couple of gun shearers were egged on to race. All work stopped, bets and shears flew and two gun shearers battled to beat the clock.

It seemed like no time before the numbers of sheep in the holding pens dwindled to a handful and the shearing gang slowed down. Tomorrow they would pack their shears away, head to town to sink a few beers and then move on to the next shed. Rangoon's cheque for the clip would be far short of the usual but at least there were sheep to shear. Many stations had either dispersed or disposed of their flocks.

Angus and Dee were sitting at the breakfast table in the homestead when the phone rang. Angus went to answer it and returned looking worried.

'That was Teddy Reed. He's arrived back in town because Bomber is in hospital.'

Deidre let out a gasp. 'Is he okay?'

'Matlock his prize bull charged him, his dog ran all the way to Ben Bangor's place and managed to bring him back.

Bomber's okay, few broken ribs and an arm but the dog should get a medal.'

'Thank goodness. Poor Bomber, he's a top bloke and is lumbered with a son who couldn't give a damn about the property,' she paused for breath and then said, 'I should ask Teddy to swap.

'I'll pack my stuff and go home and see how things are at home, then I'll go and see Bomber in hospital and, might catch up with Teddy, haven't seen him for years.'

Angus frowned. 'Look do you really have to go, you're welcome to stay here if they don't want you. Would you like me to come with you, I know your mum quite likes me.'

'Everyone likes you, Angus,' Deidre said grinning. 'Don't sell yourself short. I'll be okay and I'd rather go on my own.'

Angus blushed. He had enjoyed having her around. *She is the most honest hardworking person I know,* he said to himself. He enjoyed her sense of humour and her good nature.

Deidre packed her swag and came to say goodbye.

'I'll go home and see how things are and then I'll go and see Teddy. Then, I may come back here for a while. Maybe I could do some work around the place if that is okay?' she said.

'That's absolutely fine Dee, come anytime, you're always welcome.'

After she had left, Angus continued to think about her. She was the most unusual girl he had ever known, nothing like his sister Angela who spent all her time looking in the mirror. She had never lifted a finger to help on the property.

There was no false modesty about Deidre, Angus thought,

she didn't seem to care what she looked like. Her unruly short red hair was always jammed under a hat that came down so low it almost hid a pair of huge green eyes and shaded a turned up nose covered with a mass of freckles. When she smiles, her eyes twinkle, her nose wrinkles and the world smiles with her, he mused.

Angus was tall but Deidre was just a head shorter and had a shapely, well-built body with incredibly long legs. Her most attractive feature, he considered, was her wide mouth featuring perfect white teeth and he absolutely loved her deep earthy chuckle. 'All in all, a terrific package,' Angus said aloud.

Deidre drove slowly back into town thinking about things and when she arrived home, she stood outside staring at the stately residence attached to the imposing building that was Damengin's Bank. She hoped her father would be working in the bank at the front and she let herself in through the back door, walked around the screened verandah to her bedroom and looked in the mirror.

'What a mess,' she said out loud. Her unruly red hair clung to her head in greasy tendrils, her eyes were red and swollen from the dusty shed and she took a whiff of her underarm. 'I smell like something dead,' she groaned.

Dumping her swag on the floor she went into the bathroom and had a long hot shower. An hour later with clean hair and fresh clothes she was feeling heaps better. She made herself a strong cup of tea in the kitchen and sat outside on the verandah to enjoy it.

I'll just lay it on the line to Dad that I want to work on the land

and that's it. I'm nineteen, almost twenty, and I absolutely will not go to the bloody finishing school or any other bloody school, she said to herself.

Huw arrived home late and stressed after crunching numbers in his office in his bid to wriggle out of the mess he was in. He'd had several heated phone calls with Shifty Grey about the drought relief money and they decided to do nothing for the time being and hope something would turn up before the bank's canny auditors did.

If all else failed, Huw thought, he could somehow pass the blame to Shifty. *I'll dump the bastard right in it.*

He wandered onto the verandah and saw Deidre asleep in a chair. *Hell,* he thought, *not more trouble.* He bent down and gave her shoulder a rough shake. 'Wake up, where have you been?'

Deidre woke with a start and gasped when she saw her father standing over her.

'Dad, 'she said sitting up. 'I rang you, did you get my message? I was out helping with the shearing at Rangoon.'

'No,' Huw said, 'I've been busy and what the hell have you been doing shearing for God's sake, have you taken leave of your senses? First you go off droving and now shearing, your mother is going to have a fit.'

Deidre shrugged, her mouth set in a grim line. 'I didn't come here to have another fight. I came because I heard you'd been shot at, and what the fuck were you doing trying to sell Ben up?'

Huw went red in the face. 'How dare you speak to me like

that? It's none of your business so don't try and shove your nose in. You've been nothing but trouble. If you are staying here you can look after yourself,' he said.

Deidre watched his retreating back and muttered to herself. 'Thanks for the welcome home, Dad.'

CHAPTER 7

RETURN OF SISTER MARY

While Ben Bangor waited impatiently for Paddy, who was the district's only Justice of the Peace, to return and hopefully bail him, Paddy had problems of his own and had raced off to Brisbane to help his sister Mary.

After the council meeting where a decision was made to tackle the Federal Government face to face in Canberra over the missing drought relief funds, Paddy had gone to bed late but couldn't sleep. He tossed and turned worrying about his property Paddylea, the pub, and his trucking business. Added to the list was the dread of his mate Bomber flying them to Longreach to catch the Brisbane flight. 'Bloody idiot thinks he's still flying a MIG in the Vietnam War,' Paddy moaned.

Lightning ricocheted across the sky and was followed by an almighty blast of thunder that shook the foundations of the old pub with such a force he sat bolt upright in bed with shock. 'Christ almighty,' he moaned rubbing gnarled fingers through thick grey hair with a shudder. Then seeing Tipper his kelpie bitch scratching herself at the end of the bed, he yelled, 'and you, you little buggar stop lying on me and licking my face.'

Paddy sighed deeply, how times had changed. He had been born in and had lived in Damengin most of his sixty-one years. Parents Will and Katy had arrived in Sydney from Ireland in 1917 with war raging in Europe. Will found work as a fettler repairing the railways that spanned the west, settling Katy in Damengin and sending her his wages each week. Paddy was born in 1918 and Katy was in her forties when she died giving birth to a daughter Mary in 1934. Will was broken-hearted and hit the bottle. Two years later he finally drank himself to death leaving a teenage Paddy to take care of his infant sister Mary.

At eighteen, Paddy was built like the proverbial shithouse. He stood well over six foot and as a result of hauling beer kegs for the publican since he was twelve, was strong as an ox. He took a job shearing leaving the infant Mary in the care of the nuns at the local convent.

Paddy started as a roustabout picking up fleeces and bringing the tar jar, but he earned his shears in record time and was soon up there with the guns knocking off one hundred or more a day. He enjoyed working in the sheds.

'Best education a man can have,' he told anyone who would listen. 'I was smart enough to steer clear of the pub at the end of the clip and in a few years bought a Bedford truck for three hundred quid. I fitted her out for wool and freight and when shearing began again got the job carting the clip down to Brisbane. I loaded up with booze and produce for the trip home and made a bloody fortune.'

By the time he was forty, everything Paddy did turned to gold. His trucks travelled the length and breadth of south west Queensland and when the big drought hit in the 60s and farmers walked off their land, Paddy bought heavily.

Yep, he reflected, those were good years, the best until, well a man can't be good at everything.

His marriage to a Brisbane socialite had been a disaster. After spending a year away from the bright city lights, she fled leaving him with a baby son Bill named for his dad, William.

Bill was all his, the centre of his universe and his shadow. He followed him everywhere and mirrored his movements. When he was twelve, he packed him off to boarding school and twice the lad arrived home filthy and exhausted in the back of a cattle truck. 'This might be yours,' the first truckie said, handing him over with a grin. Everyone knew Paddy and everyone knew his Bill.

Suddenly his thoughts were shattered by the loud shrill ringing of the phone beside his bed.

'Shit,' he said rubbing his eyes and sitting up. He picked up the phone, looked at his watch and bellowed down the line, 'What the hell time is this to phone a man?'

There was silence at the other end and then a quiet refined voice said softly, 'Good morning Mr Murphy, its Sister Angelina from St Martha's speaking and yes I do know the time but this is a rather urgent matter.'

Paddy was embarrassed, Sister Angelina was Mother Superior of the convent school where his sister Mary worked as a teaching nun.

'Excuse me, Sister,' he said clearing his voice, 'I've had a bad night, what can I do for you?'

'I'm so sorry to disturb you Mr Murphy but I'm calling about your sister Mary.'

'Mary?' Paddy shaken took a deep breath, 'What's the matter with my Mary, is she ill?'

'Yes I'm afraid Mary is ill, in fact we can no longer take responsibility for her.'

Paddy let out a sigh, 'Jesus, Mary and Joseph,' he said. 'What next?'

'Mr Murphy really, there's no need to blaspheme,' Sister Angelina chastised him in her quiet saintly voice.

'Sorry Sister, such a shock. What's the matter with Mary? Is she in hospital? What happened?'

There was a slight pause on the other end of the line. 'No she is not in hospital per se, she is here with us. I think she could benefit from a spell in a rehabilitation unit, perhaps you could arrange something. Unfortunately we've done all we can for her.'

Paddy groaned, 'Rehab, Sister, what do you mean rehab, what's the matter with her, what has she done?'

'Mr Murphy, I can't discuss this matter over the telephone. I must insist you come down here as soon as you can. As I said before, we can no longer accept responsibility for Mary.'

Paddy looked at his watch. 'Right, Sister I'll settle things here and be on my way. I should be there late tonight or early tomorrow. Sister,' he said gently, 'give Mary my love and tell her not to worry.'

After hanging up the phone, Paddy jumped out of bed. If he left straightaway, it would take him at least fifteen hours to drive to Brisbane. He walked down the hall and knocked loudly on Rosie's door at the end of the passageway.

'Rosie,' he yelled, 'you awake yet?

Rosie woke with a start. 'What's the matter,' she replied looking at the clock, 'it's not even 6 o'clock.'

'Sorry to wake you but I'm off to Brisbane, Mary's crook, sick or something. The convent called and wants me to go and get her.'

Rosie opened the door, and stood facing him, her large frame enveloped in a massive nightie dotted with daises and her hair, usually restrained in a bun, a halo of grey curls around her head. She put her hand on Paddy's arm sympathetically and he looked down into the kindest eyes in the world.

'Our poor darling Mary,' she said. 'What did they say was the matter?'

Paddy squeezed her hand. 'Didn't say, just said come and get her. I'll drive straight there and all being well, be back in a couple of days.'

Rosie followed him along the corridor as far as the bathroom. 'I just hope it's nothing serious. You get dressed and I'll go downstairs and make you up some food for the trip.'

❡

While Paddy lathered himself in the shower, he thought about the message from the convent. *What did they mean, she's your responsibility.* She had been his responsibility until she was an adult.

When his father died he was just eighteen and Mary was two. He had looked after her as best he could. He had paid the nuns at St Ursula's in Damengin to take care of her. Later he sent her to boarding school in Brisbane and when she finished school she helped him with the pub and took care of the accounts and provisioning.

Yes, he had taken care of Mary, she had never done without and he had certainly missed her when she left home to live in Brisbane. He was horrified when she wrote and told him she wanted to be a nun. *What a waste,* he thought.

Mary had been an incredibly pretty girl with a happy disposition and he had hated to see her wasting her life as a nun. But it was her choice and over the years he had adjusted to it. Who was he to object?

After she took her final vows, she had been sent to teach at a convent school and during the holidays she had visited him. But for the last five years, since the start of the drought, she hadn't been home. In fact, the last time he had seen her was when Bill graduated from Agriculture College and they all had dinner together afterwards.

What Paddy didn't know was that it was shortly after Bill's graduation that Mary had broken down. She was desperately unhappy and for years had found solace in alcohol. She had nicked bottles of communion wine hiding them under her habit and polishing them off after lights out.

Recently she had tippled too much and her students found her snoring gently on her desk. She pleaded exhaustion but two of her street-smart students twigged and sniggered at her behind her back. She was terrified they would sneak to Mother Superior but worse was to come when Sister Gerhard of the long nose and nasty disposition caught her pinching the wine. A stock inventory was done and Mary stood accused. At first she denied everything but under Sister Angelina's Gestapo styled interrogation, she cracked and confessed.

Mary was sent to old Father McDill for counselling. The good Father, who was a dirty old pervert with a liking for young boys and pretty women, was hugely sympathetic. He gently stroked Mary's tear-stained face, wiped away her tears and listened sympathetically while she poured out her troubles.

Pathetically grateful for the large glasses of communion wine the priest plied her with, Mary tolerated his gentle caressing of her heaving breasts but when he shoved his hand up her leg and tried to pull down her knickers she threw the wine in his face and bolted.

Sister Angelina was not amused and believing the good Father's version, banished her to her cell, ordering her to pray for forgiveness.

A desperate Mary fled, emptied the parish poor-box and splashed out on a flagon of cheap wine from a bottle shop assuring the nosey cashier it was for a parish raffle.

ℊ

She had walked along the riverbank and sat down on a seat where she watched the moonlight throw dappled light on the water. She opened the flagon, drank deeply and felt a warm glow envelop her. How astonishing, she thought to herself, the more she drank, the better she felt. Finally, the flagon was empty and she lay down on the grass beside the seat and fell asleep.

The next morning a passing police patrol found her and, unable to wake her, were about to call for an ambulance when Senior Constable Gary Geeves bent down and smelt her breath. 'She's not sick,' he said, 'She's dead drunk. Better take her back to the lockup to sober up.'

Back at patrol headquarters Sergeant Michael O' Flynn took charge. A member of the faith, he had recently migrated from Ireland where for generations people had turned a blind eye to the weaknesses of the clergy. He was also a kindly fellow and luckily for Mary vetoed throwing her in the slammer with prostitutes, drunks and small-time crims.

'Here darling, drink this tea,' he told a mortified and awfully sick Mary. He felt sorry for the poor little thing and was amazed at the reaction he got when he telephoned the convent.

'Now come on Sister, calm down,' he said, 'For sure that's no way to carry on, she is paying for her bit of fun, and she's in an awful bad way.'

'Well she may be, she's certainly going to pay this time,' Sister Angelina said angrily. 'That's it, Sergeant, that's the absolute end, she will have to go.'

Sergeant O' Flynn smiled, 'Well Sister,' he said. 'Before she goes, you'll have to come and get her, we can't keep her here.'

But Sister Angelina absolutely refused to go to or to let any of the sisters go and she sent Harry the yardman off in a taxi to pick her up.

Mary arrived back at the convent nursing a massive hangover and after listening to Sister Angelina's tirade decided death would be a welcome release.

'You are a disgrace,' Sister Angelina raged. 'You will go to work in the parish laundry, you will not be teaching anymore and you are banned from speaking to the sisters.'

At the convent laundry where she tackled mountains of dirty washing, she was bullied and abused by the dregs of humanity. In a last desperate attempt to escape she ran to the adjoining Church, emptied the collection box, bought two bottles of gin from the corner bottle shop and went on a blinder. She was found legless behind a pew at the back of the Church by its ninety-year-old senile priest. Her skirt had ridden up around her neck, displaying her navy knickers, and her black stockings were around her ankles. She was lucky Father Gregory was way past dabbling in that sort of thing.

This was the final straw and Sister Angelina locked her in her cell and telephoned Paddy.

g

After driving through the night, Paddy arrived at the convent and was given a blow by blow account of Mary's faults and misdemeanours.

Finally he cracked. 'I've heard enough, you have made her out to be worse than the devil himself, just take me to my sister.'

He found Mary sitting on a bed clutching her few possessions looking so broken that he bent down and gathered her in his arms. 'My poor little pet,' he said. Mary sobbed and buried her face in his shirt.

'What have they done to you?' he said stroking her head.

Mother Superior shrugged. 'We've tried to help her, but she is full of sin and won't repent.'

Paddy picked up Mary's small bag and without a backward glance steered her through the door. 'Come on love,' he said. 'I'm taking you home.'

On the long road home, Mary slept with her head resting against his shoulder as Paddy gripped the steering wheel, his mouth set in a grim line.

What the hell had gone wrong, he wondered. Mary had been a lovely child, small and dainty with thick dark hair and skin like milk.

It had been more than thirty years since she had left home. 'Where have they gone,' he said to himself. 'It seems only yesterday she was the belle of the town and now she's just a tiny broken wreck.'

Paddy drove into the yard behind the pub and stopped,

'Mary,' he said giving her a little shake. 'Wake up love, we're home.'

He got out of the car, went around the other side and opened the door for her.

Mary stepped out rubbing the sleep from her eyes. Paddy put his arm around her.

'Thank you Paddy, she said looking up at him, her huge eyes full of tears, 'Thank you for bringing me home.'

Paddy choked back the lump in his throat. 'Come on love,' he said gently taking her arm, 'Rosie will be waiting to see you.'

CHAPTER 8

PRODIGAL TEDDY ARRIVES HOME

After he visited his dad at the hospital, Teddy drove out to Redlands, the family property he hadn't visited since his mum died and he inherited oodles of funds which he spent on enjoying himself. Just recently he'd become a bit bored and was enjoying the change of scenery.

'Nice little nurse at the hospital, what was her name,' he mused as he pulled into the yard. 'Pass the time away until Dad's back on deck.'

Teddy got out of the car and Bomber's dog Tessa almost flattened him. 'Hold on old girl, get down,' he said laughing. 'Yes I know you love me, just quit the licking, and let me get my stuff out.'

Tessa sat on his feet as he tried to negotiate the veranda steps and when he opened the front door she dashed ahead so he couldn't shut her out. When he still didn't take any notice of her she rolled on her back and whined until he gave in and rubbed her belly.

'Okay, yes you are a lovely girl, 'he said starting to get up but she grabbed his hand gently in her mouth and held him.

'Okay Tessa you old slag, that's enough, dinner?' he said going to the pantry and taking out a tin of food.

Tessa yelped with delight and raced into the kitchen sitting perfectly still in front of her dish while he poured the jellied contents into it.

'Right, that's out of the way,' he said with relief. 'God what a mess the place is in.' He walked through the grand old living room with its ornate fireplace and down the hall into his old bedroom. It was exactly as he had left it. His old rugby and cricket trophies spilled over on the shelves, school photos decorated the walls and a large portrait photo of his mother Caroline wearing a large flowery hat, taken at some race meeting, dominated the wall behind his bed.

Teddy threw his bag on the bed, changed into his old work clothes and followed by the still excited Tessa went outside. 'Come on girl, let's head for the paddocks,' he said.

Abandoning his luxury BMW for the old farm ute and with Tessa riding shotgun, he drove down the track to the nearest windmill, its sails moving slowly in the slight breeze pumping a trickle of water into the trough. Skinny sheep raised their heads hopefully as he drove up. He stood there speechless. This is what was left of the magnificent Redlands flock that he had known from childhood. 'No bloody wonder Dad is fed up,' he said.

Getting out he cleaned the scum off the water in the trough and looked around. Not a blade of grass, even the trees were bare. 'Enough to break a man's heart,' he sighed.

'Right Tessa into the truck we're off to sort this lot out.'

Teddy drove the 40 km into town and pulled up around the back of Gerry Fitzgerald's Produce Store in front of the loading bay and called out.

'You there Gerry?'

Gerry's son Tom leaned out of the door and when he saw Teddy his face broke into a huge grin. 'Teddy, mate, when did you get in town?'

Teddy jumped out of the cattle truck and slid back the gate. 'Great to see you, Tom. I got back just this morning, Dad's stuck in hospital. Shit, Tom when did things get this bad, I had no idea.'

'Been bad for almost three years now Ted, surprised your dad hadn't told you, whole district's in strife, some people selling up walking off their places.'

Teddy shoved his hat on the back of his head. 'I couldn't believe the state our place was in. Poor bloody sheep are on their last legs. Can't understand why Dad has let them get down so bad.'

Tom looked embarrassed. 'A case of funds or lack of, I guess.'

Teddy looked away. 'Dad should have told me. Right Tom, load up the truck with Lucerne hay and fill the bins with grain. I'll give you my cheque and settle Dad's account. Plenty in there, you can check with the bank if you want to.'

'No mate, I know you're good for it.'

Loaded to the hilt, the truck had a slow trip back to Redlands where the prize merino ewes, what was left of them, dined in style that night, their stomachs full for the first time in months.

After feeding a slavering Tessa, Teddy drove back into town, called at the pub to buy his dad a bottle of whisky and ran into Billy Murphy helping out while Paddy was away.

'Billy mate, when did you get back, thought you were up north mustering or something?'

'Finished that job, came home to help Dad, how's your old man?'

'Could be worse, I'd say he's being well looked after by the doting Maggie. But I got a helluva shock when I saw the state of our place. I didn't have a clue Dad was in such a mess.'

Billy shook his head, 'Yes, even Dad's worried and it takes a lot to upset him.'

Teddy nodded. 'Where is he?'

Bill shrugged. 'He's had to rush off to Brisbane and pick up Aunty Mary — she's very sick or something. They should be home tomorrow.'

'By the way, did you hear about Ben Bangor being locked up for trying to shoot Huw Hawtrey?'

Teddy looked at him in amazement. 'You're kidding me.'

'No, the bank wants to sell him up and he drew a gun on that shit Hawtrey, God that man's a creep. Poor Ben, he's been working twenty-four hours a day, seven days a week trying to save his place. Culling kangaroos, driving trucks anything. Now he's locked up and can't apply for bail until Dad gets home.'

'Bloody hell, poor Ben, he was my hero when I was at school, must be killing him. Bill, be a good mate and get me another bottle, I'll go and see him when I've checked on Dad.'

Bill handed Teddy his bottles and he drove out to the hospital his mind in turmoil. First he had to sort out Bomber.

He was rather miffed to find the lovely Nurse Phoebe Taylor was off duty. Relieving her was an ugly old crone who looked as if she sucked lemons for fun and who ignored him when he waved to her.

He found Bomber sitting up reading one of the *Playboy* magazines he had dropped off earlier. 'Hey Dad, you are looking better,' he said dumping a package on the bed.

Bomber's eyes lit up and he stuffed the magazine under his pillow.

'Much better, what have you got there, not bloody grapes,' he said gruffly.

'Something much better,' Teddy grinned, 'bit of liquid refreshment. Hold on to this while I find some glasses.

Teddy emptied out Bomber's water glass and tipped his toothbrush from its container.

'Here we are, to your health and good times,' he said clinking his glass with Bomber's.

'Dad,' he asked sitting down next to him on the bed, 'Why didn't you tell me how bad things were? I would have come home sooner.'

Bomber shrugged. 'Didn't want to worry you and, I

thought we'd get through it, always have.'

'Not this time though,' Teddy said taking a sip of his drink.

He stood up as Matron Maggie walked in. She smiled when she saw who it was.

'Teddy, so you finally gave the city folk a miss and came home to see us.'

Teddy gave her a kiss, 'Maggie, you old bossy boots, you don't change.'

Maggie took Bomber's glass from him and smelt the contents. 'What do you think you're doing giving my patient alcohol,' she said sternly to Teddy. 'Totally against the rules and anyway, where's mine?'

Teddy laughed and offered her his glass. 'You take mine, I'll swig from the bottle,' he said. 'I hope you're off duty Matron.'

Maggie clinked her glass with Bomber and sat down on the chair Teddy offered her.

'Always on duty, hope you are going to be here for a while Teddy.'

'Looks like I'll have to stick around. I was just asking Dad how long he's going to be cooped up in this hell hole.'

Maggie smiled. 'That all depends on how he behaves himself but with you home to look after him, I may allow him to leave at the end of next week. Mind, I said, if you look after him. He has broken ribs and pelvis as well as a fractured arm and is not allowed to lift.'

Bomber groaned. 'How long before I am back on my feet totally Maggie?'

'Can't really say, you're such a tough old buggar but give yourself at least a month.'

Bomber looked at Teddy and his voice cracked. 'Would really appreciate it if you could hang around a bit Teddy, looks like I need a bit of a hand.'

Teddy's eyes filled with tears and he turned away. This was the first time his dad had asked him for anything and he knew how hard it was for him.

'Dad,' he said, 'I'm staying as long as you need me. A change of scenery will do me good. Anyway I was getting soft down there.'

'Change of subject, did either of you know Ben Bangor is locked up?'

Bomber choked on his drink 'You're joking, what happened?'

'Hawtrey told him he was going to sell him up and the silly fool lost his cool and fired a shot at him. Hawtrey went to the cops and Percy Plod went out, arrested him and threw him in the slammer. Poor buggar can't even get bail because Paddy's away so he has to stay there until he gets back. I'm heading over there now to see him.'

Maggie got up her mouth set in a grim line. 'I don't suppose Ben should have shot at him, but I never liked Huw Hawtrey, he's an arrogant little man and that wife of his is a stuck up cow.'

Teddy smiled. 'His daughter's a cracker though and an amazing rider, wonder what she's doing now?'

Maggie cleared her throat and smiled. 'I can tell you that,

she's having the time of her life working as a shearer's cook and I might add, Mummy and Daddy are not amused.'

Teddy laughed, 'Trust Deidre, love to catch up with her while I'm home, she's lots of fun.'

'Well, he said getting up, 'I'm off to see Ben Bangor before it gets too late, leave you two drunks in peace.'

He drove to the police station saw the sign saying it was closed and banged on the door until Percy Plod the town's police sergeant yelled out.

'Can't you read the sign, we're closed until 8 am tomorrow unless it's an emergency.'

Teddy banged again, 'Percy, it's me Teddy Reed I want to see Ben, come on mate let me in just for a couple of minutes.'

Percy opened the door, waved him inside and stood behind the counter.

'Can't you wait until morning Teddy? I was just cooking tea.'

'What the hell's going on Percy? What have you got Ben locked up for?'

'What else could I do? Bloody Hawtrey's going to press charges.'

Teddy opened his wallet. 'What's the bail? I'll put it up, you can't just lock him up, he's got stock to feed. Here you are take what you want.'

Percy shook his head. 'Can't do it mate, have to wait till Paddy comes back to front court, then we can talk about bail money.'

Teddy shoved his wallet into his back pocket, 'Percy mate,

just let me have a few words with him?'

Percy shook his head and then seeing the look in Teddy's eyes sighed. 'Follow me and just for a few minutes while I get my tea ready.'

He led the way to the small lockup at the far end of the police station and unlocked the door.

Ben was lying on the bed. When he saw Teddy, he stood up.

'Teddy, great to see you mate,' he said offering his hand.

Teddy shook his hand vigorously, 'Well this is a bloody mess.'

Ben grinned, 'That's the understatement of the year, but what the hell are you doing here?'

'Had to race home, Dad's in hospital with busted ribs and God knows what else. Thought I'd check and see if I can do anything for you at your place.'

'Thanks mate, Sid's been here with Billy Murphy, they were going to go out but if you could just check. The feed or what's left of it is in the shed and the mob is out about a kilometre away at the first windmill. Just check the water's coming through okay and feed the dogs. Give them a couple of bones or they'll fret.'

Percy banged on the door of the cell. 'Time's up.'

Teddy patted Ben's shoulder, 'Not a problem, I'll make a few phone calls got some good mates who are legal eagles. I'll be back tomorrow, with some clean clothes and stuff. Now settle down and take it easy, have a rest. God knows you've earned it.'

After the cell door shut Ben lay back on his bed, his head throbbed and he closed his eyes. What a mess. Where was he going to find the money to keep the bank at bay, he couldn't stand the thought of losing Abington.

92

CHAPTER 9

WOE AND WORRY

Since his altercation with Ben Bangor, Huw Hawtrey had been tormented with worry. He knew Ben had no intention of hurting him and he also knew there were no grounds for the bank to sell him up.

How could they? Ben had been steadily banking small amounts earned from truck driving for Paddy and from kangaroo culling into the bank. As a result, Huw's prospects of promotion varied from zero to double zero and he knew he would be lucky to have a job if the bank discovered what he'd done.

He slumped over his office desk and put his head in his hands. His only hope was if Paddy sent Ben to jail for firing a gun at him even if it was over his head. But Huw knew this wasn't going to happen; Paddy was too honest and Ben was a mate who had been working his butt off driving trucks for him.

He got up, poured himself a strong drink and paced the office floor racking what little was left of his brain for a solution. God things were bloody difficult. It was the fault of his social climbing wife Audrey and her ambition to mix with those nobs the Wilton-Smiths. Even their 50,000 acres were badly affected by the drought and they should have tightened their belts but Millie and Malcolm were off enjoying themselves leaving poor Angus flogging himself to death trying to keep the place together. His little sister, the dippy Angela, was in Switzerland attending the posh finishing school bloody Deidre refused to go to. Audrey had nagged him to death saying they must have something for Timothy who, after pleading with her to let him be a hairdresser, had been shunted off at huge expense to the state's finest agricultural college.

The poor lad had spent the most miserable three years of his life at the college where he had failed every exam except art expression and ultimately been caught in bed with the art master. After being thrown out and equipped with a beautifully forged reference he had been hired as a first-year jackaroo at Somerset Downs Station in western New South Wales.

Then yesterday he had arrived home, fired from his job when the manager found him blow-drying the cook's hair instead of branding steers. The manager said, 'He was as useless as tits on a bull' and that, thought Huw, just about summed it up.

Only this morning at breakfast Tim had wandered in

looking very pleased with himself wearing a pair of brilliant red-hot pants and a pretty floral shirt. He told Huw, who was unable to say anything because he was choking on his cornflakes, that he was heading to Sydney to take part in the gay Mardi Gras and then going to try for a hairdressing apprenticeship.

Huw was too stunned to say anything and was still sitting at the table when he heard Tim speed off down the drive in the car his mother had bought for his birthday.

'So much for the sheep station I ruined myself trying to get for him,' Huw said furiously. 'Anyway, who gives a rat's arse what he wants to do, it's his life.' But he knew Audrey would be devastated, all her dreams of him being a station owner and marrying dippy Angela Wilton-Smith were now completely shot.

It was all Audrey's fault, he had been pressured into foreclosing on Ben's property so he could nab it at the bank's mortgagee auction for peanuts. And he knew he had needed to be quick before the bloody drought broke and prices skyrocketed.

Now there was the matter of Deidre, he thought. *Nothing but trouble.* He had reluctantly paid for a fiendishly expense boarding school but she hitchhiked back to her horse and was expelled. Then her godfather paid for her to go to a school down south where she could take that clapped-out old horse with her and where her only achievement was to star in the Polocrosse team. There was a furious row when she came home on holidays because her mother refused to allow her to go droving. She went anyway and no one heard from her for weeks. Then Audrey and her awful mother Edith concocted another horrifically expensive scheme to have her finished at a Swiss finishing school and that had almost finished everyone.

Just yesterday he had bumped into Sid Luxton down the street and the old fellow had congratulated him on Deidre's talent in wool classing.

He said she was working for Bert Hoffers shearing gang where she was a great favourite with the shearers. 'I'll just bet she is,' Huw groaned. Deidre had always been popular with the blokes. Her mum had fainted and had to be revived after reading her diary and finding bumper sized packets of condoms hidden in her knickers drawer.

Huw slumped in his chair. 'Bloody kids — son a raging poofter and daughter as rough as old boots.'

Shit, bloody shit, it was no good, he would have to call in a favour. He picked up the phone, dialled a number and a voice answered.

'Morning Shifty, Huw here. Look I need to see you about something. Don't want to discuss it on the phone, how about fifteen minutes in your office?'

'Right see you then,' Shifty said replacing his receiver slowly.

Fifteen minutes later there was a knock on his office door and his delicious secretary announced, 'Mr Hawtrey to see you, Mr Grey.'

Shifty ushered Huw into a chair opposite his massive desk

which was remarkably neat and tidy.

'What's the problem mate, you sounded worried,' he said.

Huw took out a large white hanky and wiped the beads of sweat gathering around his face.

'Big problems Shifty, I jumped the gun and issued a foreclosure notice on Ben Bangor. Bloody Audrey's been at me to buy her a sheep station and I knew from looking at his account that he couldn't last much longer so I thought I'd get in early and sell him up.'

'So, what happened? Sounds like a good idea,' Shifty said, moving files around his already tidy desk.

'Well I went out there to serve notice and he bloody near killed me, fired his gun at me and now he's got Teddy Reed helping him and he's called a bloody Queen's Counsel and a gun solicitor to help him. God knows what will happen if they find out what's been going on. My job will be down the gurgler.'

Shifty groaned. 'Jesus Christ what possessed you? You've dug your own grave, don't expect me to jump in with you.'

Huw got up from his chair, his face crimson with rage and leaned over him. 'Listen you bastard, I've got the goods on you well and truly. You better help me with this because if I go, I'll take you and the rest of your rotten lot with me. Now get busy and work something out.'

Huw left, slamming the door behind him and Shifty frozen with fright and with trembling hands poured himself a large drink from a bottle hidden behind a map of the shire plan on the wall behind him.

For years Huw had helped Shifty send huge amounts of money offshore to the Cayman Islands and to secret bank accounts in forged names. He shook his head and cursed. 'Trouble is coming with a big T,' he muttered.

This on top of everything else was enough to send a man up the wall. First he had to stop the Canberra trip, Bomber was still in hospital and Paddy away in Brisbane. That would slow things up a bit.

Sifting through his papers he pulled out a file and heaved a sigh of relief. He would send a message to his Works Foreman Cyril who was in Hawaii on a council junket fact-finding mission. Then if the worst happened, he could ask him to drop into the Cayman Islands on the way home and get some cash.

CHAPTER 10

TEDDY AND DEIDRE

Teddy was sitting at the kitchen table at Redlands enjoying a cup of tee when the phone rang.

'Edward Fortescue Reed here,' he said in his deep voice. 'God's gift to women.'

'Teddy you idiot, it's Dee,' she said laughing.

'Deidre Hawtrey old mate,' Teddy roared down the phone. 'How the blazing hell are you?'

'A lot better for talking to you,' Deidre said. 'Now tell me, how's your old man?'

'Don't worry about that old sod, he's lying back having the time of his life, pampered by the gorgeous Maggie. What about you, still saving clapped out old nags?'

'Teddy, that was years ago. Look there's something I need to talk to you about, okay if I come out?'

'Sure, come now if you like, be good to see you.'

Dee put down the phone and grabbed her hat. 'Come on

Rusty,' she called to the red cattle dog snoring under her feet. 'Get up you lazy buggar, we're off to Redlands.'

Back at Redlands, Teddy wandered into the kitchen and filled the kettle. He guessed Deidre wanted to talk to him about the bust up. She was a good stick, God knows how a miserable runt like Huw Hawtrey had sired her. Brother Tim's an odd sort, scared of anything on four legs. Waste of money sending him off to ag college, should have sent Dee, she's a cracker.

Meantime Dee's old red ute was churning up the kilometres to Redlands leaving a trail of dust in its wake. 'Bloody Dad trying to stuff up Ben Bangor,' Dee muttered, wrestling the wheel over the corrugated iron ruts. 'Bloody parents. Who needs them? Be good to see Teddy again.'

Dee worshipped Teddy who had helped her to rescue her beloved horse Knacker.

From day one she had dreamed of owning her own horse. But the only horses she saw in the city were owned by the Police.

When the bank had sent a disgraced Huw to Damengin she was the only family member to be excited at the thought of leaving the city. Every afternoon she ran from the Damengin Primary School gates to the stockyards on the other side of town and spent her pocket money buying carrots and hay for the horses yarded there.

These were mostly owned by the stockmen who worked at the yards but they felt sorry for the horse-mad kid and often let her ride them around town.

Occasionally some old and worn-out horses arrived, destined for the local knackery to be turned into dog meat. When the trucks arrived to take them away Dee would shed buckets of tears and plead with the drivers to let them go.

The day after her thirteenth birthday Dee trudged to the stockyards in the blazing heat armed with a bag of carrots nicked from the fridge and found the main yards empty but for a lone horse sheltering under the only tree, a half-dead gum. A poor skinny wreck of a thing, a white blaze on his fly bitten head his only distinguishing feature. His eyes were hidden under a matted mane and he was so stooped his head almost touched his knees. Bones stuck out in his shanks and all his ribs were visible on a hide encrusted with dirt.

'You poor old thing,' she said opening the gate and walking slowly towards him in order not to frighten him. But the horse barely lifted its head.

Stroking his neck, Dee gently offered him a carrot. He lifted his head and sniffed the offering.

'Go on,' she urged, 'have a taste.'

The horse took the carrot and began to munch. When he had finished, he looked up at her as if to say, 'any more?'

'Here you are old thing,' she said giving him another. The horse took it gratefully.

When the carrots were finished Dee noticed the water trough was empty. 'Animal cruelty, that's what it is, someone should be jailed,' Dee muttered.

She walked over to the fence where the tap was and dragged the hose over to the trough, as water gushed out.

Hearing the water, the horse whickered. He walked over, put his head down and drank huge drafts. When he had finished, he shook his head, gave a great shudder and stared at Dee with huge sad eyes.

Her eyes filled with tears. 'You're starving you poor thing. I'm going to get you some hay. Just you wait here.'

Ten minutes later Tom Fitzgerald, son of the proprietor of Damengin's Produce Store, was talking to Teddy Reed when Dee rushed in. 'Tom,' she said breathlessly, 'I absolutely desperately need a bale of hay for a poor starving horse in the stockyards,' she pleaded. 'I haven't got any money with me but I can pay you back later, it's a matter of life and death.'

Tom looked her and winked at Teddy. 'Life and death is it, Dee. Sorry but I can't do it and how are you going to carry a bale of hay over to the yards? I can't leave here, my dad would kill me.'

'But it's desperate,' she said her eyes brimming with tears. 'I have to save him.'

Teddy, who knew Deidre by sight, felt sorry for her. 'Where is this horse that's starving?' he asked.

'It's at the yards,' she said raising a dirty tear-stained face to him. 'Please Tom, you have to help me, please Tom he will die.'

'Give her the hay, Tom,' Teddy said feeling sorry for the red-headed freckled face kid. 'Put it on our bill and I'll drop it over to the yards for her.'

Dee turned to the tall smiling fellow. 'Thank you sooo

much,' she said, 'it means the world to me and I'll pay you back every cent.'

'That's okay,' Teddy said nodding his head. He picked up the bale of hay and carrying it outside, dumped it into the cattle truck.

'Come on, horse saver, get in the front, okay you too,' he said to Rusty.

Dee settled herself in the passenger seat, with Rusty on the floor at her feet and Teddy drove them to the cattle yards.

'There he is,' Dee shouted, jumping down from the truck and running over to the yard.

'Whew,' Teddy whistled when he saw the horse. 'Poor buggar, some people need shooting for letting a horse get in that state.'

He unloaded the hay and carried it into the yards. Dee broke some off and took it over to the horse.

He sniffed it hopefully then began to eat, Dee feeding him blissfully ignorant of his slobber running down her arms.

'What mongrel would treat a horse like this?' Teddy asked shaking his head. He examined the horse while he was contentedly eating. 'He's nothing but a young fella, I'd reckon no more than three and not much wrong except he's been badly treated. Look at these scars on his girth, someone's give him a helluva time.'

Teddy wondered if Dee knew that the horse was destined for the knackery.

Just then a door slammed and Brett Tuttle the yard manager walked down the laneway towards them.

'What the hell are you doing, Deidre Hawtrey?' he yelled. 'You're wasting your time feeding that horse, he's off to the knackers tomorrow.'

'No way' she yelled back. Sobbing, she threw her arms around the horse. 'You can't kill him, he's not even old, it'd be murder. Please Mr Tuttle, let me have him, I've got almost $50 saved up, you can have all of it, I can get it for you now.'

Greg Tuttle shook his head. He liked Deidre, she was always hanging round the yards mad about the horses. Her miserable old man should buy her a horse, she deserved one. Anyway this horse wouldn't fetch more than $20 as dog meat. Let her have it.

'Look Deidre,' he said patting her heaving shoulders, 'I tell you what, you square it with your folks and give me $20, you can have the horse and I'll throw in a bridle. But you'll have to work out where to keep him, there's no room at the bank house and he can't stay in the yards. I've got a load of cattle coming in tomorrow.'

Dee's face lit up and she wiped her eyes with her fists. 'Oh thank you, thank you, Mr Tuttle, I'll look after him. You can have all my money and I'll find somewhere to keep him.'

Teddy who had been sitting on the gate watching the action felt sorry for her. She seemed a nice kid.

'Dee,' he called out to her, 'you can keep him at our place until you find somewhere closer. But you'll have to come out and look after him.'

Deidre rushed over and grabbed his arm. 'Teddy thank you. I'll work for his food, I'll do anything to keep him. I know he looks a mess now, but so would you if you were starving. I'm going to call him Knacker because saving him from the knackery was the best thing I've ever done in my life. Could you please drive me home and I can tell Mum and Dad and get my money?'

'Okay, we'll load him up and after you've told your folks, you can come with me out to Redlands and we'll settle him in.'

When they had left Greg shook his head. 'Who the hell would want a skinny clapped-out old nag like that? Good luck to her.'

Teddy's presence with Dee when she explained her acquisition of Knacker eased their objection. Her mum was particularly pleased that she was hobnobbing with the mayor's son.

So Knacker lived at Redlands and Deidre went out every day during the holidays to visit him until she found a paddock closer to home. Cocooned in love and lavished with oats and hay, he regained his health and turned into a rather handsome fellow.

Dee and Knacker became inseparable and legends on the Polocrosse circuit. When she was sent kicking and screaming away to boarding school, he was so devastated he raced up and down the fence screaming his head off. But Dee only lasted two weeks before running away sparking a state-wide search. She was found when the owner of Knacker's paddock thought he was unusually quiet and found Dee asleep in his stable.

Refusing to be parted from Knacker, Dee's godfather paid

for her to go to a school down south where she could take Knacker.

That was six years ago but Deidre remained forever grateful to Teddy for saving Knacker and now that he was home and his dad was in hospital she wanted to help him. Despite her rough exterior Deidre had the softest heart and couldn't bear seeing people, especially friends and animals badly treated and she was furious with her dad for trying to take Ben's property away. *How could he when Ben worked so hard?* she thought furiously.

As she drove along the rutted track and changed gear to go over the cattle grid that led to Redlands she thought how lucky Teddy was to have a father like Bomber. *He should have come home sooner to help at the station, I would have given anything to have the chance,* she thought to herself wistfully.

Teddy saw Deidre's ute drive up and walked over to open the door. 'Great to see you Dee, you haven't changed much,' he said giving her a hug. 'Hey, call your bloody dog off,' he said laughing as Rusty tried to lick him to death.

'Get down Rusty, in the back,' she said letting down the tail gate of the ute. 'Now stay there.'

Teddy led the way to the house. 'I don't understand it Dee, and how the hell did Ben get himself into such a mess that your dad could sell him up. Ben's so careful with his money and has always been such a hard worker.'

'There's something funny going on,' Deidre said following him into the kitchen.

Teddy filled the kettle and put it to boil on the wood stove.

'I spoke to Ben when I visited him in the lockup and he said he had been banking regular amounts off the overdraft, money he earned driving for Paddy and the returns from roo culling. Paddy's going to speak to the bank and see what he can do.'

Deidre sat down at the table and waited while Teddy made the tea. 'I'm with you Teddy, I don't know how it happened but, change of subject, how's your dad?'

'He's raring to come home, the shearing's due next week and there's only a few hundred left so he was going to do them himself. Now he can't so he's getting really stressed.'

Deidre took a sip of her tea. 'Why don't you do it?' she asked.

Teddy looked at her in astonishment. 'Me, I haven't been near a sheep for years, wouldn't know where to start.'

'It's about time you did. I'll give you a hand, and surely you helped out when you were a kid?'

'Sure I did a bit of crutching with Dad but we always had a shearing gang to do the big stuff and all I ever had to do was mustering and cleaning up after everyone.'

Deidre stared at him. 'You know all I ever wanted to do was work and live on a property, you are so lucky. Look, I've been working in shearing sheds and between us we can easily do the few sheep you've got here. We'll go and talk to Bomber about it, he can tell us where everything is and supervise from his hospital bed.'

Teddy grinned at her. 'You always were a bossy buggar. Finish that tea, we'll go out to the troughs with the feed and you can take a look at what's left of the famous Redlands flock — pretty bloody depressing.'

They drove out to the flock that had perked up amazingly since Teddy's last overgenerous feeding when they almost knocked him over in their hurry to get at the grain pouring into the troughs.

'There they are, the last of the Redland prize ewes,' he said looking at them. 'If we can save these, Dad will at least have something left to start again with. I wish I had known how bad things were, the silly old buggar was too proud to tell me he was out of funds.'

'How is Ben Bangor going?' Deidre asked enjoying watching the sheep eat their fill.

'He's in a really bad way. I went out and fed his flock and topped up his feed bins but once that's gone I don't know what he'll do. He's too proud to accept or ask for any help from anyone.'

Deidre sighed. 'Bloody Dad and the bloody banks, we've got to find a way of helping Ben. I'm going to see if I can find anything out when I go home, that's if Dad doesn't throw me out again. Mum's away on a cruise with Millicent McDonald, I was working at Rangoon recently and Angus told me.'

'Would your dad really throw you out?' Teddy asked in amazement.

Deidre shrugged. 'Wouldn't worry me if he did, I can look after myself.'

'You can always stay here. Plenty of beds including mine,' he said looking at her and grinning.

'In your dreams,' she said. 'I've got a swag in the back of the ute that's plenty big enough for me and Rusty.'

After Deidre had gone, Teddy sat down at his dad's old roll-top desk and opened the ledger. There he saw recorded in his dad's neat hand the amounts of money he had spent on grain, hay, fuel, farm materials and household supplies. The whole lot didn't amount to as much as he spent a week on partying. He closed the ledger and looked around the large spacious room. Everything was coated in dust and cobwebs festooned the ceilings. *The old fella's really let the place go,* he thought. *I should have come home more, given him a hand.* All of a sudden Teddy was filled with remorse. He hardly remembered his mother, she had spent most of her time in the city before falling overboard while on a cruise.

There had only been Bomber and him bashing around in the lovely old homestead but there had always been a housekeeper to cook their meals and look after them. Dad must have been battling along alone for years with no money to pay for help, Teddy realised. There was nothing but a few tins of peas and some tea and sugar in the pantry. And in the large freezer usually chocked full of meat all he could find were a couple of stringy looking chooks that had clearly passed their use by date in the chook house. At least the scrawny looking chooks that survived had been given a feed and could provide a few eggs for the house.

Picking up his hat he walked out onto the verandah and gazed into the distance. A lone windmill creaked as it turned slowly in the slight wind currents. How his dad's heart must have ached to see his lifetime's work destroyed, Teddy thought sadly. He remembered the waving stands of Mitchell grass that had covered the plains as far as the eye could see and the thousands of fat sheep that looked like blobs of cotton in the lush paddocks. Over to the east the huge Brahman cattle that Bomber had been so proud of were gone, only Matlock his prize bull remained pacing his yard with frustration.

When Teddy had gone away to boarding school he had become obsessed with cricket and had made quite a name for himself as a top bat. After playing for the state team he had been picked to play for Australia and instead of going to agriculture college as his father had wanted him to, had stayed on in England and played for a county side. He was still there when his mum had died leaving him a massive amount of money. He spent lavishly on fast cars and even faster women taking his then girlfriend on a cricket tour of India, West Indies, South Africa and Pakistan where he had dozens of friends. Bored with cricket and boozy men she had left him for a far more interesting Italian stud who owned half of Rome and a little miffed he had returned to Brisbane in time for the Sheffield Shield.

He was sitting in the Cricketer's Club at Woolloongabba enjoying a beer with his mates and watching the first match of the season when he received word about Bomber. Although he had neglected him for almost five years, he worshipped his dad and abandoning the game even though Queensland was heading for an unprecedented victory over New South Wales, he drove like a madman home. His stomach churned with dread at what he would find but he cheered slightly when he heard on the radio Queensland had massacred New South Wales in the Shield. *At least there is a God*, he thought.

Good old Dee, she would help him sort out the sheep and he would make sure that Redland's would survive. That would make his dad happy.

Teddy sighed. He looked over to the west and saw the setting sun colour the wide sky a startling red. *Red sky, sailor's delight* he thought. *No chance of rain in that sky, bloody drought, it can't last much longer.*

CHAPTER 11

REPRIEVE FOR BEN

Teddy arrived at the Damengin Courthouse wearing a smart suit accompanied by a beautifully turned-out middle-aged woman. As they climbed the steps to the courthouse Teddy grinned at the motley crowd standing and watching on the footpath and called out, 'My barrister, Charlotte Cartwright QC.'

The mob cheered and an old fellow wearing a singlet and battered hat yelled good luck. They had been waiting around hoping for the fun to start. There hadn't been a serious crime in town since the local barber had cut the throat of his mother-in-law and got off after pleading insanity because everyone knew she had driven him mad for years.

Paddy, the only Justice of the Peace in the region, was so exhausted from his drive to Brisbane to bring Mary home that he arrived late and sneaked in through the back door.

Representing Huw was the town's only solicitor, Gordon

W. Slater who was so old he could hardly remember his own name and was dubbed Echo for repeating himself.

When Paddy called him to the bar to make his plaint, he droned on about his client's savage dog, stressed the importance of making a will and was nudged repeatedly by Huw to 'get on message for Christ's sake.'

Finally Ben's barrister rose majestically, winking provocatively at Paddy and calling him, 'Your Honour,' she began. 'My client had been simply cleaning his gun when it went off accidently,' she told the mesmerised audience. Turning, she fixed Huw and his solicitor with a deadly stare and said, 'He had absolutely no intention of frightening or harming Mr Hawtrey.'

Paddy looked at the notes in front of him and addressed the court. 'Knowing the defendant as I do,' he said glaring at Huw, 'I find it hard to believe that if Mr Bangor had intended to shoot the claimant he would have missed.'

'Hear, hear,' yelled one of the crowd who had crushed into the tiny court and his mates began clapping and yelling support.

'Order in the court,' Paddy shouted.' If you don't be quiet I'll have the lot of you thrown out.'

Turning to Ben he said,' Mr Bangor, will you please stand.' Ben stood up looking very smart in a new blue shirt and wearing his rugby tie.

'The judgement of this court is you are not guilty,' Paddy said banging his hammer on the gavel. 'And next time Ben, be careful when you are cleaning your gun. I award costs against the plaintiff.

'Court dismissed.'

A great cheer went up and Ben was mobbed as he made his way through the door.

Paddy led the way to the pub where he shouted beers all round and Teddy drove Charlotte Cartwright QC back to Longreach to catch her plane. Much later, tired and relieved, Ben went home to a rapturous reception from his dogs Lucy and Pippa.

The two kelpies were from the same mother but born years apart. Pippa the elder was the boss and Lucy with her huge brown eyes and sweet face, the follower but a brilliant worker.

Ben adored both bitches but Lucy was his favourite. She slept beside his bed and was his shadow, following his every move devotedly. She was the gentlest dog he had owned, not a mean bone in her body, even old Misery the cat, who never let anyone pat him loved her.

That night Ben decided to go kangaroo shooting to earn some much-needed funds. He packed his guns and ammunition, checked the ute's spotlight and loaded the dogs in the back.

He drove out on dusk following a track that led to a bunch of mulga that had survived the drought and where hundreds of kangaroos stole the miserly scuds of foliage that were left.

Ben had no war against kangaroos; in the good times, they had been welcome to share the paddocks with the flocks. Not like the dingoes that preyed on the young lambs, ripping their guts out and leaving them to die just for the sake of killing.

But times were tough, it was a choice of them or the sheep

and he needed the money from culling and selling them to the local abattoir. Ben only shot the large males, dazzling them in the spotlight and aiming for a head shot to kill them instantly.

His first shot took down a beauty and he drove over to throw it onto the back of the truck. He had shot over a dozen when the spotlight picked up another huge male. He took the head shot and climbed out to add it to the pile in the back of the truck. As he bent down to drag it into the truck it suddenly reared up and knocked him over. His dogs Lucy and Pippa launched themselves at it barking madly but the kangaroo fought back. A courageous Lucy kept up the fight but it was too powerful and attacked fiercely, kicking her cruelly with its huge back legs. Ben, by this time, had retrieved his gun and put a finishing shot to its head but it was too late for Lucy.

Screaming in agony she squirmed on the ground, her back legs paralysed. A horrified Ben knelt beside her and assessed the damage. Calmly he picked up his gun and put her out of her misery.

Then he dropped to the ground. 'You bastards, you fucking bastards,' he yelled. He gathered the limp Lucy to him and his huge frame began to shake. Sobs wracked him as he stroked her soft head.

Lucy was the last straw in his bundle of misery.

Fee Fluke had heard the shots from her place and realising Ben was shooting kangaroos decided to front him and put a stop to it. When she heard Lucy's screams, she started to run and almost fell over Ben who was sitting on the ground cradling Lucy in his arms, his big chest heaving and tears coursing down his cheeks.

Fee was horrified; she hated Ben killing kangaroos but when she saw the state he was in she was filled with pity. Instinctively she put her arms around him and held him against her.

'It's Lucy,' he said. 'She tried to save me, she didn't deserve this, it's my fault,' he choked.

Fee's eyes filled with tears. 'Oh the poor little thing, she was the sweetest pet. She used to visit me when you were out and was so gentle and friendly.'

Ben took a deep breath and rubbed his eyes. 'You know Fee, sometimes life just isn't fair. Poor little Lucy, never did a thing wrong in her life and now she's gone. All my sheep have just about gone, dead or sold for dog meat and now the property's going to be sold from under my feet.'

Fee was appalled. 'Who's going to take your farm away? How can they when you've worked so hard. They know we've got a drought.'

Ben stood up and placed Lucy carefully on the front seat of the ute. 'It's the banks,' he said. 'I haven't been able to pay much off since the drought really took hold. The roo shooting and a few truck driving jobs were the only income I had and now times running out. I've got to start making a dent in the mortgage or they'll sell me up.'

Fee followed him over and touched his arm. 'Ben,' she said softly, 'I had no idea, I know how much the farm means to you. What will you do?'

Ben took a deep breath. 'You know what Fee, I have no idea, and I really don't. This place has been in my family for generations. I just don't have any idea.'

'Ben I am really, really sorry. If I could help I would,' Fee said. 'I'll come back with you and help you bury Lucy.'

Ben looked at her. She looked genuinely upset, her huge dark eyes were filled with tears that trickled down her cheeks and her thin face was framed by clouds of black hair. *She wasn't a bad person,* he thought, *just misguided and it was kind of her to offer.*

'Sure, Fee,' he said kindly. 'Come back and help if you like.'

They drove back to the homestead where Ben dug a hole in the hard ground under a large gum tree near the tractor shed. Fee wrapped Lucy in her favourite blanket and Ben placed her gently in the ground.

'Goodbye little Lucy,' he said softly, tears coursing down his cheeks. 'You were the sweetest natured little mate I've ever had the luck to know. I know you'll go straight to heaven because you never did a thing wrong. God bless you.'

Fee found herself nodding her approval and although she was a total atheist, even managed to say amen in a voice choking with emotion. She walked over and took Ben's arm and led him back to the house.

'I'll put the kettle on,' she said. 'You have a rest.'

'No way,' Ben said wiping his eyes, 'we are going to give Lucy a proper send off,' and he walked into the living room, took a bottle of whisky and two glasses from the glass fronted cabinet.

'We both need a drink and a bloody strong one,' he said, filling both glasses to the brim.

'To Lucy,' he said raising his glass, 'the best little mate a bloke ever had.'

Fee took a tentative sip. 'To Lucy,' she said choking. 'God that's strong Ben, can I have some water?'

'Drink that first,' he said downing his in one gulp. 'Lucy deserves a decent send off.'

Fee took a large swallow and before she could put the glass down, Ben had filled it up.

'To hell with the banks and all who serve in them,' he said raising his glass and tossing back the contents.

Fee raised hers, took a deep breath and said, 'To hell with the banks and to hell with bank managers,' she said.

Ben refilled the glasses. 'Buggar the politicians and buggar their hangers on.'

Fee who hadn't eaten since the day before when she gave her last loaf of bread to some rabbits who were scratching among her derelict vegie patch, was feeling woozy.

'No more for me,' she pleaded leaning back in her chair which threatened to fall over.

'Hang on there, mate,' Ben said pulling her upright and half-carrying her to the sofa. 'You're not pulling out on me yet, have just one more for poor Lucy.'

But one more was one too much for Fee who took one look at the brimming glass and passed out.

Recognising defeat, Ben sadly finished off the rest of the bottle, picked her up and dumped her on the bed in his bedroom where she buried her head in the pillows and began to snore gently. Overcome with grief, exhaustion and grog, Ben lay down beside her and fell asleep.

Fee woke several hours later with a little man smashing a bloody great big hammer inside her head which was so heavy she had to put it between both hands before she could raise it from the pillow. Even then, she couldn't move because there was a huge hairy arm lying across her chest.

Wriggling she tried to escape but the arm tightened and Ben, turning, groaned and pulled her close with both arms and nuzzled into her neck.

'Ben, wake up, move your arm,' she said pushing herself away and falling off the bed.

'No way,' Ben said as he grabbed her and pulled her next to him. 'Stay here, I need company, go home in the morning.

'You know Fee, I'm really grateful for what you did today, meant a lot to me. Now come on, I'm too sloshed to do anything to you. Have a kip. You look like you need one.'

Fee lay down beside him. He was right, no point in going home, no one there and he needed her. Ben pulled her to him and cuddled up next to her. Women had played no role in Ben's life for years, he'd been flat out keeping the banks at bay. Fee had been celibate since she abandoned a hippie commune fifteen years ago to go traipsing around India.

Cuddling could only lead to one thing and they came together slowly and tenderly quenching the fires that consumed them before falling into dreamless sleep.

Ben woke up with the sun on his face and smiled down at

Fee who smiled back.

'My head's cracking and I could drink the tank dry' she said. 'What about you?'

'I will die of dehydration if I don't get a drink,' he replied getting out of bed and putting on his work pants. 'I'll make us a cuppa.'

'Bathroom's down the hall and there are clean towels in the cupboard.'

Fee waited until he had gone before finding the bathroom where she had a quick shower and washed her hair. She felt much better when she wandered into the kitchen where Ben was making breakfast.

'Ben,' she said sitting down at the kitchen table, 'about last night, I don't want you to get the wrong idea.'

Ben looked up from the stove where he was scrambling eggs. 'What wrong idea, we were just saying goodbye to an old friend. Here have some tea,' he said, pouring her a mug full and spooning four large spoons of sugar into it. 'Sugar is great for hangovers, and you need a big feed.'

Fee took a gulp of her tea before putting it down in front of her. 'What I meant was, oh, I don't know what I mean,' she said, resting head in her hands.

Ben put a large plate of scrambled eggs, bacon, sausages and toast in front of her.

'Now get that into you and after you've finished we'll have a talk.'

Fee smiled at him. 'I can't eat all that and anyway, I'm a vegetarian.'

'To hell with that, just eat it and stop complaining, you need meat on your bones, come on start it's getting cold.'

It smelt so delicious that Fee couldn't help herself and ate ravenously.

'You know Fee,' Ben said looking at her, 'you really saved my sanity last night. It wasn't just the sex; it was you being there with me. You know losing Lucy was the final straw after the bank. But after last night, I've decided I'm going to fight all the way. I can get through this, we both can.'

Fee looked at him and smiled. *Yes, she thought to herself, this is a good man, someone I would like to have as a friend, or perhaps a lover.*

She leant over and took his hand. 'Ben, I know in the past we've had our differences and I don't think I'll ever be able to condone the killing of kangaroos but I'm glad we are friends.'

Ben smiled at her and his cobalt blue eyes almost disappeared into the wrinkles around them. 'Fee, what brought you to this neck of the woods?'

Fee took a sip of her tea. 'I don't often talk about myself but I guess I was escaping my background, wanting to get back to nature when I came here.'

'I was born in Sydney, my parents were old when they had me and were anthropologists, always off somewhere so they put me in boarding school when I was eight.

'I spent my school holidays visiting them in different places, South American Indians, lost tribes in Uganda. Then I went to Sydney Uni and studied environmental science — then on to England to Oxford University.'

'Shit, how the hell did you end up here in the back of beyond. Didn't you miss your friends?' Ben said looking at her with new respect.

Fee sighed. 'I was too busy to make friends, no time for anything really except work. I could have just played around but I was really interested in my work. When I graduated, I came home via India and was staggered by the poverty. There were kids scrabbling among the rubbish dumps for food, beggars on every corner, indescribable.

'I ditched the idea of going home and stayed there for two years helping where I could until I got seriously ill and ended up in hospital and that was an experience. If it wasn't for a savvy doctor, I would have died. He rang the Australian Embassy who contacted my parents who were working in Egypt and they flew over and took me home.

'I had a massive infection which knocked me around and it took me ages to recover. I hated living in the city and was bored and depressed. I wanted some fresh country air so headed west until I arrived at Damengin. I met Sid Luxton in the bar and he kindly offered me the use of his place, said I could use the house but I'm happier in the shearer's accommodation, less to look after. I fell in love with the kangaroos, they're such lovely animals and I can't bear to see them killed.'

Ben shook his head. 'I don't like killing them Fee but there's bloody thousands of them all fighting for survival with the sheep. It's either cull them or they'll starve like the sheep. You'll have to toughen up if you're going to live out here. What do you think happens to the sheep when we send them off?'

Fee shook her head. 'I can't bear to think, that's why I'm a vegetarian.'

'You know, a bullet in the brain is a quick way to die. Wish I knew I'd end up like that instead of lying in agony attached to a bloody machine. All this vegetarian stuff is rubbish, you need a good feed of steak to put some blood in your veins and meat on you. It's like cuddling a bag of bones,' he said, grinning and pulling her to him.

Fee's eyes filled with tears and she nestled against him. 'You know, Ben, it's been a long time since anyone has been nice to me.'

'Well get used to it, it's time someone looked after you because you've made a shocking job of looking after yourself.'

CHAPTER 12

FOR THE LOVE OF MARY

Billy walked into the pub kitchen and saw his Aunt Mary's small frame hunched over the kitchen table, holding a cup of tea in her shaking hands. *God she looks like an old woman, and she couldn't be more than fifty,* he thought staring at Mary's dark hair that hadn't seen a shampoo for years and hung in straggles around a face grey with tiredness.

'How are you feeling today, Aunt Mary?' he asked bending down and planting a soft kiss on her cheek.

Mary looked up and her sad face creased into a smile. She had always adored Billy.

Her hand touched his face lovingly as she looked up at him with eyes red from crying and glazed from a late-night binge on rum she had pinched from the bar.

'Sorry to be like this,' Mary said tears coursing down her cheeks. 'I don't know what I'm going to do.'

Bill sat down next to her and squeezed her hand. 'We'll take care of you.'

Rosie looked over and saw Mary with her head on Bill's shoulder, Billy frowning with concern.

'Now you listen to me, Mary Murphy,' Rosie said marching over to the table and standing in front of her, arms crossed over substantial breasts. 'What you've got to do, is pull yourself together and stop feeling sorry for yourself. You're no good to anyone as you are.'

'Come on Rosie, she's upset, don't be so hard on her,' Bill said protectively.

Mary lifted her head from Bill's shoulder and wiped her eyes on a tea towel. 'She's right Billy, I'm nothing but a drunk.'

Rosie shook her head. She felt sorry for Mary but she had no patience with her upsetting Paddy and Billy. She took a plate of bacon and eggs from the stove and put it in front of her.

'Right Mary, eat this, it'll dilute that poison you put into yourself last night and don't think I didn't notice you pinching that bottle.'

Mary shrugged resignedly. She picked up her knife and fork with shaking hands and ate a mouthful. After a moment of chewing, she gave up. 'I suppose you couldn't give me a small drink to help this go down,' she asked.

'Not a chance,' said Rosie glaring at her and pointing her finger towards the door. 'Now I'm taking you upstairs, you will have a bath and wash your hair.'

Admitting defeat Mary stood up. 'Alright, I'm coming but I've nothing to put on.'

'Don't worry about that, I'll sort it out, 'Rosie said pushing her ahead of her.

'Billy, your breakfast is in the oven and Paddy won't be back until later. Don't stress worrying about this one, I'll take care of her.'

Mary slowly walked towards the stairs, she knew better than to argue with Rosie.

After seeing Mary into the bath, Rosie came back from upstairs, wiped her hands on her apron and started clearing the table. 'Billy, we've got to stop feeling sorry for her and stop her drinking. When you've finished eating, head back to Paddylea, I'm going over to see Maisie Matten at her shop. Her daughter Chloe is about the same size as Mary and she might lend us a few things at least until we can get to Longreach and buy her some new ones.'

Leaving Billy to his breakfast, Rosie combed her hair and walked along the street to the IGA Store. Maisie was sitting at the counter in a skirt that showed off her amazingly long legs, reading a magazine.

'Morning Maisie, I've got a bit of a problem,' she said folding her arms across her chest. 'Mary Murphy, Paddy's younger sister, is at the pub, she's left the convent and has nothing to wear. Do you think Chloe might have something she can borrow until we get her to Longreach shops?'

'What happened?' Maisie said, her face lighting up with interest.

'It's a long yarn lovie, could we get her some clothes so she has something to put on and then we'll have a gab?'

'Sure, I'll just close up and we'll rake through Chloe's stuff.'

Maisie shut the shop, which hadn't had seen a customer all day, and led Rosie through to the house at the back where a fed-up Chloe was tossing a coin to see whether she'd go to school or not.

'Chloe, what the hell are you doing?' Maisie asked.

'Tails — no school,' Chloe said pocketing the coin.

Chloe, aged sixteen and looking like twenty-five, was in her final year at Damengin's State High which she hated because all her girlfriends were at posh boarding schools.

And Maisie, whose shop was carrying half the district on credit because of the drought, was consumed with guilt because she couldn't afford the school fees.

Chloe was wearing a skirt barely skimming her bum, a blouse nipped in with a safety pin and a battered hat rescued from the cat's recent kittens.

Maisie looked at her. She was such a bright pretty girl but she was bored out of her brain at school. Last week the school principal had telephoned. 'Chloe is undisciplined, rebellious, untidy and unteachable,' he said. 'And if there is any further trouble, Miss Mattens,' he said emphasising the Miss, 'she will be expelled.'

When Maisie told Chloe she just shrugged and said, 'Don't worry Mum I'll just work for the *Star*.'

Last year Chloe had done work experience for the *Star's* editor Sam Spink who spotted a good yarn teller and offered her a part-time job at the paper writing short pieces about the district. Within weeks she had taken over the features section and could lay the paper out better than he could. Sam was very fond of her and dreaded the time when he knew she would leave in search of bigger and hopefully better things.

'Chloe, Rosie is here because she wants to know if you can lend Mary Murphy some clothes.'

Chloe looks surprised. 'You mean the nun?' she asked Rosie.

'Yes Chloe, it's a long story and I'm not going to share it with you but poor Mary has nothing but the clothes she had on when she arrived. You're nearer her size than me or your mum. Can we borrow something until we get her to Longreach?' Rosie asked.

'That's Billy Murphy's Aunt Mary,' Chloe said smiling. 'Of course I can give you some clothes, I've got heaps.'

Chloe had a crush on Billy Murphy who she considered the only fish worth catching in Damengin's stagnant pond. She had a picture of him winning Champion Steer Wrestler cut from last year's *Star* on her bedroom wall.

'Is Mary sick?' Chloe said returning with a pile of clothes and dumping them on the table in front of Rosie.

'I can't tell you much Chloe because I don't know,' Rosie told her truthfully. 'Paddy brought her home last night and Billy's going to take her with him back to Paddylea.'

Chloe's eyes lit up. 'Billy's home then?' she asked hopefully.

'Yes, he's back to help his dad. Thanks for these,' Rosie said. 'Mary's lost so much weight they'll probably swim on her but they'll get her through until we can go shopping.'

'You're welcome, I'll never wear them. Mum bought them

and her taste's in her bum,' Chloe said poking her tongue at Maisie.

Rosie laughed and gave Maisie a hug, 'You've got a good mum, you should appreciate her more, and she works very hard.'

Chloe shrugged and gave Maisie a peck on the cheek. 'She's not a bad old stick I suppose. I'm off to the *Star*. See you later Mum, bye Rosie.'

Mary was still in the bath when Rosie arrived back at the pub. She was lying back in the warm soapy water relaxing.

'You haven't drowned in there have you?' Rosie asked banging on the door.

Mary sat up in the bath. 'Almost done, give me five minutes,' she called out, wringing the water out of her hair.

Wrapping a towel around herself Mary walked into her bedroom and found a heap of clothes on her bed. It had been decades since she had worn anything but a nun's garb and she carefully sorted through the pile. Chloe was a good size bigger than Mary but the same height and although there was plenty of clothes, there was little to suit a middle-aged woman. After discarding several skirts that left nothing to the imagination and tops that exposed rather than clothed, she selected a pair of dark blue jeans and a navy sweater. When she put them on she hardly recognised the slim brown haired person reflected in her bedroom mirror.

'That's better,' Rosie said when she walked into the kitchen. 'I've made an appointment to get your hair cut this afternoon. Here's a pair of shoes Maisie said might fit you and a pair of boots from Chloe.'

Mary smiled, she still felt a bit groggy but the bath had helped and Rosie was like a shot of tonic minus the gin.

But her head still ached and she wanted something to lift her from the misery that consumed her. As soon as Rosie went out, she would grab something from the front bar and hide it in her room, just for emergencies.

'Wait till Paddy sees you, he won't recognise you,' Rosie said. 'You look like the old Mary, almost as pretty.'

'Thank you, where is Paddy? I haven't seen him since yesterday,' Mary asked.

'He got up early, some problem at Paddylea and then he was going to see Bomber at the hospital, he had an accident.'

'Oh no, what happened,' Mary asked eyes wide. 'Is Bomber okay?'

'Yes, he's alright, few broken bones but he'll recover,' Rosie said watching her carefully.

When she was a teenager, Mary had been mad about Bomber but then he married a girl from the city and she went into the convent.

'I think I'll go and help Annie in the bar,' Mary said getting up.

Rosie walked over and pushed her back in the chair. 'Oh no you don't, you are not drinking anymore. Not a chance. Paddy has told Annie the bar's off limits.'

'I don't feel very well,' Mary moaned, 'I just want one little drink please Rosie.'

'No. If you feel sick, I'll call Dr Dickie and he can give you something but you can forget drowning your sorrows my girl. If you take another drink I'll drown you in the creek.'

Mary began to cry just as Paddy walked into the kitchen.

'I heard that Rosie and it goes for me too,' he said staring hard at Mary. 'You almost killed yourself with your last binge and you won't be having another under my roof.'

Mary looked at him with big blue eyes filled with tears. 'I'm sorry, Paddy,' she said.

'Mary,' he said sitting down next to her and cradling one of her soft white hands in his own, 'we all want to help you, that's why I'm sending you out to Paddylea with Billy. He needs a cook and you used to turn out some good tucker. It's nice and quiet out there so you can read a few books, help Billy with the sheep. There's peace and quiet so you can get yourself off the drink and be the girl you used to be.'

Mary nodded. 'I'll try, when will you take me?'

'Rest here today and I'll take you out tomorrow. I bumped into Annabel Grey at the hospital and she said she was going to pop in and see you. You could visit Bomber in hospital with her, cheer him up.' Although, Paddy thought to himself, seeing Mary in her present state would more likely send Bomber into depression.

'I've booked Mary an appointment at the hairdresser this afternoon,' Rosie said. 'And when you get time I want you to drive her into Longreach to get some decent clothes. It's too far for her to go on her own.'

Paddy shook his head. 'No way, that's a job for Annabel, she loves shopping.'

Mary shook her head. 'I don't have any money to go shopping. You don't understand, I'll have to get a job.'

'Don't be bloody ridiculous, you are my sister, my responsibility, I'll go and open a bank account this afternoon, you buy what you need, do you hear me? In the meantime, take this,' he said opening his hand and slapping a fistful of money on the table.

Mary stared at it. 'Thanks Paddy,' she said quietly. 'I don't deserve it.'

Paddy sat down and pulled her into his arms. 'For God's sake Mary, why didn't you tell me you were so unhappy. I would have brought you home years ago.'

'I was so ashamed I couldn't, I can't explain but I just couldn't.'

Paddy stroked her back. 'Well you're here now and we're going to look after you and get you well, bring that smile back onto your face.'

After Paddy left, Mary was peeling vegetables in the kitchen with Rosie when Annabel Grey breezed into the kitchen smelling deliciously of Chanel No. 5 and enfolded Mary in her arms.

'Mary, it's wonderful to have you home, Paddy says you are here to stay, I'm so glad you've come home. Paddy is so worried about you,' she said hardly pausing for breath.

Mary hugged her back. It was lovely to see Annabel again. They had been best friends all through school but had lost touch when she left Damengin.

Rosie looked over and saw the two old friends standing

looking at each other. 'You two go out onto the verandah and have a nice chat,' she said. 'I'll bring some tea out for you.'

Mary led the way through the kitchen out onto the verandah which was bathed in soft sunlight. She pulled up a chair for Annabel and sat down facing her.

'Well, I'm home for good, if they can put up with me,' she said. 'Paddy has asked me to go and help look after Billy at Paddylea.'

'That'll be a nice change for you after the city,' Annabel said. 'If you like I'll come out and visit, bring you up to date with the town gossip. I imagine you know Bomber is in hospital, had an accident and broke a few bones but he's on the mend. And the good news is, Teddy's come home. He's taking care of Redlands and I really think he might stay this time. Just having him home has perked Bomber up.'

'What about you, Annabel?' Mary asked. 'How's Geoffrey and the council?'

Annabel frowned. 'I'm afraid Geoffrey and I have very little to say to each other. I have my life, and he has his. Thank God for my roses and community work. I've plenty to keep me busy and out of trouble.'

What Annabel didn't tell Mary was that Geoffrey rooted anything in a skirt that was silly enough to let him and she had tossed him out of their bedroom years ago when she found him bonking his then secretary on the kitchen table. After scouring the table with bleach, she carefully stirred a can of Miaow cat food into his fish pie for tea and smiled while he ate it. Yes, she considered there was no love lost there.

She leaned over and took hold of Mary's hand. 'When you settle down, you can come and help me, be like old times.'

Mary smiled. 'I'd like that.'

After Annabel left Mary ate some of the delicious pie Rosie had set out for lunch and went down the road to have her hair done. Doris the town's only hairdresser and barber, cut, shampooed and blow dried her hair which was in shock enjoying its first attention for thirty years.

Feeling and looking like a new woman and a hundred times better than she had when she first arrived, Mary wandered into the chemist with her fistful of money and spent lavishly. She bought cream and lotions guaranteeing wrinkle banishment and rejuvenation. Then, clutching a large package containing powder, lipstick and perfume that reminded her of the gardenias that filled the evening air at Paddylea, she walked back to the pub.

While she was away, Rosie had been warned by Paddy to keep an eye on her.

'We have to keep her occupied so that she doesn't start drinking,' he said. 'We'll watch her while she's here and tell Billy to lock up the grog at Paddylea.'

'Don't worry, she'll be safe at Paddylea.'

CHAPTER 13

SAM'S STORY HITS HOME

Sam Spink was asleep in a drunken stupor in his flat above the *Damengin Star* when Chloe Mattens let herself into the office to write her weekly column, the 'Star Scene', outrageous gossipy tripe about anyone or everyone in the district. Sitting down at her untidy desk, she tossed her schoolbag against the far wall and clearing a space with the back of her hand, laid the day's Brisbane newspaper in front of her looking forward to a good read.

'Shit,' she said turning the pages frantically and shaking with excitement, 'wait till Sam sees this.' But, before she could race upstairs and tell him, the phone began ringing and she was kept busy frantically writing down messages. With each call Chloe got more and more excited until finally she dropped the receiver down on her desk, dashed up the rickety stairs and banged furiously on Sam's door.

'Sam get up,' she shouted. 'Come on Sam, get out of bed,

it's after 9 o'clock. This is really urgent, big news, come on Sam.'

Inside, the tiny bedroom that faced the street, Sam was waking with a fuzzy head caused by his usual indulgence in the rum bottle. He tried to ignore the constant pounding until Otto his smelly dog joined in howling ecstatically.

'For God's sake stop that racket, both of you,' he yelled, kicking a disappointed Otto off the bed. Heaving himself up and groaning loudly with the effort, Sam got out of bed and opened the door.

'This had better be good Chloe,' he said scowling at her. 'And what are you doing here today, you should be in school.'

'Never mind that, this is more interesting,' Chloe said her eyes shining with excitement. 'Look, we've hit the jackpot, here read this,' she said shoving the paper into his hands. 'It's a scoop, a real scoop, the city papers are going crazy about your story, a Brisbane television crew is flying up to do a feature story, and the phone hasn't stopped ringing,' she said breathlessly.

Sam grabbed the paper. 'What story?' he asked.

'Sam,' she said shaking her head in exasperation at him. 'It's your story about the drought. Look,' she said pointing at the paper, 'they've even got your pictures of dying sheep on pages one, two and three and you should read the editorial it's amazing ...'

'Okay Chloe, settle down. You go downstairs, I'll have a quick shower and get dressed. And,' he called after her, 'put the kettle on and make me a strong coffee.'

Chloe bounced down the rickety staircase and went into the tiny kitchen where, in a spirit of generosity, she filled the sink with hot sudsy water and gave the mugs a much-needed wash.

By the time Sam made his way downstairs, showered, shaved and looking a lot brighter than Chloe had ever seen him, she had a mug of strong black coffee ready and a plate of buttered toast.

'We've had heaps of phone calls from media all over the place, even from Sydney,' she said handing him a pad full of numbers, 'and there's another television crew coming who want to do a feature story for national television.'

'Sam,' she said pulling his shirt sleeve, 'we've got a real scoop, can't you show some reaction?'

Sam sat down at his massive old desk and picked up the paper with trembling hands. As he worked his way through the pages, he absentmindedly gulped his coffee and fed the toast to a slavering Otto.

After a few minutes of reading, he leaned back in his chair and smiled. Chloe was darned right, it was a scoop, the first for a very long time. And it was thanks to Chloe for ensuring the story and film had caught the afternoon bus.

Over twenty years ago Sam had been sacked from his job as editor of a major daily for exposing a corrupt and very wealthy politician who was a close friend and financial contributor to the paper's owner.

Frustrated and furious Sam had gone on a bender and ended up in Damengin where he completely cracked up and was hospitalised in the care of his darling younger sister Maggie, the matron of the local hospital. Maggie had cared for him until he was able to work and using his payout from the paper he had bought the small shop in the heart of town and started the *Star*.

Boredom and hatred of the bastards who had wrecked his career had caused him to seek solace in his friend the rum bottle. But although barely coherent after lunch, he was a giant in the morning.

Chloe had been working for him for almost two years and had huge respect for him. Many times she had helped him upstairs to bed and returned to his desk sorting through his typed pages, retrieving notes from the overflowing rubbish basket under his desk and piecing stories together. Sam had taught her to lay out the paper and place the advertisements and she had become adept at placing the stories and editorial to his prepared layout and sending it off to the printers.

If only he would chuck the grog, she thought wistfully, *then he could give me a proper job with wages and I could leave crappy school.*

Chloe looked over at Sam reading through her list of calls. 'Want another coffee, boss?' she asked.

He looked up at her and smiled. 'Thanks matey, I'll just return a couple of phone calls and then I'll go and see Ben, tell him the good news.' Sam picked up the phone, dialled Paddy's number and talked quickly down the phone.

'Right Chloe, you coming?' he said picking up his car keys.

Ben Bangor was busy sorting out the massive amount of hay and grain Tom Fitzgerald had delivered courtesy of Teddy Reed's generosity. He had no idea how he was going to repay him but if he could keep his flock alive for a few more weeks, he would think of something.

A blast of horn and hysterical barking interrupted his thoughts and walking over towards the house he saw Sam Spink getting out with that little sexpot Chloe Matten.

'Good to see you, Sam, Chloe,' he said, nodding to her and wiping his hands on his pants before shaking Sam's outstretched hand. 'What brings you out to these parts?'

Sam waved the paper at him. 'We've had a win, here take a look at this. That story we did out here last week stirred the buggars up. Hit the front pages of the city dailies and we've had a call from a television crew who want to come out tomorrow and do a documentary.'

'Great stuff,' Ben said reading the headlines and looking at the pictures of skinny sheep they had taken. 'What do you reckon Sam, where to from here, will it do any good?'

'Certainly can't be bad. If we can get a sympathetic reaction from the city folk then that might pressure the government into handing out some relief.'

'Come into the house and have a brew,' he said leading the way.

'I'll do it,' said Chloe walking to the sink and filling the kettle.

'Any biscuits, Ben?' she asked.

'No mate, but there's some tinned milk in the pantry if

anyone wants it. I'll take mine black.'

The kettle whistled and Chloe went over to the wood stove, filled the teapot with the scalding water and handed out the mugs.

Ben took a sip of his tea and poured over the pictures of his starving sheep. 'What's the next step Sam?' he asked.

'I'll make arrangements for the television crew to come out here and I'll talk to the newspapers with a follow up. They sounded pretty keen, may be up here tomorrow, that okay with you?'

Ben nodded, 'Give me a call and leave a message.'

Chloe nudged Sam, 'Can I come with you?' she asked. 'I'll bring some food out for the crew from Mum's shop.'

Sam smiled. 'Sure you can, might learn something.'

'Fine with me,' Ben said, 'I'll give you some money, we don't want you getting into trouble with your mum.'

Chloe was over the moon, not only would she see a top television crew at work but she would spend the morning with Ben who she had a tremendous crush on.

Back at the *Star*, Sam settled down to return the long list of phone messages and gave directions to the television crew who, as he predicted, couldn't wait to do their story. They would fly into Longreach, the nearest major town, hire a car and be in Damengin by 11 am the next day. When he told Chloe, she made a mental note to get rid of the rum he kept in his desk or he would be sloshed and useless when they got here.

Next day Chloe spent over an hour in the bathroom washing her hair and drenching herself in Maisie's horribly expensive creams and perfume. When Maisie went to the shop, she rifled through her cupboard and found a skin-tight top that was so low it almost reached her waist. She squeezed herself into her jeans and after pulling on her boots, grabbed the lunch basket she had made earlier and walked down town to Sam's hoping he would be sober and ready to go.

To her surprise, she found Sam sitting at his desk washed, shaved and wearing a rumpled but clean shirt.

Chloe dumped her basket on the floor and gave him a dazzling smile that lit up her tiny heart-shaped face. 'Morning Sam, I've made some corned beef and pickle sandwiches for lunch and Mum gave me a fruit cake and some biscuits for morning tea. What time is the crew coming?'

Sam looked at his watch. 'They should be here any minute, we'll go straight out to Abington when they arrive. Don't let Otto near those things Chloe, he's a sod for scavenging.'

Chloe lifted her basket up onto the table away from the snuffling Otto who immediately started barking. 'That will be them,' she said looking through the window.

A large car with three passengers had pulled up outside. Sam opened the door and waved to them. 'Television crew?' he asked and received a chorus of agreement. 'I'm Sam Spink, don't bother getting out, we're ready so just follow us out.'

Churning up a dust spiral that could be seen for miles, the two cars arrived at Abington in just under an hour where Ben, who had been alerted by Chloe, was waiting for them. After the introductions were over, he took them on a tour and they were shocked at the devastation. The cameraman spent hours filming starving sheep around the tanks, the hordes of kangaroos competing for the scant feed and the endless dusty landscape.

During lunch, which Chloe set up on the verandah, Vincent the producer, a stunningly handsome and charming individual, found getting Ben to talk about the struggle he was having was a bit like pulling teeth. But later when he invited Chloe to drive back to town with them, she spilled out in graphic detail the story of Ben's fight for survival including the Hawtrey incident and his time in the slammer.

'He almost killed himself roo shooting at night, driving trucks during the day struggling to keep his breeders alive, then those swine at the bank tried to sell him up,' she said. 'Poor Ben,' she told them her large blue eyes glistening with unshed tears and her delightful little breasts heaving with emotion, 'he doesn't deserve to lose his property.'

The photographer who was sitting next to her in the back of the car was overcome with sympathy and offered a rather grotty hanky. The driver who was equally impressed was so jealous, he careered off the road and almost wiped them out.

After a terrifying drive, they arrived back at the newspaper office where the two men insisted on giving her their cards and getting her phone number. Sam, who had arrived before them, thanked them and asked them to ring him when the film was going to air.

He was bent over his desk typing instead of slouched over a bottle of Rum and Chloe was on cloud nine. *Things were looking up,* she thought to herself, *and for me too, there was plenty to write about in the Star this week. To hell with school, I'll just tell Mum I'm leaving.*

CHAPTER 14

DEIDRE AND TEDDY

Teddy walked into his dad's hospital room, dumped a bottle of whisky on the side table and a bag of grapes on his tray. 'How are you feeling today?' he asked sitting down on the chair at the side of the bed.

Bomber's eyes lit up when he saw Teddy and he pulled himself into a sitting position. 'Much better, thanks for that,' he said pointing to the whisky. 'I'll have to hide it from Nurse Phoebe, she's getting to be a little tyrant. How are things at home?'

Teddy, who was eating grapes, swallowed. 'Sheep have all got full bellies, I gave Matlock a good talking to and told him if he mends his ways we'll get him a few cows to play with and Deidre Hawtrey is coming out to help me with the shearing.'

'Deidre Hawtrey, when did she get to be a shearer?' Bomber said in astonishment. 'Last I heard Audrey was banishing her to some finishing school or something.'

'Well Dad, you've got it wrong, Deidre's been working with a shearing gang and says she is a gun classer and top shed hand. Anyway, she's a lot of fun and an old mate so I don't mind having her around. And, I think I can remember how to shear sheep, what's left of the poor buggars.'

Bomber shook his head sadly. 'You're right about that and the wool won't be up to much either.' He turned, looked at Teddy and said in a gruff voice, his eyes suddenly bright, 'Thanks son for helping out and filling the food bins. I'm running a bit short at the moment and I don't know when I can repay you.'

Teddy got up and looked out of the window. 'Don't you dare talk about paying me back,' he said angrily. 'I'm bloody furious you didn't tell me how bad things were, I would have been here in a second.'

Bending down he gripped his father's good arm. 'Look, I'm going back to Redlands to start things rolling and I probably won't be back for a few days. Do you need anything before I go?'

Bomber shook his head. 'No thanks son, between Annabel who has been in and out every day doing washing and so forth and Maggie who looks after me like a baby, I'm very well cared for. Just give me a ring and let me know how you are getting on. And,' he said smiling, 'tell Deidre I sent my regards.'

Walking out through the hospital, Teddy bumped into the gorgeous Nurse Phoebe who had been secretly waiting to waylay him.

'Sorry Nurse,' he said taking her arm and holding on to it.

Phoebe smiled up at him. 'My fault,' she said, flashing a brilliant smile which showed off her beautiful white teeth and gorgeous dimples.

Teddy smiled back. 'Thanks for looking after Dad so well, he's getting spoilt rotten,' he said.

'He's a tough cookie, your dad,' Phoebe replied thinking how attractive he was and how much she would like him to whisk her off to his sheep station.

Teddy laughed, 'He's certainly that. Look I'm busy for the next week but after that, would you like to go out for a meal one night. There's not much to offer around here but we could go through to Longreach?'

Phoebe didn't hesitate. 'Love to, you can ring me at the nurses' quarters.'

'See you in a week or so,' Teddy said.

Before heading back to Redlands he called at Fitzgerald's Produce Store and picked up oil and other bits and pieces and then drove round to the bank residence to see Deidre. As he parked his car, Rusty ran up and wagged his tail furiously.

'Where's the boss?' he asked patting him on the head. 'Under here,' a muffled voice answered and he saw a pair of legs he recognised as Deidre's scrambling from under a ute.

'Just changing the oil,' she said wiping her face with a dirty rag. 'Nearly finished, how's Bomber?'

'Great and I'm ready to start the shearing if you really want to help,' he said.

'Certainly do, I'll be another half an hour and then I'll be out at your place. Have you got everything you need?'

Teddy nodded. 'See you back at Redlands,' he said driving off.

Deidre had finished the ute and was stowing her gear when her dad walked into the backyard.

'Where are you going to this time?' he asked.

'I'm off to Redlands to help Teddy with the shearing.'

'No you are not, you can stay here. Your mother will be back tomorrow and I am not going to have to explain where you are.'

'Sorry Dad,' Deidre said, turning on the engine. 'I couldn't care less what you or Mum want, I'm going.'

'How dare you?' Huw yelled after her, 'After all we've sacrificed for you.'

He watched her leave, grinding his teeth and clenching his fists. How he would like to slap her right across the face. Now he would to have to put up with Audrey screeching at him when he picked her up off the plane in Longreach tomorrow.

Deidre hated fights and was relieved she wouldn't be there when her mum arrived home. Defiantly she turned the music up full volume and sang along happily in her deep husky voice. She was looking forward to the next few days but had absolutely no idea what she would do after that. She had saved some money from the shearing but that wouldn't last long and she knew there was little hope of getting work with the drought. 'Not to worry Rusty old mate, something will turn up, always does,' she said stroking his head which was resting on her lap.

Teddy was waiting for her when she arrived and after she dumped her swag in a spare bedroom, they drove out to feed the sheep. 'We'll start early in the morning,' Teddy said doling out feed. 'The dogs can bring them in and we can set up the stands when we go back.'

They set up two stands with shears and cleaned up the shed and sheep yards before leaving to feed Matlock the bull who was still irate about his lack of cows and tried to charge Teddy when he opened the gate. 'Buggar off,' Teddy said throwing the hay in his face and jumping for the rails.

Deidre laughed so much she got a stitch in her side. 'Nearly got you that time,' she said.

'Not funny,' Teddy said grinning. 'You can feed him tomorrow.'

'No way,' she said punching him on the arm, 'your bull, your job.'

Back at the homestead they relaxed on the front verandah drinking beer and watching the sun set over far distant horizon.

'It's just magic out here,' Deidre sighed. 'I don't know how you could ever leave and live in the city.'

Teddy took a sip of his beer and looked at her. 'I had some fun, met some interesting people, saw places,' he said. 'Sometimes you need to leave to find out how much you miss a place.'

Deidre looked at him hopefully. 'Does this mean you're home for good?'

'Not sure yet, but coming back this time and seeing what Dad has gone through, it really affected me. He's a great guy, Mum was okay, but she was never happy here, always off visiting friends in the city or going on holidays with her girlfriends. You know how she died I suppose?'

Deidre frowned. 'Didn't she drown or something?'

'Sure did. I'm not supposed to know but I overheard Dad telling Paddy about it. She was on a cruise to New Zealand with her girlfriend Susie and there was a storm in the Tasman, passengers were told to not to go outside, but Mum, who was tanked up to the eyeballs, decided to wander outside and was washed overboard.'

'I wonder why your dad didn't marry again, he was a good looking bloke,' Deidre mused.

'Always too busy. Now let's go and get something to eat, I'm starving.'

Teddy had bought two huge steaks which he threw into a sizzling frypan and served with two eggs each on top. A ravenous Deidre demolished her steak and wiped the remains of the eggs up with a large slice of bread and butter.

Teddy smiled as he watched her. 'No doubt about you, Dee, you can certainly enjoy your tucker,' he said.

'You bet I do,' she said giving a huge sigh of contentment before offering Rusty a hunk of fat.

Deidre washed the dishes while Teddy fed Rusty and Tessa a tin of Pal and put a bowl of milk and some cat biscuits out for Star, the black cat that lived in the shed. 'She only comes out at night,' he said grinning.

Teddy's alarm went off at 4.30 am and he jumped out of bed. 'Rise and shine,' he said banging on Deidre's bedroom door.

'I'm in here,' she called from the kitchen, 'beat you and breakfast's ready.'

By the time they got over the shearing shed the sun was up and they could feel its heat on their backs.

'It's going to be another hot one,' Deidre said as they drove out to bring in the sheep.

She whistled to Rusty and taking his lead from Tessa who was frantically excited to be working again, jumped out of the back of the ute and began running in a large circle around the sheep drawing them together.

The old trouper was a delight to watch as she expertly weaved her way around the sheep back and forth pushing them slowly towards the pens. Rusty, new to the job but keen as mustard and showing his breeding, ran the opposite flank and mimicked her as she raced back and forth crouching down and eyeballing into submission any sheep foolhardy enough to break the link.

The two professionals had the small flock yarded and penned in under an hour.

'These dogs are fantastic, absolutely brilliant,' Teddy said, patting the head of a grinning Tess while Deidre hugged an excited Rusty.

'You sort the sheep and send them up the chute when I tell you,' Teddy called jumping up the steps and into the shed.

'Right, send one up,' Teddy called. The two dogs jumped on the sheep's back barking and nipping as they forced it up the chute. Grabbing it behind the front legs, Teddy clamped it between his legs and began to shear starting at the head and working his way down the back with long sweeping strokes.

Deidre picked up the tin of tar and dumped it beside him. 'Hope you don't need too much of this,' she quipped.

'I'm guaranteeing nothing — anything could happen.'

It took Teddy almost an hour to shear the first sheep and when he straightened up afterwards his back felt like it was broken.

'Bloody hell, how do those shearers manage a hundred a day,' he moaned as he wiped the sweat from his face with an old rag.

'Quit complaining, you're just soft, let me show you how to do it,' Deidre said attaching another set of shears to the stand next to his. She grabbed a sheep and expertly had the fleece off in minutes.

'How's that,' she called showing off the snowy white effort.

Teddy looked at her in amazement. 'Bloody terrific, if you're not careful, you can do the lot.'

'Thanks mate,' she said grinning. 'Give you a race?'

Teddy threw his oily rag at her and grabbed another sheep. 'Jesus you're a show-off. Okay then, whoever loses makes smoko,' he said starting shearing.

'Hang on I haven't even got my sheep yet.'

'Too bad, I've won, now pass me the tar I've got a bloody cut on this one and it's your fault entirely.'

Deidre laughed and dabbed some tar on the cut. 'Alright, I'll go and start sorting the wool out and I'll make smoko but not until you've done at least a dozen.'

When they stopped for smoko Teddy's back felt like it was on fire and he didn't know how he was going to get through the day.

'God you're walking like an old fogey,' Deidre teased. 'I haven't had this much fun for ages. Here, have a biscuit to dunk in your tea poor old sod.'

'You're bloody hard on a bloke,' Teddy said clutching his back.

By the end of the day they had managed to get through seventy-six sheep and Deidre had collected the fleeces from the floor and sorted and graded them.

'The quality is not much and the cheque will be buggar all,' Deidre told him.

'Well it's better than nothing and at least we'll have some breeders left to restart the flock with,' Teddy said.

As the sun was setting, they fed the rest of the sheep in the holding pens and cleaned up the dung, dust and wool residue before going back to the homestead. By this time Teddy could hardly stand and Deidre was flagging.

'I'm too stuffed to cook,' Deidre said. 'We'll have some corned beef and pickle sandwiches.'

'Fine with me, I could eat a horse, just pour me a bottomless cup of tea, I'm parched.'

After eating Deidre refused Teddy's offer of help and sent him off for a shower.

'Call me when you've finished and I'll rub some liniment on your back.'

Teddy stood under the hot water for ages and let it blast

into his aching back. How the hell did Dad do this on his own, he wondered. When he had finished he wrapped a towel around his waist and wandered into his bedroom where Deidre was waiting.

'Lie on your back and take off the towel,' she ordered.

'You asked for it,' Teddy said winking at her and dropped his towel on the floor.

Unfazed, Deidre picked up the liniment. 'Not bad, but I've seen better,' she said turning him round. 'Now lie on your front.'

Deidre rubbed and massaged his back easing out the pain and Teddy groaned in pleasure. He was so relaxed when she finished that he was floating and vaguely heard her singing in the shower. He should have offered to do her back but was too fagged out to get up. *Maybe tomorrow*, he thought, and fell asleep.

That night Deidre lay awake thinking about how nice it would be to cuddle up to him. He really was a likeable fellow and it was fun working with him.

The next day Bomber rang from the hospital to see how they were going and laughed so much when Teddy told him about his aching back and Deidre beating him that Matron Maggie worried he might re-break his ribs.

'Don't worry Dad, we might take a bit longer than you, but we'll get there,' Teddy reassured him.

A few days later Teddy found his rhythm and his back had stopped aching. Most of the flock were back in the paddocks looking like fluffy white clouds and the last lot were waiting in the holding pens. Teddy calculated that if they had a good run, they could finish by Friday night in time for him to take Nurse Phoebe out for dinner on Saturday.

Deidre was enjoying herself so much she dreaded the finish and she wasn't looking forward to going home and facing her parents.

When the last ewe was pushed out of the shed, Teddy unhooked the shears from the stands and heaved a sigh of relief.

'Come on Dee, let's go,' he said, and they followed the two dogs as they herded the last sheep out to the far paddock where the rest of the flock were camped.

As they walked back to the homestead Teddy put his arm around Deidre's shoulders and gave her a hug.

'Dee, you're a champion, I couldn't have done it without you. You jump in the shower first and I'll sort out the feeds.'

Deidre stood in the shower and sighed with pleasure as the hot water cascaded over her tall well-built body, flushing the dust and grime from the sheds down the drain. She shampooed her short wavy hair and scrubbed her hands which were black from the oil and dust of the shed until they bled. Turning the cold tap on full she blasted herself with cold water — 'Bliss,' she moaned.

By the time she had dressed, Teddy was in the shower and she went into the kitchen to throw something together for tea. Their usual fare was steak and eggs but tonight Teddy had been in earlier and put a leg of lamb in the oven. 'Mmm delicious,' she said, inhaling deeply. She scrubbed some potatoes and put them around the lamb and found some frozen peas in the top of the fridge. 'Perfect'.

Teddy walked in shaking his wet hair, squeaky clean from the shower. 'Smell me, I'm gorgeous,' he said, offering her his arm pit.

'Mm,' Deidre said sniffing, 'but not as gorgeous as the smell that's coming from the oven.'

'Aha, I've got a surprise for us, 'Teddy said opening the fridge and taking out a magnum of champagne. 'This deserves special glasses which I will fetch from the dining room and we will adjourn to the verandah to celebrate our achievements.'

Deidre was standing at the verandah when Teddy returned with two exquisite crystal glasses filled to the brim with champagne.

'A toast, to us, we did it,' he said handing her a glass.

'Not only did we do it, we did it magnificently,' she said. 'We are the greatest.'

'No Dee, you are the greatest, 'Teddy said downing his drink. 'To Dee, the best shed hand and shearer in the district.'

Deidre took a huge gulp of her drink. 'To the best offsider,' she said laughing.

'To the best masseuse,' Teddy said downing his drink and pouring two more.

'A toast to the dogs, Rusty and Tessa,' Deidre said slurring slightly and sitting down on the verandah sofa with a bump.

'To Rusty and Tessa,' Teddy said sitting next to her.

Deidre was feeling dizzy; they hadn't stopped to eat at

lunchtime because they were so keen on finishing the shed.

Teddy filled up the glasses again. 'A toast to Dad for being such a great guy.'

'Great guy,' Deidre said groggily finishing her drink and getting up. 'Have to see to the lamb.'

The lamb, which was just as mouth-wateringly delicious as it smelled, was cut into large hunks by Teddy with a large carving knife and accompanied with crisp roast potatoes, gravy and peas.

'What, no mint sauce?' Teddy moaned.

'You'll be lucky, I've only just managed the gravy,' Deidre laughed.

Ravenously hungry they demolished the lot and afterwards Teddy produced a bottle of his dad's vintage port. 'This is really good stuff,' he said pouring two glasses.

'Not as good as the lamb,' Deidre said accepting a glass.

'Buggar the lamb, drink that down, you deserve it,' Teddy said wrapping his arms around her. 'Now my dear I am going to reward you handsomely for all your hard work. Come with me to the bedroom and I will inject some culture into your rough exterior.'

Dee giggled and allowed him to lead her to the bedroom where he pulled her onto the bed. But after lashings of champagne and the best part of a bottle of port she was busting for a wee.

'Have to go to the loo,' she said apologetically pushing him away. 'Back in a minute.'

But when she returned, she was devastated to find him

sound asleep and snoring.

'Buggar,' she said giving him a shake. 'So much for that.'

The next morning feeling a bit embarrassed at last night's anti-climax, she left before Teddy woke up and returned to face the music at home.

CHAPTER 15

PHOEBE AND TEDDY

Nurse Phoebe Taylor's ultimate goal in life and the reason she had quit her job in a large city hospital to work at the tiny Damengin Hospital was to marry a rich grazier. Surely, she imagined the heartland of the nation's wool industry would have men thick across the ground.

But when she arrived, she was horrified to find the only thing thick across the arid land was a metre of dust. All the eligible blokes had headed north or south looking for work so they could send money home to their families. Those that were left were fighting the elements and far too busy to bother with her.

Although Phoebe enjoyed working at the hospital and was popular with both staff and patients she was bored to tears and spent her spare time sitting in the kitchen drinking endless cups of tea with Joyce the hospital cleaner and Violet (Vi) the cook, both serial gossips. Romantics at heart they enthusiastically took up the challenge and compiled a list of suitable targets for her to aim at. These included the drop-dead gorgeous but horribly shy workaholic Angus, only son of Malcolm and Millicent Wilton-Smith of Rangoon, the largest property in the region; Paddy Murphy's son Billy, who was 'lovely' but they thought still a bit young; and Teddy Reed, also fabulously wealthy, a cricket tragic, bit of a playboy, and who was unfortunately off somewhere sowing his wild oats and consequently missing in action.

So when the schemers, Joyce and Vi spotted Teddy's large frame arriving at the hospital to visit his dad, they immediately tipped off Phoebe, who in a panic to tart herself up almost took her left eye out with her mascara wand.

Trembling with excitement she doused herself in Miss Chanel Cologne and checked herself in the mirror. 'This could be the ONE,' she confided to Joyce, who told her Teddy was drowning in money inherited from his mum and, Vi added, he was set to inherit one of the largest stations in the district when his dad 'croaked it'.

Not that Phoebe wanted anything to happen to Bomber, she adored him. He never made as much as a squeak when she plunged the incredibly long needle in him and he was always giving her his chocolates and flowers. 'Lovely flowers for a lovely lady,' he would say.

When Teddy arrived for the first time, he met Phoebe (who had told the receptionist to buzz off) manning the front counter looking terribly sweet and efficient in her snowy white uniform and pale pink lippy.

Since then she had managed to pop in each time he was visiting his dad, plumping the pillows and taking away the dishes. At first Teddy was too preoccupied to notice her but who could ignore the sweet smiles and pretty face for long.

On his last visit he had collided with her in the hall and after helping her up and holding onto her soft little hand a little longer than necessary he had decided to ask her out.

For years Teddy, who could charm the birds off the trees without even trying, had his pick of girls. His easy manner and slow drawl attracted them like flies but he had avoided entrapment and firmly believed in the saying 'love em and leave em'.

Of course, Phoebe knew none of this and if she did it is debatable whether she would continue with the chase. She was thrilled her action plan of hiding in the hall cupboard and bumping into him had worked and delighted when he said he would ring.

Almost two weeks later Phoebe was sitting in the nurses' quarters watching television wondering if she would ever hear from him again when the phone rang.

'Nurses quarters, Nurse Taylor speaking,' she said.

'G'day Phoebe, its Teddy Reed, you free for a meal tomorrow night?'

Phoebe could hardly speak for excitement. 'I'd love to,' she said.

'How about I pick you up at say, six, take us an hour to get there. The pub's good on a Saturday night, bit of fun and lots of people.'

'Sounds wonderful, thank you Teddy, I'll look forward to it,' she said dropping the receiver and dashing off to tell the 'schemers'.

Teddy put down the phone and went out on the verandah. He liked Phoebe. She was a pretty girl and it would be good to go out and have some fun.

Phoebe shared news of her date with Joyce and Vi and when she went in to change Bomber's dressing she couldn't help telling him.

'You watch out for that fellow,' he warned Phoebe, grinning. 'Tell him I'll break his neck if he doesn't treat you properly.'

Teddy arrived at the hospital early, sat down next to Bomber's bed and told him about the shearing.

'Couldn't have done it without Deidre, she's an absolute cracker,' he said. 'Tough as nails and bloody strong. Have to admit though, she's a hopeless cook, the mob at Rangoon were ready to string her up after her first effort but, she's worth her weight in gold in the shed.'

Bomber laughed with him. 'How the hell did the Hawtreys breed a girl like Deidre?'

'God knows,' Teddy said. 'She can down a beer with the best of them but I outclassed her last night. You should have seen her this morning, looked like something the cat brought in.'

Bomber smiled, 'Sounds like you got along well. What's she doing now?'

'Don't know Dad. I hope she's okay and her parents are not too bloody with her. God she worked like a trouper. I thought I'd leave it a couple of days and ring her.'

'You do that, those Hawtreys need a wakeup call. So you're taking the charming Phoebe for a night out I hear, I hope you behave yourself.'

'Sure Dad and tomorrow I'm going over to Paddylea to see Billy, told him I'd catch up after the shearing and give him a hand if he needs it. Paddy's off driving the trucks and he's got his Aunt Mary looking after him, be good to see her again.'

'Give my regards to Mary, I haven't seen her in years.'

'Will do, let me know if you need anything,' Teddy said as he left.

He walked around to the nurse's quarters, knocked on the door and was almost knocked over by the sight of Phoebe. Her pale blue silk dress flowed caressing her slender frame and her long blond hair released from imprisonment, cascaded like a river of gold down her back.

She lifted her head and smiled at him, he was enchanted, she was an absolute stunner.

Bestowing a peck on her cheek, Teddy guided her to his newly washed BMW sports car and settled her into its deep leather upholstery. Phoebe sighed with pleasure.

As they drove along, Teddy regaled her with tales of the shearing and had her in fits of laughter. It seemed no time at all before they drew up in front of a long low building in what seemed to be the middle of nowhere.

'This is it,' Teddy said opening the door for her. 'The Rafferty Pub where it's all happening.'

Inside the place was rocking. 'Over there,' Teddy pointed pushing his way through the crowd and leading her through a door at the end of the bar that led to a rather smart dining room where a waiter led them to a table by the window.

'This looks nice,' Phoebe said.

'Best we can offer around here,' Teddy said picking up the wine list. 'Right Phoebe, what would you like to drink?'

'A glass of dry white please,' she said looking around the packed room.

'Make that two,' Teddy said handing the list to the waiter. 'We'll have a drink and then order.'

'Now,' he said leaning over, 'what is a gorgeous looking girl like you doing in a hick town like Damengin?'

Phoebe blushed. 'Well, I was sick of working in a big hospital, and wanted a change, somewhere I could get back to basics. When you are in a big hospital you are a small cog in a very big wheel but in small hospital, its more hands on, you have to be a jack of all trades and I like that. I like being able to interact more with the patients.'

'What about your family, don't you miss them?'

Phoebe, thinking of her mum who was addicted to poker machines and her dad a professional bludger who sat around watching the telly all day and whose biggest effort was getting more beer from the fridge, said quickly, 'all dead,' and wished they were.

Teddy took both of her soft hands in his. 'You poor love,' he said softly.

Phoebe opened her beautiful blue eyes wide and looked at him. 'I'm fine, but you are so lucky having such a kind and caring dad.'

'Yes, Dad's a great bloke, wish I'd been around more for him.'

'I hope you will stay around now,' Phoebe said in a small voice.

'With you around, it could be worth it,' Teddy said stroking the inside of her arm. God she was lovely so soft and caring. He longed to take her in his arms and crush her against him.

After dinner he took her hand and led her back to the front bar where a boisterous crowd was dancing to booming music. Everyone seemed to know him and kept coming up and slapping him on the back. They all made a fuss of Phoebe, nurses were like gold in the bush and she felt marvellous.

Everyone was so friendly, not like the city where people hardly spoke to you, Phoebe thought. She had never felt so happy.

On the way home, Teddy told her about his cricketing career and his travels.

'Do you miss that life?' Phoebe asked, hoping that he didn't.

'Sometimes, but by the time I was back in Brisbane I knew I didn't have what it takes anymore and I was sick of living out of suitcases. I guess it was time to do something else. Dad getting hurt really got to me and I realised it was time to make a decision about my life. I don't know whether I could settle down on the property, but I'll give it a try for his sake.'

Phoebe determined that she would move heaven and earth to make sure he did settle down. *Whatever it takes,* she thought, *I really like him.*

Teddy walked her to the door of the nurse's quarters and

bent down and kissed her. 'Thank you for a lovely evening,' he said, 'I'll ring you, sleep well.'

Phoebe went to bed floating on a cloud dreaming of their next meeting.

Doing her rounds next day Phoebe copped a teasing from Matron Maggie, who had been thoroughly briefed on her night out by Bomber. 'Don't you be taken in by that playboy nurse, he's a real tease and a womaniser.'

Phoebe smiled to herself as she went about her day handing out pills and changing dressings. She wondered what she would wear next time and would he want to take her to bed — should she let him? It was such an ecstasy of agony making decisions.

Teddy was oblivious to Phoebe's plans and after leaving her went home and slept like a log.

CHAPTER 16

MARY'S LITTLE LAMBS

When Deidre had arrived home from Redlands nursing the daddy of all hangovers her parents, who'd had an almighty row before she arrived and were not speaking to each other, unleashed their frustration.

'Where have you been?' Audrey said. 'I arrived home and the place was a mess, dirty clothes everywhere, the cat hadn't been fed and your father was nowhere in sight. He is so inconsiderate he completely forgot to pick me up at Longreach and Angus Wilton-Smith, who picked up his mother, was kind enough to give me a lift home. Then he told me you had been out there working in their shearing shed, how could you?'

'Better than sitting around here and copping abuse,' Deidre replied taking out a can of lemonade from the fridge and slamming the door.

'Don't do that,' Audrey yelled. 'You are an absolute disgrace. You look and speak like a common tramp.'

'Takes one to know one,' Deidre replied.

A screaming match between Audrey and Deidre erupted and the racket was so horrific that Huw, terrified his staff in the bank next door who he knew would be listening, would ring the police, tried to intervene but was shouted down.

After fielding a particularly nasty torrent of abuse, Deidre lashed out at her mum calling her a 'stuck up bitch'.

'How dare you,' Audrey screamed and rushed at her, slapping her across the face.

'Stop that,' Huw cried, catching hold of her arms and pinning them to her sides.

'Let me go,' she shrieked struggling.

Deidre rushed at him. 'Don't you touch my mum, you bastard,' she yelled letting fly with a massive punch to his face.

Huw fell to the floor groaning, his nose bleeding and blood pouring down his face.

'You wicked girl, you've killed him, call the ambulance,' Audrey shrieked kneeling down and cradling his face in her lap.

Deidre bent down and tried to help him up.

'Get away from me,' he said pushing her away. 'You've done enough, just get out of here.'

Deidre stood up. 'He's alright, the only thing hurt is his bloody ego. And you,' she said scowling at her mum, 'you're fucking ungrateful. I was only trying to protect you.'

'Don't you speak to me using that language,' Audrey shrieked dabbing Huw's nose with a frilly lace hanky. 'All the money we have spent trying to make you into a lady and you come out with that.'

Deidre shrugged. 'If ladies behave like you, then I'll stay as I am and as for him,' she said pointing at Huw, 'he's the biggest crook this side of the black stump for trying to steal Ben's station from him.'

Huw jumped up spattering blood over Audrey and shoved his face into hers. 'Who told you that,' he demanded. 'It's a damned lie, don't you ever accuse me of stealing.'

Deidre put her hands on her hips and glared at him. 'Why else did you try to foreclose on Ben when he was up to date with his payments.'

'For your information, it was a bookkeeping error, easily made and if I hear you spreading this filth around I won't be responsible for what I'll do to you.'

'Oh yes, well you better start eating some spinach Dad because if it comes to a fight, all the money would be on me. Anyway, I'm sick of the fights, I'm off and I'm not coming back this time,' she said walking into her bedroom.

'You'll be back, you always are,' her dad called after her. Ignoring him, Deidre went into her bedroom and began shoving clothes into her backpack.

'This time it's really for good,' she said, before calling Rusty and roaring off in her ute.

'Doesn't matter where we go, Rusty mate,' she said to him as they drove along, 'we'll be right.'

Turning on her radio, Deidre calmed down and began to think through her options. She still had the money Teddy had insisted she take for helping him and he might have some more work for her while Bomber was in hospital.

As for her parents, she was sorry about her mum but glad she had told them what she thought. Serve them right for the way they had treated Ben and her brother Timmy. *Poor Tim,* she thought fondly, *all he ever wanted was to be a hairdresser or a male model and they forced him to go to ag college where he was given hell by the macho blokes.*

'It's just not fair,' she said sadly to a doting Rusty who leaned his head on her shoulder. 'So what if he's gay?'

It was getting dark when she took the turnoff to Redlands to see Teddy and by the time she drove into the homestead yard, he had already left to pick up Phoebe at the hospital. The house was locked so she drove down to the large feed shed and parked under the awning. Unrolling her swag, she fell into a deep sleep in the back of her ute with Rusty to keep her warm.

In the morning when she woke up she walked over to the homestead and was relieved to see Teddy's car parked out front and the front door open.

'Wake up you lazy buggar,' she said walking down the hall and banging on his bedroom door.

Teddy, who had been having wonderful orgasmic dreams of the gorgeous Phoebe was hugely disappointed to be woken up.

'Who the hell is there at this time of day?' he yelled.

'It's me, Deidre, get up you lazy buggar it's time for work,' she said walking into the bedroom.

Teddy grinned. 'Okay Dee, give me a chance to get some gear on.'

'Don't worry about that, seen it all before,' Deidre said grinning. 'Where have you been?'

'None of your bloody business,' he said shocked by her appearance. 'You look like shit mate, what's happened?'

'Had a bit of a brawl with the parents, landed a punch on Dad and Mum freaked. Dossed down in the shed. Is that okay?'

'Sure mate, long as you like, what brought the row on?'

Deidre grimaced. 'I thought Mum was okay but she is a bloody snob. They pick on Timmy because he wants to be a hairdresser and they try to make me into something I'm not.'

Teddy grinned. 'They'd have to try bloody hard to change you Dee. You got to admit you did buggar off without telling them where you were, your mum was probably worried sick.'

'Nah, the only person she worries about is herself, as for Dad, that goes double,' she said angrily. 'He's an absolute shit, look what he did to Ben?'

Teddy put his big hand on her shoulder. 'Let's have some brekkie, I'm starving. You can stay here as long as you like and not in the bloody shearing shed. There's plenty of room in the house.'

Deidre sat at the kitchen table drinking tea while Teddy cooked them breakfast.

'Are you sure Bomber won't mind me staying here for a bit?' she asked.

'Don't be silly,' Teddy said dropping four eggs into the

sizzling pan, 'Dad thinks the world of you and look how you helped me. Just get that toast will you and butter it. This is almost ready.'

Deidre's mouth watered as Teddy served out deliciously crisp bacon with eggs, tomato and fried potato.

'You know Dee,' Teddy said between mouthfuls, 'that was a bloody dirty trick of your old man's considering Ben wasn't behind in the loan repayments. How the hell could he have made a mistake like that? Your dad could be in a whole lot of trouble if he stuffed up.'

Dee put down her knife and fork and looked across the table at Teddy, 'Remember what he said in court, he claimed it was a bookkeeping error and to be honest, I hate to think of him as a crook. It would be awful if he went to jail, Mum would never get over it. Teddy, do you think he had an ulterior motive?'

Teddy shrugged. 'I reckon he did, jumping the gun like that. Something odd is going on. Proving it's going to be hard.'

Deidre wiped the egg off her plate with a piece of toast, popped it into her mouth and sighed contentedly. 'I guess things will have calmed down by next week and it's Mum's birthday so maybe I'll drop around with some flowers, see if she knows anything. But it's not like he's going to tell her he's a crook is it, and one thing I know about Mum, she might be dippy, but she's honest.'

After they had washed up, they drove out to the windmills where the sheep were gathered and distributed some bales of hay.

'Don't they look lovely now that they're shorn, so clean and white,' she said. 'You know Teddy, even though the drought has been so terrible and hurt so many people, you can't help loving the place. I couldn't live anywhere else, could you?' she asked, squinting her eyes against the glare and looking to where the cloudless blue sky met the red dusty plains.

'I don't know. I had a great time playing cricket and travelling, met lots of interesting people but I'm beginning to think it is time to come home,' he said. 'But I'd like the place a bit more if we had some feed,' he said pulling the hay apart.

'Look there's not much to do here at the moment, how about we go out to Paddylea and see how Billy and his Aunt Mary are getting on? Billy told me she was in an awful state when Paddy brought her home.'

'Great idea,' Deidre said closing the tray of the ute, 'be good to see Billy again. Give them a call and let them know we're coming.'

Paddylea Station was a good hour's drive to the west over a road made up of corrugated ridges and large open cracks. A wind was coming from the south whipping up red dust which coated the windows of the ute and made driving uncomfortable and along the side of the road, gluttonous fat crows fed on rotting carcasses of kangaroos.

'God they stink,' Deidre moaned, holding her nose.

'They sure do,' Teddy said grimacing. 'What happened to those miles and miles of Mitchell grass for as far as the eye can see?'

'Long gone,' said Deidre sadly, 'but when the rains come

as they must eventually, then you'll see them again.'

'Let's hope we don't have to wait too long.'

Mary and Billy were looking forward to seeing them and were waiting on the verandah when the ute drove up.

'Welcome to Paddylea,' Billy said giving Teddy a slap on the arm and hugging Deidre.

Mary stood back and smiled shyly at them. 'I haven't seen you Teddy since you were at boarding school with Billy and I don't think I've ever met you Deidre, but it's so nice to see you and as Billy says, welcome to Paddylea. Now come inside and have some tea, I've made some scones,' she said leading the way into the kitchen.

'Yes come on in, Aunty Mary's put a roast on for lunch and she wants to show you her pet project, don't you Mary?'

As Mary poured out the tea, she smiled to herself thinking she was feeling the best she had for ages. Billy's 'no grog' stance had worked wonders with her since they'd arrived two weeks earlier for the start of the lambing.

The effects of the drought had taken their toll on the skinny ewes and many were so weakened by the ravages of the drought they died giving birth. Their lambs, with no chance of survival, were quickly dispatched by Billy.

When they first arrived Mary, who was suffering alcohol withdrawal was a mess, shaking and vomiting; then, after a few days, the shakes eased, the vomiting stopped and she was able to eat. One day she had wandered off to the first feeding station nearest the homestead and found a newborn lamb bleating pitifully next to its dead mother. Consumed with sadness for its pathetic little bundle whose only future was a bullet, she picked it up and carried it back to the house. There she carefully wrapped it in an old blanket and made up a bottle of powdered milk. It was so famished it polished off the lot in a few seconds and was cheeky enough to butt her for more. 'You greedy little tot,' Mary said stroking its soft woolly head and made it another bottle. Replete, it settled comfortably in her lap and when Billy arrived back he found the two of them asleep next to the stove.

He looked down at them and smiled. 'Poor thing, she just needed something to love,' he said tenderly.

After that, the orphan lambs became Mary's salvation and each day she followed Billy when he did the rounds and adopted the little souls.

Teddy and Deidre made short work of Mary's delicious scones and needed no persuasion to follow her to the shearing shed where she was keeping her lambs. A large area had been fenced off and inside were dozens of tiny lambs. As soon as they saw Mary they began bleating, the noise was horrific.

'Yee Gods,' Deidre said laughing. 'It's bedlam in here.'

Mary laughed. 'They're wonderful and more than half are females,' she told them proudly, 'so at least Paddy will have a few more breeders to add to his flock. I'll make up the bottles. Billy bought 44 kg bags of milk powder and I just mix it with water, we bought some feeding units and I do them in shifts of ten at a time.'

'I'll give you a hand,' Deidre said following her to the water tank outside.

'What news of Paddy?' Teddy asked watching the feeding frenzy as Deidre helped Mary put out the milk.

'He should be back tomorrow,' Billy said. 'He took a truckload of roos down to the abattoir and he's bringing stuff back for the pub and Tom Fitzgerald. Then he wants to sort out the drought relief. He said when Bomber had his accident everything went haywire and they had to change their plans. Now he's thinking of taking Maisie Matten and Sid Luxton and if he has to Shifty Grey.'

Billy took them out to see the rest of the flock and to check for more lambs and then they drove back to the homestead where Deidre helped Mary serve lunch.

They were tucking into roast mutton and white sauce with potatoes and peas when the phone rang and Billy got up to answer it. 'That was Chloe Matten,' he said excitedly, 'you're not going to believe this but Damengin is on the front page of the city papers and some mob have just done a television film at Ben Bangor's place. Chloe said the phone hasn't stopped ringing at the *Star* with people wanting to help. Sam is talking to Huw Hawtrey at the bank to set up a fund so people can put money in and everyone is asking how they can help. There's a mob wants to set up a pool so people can drop off lawn clippings and truckies are offering to bring them out for nothing, others want to donate bales of hay.'

'That's wonderful,' Mary said her eyes shining. 'Think what a difference this will make.'

'Don't know if I'd trust my dad to set up a trust fund. Mistrust, more likely,' Deidre muttered.

'I hope Ben knows,' Billy said. 'This could mean the difference between life and death to his place. I'll give him a call.'

Ben already knew. 'Chloe rang and I told her I'll believe it when it happens,' he told Billy.

'This calls for a celebration,' Billy said opening a bottle of beer and pouring out three glasses. Mary poured herself a lemonade.

'To the *Star*,' he said raising his glass.

'To the *Star*,' they replied.

CHAPTER 17

ANNABEL AND SHIFTY

Back at the Damengin Pub Paddy had finished unloading his truck with help from Joseph the yardman and decided to telephone Shifty Grey to find out the latest on the Canberra trip when Annabel Grey stormed in.

'That bastard,' she cried throwing her substantial self into Paddy's arms and bursting into noisy tears. 'I caught him red-handed or red bottomed with that slut Dolly McIntyre in my bed, my beautiful pristine bed made with my mother's hand embroidered sheets,' she said, tears streaming down her bright red face and saturating the front of Paddy's dusty shirt.

Paddy held her close and gently stroked her back. *Bloody Shifty*, he thought, everyone except his wife knew exactly what a shit he was.

'I didn't want to go to Bomber and upset him,' Annabel said between sobs. 'I want him out of my house, out of my life and I want her sacked, the slut. When I think what I've put up with for years, how could he?'

Paddy sighed. What a bloody mess this was. The last thing he wanted was Shifty to leave town when they were in the middle of trying to get the drought relief. And, thank Christ Bomber was stuck in hospital or he would be locked up for murder.

Holding her away, he looked in her eyes. 'Annabel, I could go over and throw him out for you but how about you stay here for a while until I can sort things out. Everything is a bloody disaster and we need to keep him on side, just until we can sort out things at council. We really need him to follow up on the drought relief.'

'Oh, you can kiss that away,' Annabel said angrily. 'He's more interested in following up Dolly's knickers. Anyway he'll have a bit of explaining to do, he's nursing a dirty great black eye.'

Paddy laughed. 'You little beauty. Annabel, my advice is bide your time, believe me he'll get what's coming to him.' *That is, if she doesn't take the slimy little shit back again,* he thought to himself. This wasn't the first time Annabel had walked out on Shifty. It was just the latest in a long list of partings where the vow 'never to meet again except in the divorce courts' featured. Usually, within a few days, Shifty went crawling back and Annabel, who was basically lazy and couldn't be bothered with the fuss, took him back.

Although Paddy was fond of Annabel she had been spoilt by doting older parents and was used to having her own way. Over the years she had left Shifty to his own vices and chose to gallivant around socialising. Mind you he thought, he couldn't blame her for that — who would want to stay with that lowlife? And the truth of it was, the only thing the pair had in common was the date they got married.

While Paddy went off to let Rosie know Annabel would be staying and to make up a room for her Annabel wandered into the downstairs loo to tidy herself up. 'What a mess,' she said, looking into the mirror over the sink. She pulled a comb through her unruly curls, dusted her shiny nose and under her eyes, red from crying, with powder, applied frosted pink lipstick (her favourite) and dabbed a touch of Eau de Lancôme behind her ears. 'That's better,' she said smiling.

Unbeknown to Paddy, Annabel had carried a torch for him since she was a girl and thought that if she was going to ditch Shifty, it was only sensible to cover all options. She had never been in love with Shifty, in lust maybe but not heartbreakingly adoring love. He (realising he was on to a good thing) had rushed her to the altar, and they had spent the last twenty years repenting at leisure only it hadn't been the least bit leisurely.

When Paddy got back she took hold of his arm and looked up at him. 'Paddy you are such a good friend to me,' she said in a low sweet voice, 'I am so sorry to be a nuisance and I will accept your invitation to stay here for a few days but I'll have to go back and collect some things because you see Paddy, this is really the end. Geoffrey Grey and I are finished.'

Paddy put his arm around her shoulder. 'Good, Annabel, stay as long as you like. Do you want me to come with you when you collect your things?'

Annabel nodded. 'Would you?' she said.

'Sure, then we'll go out and see how Bill and Mary are coping at Paddylea. I told him I'd see him when I got back.'

By the time they got over to Annabel's magnificent home set on five acres of rolling lawns just outside the town, Shifty had gone so Annabel threw some clothes in a bag and picked some roses from her garden for Mary.

As they drove along, Annabel felt a load had been lifted and entertained Paddy with tales of Shifty's adventures.

'Last year he booked for a Local Government Conference in Cairns and told me no partners allowed. I didn't believe a word of it and when he arrived in Cairns with Dolly in tow I was at the airport waiting for him. The look on his face was to die for. Poor Dolly panicked and hid in the loo. I felt quite sorry for her.'

'What happened next?' Paddy chuckled.

'I told him I would tell Bomber who would sack him and the little shit went to water. Gabbled on blaming everyone in his office. You know Paddy, I should have left him years ago,' she said shaking her head. 'I always wanted children but the bloody fucker couldn't even do that right.' What Annabel didn't know was that Shifty, who was far too mean to be stuck with children had had a vasectomy before he left New Zealand. A randy little runt, he was more than happy to jump on Annabel at every opportunity with the excuse they 'must keep trying' and poor Annabel was over serviced to hell with nothing to show for it.

'Why didn't you leave him?' Paddy said looking at her sideways.

'Well I suppose there was always plenty of money and I was free to do what I liked.'

When they arrived at Paddylea, Mary and Billy gave them a huge welcome and while the men unloaded the grain and hay the two women went off arm in arm. It had been years since they had spent time together so they had plenty to catch up on.

Mary was excited to see Annabel and even more thrilled with the beautiful roses she brought. 'Oh the perfume,' she said, hugging Annabel and almost crushing the huge bouquet. 'I'll find a vase and then we'll have some tea.'

'It's so lovely to have you back after all these years,' Annabel said hugging her back.

Mary finished arranging the roses and sat down next to her. 'Annabel, it is so good to be here, I wish I had come home sooner. You have no idea how awful my life has been, one day I'll tell you about it. I don't know what I would do without Paddy, he has been wonderful.'

'Paddy is a life saver. I'm glad you came home, Mary, it will be good to have a friend I can trust. My life has been pretty useless too. Geoffrey and I, well we're finished and I'm glad I finally made the decision. He's a shit, and that's really a compliment. Darling Paddy has rescued me and I'm going to stay at the pub until Bomber is allowed home and then I'll stay at Redlands and look after him until I work out what to do with my life.'

Paddy and Billy took hay out to the troughs. 'Bit of a worry that Annabel,' Paddy said. 'She's had a hell of a fight with Shifty, blacked his eye, and I've got her staying with me until Bomber gets better. She wanted me to go over and sort the buggar out but I don't want to rock the apple cart at the moment not with the drought relief pending.'

'Couldn't she go and stay with Teddy at Redlands, after all he is her nephew, instead of hanging around the town?'

'Hadn't thought of that, I forgot Teddy was out there. I'll mention it to her when we get back, probably suit her better and it would get her out of the way until things are sorted out. How's Mary coping?'

'You wouldn't believe the difference, Dad, she is a changed woman. I removed all the grog and she's eating, even cooking, sleeping and absolutely dotes on the lambs. Poor thing she must have been through hell to get herself in a mess like that.'

'You know Billy she was the prettiest little thing when she was young, full of fun, broke my heart when she left the way she did. I'm glad she's so much better. I think we'll leave her settle down out here for a while, the peace of the place is what she needs.'

When Paddy and Billy arrived back at the homestead they were greeted with the fabulous smell of roast lamb.

'Something smells good,' Paddy said removing his hat and sitting down at the kitchen table.

'You can thank Annabel,' Mary said smiling. 'I put the

roast on earlier but she did the rest, roast potatoes, carrots, peas and gravy and even a baked custard to go with the apples I stewed.'

'Wonderful, thanks Annabel, way to a man's heart, you'll have to give Mary some cooking lessons,' Paddy said.

Annabel served out large plates loaded with tender lamb dripping with gravy and vegetables and they all sat down to eat at the large table on the shady front verandah. The kitchen with its fuel stove was far too hot during the day but was a haven of warmth in the cold winter nights and mornings.

'This is delicious, Annabel,' Paddy said between mouthfuls. 'How would you like to spend some time at Redlands with Teddy? It would get you right out of town for a while until we can sort out the council problems.'

Annabel looked at him with her head on the side. 'What's the matter Paddy, do you want to get rid of me already?'

'No way, not if you can turn out food like this. Seriously though, you need to get away from that loser you married and I'm sure Teddy could do with a decent feed out at Redlands.'

Annabel nodded. 'You're right, it's a great idea. I'll stay at the pub tonight as Rosie's already made the bed up and then I'll drive out there tomorrow. Geoffrey won't have a clue where I am so don't tell him will you?'

'You can rest assured I won't be telling him anything, I just want to make sure the little creep gets on to that drought money.'

After lunch Mary took Annabel to see her little orphaned lambs.

'I haven't been much help to my brother and he's always been marvellous to me,' she told Annabel,' this is helping in a small way and it's lovely to see the little things thriving. You know I was never interested in the property when I was young but I feel right at home here now.'

Annabel bent over and stroked one of the tiny creatures. 'They are so soft and so cuddly, little bundles of fluff. I'll take some powdered milk and bottles out to Redlands and see if I can save a few of Bomber's lambs.'

Later that afternoon, they said goodbye and headed back to town. As they drove along Paddy explained the problems they were having in getting funding from the Federal Government. 'We need Shifty to follow through with this Annabel, that's why I'm asking you not to do anything until things are settled.'

'I understand what you're saying but I tell you when it's resolved, I'll squeeze the little bastard so hard he'll fit through the eye of a needle,' she chuckled. 'He thinks he's getting away with this, like hell he is. He'll leave town the way he came with nothing but his bare arse.'

Paddy grinned. Shifty had it coming and he was looking forward to seeing Annabel in action.

Down at his council office Shifty tentatively pressed an ice pack on his left eye which had swollen to three times its size and was a multicoloured slit in his thin weasel face. Bloody Annabel, she packed a powerful right hook. He'd have to remember to duck next time, if there was a next time, he thought, miserably.

His voluptuous secretary Dolly came in with a cup of tea and a ginger nut biscuit.

'You poor love,' Dolly said sympathetically sitting on the edge of his desk and resting her foot in his crotch. 'She's such a bitch your old bag of a wife, you should have given her one back.'

Shifty glared at her out of his one good eye. 'Don't be bloody ridiculous and have her giant of a brother on my back. Shove off Dolly, leave me in peace. I've got to think.'

Dolly shrugged her shoulders, got up and walked out slamming the door behind her.

Shifty groaned. 'Bloody women,' he muttered, now he would have to go crawling to Annabel or she could get Bomber offside and there really would be strife.

He arrived home that night weighed down with flowers, chocolates and wine to a dark and empty house. Annabel's late model car was gone, and in the kitchen, Tiddles the cat was yowling for food. Taking a tin of kittycat from the cupboard Shifty miserably spooned it into her bowl.

'Where the hell has she gone, Tiddles?' he asked the cat, who was far too busy wolfing down his dinner to care.

Meanwhile Annabel and Paddy were enjoying more than a few drinks in the private quarters upstairs in the pub.

'You know what, Paddy,' she said leaning her head on his shoulder, 'I haven't enjoyed myself so much for years. To hell with the little shit, he'll get more than a black eye if he comes near me again.'

Paddy looked down at her and laughed. 'Annabel, there's

no doubt about you,' he said giving her a hug.

'I'd be happy to go anywhere with you Paddy,' she said cuddling into him.

Paddy smiled and tipped her chin up to him. 'Would you now,' he said kissing her firmly and drawing her close, 'well we might be able to do something about that. Follow me,' he said taking her hand and leading her into his bedroom.

The next morning Annabel said she had a hangover and was too ill to face the trip to Redlands and Paddy, consumed with lust, had no intention of letting her go so they stayed in bed which worked out to be the most effective remedy for both ailments.

CHAPTER 18

DEIDRE TO THE RESCUE

When Dee and Teddy arrived back at Paddylea from their visit to Redlands, Dee was in a quandary about her parents. 'Teddy what do you think I ought to do about Mum and Dad. I can't stay here forever.'

Teddy looked at her worried face. 'Stay as long as you like but maybe you need to see how things are. I know I've given Dad a bad time over the years and when I see how he's struggled I feel a right shit. All the money I blew having a great time while the poor buggar was battling to keep the place going.

'Tell you what Dee, if you do decide to go back and see how things are, try not to lose your cool. I know you think your dad did the wrong thing by Ben, but maybe there was a mistake in his bookkeeping.'

Deidre sighed, it wasn't in her nature to be angry, she loved life too much and all the hatred she had felt towards her parents had dulled.

'Maybe you're right,' she said. 'It's Mum's birthday tomorrow, no idea how old she is because the vain old biddy never admits to her age. I might take her some flowers for a peace offering. Now let's go to bed I'm stuffed.'

Teddy put his head on the side and looked at her smiling wickedly. 'Is that an invitation?' he said, 'or are you too lazy to make up a bed in the spare room?'

Deidre punched him on the arm. 'Well, it gets bloody cold in this place at night and I figured a big bloke like you should be able to keep Rusty and me warm.'

'Buggar Rusty and I'll do more than keep you warm,' Teddy said taking her arm and rushing her down the hall and into his bedroom. 'Out,' he said closing the bedroom door on Rusty and pulling Deidre inside.

'Now Dee, the last one to get their gear off makes breakfast.'

Deidre immediately stepped out of her jeans and knickers, whipped her jumper over her head, threw boots and socks in the corner of the bedroom and jumped into bed before Teddy could get his boots off.

'Beat you,' she called smirking with the sheets pulled under her chin.

'And that's just what I'm going to do to you so watch out,' Teddy said as he launched himself on top of her.

Yelling in protest, Deidre surrendered herself to his arm wrestle and pushed herself against him.

'This is the type of beating I like,' she said giggling hysterically.

'Just shut up will you and concentrate, I can't do anything

with you laughing. Alright you minx let's see if this will keep you quiet,' he said lying on top of her.

An hour later relaxed and totally satisfied, Teddy looked down at her. 'You're pretty good at this. If I remember rightly, you've had some serious practice.'

'Aha,' Deidre said grinning at him, 'those long trips home on the boarding school train were never boring.'

Teddy burst out laughing. 'No doubt about you Dee.'

'Ready for a replay,' she teased, 'or do you only come once?'

'Want more, you little hussy, right.'

The sun blasting its way through the French windows had no effect on them the next morning as they lay completely shagged out. Rusty, who after he was so rudely ejected by Teddy had camped outside the bedroom door, decided enough was enough and threw himself against the door which buckled under his weight. Overjoyed he launched himself on top of them.

'What the hell,' Deidre yelled, 'get off you monster,' she laughed, pushing his slobbering face away from her.

Teddy escaped by diving under the bedclothes but Rusty jumped on top of him and sat on his back.

'Get off you bloody mongrel,' Teddy groaned pushing him off the bed. He pulled a giggling Deidre towards him and began planting wet noisy kisses on her neck.

'You're insatiable,' she said.

'Stop calling me names and start cooperating or I'll keep you here all morning and don't forget you're making breakfast.'

'No way, you lost that bet and you'll be bloody sorry if I do, I can't cook.'

'About time you learnt, I like my women domesticated.'

'You can't have everything,' Deidre said. 'Now stop complaining and get on with it for God's sake, I'm hungry.'

It was midday before Deidre finally waved goodbye to Teddy and drove back to Damengin to face her parents. As she drove along she decided she would take Audrey to lunch at the pub to avoid another screaming match.

But when she got there all was well because Huw who had been relegated to the spare room since the last awful row with Deidre and keen to get back in Audrey's good books and comfortable bed had got up early, made a pot of tea and toast and taken it in to her.

'Happy birthday Aud,' he said bending down to kiss her. 'Something special for a lovely lady,' he said handing over the beautifully wrapped box.

Audrey, fed up with the tension in the house and terrified no one would remember her birthday, was ready to make peace accepted his gift graciously.

'Thank you, Huw,' she said smiling. She carefully undid the ribbons and removed the wrapping paper to reveal a little red velvet box which contained two beautiful and very large diamond earrings.

'Oh they are absolutely beautiful,' she gasped holding them up to the light to check the size of the diamonds. 'Thank you darling, you'll have to take me somewhere really special so that I can show them off.'

'I would be delighted,' Huw said. 'I'll book a table at the pub tonight.'

Audrey grimaced. 'Really Huw, is that the best you can offer?'

'Well there's nowhere else to go unless we drive into Longreach. I suppose we could make a night of it and stay over at the motel,' Huw said, hopeful he could be rewarded for his efforts.

'Yes, that would be nice,' said Audrey. 'I'll wear these with my new blue silk I bought in Bangkok last year.'

Huw went off to work and Audrey showered and was just getting dressed when the phone rang.

'Happy birthday Aud, Milly here, I've got something for you but I can't get into town today, can you come to lunch tomorrow?'

'Thank you Milly, that would be lovely. Huw bought me a beautiful pair of diamond earrings, at least one carat, and he's taking me to dinner at Longreach. I think he's got the message at long last.'

Millicent Wilton-Smith, who was Audrey's best friend and had already received a blow by blow description of the row with Huw and Deidre, was delighted with the news.

'Well done, Aud. As I said, threaten to leave and demand half of everything and he'll just go to water. They all do, the bastards.'

After chatting for over an hour to Milly, Audrey had just put down the phone when Deidre walked in, her arms filled with flowers and clutching a gigantic box of chocolates.

'Happy birthday Mum,' she said thrusting them into Audrey's arms and giving her a peck on the cheek.

Audrey looked at her in disgust. She was wearing a ripped pair of jeans, an old shirt of Teddy's and an ancient sweat stained hat. She hadn't even removed her boots which were filthy and had left mud on the best cream Wilton carpet.

'Look what you have done' she shrieked, 'you've ruined the carpet. Take your disgusting boots off before you come in here, it's not the cattle yards.'

'For God's sake, Mum, is this the thanks I get,' Deidre said taking off her boots and throwing them through the door just missing Rusty who had been gazing in hopefully through the gauze screen.

'Sit down, I want to talk to you,' Audrey said, calming down slightly. 'Thank you for the flowers but you know I don't eat chocolates and neither should you, just look at the size of you.'

Deidre sat down opposite her. 'Look Mum, I didn't come here to talk about myself, I came to try to sort things out with Dad. What the heck do you think he was doing when he tried to foreclose on Ben Bangor when Ben was up to date with his payments?'

'What did you say?' Audrey hissed. 'Your father did no such thing, Ben Bangor was well behind in his payments.'

'No he wasn't, he'd been working his butt off roo shooting and driving for Paddy and I know for a fact he was making the payments. Dad will be in big trouble when the bank auditors check because Ben is going to lodge a complaint.'

Audrey stared at Deidre with her lips pursed. How could Huw do something so dreadful, she thought? But, deep down she knew he could and she knew she was partly to blame for pressuring him to buy a sheep station for their son Timmy. For years she had dreamed of joining the landed gentry to be on a par with her friend Millicent Wilton-Smith. And, since the drought had caused such havoc and prices had hit rock bottom Huw had agreed it was the ideal time to buy. He had mentioned Ben was struggling to pay his mortgage to her before she went on the cruise and Babington was one of the most sought-after properties in the district. If he had jumped the gun and done something illegal, he could be sent to jail. Audrey went white with shock. How on earth would she ever face Millicent again?

'Right, I'm calling your father and we'll have this out,' she said picking up the phone.

'Mrs Hawtrey speaking, please tell Mr Hawtrey there is an emergency at home and he is to come immediately,' Audrey said, slamming down the receiver.

Huw arrived minutes later through the interconnecting door from the bank.

'Audrey, what on earth is the matter? I have important people waiting to see me,' he said looking at his watch.

'Hello Dad,' Deidre said quietly from her position by the door, ready to make a quick exit if things got rough.

'Deidre,' he said nodding. 'Now what's all this about?'

'Huw Hawtrey, just answer this question honestly,' Audrey said fixing him with an icy stare. 'Did you foreclose on Ben

Bangor when he was up to date with his mortgage payments, yes or no?'

'Don't be ridiculous,' Huw said grinning.

'Yes or no, I want a straight answer,' Audrey said. 'Our future together depends on it. If you lie to me, I am leaving you and I'm taking you for everything you have.'

Huw was silent. If he said yes, he was in big trouble, if he lied and said no, he could be found out and then he would be in seriously big trouble.

'I did it for you Aud,' he said his voice quavering. 'You kept on nagging me about buying a sheep station for Timmy and we just didn't have the money so I thought if I could sell him up we could buy it for next to nothing.'

Audrey stared at him in horror. 'How could you, you absolute idiot? You'll go to jail and Millicent will never speak to me again. I won't be able to hold my head up in this town. That does it, I'm leaving you and I want half of everything. You can pay your own legal bills and don't think I'll come and visit you in jail,' she said bursting into loud sobs.

Terrified Huw dropped to his knees and grabbed hold of her, 'Please Aud,' he pleaded, 'don't leave me, I love you, I only did it for you and for Timmy.'

'Don't blame me,' Audrey sobbed. 'I didn't ask you to break the law, and you have ruined my life.'

'I really love you Aud, I am sorry. Please don't leave me.'

Deidre shook her head in disgust. 'Bastards couldn't give a damn for me,' she muttered. 'All they want is a place for Timmy, what a joke that is.'

But the sight of Audrey bawling her eyes out and Huw on his knees begging her not to leave him was so ridiculous and so tragic that despite herself Deidre felt sorry for them.

'Come on now, pull yourselves together, it's not the end of the world,' she said walking over and sitting next to her mum.

'Look, I'll go out and talk to Ben, tell him the truth and maybe he won't press charges. After all Dad, he did pull a gun on you so it's a bit of tit for tat. And both of you can forget about buying a station for Timmy because he's gay and he doesn't want one. He's been trying to tell you for years and you need to know that he's gone to Sydney to the gay Mardi Gras and to find a job as an apprentice hairdresser.'

Audrey jerked her head up and looked shocked. 'My poor darling Timmy is gay?' she said wiping her eyes, 'Now I know why he was always borrowing my face creams and waxing under his arms. He was always making such an awful mess in the bathroom.'

'Of course,' she said brightening, 'he would be a brilliant hairdresser, and he's got such wonderful taste. Huw darling, we must buy him a lovely place to live and a beauty salon somewhere trendy like the North Shore.'

Huw stood up and wiped his eyes with a large very white beautifully ironed hanky. 'Anything you say Aud, as long as you don't leave me.'

Turning to Deidre his eyes still red from crying, he said, 'Thank you Deidre, but it is for me to talk to Ben not you.'

'No Dad, you look after Mum, I'll go on my own, see how things are and I'll let you know. Now cheer up and if the worst comes to the worst, you can always move to Sydney and live with Timmy.'

Audrey smiled happily at the thought. 'I would really like that. We could go to the theatre and art galleries, Sydney is such a beautiful place. Huw we must go down and set him up, make sure he chooses the right people to get in with.'

Huw shook his head sadly as he walked Deidre to the door. 'Your mum has no idea the seriousness of this. Let me know how it goes with Ben, I'll see to your mum and Dee, thanks.'

'Okay Dad,' she said getting into her car. *For God's sake, she thought, what a hopeless pair.* Did her mum ever think of anyone but Timmy? *What about me, what about my life? Where was Timmy today when it was Mum's birthday, not even a phone call?*

Huw walked back to the bank and told them to cancel his appointments because he had 'urgent business to attend to'. He could see the merit in Deidre's proposal because after all, Ben did pull a gun on him but he needed to make plans.

When Audrey had threatened to leave him, he was horrified because all of the money he had made from the syndicate had been salted away in her name without her knowledge. In fact she was wealthy enough to buy any reasonably sized station in the district. He had chosen Ben's because it would sell for a fraction of its worth. The big problem now was that if she left him, she would be a very wealthy woman and he would be left with his arse out of his pants and nothing but his miserable bank pension which could also be under threat.

He stood shaking at the thought. *Thank God she has*

forgiven me, at least if I go to jail I'll have something to look forward to when I get out.

Then he shuddered remembering. Christ, what about Shifty? If things went bad with those bikies, jail would be the least of his problems.

CHAPTER 19

TRUCKLOADS OF FODDER

Paddy arrived home after delivering a truck load of skinny ewes to their final destination, a New South Wales abattoir, to find a huge semi-trailer loaded with fodder blocking the yard at the back of the pub.

'Bastards,' he muttered as he wearily made his way into the bar. 'Who the bloody hell owns that truck out back?' he roared.

A scruffy looking fellow with a fag hanging off his bottom lip lifted his hat. 'Ya talkin to me mate,' he said putting his beer on the counter in front of him. 'Stan Davis, from Davis and Watson carriers.'

'Is that right,' Paddy said. 'And who gave you the right to park there? I can't get my bloody truck in.'

Annie the barmaid leaned over and grabbed Paddy's arm. 'Paddy listen, he's brought us a truckload of fodder from Brisbane, for nothing, free.'

Paddy's mouth fell open and he turned to the driver. 'That right mate?'

'Certainly is, now how about settling down and showing a little gratitude, been a bloody long drive and I could go a few beers.'

Paddy shook his head and offered his hand. 'Sorry mate, the beer's on me, have as many as you like. Now tell me what's the story, how did this happen.'

Stan downed his beer and put it across for Annie to refill. 'Well it's like this. When the city folk saw the television report of those starving sheep, they fell over themselves wanting to help. Any rate, the TV station set up a fund and they got an avalanche of money. Came from mums, dads, little kids, pensioners, community groups, service clubs, just about anyone. People donated fuel, others offered to deliver, it was amazing. Shows the sort of spirit there is out there. Well, work was a bit slow so I stuck up me hand to deliver the first lot of fodder and here I am and there's plenty more to come.

'Now, where do you want me to park me bloody truck you miserable old sod?'

Paddy laughed. 'Stan, you're a great bloke and you're dead right about me putting me foot in me mouth without thinking. Park where you are and I'll get a few blokes to help me stack the stuff in the big shed. I don't know how to thank you mate, and this is going to make one hell of a difference to us. It'll buy us more time until hopefully the Big Fella up there sends down some bloody rain.

'Have as many beers as you like and I'll get Rosie to rustle you up a feed.'

Paddy walked into the kitchen and asked Rosie to cook a large T-bone steak and some chips for Stan then picked up the phone and called Sam Spink.

'Sam,' Paddy roared down the phone, 'you're a bloody beauty. A dirty great big load of stock food has arrived courtesy of our generous hearted city cousins and it's all thanks to you and those stories you wrote.'

'That's fantastic,' Sam said. 'But hang on a minute Paddy. It wasn't just me. Young Chloe is the one to thank, without her nagging me to do the story and working with the television crew it wouldn't have happened.'

'Well, you give Chloe a big kiss from me,' Paddy said smiling. 'Now our biggest problem is to get this stuff out to those who need it before the next load arrives. Any ideas?'

'Right, why not let the stations know what we have and then work out a system of need. I think Ben Bangor would have to be near the top of the list,' Sam said. 'Look I've got Chloe here helping me. How about I get her on to it straightaway?'

'Thanks Sam, that will be great, I'll get this lot unloaded into my shed and we can sort it out from there. One thing though Sam, we need to show our appreciation in the best way possible, what do you think?'

'I'll think on it and let you know. First thing is to work out who gets what.'

By the time Sam had replaced the receiver, Chloe, who had been listening and was already making out a list, looked up.

'Sam, I know how we could demonstrate how much the fodder is appreciated,' she said. 'How about we do a picture of the fodder being delivered and the sheep rushing to it and send it off to the papers? And,' she said smiling cheekily, 'we could ring the television crew and they could do a follow up. I've got their numbers.'

'Chloe, that's a great idea, 'Sam said. 'Give me that list, I'll finish it and then I'll get it over to Paddy and tell him what we're doing.'

Chloe spoke to Phil at the television station and told him what had happened.

'You're not going to believe what happened, thanks to your film,' she said excitedly, 'we have just received a massive food drop, incredible boost for the people out here.'

'Fantastic, Chloe, thanks for letting us know.'

'One thing Phil, we wondered if you would like to do a follow up good news angle. It would be a way of letting people know how much we appreciate their help.'

'Great idea, I'll talk to the manager and ring you back.'

Ten minutes later Phil called and said they would arrive the next day and probably stay the night in the pub.

'Can you do the same trick and show us the way and maybe you and Sam could have a meal with us tomorrow night.'

'That's terrific, I'll look forward to it, Sam too,' she said. 'See you tomorrow.'

Chloe rushed into Sam's office to tell him the news but he had already gone to see Paddy so she telephoned the pub and left him a message with Rosie that the television crew were coming the next day.

Walking into the tiny washroom at the back Chloe checked herself in the mirror and pushed her unruly curls off her face.

'Well Miss Mattens,' she said batting her sooty eyelashes and smiling wickedly, 'if you want to make headway with this bloke, you'll have to be extra nice to Mum or she'll twig something is going on.'

But Maisie, Chloe's mum, was so busy running the local IGA store, attending council meetings and having clandestine meetings with Shire Treasurer Simon 'Scrooge' McKay in her bedroom above the shop, that she was completely oblivious to her darling daughter's goings on and in particular her goings out.

Maisie was unconcerned that her clever and very pretty little daughter hadn't been within sight of the school for months and spent most of her time working at the *Star*. But the school's Principal was peeved his brightest pupil was rejecting the education he offered and wrote to her mum to complain. Luckily Chloe intercepted the letter and sent one back saying she was being privately tutored.

When Sam arrived at the pub, he found Paddy sitting in the kitchen with Stan the truckie who was polishing off a large juicy steak and a pile of hot chips.

'Sit down Sam, this is a great day for Damengin and meet Stan Davis. We have him to thank for bringing the first load of fodder.'

'Good day, Stan,' Sam said shaking the outstretched hand before taking a seat at the table.

'My pleasure, my folks were on a farm and I know how they struggled in the bad seasons. Glad to help.'

'This is great tucker, Paddy,' Sam said between mouthfuls. 'Worth the trip.'

Paddy sat down opposite him. 'Plenty more where that came from and a bed for the night if you are staying on.'

'No mate, I'll start back after this but thanks for the offer. I'll bring another load out in a couple of days.' He mopped up the juice with a large piece of bread and popped it into his mouth. 'Absolutely delicious,' he said pushing his plate back. 'Tell that cook of yours she's a champ. Have you worked out how you're going to distribute the stuff?'

'Sam here has worked out a list based on need and there's plenty of that. We also want to get some publicity so that people can see it's going to the right places so he's sorting that out.'

Sam handed over the list Chloe had made and told them she was trying to contact the television crew. 'Chloe is all worked up about it,' he said with a grin. 'I think she's keen on one of the young fellas.'

Paddy laughed. 'Like mother, like daughter, she's a pretty little minx.'

'She's also bloody smart,' Sam said. 'If I could afford it I'd take her on full time, she's got stacks of talent as a writer and is as keen as mustard.'

'If we can get the television crew here, I thought they could follow you out to deliver the first load to Ben Bangor's where they did the original film,' he said shoving a sheaf of paper into Paddy's hands. 'I've already sent off a press release to the Brisbane papers from the community thanking them and I thought we could get Bomber as mayor to say something.'

Paddy nodded his head. 'Good idea. Look it's getting late, come on in and have a feed with me and then we can go over to the hospital and tell him what's going on. He can say something on behalf of the council. Shit I hope Redlands is up there on this list, the poor devil's been having a hard time of it too although now that Teddy's home and pulling his weight things have improved.'

Paddy was worried about how Bomber would react to Annabel leaving Shifty and decided to tell him later after Sam had left. *At least he can't shoot the buggar while he's tied to the bed,* he thought frowning. 'It might be a good time for her to go and see him and tell him herself.'

After tea, Paddy and Sam went to see Bomber who was totally absorbed reading a trashy porno magazine Teddy had dumped on him and didn't see them.

'What's that you're reading?' Paddy said snatching the magazine and breaking into a wide grin. 'So this is how you're spending your time.'

Looking sheepish Bomber took off his glasses and his eyes lit up. 'Well, look who the wind's blown in,' he said. 'Grab a chair Sam, you too Paddy. To what do I owe this unexpected honour?'

Paddy dragged a chair over from the wall and offered it to Sam and then sat down on the end of the bed.

'We are the bearers of good news, in fact you could say, it's bloody good news. There are tonnes of fodder in my shed courtesy of our city cousins, bloody heaps of the stuff and more on the way. And, we want you, as our mayor to let them know how much we all appreciate their generosity.'

Bomber was speechless. 'This is amazing, and how did all this happen?'

'It's a long story but the upshot of it is unlike the bloody government, the good citizens of Brisbane have opened their hearts and their wallets for us. Mate, we start deliveries tomorrow and Ben out at Abington will be one of the first on the list. There's a TV crew coming out to do a follow-up story and we thought they could get a message of thanks from you on behalf of the district. That okay?'

'Of course, anything, that's bloody marvellous,' Bomber said shaking his head in wonder.

'Right then, Sam here will get a quote from you and send it off to the city papers tonight and we'll get the TV crew to come and see you sometime tomorrow.'

Sam, who was usually plastered at this time of night, was having trouble stopping his hands from shaking and crouched over his notebook as Bomber cleared his throat and began to speak.

'As Mayor of Damengin I would like to say on behalf of our town how grateful we are to our city cousins for their outstanding generosity, you got that Sam,' he said rattling on for another five minutes with Sam frantically trying to keep up with him.

'Sure, Bomber, 'Sam said mopping his face. 'That's

probably enough so I'll say goodnight and go and file this copy.'

'Look mate, don't worry if you didn't get what I said, just put something together from me, you're the educated one,' Bomber said, feeling sorry for him.

Sam nodded. 'Thanks mate, must have a touch of the flu.'

Bomber smiled. *Nothing a nip of scotch won't fix mate*, he said to himself.

Sam stood up and went over to door. 'Thanks Paddy for letting me know and for the meal,' he said.

'Night Sam,' Paddy said opening the door for him. 'See you tomorrow morning.'

'Good bloke, shame the grog has got him,' Paddy said sitting down on the chair Sam had vacated.

Bomber nodded. 'Don't know what happened to him but his sister's a saint, runs the hospital like a dream.'

Paddy smiled, everyone except Maggie knew Bomber was mad about her.

'Look mate, I know what you think of her, why don't you ask her out sometime?' Paddy asked.

'Don't be stupid, she's much too good for me,' Bomber said shaking his head. 'Now change the subject, how is everything else going on, what's happening your end?'

'There is something I'm going to tell you,' Paddy said leaning over. 'It's about Annabel, she had a big fight with Shifty, caught him at it with Dolly.'

'The bastard,' Bomber roared. 'I'll bloody kill him.'

'No you bloody won't. Settle down,' Paddy said pushing

him back onto the pillows. 'She's fine, I took her out to Paddylea and Mary is looking after her or, I should say, they are looking after each other. What I want to find out is what the hell is going on with the bloody rat fink?'

Bomber was fuming. 'He's been living way above his means for years and until the drought hit he was always scrounging funds from me. I just hope Annabel's name is on the title of that house they live in or she'll be left with nothing if he shoots through.'

Bomber's face suddenly went bright red and he sat upright in the bed as Matron Maggie bustled in with a tray of bottles.

'Good evening gentlemen,' she said, her round plump face breaking into a smile that showed off heartbreakingly lovely dimples. 'Visiting time is over Paddy, this fellow needs some rest.'

Paddy stood up. 'Right Maggie, I was just going. Bomber, I'll let you know how things pan out,' he said walking through the door.

Maggie Spink was a highly intelligent woman who had been married briefly in her youth to a womaniser and had arrived to be matron at the hospital twenty-five years ago. She was well aware Bomber was besotted with her which she found incredibly flattering. In fact, she considered, he could put his shoes under her bed anytime. Problem was he was so awfully shy, he just would not make the first move.

Ah well, she thought leaning over him so that her ample breasts rubbed against his arm causing him to go start like a rabbit, *it is a leap year.*

'Time for sleep, my lad,' she said plumping his pillows and smoothing his thick grey hair out of his eyes. 'Do you need anything to help you sleep?'

'Only you Maggie,' he said, looking into her lovely green eyes.

Maggie chuckled. 'Wait until you're not trussed up like a chook and I might take you up on that,' she said.

Bomber took her hand and placed it against his cheek. 'With that to look forward to, I'll be out of here before you know it.'

'Goodnight, Bomber, sleep well,' she said walking out.

'Goodnight Maggie my love,' he whispered.

Sam arrived back in his office to be greeted by an overjoyed and ravenous Otto who almost knocked him over. Chloe was still working and was hugely relieved to see him. 'I wondered where you had got to,' she said.

'Went to see Bomber. Look could you put this together for me, Chloe love,' he said, handing her his jumbled notes. 'I've got to feed Otto and a few things to sort out and then I'll be back.'

'Right,' she said looking at his scribbles. 'The only thing you're going to sort out is a glass of scotch,' she muttered to herself. But despite his drinking, Chloe liked and respected Sam. He never complained and had the kindest heart. No matter how sloshed he was he always made sure he fed smelly old Otto.

While he was attending to Otto, Chloe knocked up a press release from Sam's messy notes and walked into his office to find him snoring at his desk with an empty glass beside him. She sighed with exasperation and nudged him.

Sam opened his eyes and sat up. 'Sorry love, I must have dozed off, it's been a hectic day. Let's see what you've got.'

He scanned the copy briefly, changed the heading and handed it back.

'Well done Chloe, send it down the line and then lock up. I'll see you here bright and early tomorrow morning and thanks. I don't know what I'd do without you.'

CHAPTER 20

PHOEBE BAGS HER MAN

Phoebe had seen little of Teddy since their first date because he had been flat out with the shearing and getting things sorted out before his dad came home from hospital. Then out of the blue he telephoned and asked her out to Redlands for dinner and she was over the moon with excitement.

'I didn't hear a peep from him for ages and thought he had forgotten about me,' she told her scheming fans, Joyce the cleaner and Vi the hospital cook. 'Then he rings and asks me to his property. Will I go casual or dressy, what do you think?' she asked, fossicking through her tiny wardrobe in the nurse's quarters.

Watched by her two fans she tried on a pretty pink sundress and teamed it with matching high heeled sandals. 'Teddy is very tall and has very big feet,' she said winking.

'Lovely,' was the judgement from her fans as she twirled. But Phoebe was nervous.

'I really like him and I don't want to put him off by coming on too strong,' she said. 'Maybe,' she said stepping out of the dress, 'I'll just wear jeans and shirt instead.'

'Make sure you're wearing your best underwear,' Vi said, cackling mischievously.

'If she plays her cards right, she won't need it,' Joyce butted in.

'Look you two, it's just dinner. He's probably bored and wants someone to talk to,' Phoebe said pulling on her jeans.

'Come off it, this is your big chance,' Vi said picking the dress off the bed, 'Now put this back on. The last thing he wants is a cowgirl.'

The doorbell rang and Phoebe hesitated. 'Can you get that Vi? Tell him I won't be a minute, I will put the pink dress on.'

Phoebe dressed quickly, splashed on some perfume and grabbed her bag.

'Wish me luck,' she said, giving Vi and Joyce a big hug.

'You won't need it,' Vi replied. 'Knock him dead.'

'Good luck lovie,' Joyce said, winking at her.

Phoebe raced down the steps and paused when she saw the battered old ute waiting for her instead of the shiny BMW sport.

'Brought the ute. Hope you don't mind, but Tessa gets really upset if I leave her behind. She's been fretting for Dad.'

'Not at all,' Phoebe said settling down in the front seat next to a slavering Tessa and immediately regretting her choice of outfit.

'I love dogs,' she said smiling sweetly at him, 'and she

deserves a medal for saving your dad. That was incredible running all that distance to get help. It's a pity we can't take her inside but Matron would really freak.'

Tessa rested her head in Phoebe's lap as they drove along and Teddy kept her in hysterics with tales of his travels. 'I was a cricket tragic and followed the Aussies around the place for a couple of years. We had some hilarious experiences, got caught climbing into the harem of some sultan's palace and were slung in some foul smelling cells. Only the fact that the Pakistani Captain Ali Khan was related to the bloke saved us,' Teddy said with a shudder.

'God-awful place and the women weren't that hot either.'

'Serves you right,' Phoebe said. 'Did you meet anyone interesting?'

'Certainly did, met everyone who is anyone, top spin bowlers, even bumped into an old Pom who had clean bowled Bradman. He was a cracker of a fellow.'

Phoebe smiled. *Bradman who?* she wondered.

Finally they passed through the entrance to Redlands and outlined against a background of a merging red and orange sunset, she saw the majestic old homestead.

'Wow,' she said catching her breath, 'it's simply lovely. A perfect picture like you see in magazines, only better'.

Teddy laughed and pulled up at the front steps. 'I take it for granted but I suppose it is a grand looking old place. My great grandparents bought the land at the turn of the century and built the homestead using local hardwood and imported oak. The iron railings for the verandah were made by their resident blacksmith and the bricks for the chimney were carted by bullock train from Newcastle.'

'Come inside and I'll show you through,' Teddy said, taking her hand and leading her into the beautiful hallway.

'There are so many rooms I lose count but families were big in those days and the jackeroos, they were the farm apprentices and usually came from other grazing families, always ate with the family.

'This verandah goes right around the house and is essential in the kind of weather we have out here. It provides shelter from sun and rain and is a great place to sleep in the middle of summer. I often used to throw my mattress out here.

'The sitting room, dining room, library and music room are at the front overlooking the gardens and the small dam. We use it to water the gardens and service the lavatories.

'The main bedrooms are on the east so they get the morning sun and the kitchens, pantry, office and bathrooms are at the back, the spare bedrooms and storerooms are on the west.

'You can see the tennis courts to the right beyond the dam. They haven't been used for years but we used to have great tennis parties when I was a teenager.

'There's a couple of old cottages on the place that Dad has preserved. His two spinster aunts Grace and Clare lived in one of them. They were well into their nineties before they died and the old biddies used to drive an ancient old Rolls into Damengin every week to go visiting. Everyone knew them ... Aunty Grace was president of the Country Women's

Association until she died and she ruled them with an iron fist. When I was away at school they used to send me boxes of homemade cakes and biscuits, the other kids were green with envy. Fabulous old birds.

'I'll take you over and show you their house tomorrow, it's built along the same lines as this but much smaller. Dad has always made sure it was looked after, he loved the old chooks.'

'This place is magnificent,' Phoebe said looking round in wonder. 'A palace.'

'Bit untidy at the moment,' Teddy said looking round. 'Dad usually has a housekeeper but things have been tough for him lately. I'll get someone from town to come out and clean before he comes home. Oh, by the way there's a loo in the bathroom down the hall. Now come onto the verandah and I'll pour you a drink, what would you like?'

Phoebe settled for a glass of iced champagne and stood looking at the view from the front verandah while Teddy went back to the kitchen. He came back carrying a tray of cheese with some biscuits.

'I'm not much of a cook so don't expect anything special,' he said. 'I've got some steak out and stuff to make a salad, we can always throw a few spuds on.'

'Anything's better than hospital food. Do you want some help?'

'I wouldn't say no to that, don't tell me you can cook?'

Phoebe smiled, showing off perfectly straight white teeth. 'I worked in a bistro café after school and every weekend from the time I was fourteen until I went nursing. It was washing greasy dishes at first then onto the cooking. I really enjoyed it and even thought of becoming a chef but changed my mind. Now to answer your question, yes I can cook.'

Teddy looked surprised. 'God you had it tough, why did you have to work so hard? But of course your parents died, didn't they?'

Caught out, Phoebe almost choked on her drink. In truth her parents were very much alive and living off social services in a run-down housing commission home in the western suburbs. Along with five of her brothers who had spent more time in the slammer than on the outside, they spent their days fighting, drinking and gambling in that order.

After slogging herself in the café for three years without a break and having most of her pay nicked by her family, Phoebe had decided to change her name when she left to go nursing and draw a line under her family.

But her eldest brother Lionel, who had escaped the family fiasco by winning a scholarship to university and becoming a highly respected magistrate, was not so smart and spent half his time absenting himself when one of his 'bros' turned up in the dock.

As far as Phoebe was concerned her folks were dead but sometimes, with a few glasses of champers under her belt, she let down her guard. 'Have to be more careful in future,' she scolded herself.

'Right, come with me and I will show you where it is all going to happen,' Teddy said, taking her hand and leading the way to the huge kitchen which featured a large wood stove.

'I lit this especially for you,' he said winking. 'Not only does it have every cook's desire, a double oven but it also provides us with an endless supply of hot water. Nice when it's a cool night like tonight, a bit of a worry in the summer.

'We've also got a gas stove over there, if you prefer,' Teddy pointed out.

Phoebe was in raptures. 'I love cooking on these stoves, the heat is so even and it's great in the winter for soups. Have you got an apron?'

Teddy shook his head. 'Got me there, how about a tea towel?'

Phoebe wrapped a tea towel around her waist and began chopping garlic and onions, and dicing mushrooms while Teddy wandered round finding things for her and pouring drinks.

'It must have been lovely growing up here,' Phoebe said, throwing lettuce into a colander and washing it under the tap at the sink.

'Yes, I guess I didn't appreciate it at the time, but when I look back it was. You know Dad was a top sportsman, he played rugby for Australia and spent a lot of time coaching the local Damengin Crushers. He was mad about sport and when I went down to Brisbane for school he'd drive all night to watch me play cricket then drive home afterwards. Incredible really.

'When I finished school I know he wanted me to come onto the property but my grandparents, Mum's people, thought I should see the world first and I did. It was intoxicating and when I turned twenty-one, I got access to the money Mum had left me so I could pretty much do what I liked.'

'You're very lucky,' Phoebe said pulling out two plates that had been warming in the bottom oven and setting them on the table.

'Dinner is ready, steak béarnaise with mushrooms, pommes frits and tossed salad.'

'Bit of an improvement on what you could have expected from me,' Teddy said taking the plates and leading the way into the adjoining dining room.

'We dine in style tonight,' he said pulling out her chair and laying a napkin across her knees. 'For you,' he said, waving his arm to show off the gleaming cedar table that he had set with old silver and fine crystal glasses.

Teddy filled her glass and raised it. 'To the prettiest cook to ever grace the table at Redlands.'

Phoebe blushed and raised her glass. 'Thank you, I hope it tastes okay.'

After dinner, they left the washing up and went out on the verandah where it was getting quite cold.

'Come and sit over here with me and I'll keep you warm,' Teddy said, patting the seat of an old sofa.

Phoebe sat next to him and he put his arm around her. 'You have the most beautiful skin, so soft it's like silk,' he said stroking her cheek. He pulled her head round and kissed her long and deep his hands caressing her neck and bare shoulders.

'You're just beautiful, all of you' he said, sliding his hand over her breast. 'Come to bed with me?'

Phoebe smiled and nodded.

He picked her up as if she were a feather and carried her into his bedroom. Laying her gently down on the bed he began undressing her, all the while his hands were caressing her moving slowly down her body. By the time he had slid her knickers over her feet she was panting softly and he quickly undressed and lay beside her.

Smothering her face with feather-like kisses he found her mouth and kissed her deeply. He moved on top of her and slowly and gently he entered her finding his way so as not to hurt her. But he found her more than ready for him and putting his strong hands underneath her he pulled her towards him and drove himself until they were both panting and sweating. Crying out, she reached her climax and jubilantly he raced to meet her.

Afterwards, they lay back on the bed exhausted but replete.

Teddy turned to look at her. 'You are really something special,' he said stroking her wet hair. 'And when I get my breath back I'll go and get us both a drink, or maybe not,' he said, noticing she had gone to sleep.

When Phoebe woke up Teddy wasn't there. She looked at her watch and, realising it was early, had a shower before going to look for him.

If he didn't come back soon, she knew she would be late for work and just as she was thinking about ringing the hospital to explain, Teddy walked in with a big smile on his face.

'Up already, you were dead to the world when I left you,'

he said giving her a kiss.

'You wore me out,' she said smiling at him. 'I hate to be a spoilsport but as I'm on duty at 8.30 am and it's after 7 am, will you please deliver me back to the hospital?'

'So soon, I thought I might take you for a drive and show you the rest of the place. What about some breakfast?'

'No really, I haven't got time, I'll get something later. I don't want to let Maggie down and I have to do rounds this morning.'

They didn't talk much on the drive into town. Teddy was feeling rather miffed because he had been looking forward to spending the day with her and having at least a repeat of last night's lovemaking. But when she got out of the ute, he gave her a long passionate kiss in front of the nurse's quarters much to the delight of Vi and Joyce who were watching.

'Thank you for dinner and a wonderful night. I want to see you again soon. When can you get a couple of days off?' he said, stroking her face.

'I'll ring you, hopefully next week,' she said dashing up the steps.

Back in the nurse's quarters Phoebe put on her uniform and raced over to the hospital to do her rounds. It was her job to distribute the morning pills and injections and first on the list was Teddy's dad, Bomber.

'Morning Mr Reed,' she said smiling.

'Nurse Phoebe, how many times have I told you to call me Bomber, everyone else does,' he told her shaking his head.

'Now some little bird told me you went out with my son last night. I hope he behaved himself.'

Phoebe blushed bright red and almost dropped her tray. 'Nothing is sacred in this place. Who told you?'

'I have my spies. So what did you think of Redlands, did Teddy manage to cook something for tea or did he get some pies from the bakery?'

'Now don't be cynical. I had a lovely evening and you have the most beautiful home, I just love it.'

'You know Phoebe when my dad was a young lad, there were upwards of thirty people living and working at Redlands. There was a fully operational blacksmith, half a dozen farm workers and their families and a store. It was a real community, even had a school. During the shearing the place was buzzing.

'Then over the years things became more mechanised and we got by with less staff. But even in my days Mum often used to have fifty people sit down to dinner. Everyone would be all dolled up in their dinner jackets, the women in long dresses. They would travel for miles to come and most stayed the night. The women used the bedrooms and the men camped on the verandahs or if it was really crowded, in the shearer's quarters. In those days Mum had a full time cook and a couple of house maids. Everything was a lot more social.'

'I would have loved it, 'Phoebe said. 'The kitchen with its huge stove and pantry is ideal for catering and I can just imagine what it must have been like. Did you ever do much entertaining?'

'The last big function we had at Redlands was my sister Annabel's 21st. People came from everywhere and the celebrations went on for two days.

'My wife Caroline, Teddy's mum, wasn't really interested in entertaining. She was a city girl and couldn't settle. It's a bit of a lonely life out here,' he said watching her carefully.

'I don't think I could ever be lonely in a place like Redlands,' she said dreamily. 'Life is what you make it or what you choose to make it. Now pop these tablets into your mouth and drink this.'

Bomber watched her trim figure walk out and thought about what she said. It was about time Teddy settled down and she was certainly a lovely girl. If he was thirty years younger he'd be after her himself, he thought, as he drifted off for a snooze.

When Teddy arrived back at Redlands, he found Deidre sitting on the front steps waiting for him. *Shit*, he thought, remembering the last time they had spent together, *I hope she doesn't want a replay, I'm shagged out.*

But Deidre had other things on her mind, in particular how to approach the problem of her dad and Ben Bangor.

CHAPTER 21

HELP ARRIVES

Over at the flat on top of the 4 Square Store, Maisie Matten dragged herself out of bed and was astonished to see her daughter Chloe already up and hogging the bathroom instead of buried under the covers in her bedroom.

'Chloe, hurry up in there or I'll be late,' she said, banging on the door.

Chloe, who was shaving her legs in the bath, ignored her.

'What are you doing in there?' Maisie yelled.

'Ouch,' screamed Chloe, 'now look what you've made me do. I've cut myself, probably bleed to death for all you'd care,' she yelled hauling herself out of the bath and wiping off the blood on her mum's white towel.

She opened the bathroom door scowling. 'Couldn't you wait for just a few minutes?' she said running past her mum into her bedroom and slamming the door.

'No I can't,' Maisie called after her. 'Unlike you, I work to put food on the table.'

Chloe dried herself and rubbed body lotion into her legs and arms. Then she ran a brush through her wet tousled hair and searched in her cupboard for something to wear.

'This will do,' she said wriggling into a shockingly short blue denim skirt and teaming it with her mum's new blue top that she had whipped from her cupboard the night before.

Pirouetting in front of her mirror Chloe studied her reflection. 'This should do the trick,' she said grabbing her bag and opening the door.

'Where do you think you're going in that outfit?' Maisie said emerging from the bathroom with a towel wrapped round her. 'And isn't that my top you're wearing and Chloe, what about school?'

'Got a leave pass from school, Mum, Sam wants me on a job with him. The television crew are coming up to do another story.'

Maisie frowned, she knew all about Sam and Chloe's scoop and was proud of what they'd done. Oh what the hell, she thought, it wasn't worth the fight to stop her going and knowing Chloe, she'd defy her anyway.

Maisie smiled, accepting defeat gracefully and called after her, 'Go on then, good luck and don't get into any trouble.'

'Thanks Mum, sorry I was bitchy this morning,' Chloe called back and hurried down the street to the *Star*.

Out at Abington, Ben Bangor was both excited and nervous about the pending visit of the TV crew and the arrival of fodder. Fee, who had remained glued to him since the night Lucy died, was also tense.

'Will this be enough to see you through the drought?' she asked.

'It'll go a good way towards it, particularly now that there are so few sheep. I can't believe how generous those people have been, gives you a good feeling,' said Ben, putting his arm around her.

Ben had become totally besotted with Fee and used any excuse to stop her from leaving. He told her he was worried about her living by herself at Sid's but the truth was he couldn't bear to let her go. She reminded him of the skinny ewes that were so dependent on him and he wanted to protect and care for her. Making love to her was a joy and afterwards when she cuddled into him, he had been able to sleep for the first time in months. He knew she spent her tiny stipend from the council on food for the kangaroos which he thought was crazy, but he couldn't help admiring her for it.

In exchange for her staying, Ben had agreed to stop shooting the roos but as this was his only income, he was desperately worried about servicing his overdraft.

God help us if Huw Hawtrey comes sneaking out again, he thought to himself. He would have to ask Paddy if he had any work when he came out.

Fee was incredibly touched by Ben's tenderness towards her and, if she was honest, mad about him. Even if he hadn't agreed to stop shooting the roos, I would still have stayed, she admitted to herself.

All her life Fee had longed for affection and love which

she certainly hadn't had from her totally selfish elderly parents. Her mother, who was deliberately barren at forty-nine, thought she was experiencing an early menopause when she collapsed with stomach cramps on the site of the dig the couple were working on in Egypt. Rushed to hospital she delivered a screaming Fee into the hands of the midwife and promptly abandoned her. She was left in the care of a series of nannies and sent off to boarding school in Australia when she was eight. And apart from spending a few holidays at archaeological digs in far flung places, she hardly ever saw her parents. The last contact had been a Christmas card last year with a cheque for $1000 inside; sadly it was unsigned.

Although Fee had slept with dozens of men during her university days and travels, it had been more lust than loving. The only real love and affection Fee had ever received until now was from animals, hence her passionate support of kangaroos.

Fee was busy in the kitchen baking bread to go with a huge pot of lamb and vegetable soup she had lovingly prepared and which was simmering away on the stove for lunch when she heard a truck engine and Ben called out to her.

'Be there in a minute, just putting the bread in the oven,' she called out slamming the oven door.

Paddy manoeuvred the huge truck into the yard pulled up in front of the homestead and jumped down from the cab.

'Mate, you don't know how welcome you are,' Ben said pumping his hand. 'I can't believe those people — how can we ever thank them?'

'Well you'll have your chance with the lot that are following me, they're going to do a film clip of you receiving the stuff and it will go nationwide.'

Taking in Ben's worried look he said, 'Just be yourself, and they'll do the rest.'

'Hello Paddy,' Fee said walking over to him.

'Fee,' Paddy said, 'you're looking well, come to share the good news?'

Fee blushed and Paddy looked at her in surprise taking in the shining hair and glowing pink cheeks. *My God,* he said to himself, *she looks almost pretty, what's going on here?*

Ben walked over. 'Fee is staying here, she's been helping me out,' he said putting a protective arm around her shoulders. 'She's got some good ideas about the drought relief. Her uncle's Director General of the Department of Agriculture in Canberra and she's already written to him stating our position.'

Paddy looked at them in surprise and said to himself, *what a turn up for the books, the unification of the rabid greenie and the roo shooter, wait till I tell Bomber.*

'Hell, that's a bloody good contact to have, let me know when you hear something,' Paddy said. 'Aha, here come the media contingent, Sam's done a great job getting this mob together and even more amazing, he's managed to stay sober enough to do it. That young Chloe's a goer, she's been a fantastic help to him.'

'She's certainly growing up fast,' Ben said, watched Chloe get out of the back door of the TV crew's rented car flashing a pair of very pretty shapely legs.

'Welcome back to Abington,' Ben said walking over to the car and helping Dexter with his photographic gear. 'Can't thank you enough for the story you did, it's made one hell of a difference to us out here, we never expected this sort of response.'

'Our pleasure, mate,' Phil the producer said, grabbing his hat from the back of the car. 'God it's hot out here, when's it going to rain?'

Ben shook his head and smiled ruefully, 'That's the big question we all want answered.'

Paddy backed the truck up to the feed shed door and Ben drove his tractor over to start unloading the tonnes of hay and grain.

Sam gave Phil an update on the response to his film and Chloe helped Dexter work out the light and camera angles while they worked. They filmed the unloading of the fodder and then loaded up the ute and followed Ben out to the sheep.

Paddy, who with Fred his offsider had helped to stack sacks of grain, paused to wipe the sweat off his forehead. 'We'll say goodbye now,' he said. 'Good luck and thanks for all your help, you've done a mighty job,' he said climbing back into the truck.

'Hang on a minute there Paddy, Fee's made smoko for you over at the house, she'll be ropeable if you don't stay,' Ben said. 'Thanks for that Paddy, we really appreciate it.'

'No worries,' Paddy said. 'We'll pop in on Fee then, could do with a cuppa.'

Back at the homestead, Fee was pulling a tray of hot scones from the oven and had the kettle boiled and tea made when Paddy and Fred walked through the door.

Paddy sat down at the kitchen table and watched as Fee poured the tea and dispensed hot scones oozing with butter and covered in jam in front of them. He couldn't take his eyes off her. Her long almost black hair rippled like silk and her thin face had a definite glow to it. Although she was wearing the same dreadful clothes, a long flowing dress from her hippy days which covered her too thin bony frame and her usual Jesus sandals, she was smiling. Yes, he decided, that was the difference — she had hardly ever smiled. It must be love. What an unlikely pair, then again maybe it will stop her driving us mad with her crackpot crusades to save bloody roos and other vermin.

Paddy put down his cup and finished off the last of his scones. 'Thanks for the smoko, Fee love,' he said getting up and collecting his hat from behind the door. 'We'll head out to Redlands, drop a load off to Teddy and then go back to the pub. Tell Ben to give us a ring and let me know how things go.'

Out at the windmill the crew filmed Ben filling up the troughs and when he distributed the hay, the skinny ewes started walking towards him trailing tiny lambs.

'Poor little buggars,' Phil said overwhelmed with sympathy. 'Breaks your heart to see them. How many have you lost since this drought started Ben?'

'Thousands, just thousands,' he said shaking out a bale of hay. 'At first I sent them off to the abattoirs, then when it got really bad it cost me more to send them than I was getting back. It was a choice of watching them die of starvation or shooting them. I shot over one thousand in one week, nearly broke my heart. Dad and Mum had spent their lives breeding the best fine wool flock in the district. When times were good, the wool cheque was fantastic. You know, Phil mate, the worst part after shooting them was getting rid of them. The ground is that hard you couldn't dig trenches even with the bulldozer and I had to leave them out there for the bloody crows. The smell was something awful.'

Phil, who was horrified shook his head. 'Who would be a bloody farmer? What's the story now, how many have you got left?'

Ben looked around at the flock, 'I've got around one thousand ewes left, maybe a dozen rams and whatever lambs we manage to rear. It's not much but with this food drop we can hopefully carry them through and when the drought finally breaks we can start again.'

'Well, you're a better man than I am, I'm damned if I could put up with the stress of it,' Phil said. 'It's been a real eye opener coming out here.'

'Well,' said Ben looking him straight in the eye, 'thanks to you, this mob are a lot better off than they were last week. Then, the crows were the only ones getting a feed.'

Sitting down at the kitchen table to eat the meal Fee had prepared Phil tackled Ben about the government's lack of help.

'Fee's on the Damengin Shire Council and they applied

for drought relief years ago, didn't they Fee?' he said turning to her.

Fee nodded. 'Just after I was elected to council three years ago, I remember the Shire Clerk being asked to send in an application. They seem to have ignored us but recently there was a resolution for a delegation to go to Canberra and personally appeal to the Minister. I'm not sure when this will happen, it was held up when our mayor was hospitalised.'

Phil put down his spoon. 'That soup was delicious Fee, so was the bread thank you. Ben when I get back to Brisbane I'll try and see what I can find out.'

'Good luck,' Ben said soaking up the last of his soup with bread. 'Our mob have been hassling them for years.'

After lunch Ben and Fee went out to wave them off. 'We don't know how to thank you all,' Ben said shaking hands with the men and giving Chloe a kiss. 'This time last month I was wondering how the hell I could go on and now you've given us a new lease of life.'

'Glad to help and you look after yourself,' Phil said starting the car. 'We'll be in touch.'

When they got back to town Phil asked Chloe and Sam to have a meal with them at the pub that night.

Sam shook his head. All he wanted to do was to sink a bottle of scotch and pass out with Otto. He hadn't had a drink since the night before and his head was almost keeping time with his hands which were shaking so much he'd dropped his notebook back at the homestead when he was trying to take down Ben's story.

Spotting his plight, Chloe took over so he could go for a pee and at the same time take a swig from the flask he had stashed in his coat pocket.

'Sorry, I can't make tonight,' he said stumbling in his haste to get into his office. 'I've got important calls to make but Chloe, I'm certain, will join you.'

Chloe beamed. 'I'd love to,' she said.

'That's fine Sam, sorry you can't make it,' Phil said. 'We'll say goodbye now as we're heading off early in the morning.'

Sam opened the door and turned around. 'Thanks Phil, Dexter, we'll be in touch,' he said clutching the wall for support as an excited Otto pounced on him.

'Get down you mongrel,' he groaned pushing him away, 'Leave a man in peace.'

But Otto who had been locked up all day and was desperate for a walk was having none of it. He grabbed his lead from his basket and shook it at Sam.

Chloe laughed. 'Don't worry Sam,' she said. 'He can come with me. I'll take him for a walk and drop him home later.'

'Chloe, you are an angel,' Sam said gratefully, 'I'll leave the door open for you, lock it on your way out.'

Chloe walked down the street with Otto prancing along beside her, his red tongue hanging out of his wide mouth looking for the world as if he was smiling.

'You're such an old fraud Otto,' Chloe said breaking into a jog, 'Come on let's have a run.'

The two of them ran up the road and almost collided with Scrooge McKay who was feeling very happy with his lot after spending most of the afternoon going over the council budget with Chloe's mum Maisie and before leaving he had given her a going over in her comfortable bed.

'Whoa there, Chloe, you're in a hurry,' he said, thinking what a very pretty young thing she was becoming.

'Sorry Simon, can't stop now,' she said as Otto dragged her past him. When she got back to Sam's, the office was empty and he'd left a plate of food out for Otto who ate it ravenously.

'Night Sam,' she called before locking the door on her way out.

She walked back along the street humming to herself and thinking about what she would wear to impress Phil that night. Luckily Maisie was busy in the shop downstairs when she got home and didn't find out until weeks later that Chloe had swiped the gorgeous black lace top she had bought specially for the Black and White ball in Longreach the following month.

Chloe jumped herself into her skinny black jeans and squeezed her feet into Maisie's new leopard stilettos.

Tottering along the street on the killer heels she drew whistles of appreciation from a group of local yokels yarning and smoking outside the pub.

'Where are you off to, Chloe,' they called. 'Can we come?'

'Not this time,' she called laughing.

Phil and Dexter who were waiting for her in the bar joined the chorus of admiration from the other drinkers. 'You certainly scrubbed up well,' Phil said giving her a peck on the cheek. 'What would you like to drink?'

'I'll have a beer,' Chloe said sitting up on the bar stool to relieve the agony of her feet.

'Sorry Chloe, it's worth my job to serve you, how about a coke?' Annie said leaning over to wipe the counter.

Chloe went pink with embarrassment. 'Sure Annie, a coke would be nice.'

Phil chuckled, 'Sorry Chloe I forgot how young you are. Don't let it spoil the night,' he said taking in a woeful expression. 'You know kid, you did a fantastic job out there. When you finish school you have a great career ahead of you.'

But Chloe's night was ruined and she hardly touched the delicious meal Annie had prepared for them.

How dare Phil talk about her as if she was a child, patronising sod. For his information, she was almost seventeen, had no intention of finishing school, buggar that. And she had been almost running the *Star* singlehandedly for the past three years while Sam drank himself to oblivion. She had seen Phil as her ticket to get the hell out of Damengin and now it was shattered and so was she.

When they parted on the steps of the pub and Phil and Dexter again thanked her for her help, she could barely respond and made her way dejectedly down the street to the flat over the shop.

CHAPTER 22

MAGGIE AND BOMBER

Maggie Spink marched into Bomber's room smiling broadly and waving a piece of paper. 'Dr Davis has just finished his rounds and told me you can go home, providing you don't do anything stupid,' she said waggling her finger at him.

Bomber's face broke into a huge smile. 'Thank Christ for that, I told him if he kept me in here any longer I'd have his license suspended — must have believed me, silly old fool. Thanks Maggie, this place is worse than prison.'

Maggie dropped the paper she was holding on the tray in front of his bed. 'So that's what you think of us,' she said smiling. 'Well I've already spoken to Teddy and he said he'll be in to pick you up later today after he's collected a load of gear from Fitzgerald's. Meanwhile, Paddy rang and I told him you could leave so he said he's coming over now to take you back to the pub until Teddy arrives.'

'Right, up you get,' she said opening his cupboard and pulling out his clothes. 'First thing is to get you dressed. Now don't look like that,' she said, winking at him. 'How do you think you can pull up your pants with your arm in a sling?'

'Step out of those pyjamas,' she said taking in Bomber's hesitancy. 'Oh for goodness sakes come on, I've seen it all before you know.' *Wouldn't mind seeing it in different circumstances though,* she thought to herself. Bomber was still a fine figure of a man with a full head of hair even if it was white and he could do some damage with the equipment he was carrying.

Bomber blushed as she bent down to put his underpants on, snapping the elastic and patting him cheekily on the bottom. 'Don't you go doing anything silly or you'll be back in here like a flash,' she threatened pulling his pants up and threading his belt. 'I've just got your shirt to do now, come on lift your arm up,' she said deftly pinning the empty sleeve up with a large safety pin.

Bomber looked down at her fussing over him and before he could help himself pulled her close with his good arm. 'You've been marvellous Maggie,' he said gruffly. 'I think you should come out and check up on me — I need looking after. How about it?'

Maggie smiled up at him. 'Cheeky sod, watch out or I might just do that,' she said, tracing the lines around his mouth with her finger.

Bomber was dithering about whether to kiss her when

Paddy walked into the room, took one look at them, turned, and walked out again

'Now you've done it,' Maggie said laughing. Pushing him away she said, 'Go on get out of here before I change my mind and tie you to the bed.'

'Sounds like fun. Now you make sure you come out and visit, I've got more I want to say to you,' Bomber said following her to reception where Paddy was waiting.

'Sorry if I interrupted something,' Paddy said taking Bomber's bag from Maggie.

'Watch it cheeky,' she replied, 'and Bomber stop playing silly beggars with bulls.'

'Thanks Maggie, don't forget what I said,' he said, giving her a peck on the cheek. 'Right mate,' he said, nodding to Bomber, 'get me out of this place.'

Annabel was waiting for them at the pub and poured out the grotty details of Shifty's extra-marital activities with his over-sexed and under qualified secretary Dolly McIntyre.

'And believe me, that's not the first time I've caught him out,' Annabel said. 'He's a persistent philanderer and I'm glad it's finished.'

'Never liked the grubby little swine,' Bomber said. 'If I wasn't strung up like a chook I'd go around and take him apart.'

'No you bloody won't,' Paddy said glaring at him, 'not until we find out what he's been up to. We've got to plan this properly, there's too much at stake.'

'Well, you can come back to Redlands with me this

afternoon when Teddy picks me up and we'll sort something out,' Bomber said.

Annabel and Paddy stared at each other and Paddy came round and put his arm around her.

'What's going on?' Bomber asked.

'Nothing, I'll go and pack my things,' Annabel said.

'Come into the bar and we'll have a beer,' Paddy said leading the way.

He handed Bomber a beer and poured one for himself before sitting down on the stool next to him.

'It's like this mate, you might as well know Annabel and I have a sort of thing going.'

'What sort of a thing?'

'Well you know we like each other.'

'Look you silly old fool, are you having it off with my sister? If you are for Christ's sake come out and say so.'

'Right,' Paddy said downing his beer, 'we are,' putting his empty glass down on the counter and looking uncomfortable. 'If you must know I've had a thing about her for years, long before she met up with that creep she married. I know it's early days but I don't want to waste time, we're not getting any younger you know.'

Bomber nodded, 'You don't have to convince me, I know mate. I've been hankering after Maggie for years, maybe it's about time I made a move too.'

Annabel walked in and Paddy went over and put his arm around her. 'I've let Bomber in on our secret and all's well,' he said giving her a squeeze.

Annabel looked up at him and then turned to Bomber and smiled. 'I told him to tell you,' she said. 'Now it's all out in the open you can understand why I'll want to spend some time here. But of course I'll come back to Redlands with you until you're up and around again.'

Bomber shook his head. 'More problems, I don't know, I leave you alone for five minutes Paddy and you seduce my sister before she's even unloaded the last buggar.

'Now Annabel, the first thing we must do is to sort out your situation with that shit Shifty, then you can do what you like,' he said.

But secretly Bomber was pleased; he had always loathed his brother-in-law who he suspected had only married Annabel for her money. And he was delighted to see Paddy and Annabel together at last. He knew they had enjoyed a fling before Annabel met Shifty and if she hadn't been dazzled by him, they might have got together earlier.

Teddy arrived to pick up his dad just as they finished lunch. Bomber got a rapturous welcome from Tessa who had fretted her heart out for him while he was away. She threw herself at him, whining and licking, dancing and jumping.

'Get down girl,' Bomber said detaching her from his legs and fondling her beautiful soft head. 'Yes, I missed you too now stop slobbering me or I'll need a towel.'

'She's really missed you, Dad,' Teddy said, taking his bag and leading the way to his ute. 'She wouldn't eat for the first couple of days and slept on top of your boots. The only thing that pulled her out of it was taking her in the ute, I think she smelt you in there. And she cheered up when Rusty, Deidre's dog arrived, they were good mates.'

As they drove along followed a long way back by Annabel in her late model Mercedes so that she didn't eat their dust, Teddy brought him up to date on the sheep and had him laughing at the antics with Deidre in the shearing shed.

'She's a cracker of a girl, a big brash bundle of fun,' he said.

'Don't tell me you've finally fallen,' Bomber asked.

'Nah, I really like her but more of a mate, but there is someone.'

'I suppose it couldn't be a certain nurse?'

'Well, now you mention it, maybe it could. Only time will tell, now stop being so bloody nosey.'

When they arrived at the homestead Teddy dumped Bomber's bag in his bedroom and they went outside to greet Annabel, who was ten minutes behind them.

'Well the old place could certainly do with a bit of a clean,' she said walking in.

'Sorry about the mess Aunt Annabel, you choose which room you want,' Teddy said.

'Deidre's been bunking in one of the spare rooms and I haven't got around to cleaning up. Dad's coming home early caught me by surprise.'

Annabel laughed. 'You bachelors, I know what you're like.'

'Well at least you'll have something to keep you occupied, stop you being bored out here in the sticks,' Teddy said, grinning.

'Cheeky sod, looking after you two will keep me busy

enough. Now how about taking your dad to see his beloved stock, he's been driving everyone mad worrying about them.'

Bomber put on his old working boots and hat and followed by Tessa, who had stuck to him like glue, they drove off to inspect the sheep.

When they got near the first feeding station Bomber's eyes lit up as snowy white ewes, some with lambs at foot, came racing over to meet them looking for all intents and purposes full of the joys of spring.

'Christ, look at that, last time I saw them they were on their last legs,' Bomber said in amazement.

'Shows what a bit of tucker and a good haircut can do,' Teddy said grinning. 'Mind you I had some help, Dee was fantastic, if you ever need an offsider, she's the one.'

Bomber knew Teddy had settled his account at Fitzgerald's and was feeling very embarrassed. 'Look son, you must have spent a packet on feed and I just want you to know that as soon as the place is back on its feet I'll pay you back.'

'Don't be bloody ridiculous, there'll be World War III if you even suggest paying me back,' he said angrily. 'I'm just ropable that you didn't let me know sooner.'

Teddy didn't tell him that as well as settling the account at Fitzgerald's, he had paid off his dad's overdraft at the bank.

'Anyway,' Teddy said, 'I've really enjoyed being back here and I want to talk to you about maybe coming home permanently. I don't want to cramp your style, especially as a little bird told me you may have plans of the romantic kind with a certain matron. But I might look at some sort of partnership or maybe I'll look to buy a small place of my own. I've still got shit loads of cash left in the kitty. Anyway Dad, how about we talk about it when things have settled down?'

Bomber was delighted. He could never see himself leaving Redlands but he would be happy to take a break. *And in the good times, if it ever bloody rained, the property is more than big enough to support both of us*, he thought hopefully.

It had always been his dream that Teddy would come home, perhaps marry and start a family. If things did work out with Maggie, well who knew, there was plenty of room for two families.

Back at the homestead Annabel had been busy tidying up and was looking for something to cook for tea that night when the telephone rang.

'Just ringing to see if you've settled in alright,' Paddy asked. 'I've had your husband in here wanting to talk to you. He was in a terrible state, almost off his bloody rocker. Bloke needs certifying and locking up. I told him you weren't here and chuffed him off with a flea in his ear, or what's left of it.'

Annabel laughed. 'You didn't hit him?'

'Well I did give him a bit of help down the stairs and I don't think he'll be back for a while, at least not until he recovers.'

'Really Paddy, you don't mess around,' she said giggling.

'Anyway, what I really wanted to tell you was that the rumour is, a mob of bikies is hunting him and they lobbed a bullet through the window of his office today.'

'My God, was anyone hurt?'

'No it was just a warning, but from what I can gather, Shifty is in deep shit, right up to his eyeballs. Cyril Rowe and Dolly were there and hid under the desk. Shifty telephoned Percy Plod and he went round there but they'd gone. He telephoned Longreach and they were keeping an eye open for them.

'Look I need to talk to Bomber about a few council matters so I'll come out late this afternoon if that's okay?'

'More than okay,' said Annabel. 'Stay for tea if I can find anything worth cooking here. I don't know what you fellows live on.'

'I'm happy with anything, do you want me to bring something out?'

'Some potatoes and fresh greens would be nice or I'll be using tinned stuff.'

'Fine, if you think of anything else, just ring, see you about 5 pm.'

When Paddy arrived he and Bomber took their drinks into the office while Teddy yarned with Annabel who was cooking tea in the kitchen.

'What worries me is whether this bikie business is just the tip of the iceberg,' Paddy said frowning. 'And what else has the bastard been up to. I always said I wouldn't trust him as far as I'd throw him. And as for Cyril and the other freeloaders they'd be in it up to their neck.

'Now that you're back on deck I think we should call another emergency meeting of council before we go off to Canberra. We'll tell McKay to hand over the accounts and get an independent auditor to go over them. I could ask my accountant if you like?'

Bomber frowned. 'I feel like a bloody idiot for getting us into this in the first place, I should never have asked you to find him a job. Then again, if he had stayed here, I would have ended up having to shoot the bastard.'

Paddy leaned over and grasped Bomber's good arm. 'Never mind that, I was the one who put him where he is so let's not start blaming each other.

'Look it's Tuesday today, what about we call the meeting for next Monday at 10 am, that gives Dolly time to let everyone know?'

'I'll drink to that,' Bomber said standing up. 'Now let's go and see what Annabel cooked up for tea, I'm hungry.'

Annabel had excelled and provided a delicious meal of savoury chops cooked slowly in the oven with spices and herbs and served with baked potatoes and fresh beans.

'And for pudding, we have a baked apple pie with ice cream, courtesy of Paddy,' she said, putting out the plates.

'No, don't thank me, thank Rosie for the pie and ice cream,' Paddy said taking his plate from Annabel.

'Well I'd still like to thank the cook,' Bomber said smiling. 'Not bad, Bella, when the only thing in the freezer was the remains of a killer.'

Annabel laughed. 'Thank you for your kind words. I'll go into town tomorrow and get some groceries and I'll ring Mary at Paddylea to check if she needs anything before I leave.'

Paddy squeezed her hand under the table and said with a wink, 'I've been meaning to pop out to Paddylea, so I'll see you there.'

CHAPTER 23

ANGUS INSISTS

Teddy was in town to pick up some stock feed from Fitzgerald's and decided to have a beer at the pub before popping in to see Phoebe at the hospital, when he bumped into Angus Wilton-Smith.

'Seen anything of Deidre?' said Angus hopefully. He had been longing to see her since she helped with the shearing at Rangoon. Truth was he was fascinated by her. He had never met a girl like her. She clearly couldn't give a damn what she looked like or what she wore but she oozed sex appeal. Her sultry deep voice and sexy chuckle attracted him like hell and he couldn't get her out of his mind.

'Sure have, she was out at my place for a couple of weeks helping me do the crutching and shear the last of the stock,' Teddy told him. 'She's a cracker, tough as guts and good as a bloke in the sheds. We had a great time. Bloody awful cook though,' he chuckled. 'Char grilled everything.'

Angus almost choked on his beer. 'Know what you mean, it was bloody hilarious when she tried to pass herself off as a shearer's cook at my place, the gang nearly lynched her.'

'Yep, there's no doubt about our Dee,' Teddy chuckled. 'She's always good for a laugh. She's had a rotten time with her folks. They virtually threw her out when she went home after helping me. Poor sod had nowhere to go and tried to ring me but I was out with Phoebe, the new nurse at the hospital. Fabulous girl. Anyway, next morning Dee arrived at the door, said she'd spent the night in the back of her ute. I told her to move into the house, Dad wouldn't care, he thinks the world of her but she wouldn't, stubborn buggar.

'You know mate you can't help admiring her she's as independent as all hell. Anyway, I know she's looking for a job so if you hear of anything, give her a ring.'

Angus put down his glass and stood up. 'I'm off and if you happen to see Deirdre before I do, let her know that I might have some work for her at Rangoon. Hate to think of her stuck.' But the only place he really wanted Dee to be stuck was to him.

He drove off and decided to cruise around town and see if he could spot Deidre's bright red ute. He drove slowly past the bank house which was deserted and continued along the back road past the showgrounds where he saw it parked outside Fitzgerald's Produce Store. Just as he stopped, Deirdre came down the steps carrying a large sack of dog biscuits for Rusty who was sitting on the front seat with his head poking out of the window.

Spotting his old mate Angus and remembering the glorious days at Rangoon chasing sheep and cavorting with the friendly collies, he leaned his head out of the window and barked joyfully.

'Hi there Angus, you've scored a hit with Rusty,' Dee called out as she dumped the heavy sack in the back of the ute. 'What are you doing in town?'

Angus walked over and stroked Rusty's silky head. 'Well if you must know, I was looking for you,' he said. 'I've got a fair bit of work on at the moment and wondered if you needed a job, same pay as last time and board and keep. This time I insist you stay in the homestead, heaps of space.'

Deidre's face lit up. 'That would be great. I really enjoyed working at Rangoon.' She didn't add she had the biggest crush on him for saving her from the wrath of the shearers after she burned their dinner.

'Look I don't want to seem ungrateful, but Rusty and me are better off in the shearer's quarters. We don't want to be a nuisance to you.'

Angus grinned at her. 'You'll never be that, but whatever you prefer,' he said, thinking his mum might make a flying visit and would flip seeing Rusty romping around the pristine and palatial home.

'If you're ready, you could start now,' he said. 'Do you want to go and tell your folks?'

'Not necessary, quite frankly they couldn't care less what I do. I've got my swag and all I need in the back. Let's go.'

When they arrived at Rangoon Deidre drove over to the

shearer's quarters and threw her swag and backpack on the bed. Like everything at Rangoon, the room was meticulously clean and tidy and the bathroom at the end of the shed that had recently borne the invasion of a gang of filthy shearers was now pristine and hygienic.

'We'll be very comfortable here,' she told Rusty, who was lying on the bed with one ear up listening to her. 'Come on you lazy mutt,' she said, 'let's go and help Angus unload the truck.'

Rusty pranced along beside her and went into a spasm of tail wagging and leg lifting when he reacquainted himself with the beautiful border collies that Rangoon was famous for. They chased each other round and round the yard stirring up clouds of dust until Angus yelled at them to 'cut it out' and lie down.

Rusty parked himself under Angus' truck while he was unloading sacks of grain into the feed shed. Deidre helped him by stacking bales of lucerne hay in neat piles against the wall.

It was heavy work in the blistering hot sun. When they had finished, Deidre wiped her dirty hands on the sides of her jeans and pushed her fiery red hair out of her eyes. 'That's a good job done,' she said. 'What's next?'

Angus looked at her dirty freckled face and grinned. 'Time for a beer, come on we've earned it,' he said leading the way to the house.

Sitting on the steps of the verandah drinking a stubby with Rusty lolled next to her, Dee enjoyed the peace and quiet.

'Is your dad back from his golf?' she asked.

'No,' he replied shaking his head, 'he won't be back if he can help it, too bloody hot for him.'

'When is your mum due home? Wasn't she on a cruise?'

'Mum came here for a day or two before she left to join Dad at the Gold Coast. To be honest Dee, they're hardly ever here. Dad lost interest in the place years ago and Mum never had any. This place bored her to tears and when Julianne my eldest sister married and Angela went to boarding school, they bought the house at the coast and virtually abandoned the place.'

'Who looks after you?' Deidre asked feeling sorry for him being left on his own.

Angus shook his head. 'I prefer to be on my own, make my own decisions. Betty Davis comes out from town to clean the place and I've inherited old Chinese Charlie. He came to work here decades ago. I can remember Grandpa telling me about taking him out to run the camp kitchen during the big musters so he must be well over eighty. But, he's still the best cook this side of the black stump.'

Deidre laughed. 'You said it, he certainly saved my back,' she said. 'God that was a riot. I guess one day I'll have to learn to cook. The shearing gangs will be doing a starve with the drought, Rangoon is one of the few properties around here that has a decent sized flock left.'

Angus shook his head. 'Not for much longer. If the drought doesn't break soon I'll have to start destocking. The only reason we were able to hang on so long was because

Rangoon was well prepared. My grandparents weathered many droughts by making provision for the bad times. But, this drought is one for the books and things are bad. I was damned grateful for the grain Paddy dropped off thanks to Sam Spink and his story.'

'Hang on there, don't forget Chloe, she's been the mover and shaker on that,' Deidre interrupted. 'Chloe busted her boiler over that story, even managed to keep Sam sober enough to make sense.'

Angus nodded in agreement. 'You're absolutely right, good for little Chloe.

'Finished?' he asked, getting up.

'Yep,' she said handing him her empty mug. 'What's next?'

'We'll check the water troughs and then drive over to the eastern fence to see if any dingoes are breaking through. I found three dead ewes ready to lamb with their stomachs ripped out last night,' he said shaking his head. 'Must be a break along there somewhere.'

They drove along the fence line for over two hours checking to see if any wires were broken which would put the ewes and lambs at the mercy of marauding dingoes and wild dogs.

Suddenly, Angus slammed on the brakes and reaching under his seat, grabbed his gun. Leaping from the cab, he rested his arms on the front of the ute and took aim at a large yellow dog slinking along the side of a gully inside the fence. The shot took the dog on the shoulder and with a howl of pain he went down.

'That's one less of the bastards,' he said, stashing his gun back under the seat. 'Come on, let's have a look at him.'

They found the dog's body next to the fence, where a large hole with strands of yellow hair in it pointed to his way of access.

'Do you think any others got in?' Deidre asked, getting out her fencing plyers and pulling up the broken strand of wire.

'Don't know,' he said twisting a new piece of wire to the other end and then tying the wires together before ratcheting the fence up until it was tight.

'We'll come out tonight and check,' he said releasing the straining tools.

It was getting late when they finally drove into the homestead yard and after feeding the dogs, they washed and went into the kitchen where Charlie had set the table for tea.

Deidre, who hadn't eaten since the day before, was starving. 'Smells fantastic, Charlie. Looks good too,' she said watching him dish up plates heaped with grilled lamb chops and mashed potatoes.

'This is great, Charlie, you sure can cook,' Deidre said between mouthfuls.

Angus grinned as he watched her. 'Wait till you taste his homemade ice cream. Now that really is something. He makes it using fresh cream from old Dolores our jersey house cow and it's to die for.'

Charlie's wrinkled old face beamed at her. 'You want ice cream?' he asked.

'You bet, thanks Charlie.'

'Okay, you milk bwuddy cow, she kicks,' he said, his old, wrinkled face breaking into a huge grin.

'Charlie, I'll milk her if the ice cream comes up to scratch,' Dee said, taking a brimming dish from him.

'You know Angus, it's absolutely beautiful out here,' Dee said, spooning delicious mango ice cream into her mouth. 'You are so lucky.'

'Luck doesn't come into it,' Angus said. 'Running this place is bloody hard work, but I wouldn't change a thing except the weather. It's what I've always wanted.'

Dee put down her spoon and frowned. 'You know it really irks me that Mum and Dad wanted to buy a property for Tim which is the last thing he wants and wouldn't have a clue how to manage. Just because I'm female they think I'm useless but I can do anything a bloke can.'

Angus looked up and noticed how serious she was. 'What was it you wanted to do after you finished school?'

'I desperately wanted to go to agriculture college and what did they do, they sent Tim. Poor sod had hysterics when they started castrating the bulls and when they told him to shove his arm up a cow's arse that was the end of him, he fled,' Deidre said almost choking with laughter. 'Can't you just see him?'

Angus laughed with her. 'Poor Timmy. I can only imagine.'

Angus loved her earthy laugh, it was so sexy and infectious. She wasn't like other girls, she had no inhibitions, made no effort to tart herself up but in a funny way, he thought, that was the very thing that made her so very attractive to him.

For as long as he remembered his mum and sisters had focused on how they looked and what they wore. They spent hours preening themselves in front of mirrors and couldn't wait to fly south to the shops and theatres. He had never seen his mum looking anything but immaculate. Even during the hectic days of the shearing she always managed to look smart.

He leaned over and covering Dee's work roughened hands with his. 'These hands aren't frightened of hard work,' he said turning them over and stroking the calluses. 'What do you want to do now?'

Deidre stared at him. 'I know what I don't want and that is to live in the city. It was bad enough being shoved off to boarding school for four years. The only thing that made it bearable was having Knacker with me.'

Angus smiled. He remembered the tales of her refusing to go without her horse and also her outrageous behaviour on the boarding school train.

He also remembered his first days at boarding school when he was desperately miserable for his home and where the only compensation was being away from his bossy older sister Julianna. Fortunately by the time he graduated and returned to Rangoon, Julianna had hooked a wealthy stockbroker and moved to Brisbane and his younger sister Angela, who hated the place as much as his parents, was happily away at boarding school.

Deidre's arrival, with the shearing team several weeks ago and the attack by the furious shearers over her awful cooking was a bright spot in an otherwise rather dull life. When he had rushed to protect her, she was on the cusp of being really hurt or at least abused. But what really amazed him was that she had the cheek to even pass herself off as a cook because she didn't have a clue what she was doing.

As he got to know her and watched the way she worked and got on with everyone in the shed, he was fascinated. She was completely different from all the other girls he had met, not beautiful or even pretty, but it was her 'couldn't give a rat's arse about anything' that attracted him the most. Dressed in her work jeans, old shirt and boots with her hair scraped back off her face she exuded confidence and drove him mad with desire. He longed to plunge into her to feel her soft and yielding underneath him. He wanted to bury his head in her generous soft breasts and…'Oh God,' he groaned.

'What's the matter?' Deidre asked, absentmindedly patting his knee and thinking what a really lovely looking fellow he was.

'Nothing,' he replied putting his arm around her, pulling her head into his shoulder so she settled comfortably against him.

'How long have you been running the place?' she asked stroking his cheek with her finger.

'Oh for about five years now. In his will Grandpa left Rangoon to Dad and me. But, when I came home, Dad was fed up with the place and wanted out. He'd discovered golf and Mum couldn't wait to leave. Anyway, we made the whole thing legal. Under the agreement, I borrowed from the bank and bought their share of the place.

'Mum and Dad are hardly ever here unless there's something big happening like the show or picnic races then they drag their overbearing and snooty friends with them.'

Deidre laughed. 'Can't be that bad,' she said raising her head to look at him.

'Well, it hasn't been bad lately because most everything has been axed because of the drought. Both the show and races are off the agenda this year, thank God.

'Come for a walk with me,' he said taking her hand. They walked outside and looked out over the dusty paddocks to where the moon sent shivers over the waters of the house dam.

Angus sighed, he wished the rains would come. When he had taken over the place five years ago there had been plenty of feed in the huge silos and barns, now it was almost gone and soon he would have to start culling his prize flock or seek a loan extension to carry him forward. He knew that once the flock had gone it would take years to replace the breeders responsible for the fine wool Rangoon had produced for generations.

All the wealth that had been created by his grandparents had been ploughed back into the property. But when his parents had taken over, they had bled the place dry and invested the returns in blue chip stocks and real estate including the fabulous Gold Coast mansion they had retired to.

He knew it was futile to ask them to help. They seemed to ignore the impact of the drought on the property or the harsh reality that it might have to be sold.

They bury their heads in the Gold Coast's sand and to hell with what happens to Rangoon, he thought bitterly.

'Are you alright?' Deidre asked, noticing his frown.

'Just thinking,' he said. 'We really need some rain.'

'It'll come. Come on,' she said holding out her hand, 'let's stretch our legs.'

They walked along the track that led to the dam with Rusty bounding in front of them. Deidre picked up a stick and threw it for him to retrieve.

'There's a peace out here that is unique,' she said dreamily. 'You know Angus, I'd rather camp in my swag beside a creek than live in a mansion in the city.'

Angus grinned at her. 'You'd be such a waste in the city and please don't go and sleep by the creek, my bed is much more comfortable. Not promising you'd get much sleep though.'

Deidre looked at him and considered. He really was a lovely man, she thought.

'That sounds like a nice idea, why not?' she said, looking up at him cheekily.

Angus grabbed her and pulled her to him. 'You are on a promise now,' he said drawing her to him.

Later he discovered just how wonderfully sexy she really was.

'I knew you would be great in bed,' she said in her deep husky voice, 'but you really are insatiable.'

'Can't help myself, 'he said, running his hands down her strong thighs, rock hard from years of riding Knacker and pulling her against him so that his hardness pressed into her. 'You're like ice cream, very moreish and we fit so well together,' he said rolling on top of her.

'There's certainly plenty of me to enjoy,' Deidre moaned, caressing his back.

'I love every bit of you, especially these lovely soft things, now what do we call them, mammary glands?' he asked burying his face in them. 'You are just delicious and I wouldn't change a thing. But we have to do it again, just to make sure we are getting it right.'

'You are insatiable, you big brute,' she said giggling.

'Shut up, you've already said that, now open your legs and stop complaining.'

The next morning they were spooned together completely shagged out and dead to the world when Millicent Wilton-Smith barged in.

'What on earth is going on, who is that in bed with you Angus?' she said imperiously.

Angus sat up like a rocket rubbing the sleep from his eyes.

'Mum,' he said in a surprised voice, 'what are you doing here? I thought you were with Dad at the Gold Coast.'

Pulling herself up to her full height and with her mouth set in two thin straight lines his mother ignored him. 'Again I ask, who is that in bed with you Angus?'

Deidre, hazily aware that something was wrong but still half asleep, tried to sit up. The bedclothes fell off and Angus grabbed them hastily and threw them over her naked body.

'Good God, is that Deidre Hawtrey?' Millicent said nastily.

'What would your mother say if she could see you now I wonder. And what is that disgusting dog doing in here, get it out now.'

'Yes, it is Dee,' Angus said smiling and throwing his arm around her protectively. 'She's been helping out on the property. My best worker, strong as an ox and twice as useful.

Millicent glared at them. 'I'm very disappointed in you Angus, I would have thought you had better taste than this. You can tell that slut to get dressed and get out of here and, take that dreadful dog with her,' she said, walking out and slamming the door.

Deidre was red with embarrassment. 'What does she mean "slut", "better taste"?' she said, jumping out of bed.

'You stay right here, don't move,' he said his face contorted with rage. 'She had absolutely no right to speak to you like that. I'll fix her.'

He jumped out of bed, pulled on his pants and raced off.

Deidre was devastated and angry. She jumped out of bed and dragged on her clothes. 'Well fuck you to hell, I'm off,' she said to herself. 'I'm not staying here to be insulted by that cow.'

Angus caught up with Millicent as she was firing off instructions to Charlie in the kitchen.

He grabbed her by the arm and turned her to face him.

'Don't you ever speak to Deidre like that again,' he said quietly, 'or I won't be responsible for my actions. This is my property, you gave up any right to dictate who I choose to have here. And I want you to go and apologise to Deidre right now.'

'Angus, I only want what's best for you and you can do much better than her, she's as rough as they come. She does what she likes and is completely out of control. I feel sorry for her poor mother, she has a terrible time with her.'

Angus was enraged. 'You know nothing about her. She is one of the finest people I know and you will apologise or your days here are numbered. I remind you this is my home and I will have whoever I choose here. Now make up your mind, apologise or leave.'

Millicent looked at his angry face and realised she'd overstepped the mark.

'I'm sorry,' she said, 'she is not the right person for you.'

'Mum I have warned you — either apologise or get out.'

Millicent sighed. 'Alright, calm down and I'll go and talk to her.'

But it was too late, an engine roared to life and Deidre drove out of the yard in a swirl of dust.

'Typical snotty nosed aristocrats,' she raged, as the red ute flew along the road. 'Well they can all go to hell, all except you Rusty,' she said patting him as tears coursed down her cheeks.

DEIDRE AND BEN

When Deidre fled from Rangoon after Angus's mum found them in bed together, she didn't have a clue where to go and just kept driving. Tears of rage were coursing down her face as she remembered the rotten things Millicent Wilton-Smith had said to her. How dare she say Angus had no 'taste'?

'So what if they own the biggest property around. That doesn't give her the right to speak to me like that,' she told Rusty, who cocked one ear in sympathy. But what really hurt was that she really liked Angus and was sorry she had run off. Deep down she knew that he would have stood up to his mum but she was just too mortified to stay.

Now the problem was, where would she go? Then she remembered that she had promised her dad that she would talk to Ben Bangor and try to persuade him not to press charges on Huw for trying to sell him up.

'At least that's something useful I can do,' she said to herself and she turned the car around and headed off in the direction of Abington.

Since the night when Lucy's death had brought them together, Fee and Ben had become even closer and at Ben's insistence Fee had moved her few possessions into the main bedroom at Abington. And although it didn't matter a scrap to Ben what she wore because he was constantly undressing her to make love to her at every hour of the day, she had become more fastidious and had shaved off her armpit hair and the impressive growth on her legs. But she drew the line at Ben's pleas to shave off her bush. 'Only if you do yours,' she told him, smirking.

Just before Deidre arrived, they had been at it again in the hay shed and they hastily threw their clothes on when they heard the ute's engine coming down the lane.

Drunk with sex, they pretended they were stacking the hay into the huge feed shed which had been virtually empty except for a few resident possums for the past three years.

'Look, I know what you think of my dad,' Dee said, walking over to them, 'but I've come to see if I can smooth things out or explain things to you, Ben.'

Ben stared down at her. He had always liked Deidre even if her dad was a shit.

'That's okay Dee, you don't have to say anything. Come on to the house and have a cuppa with us, you know Fee Fluke don't you?'

'Yes sure do, how are you Fee, you're looking well,' she

said looking at her in astonishment. God she does look well, Dee thought, in fact she looked quite lovely with her hair all soft and fluffy around her face and she was actually smiling. What was going on between those two?

They sat down at the kitchen table, Fee poured out the tea and Dee started talking.

'Ben,' she said, 'I know Dad was wrong to do what he did but you did win the case and Dad had to pay the costs. He'd been under awful pressure from Mum to buy Timmy a property, she's been driving him mad and the truth is he really thought you were finished and jumped the gun. Another thing Ben, you really shouldn't have fired that gun at him, I know you didn't intend to hit him but you know it was wrong.'

Ben looked at her and took a deep breath. 'Dee I know you are loyal to your dad but there's no getting away from the fact that he did something wrong, illegal if you like. And there's no way I am going to let it go.'

'Please, Ben — Mum and Dad have had the most awful row,' Dee said running her hands through her hair. 'Dad's terrified the bank auditors will sack him or he'll go to jail, Mum's threatening to leave him.

'When I left, he was down on his knees begging her to stay. I've had my fights with him but I can't help feeling sorry for both of them. He wanted to come and see you himself but I told him I would see if you would accept an apology. The thing is he's told Mum he'll resign from the bank and they'll move to Sydney.

'I told them Timmy was gay and Dad already knew. He said he didn't mind at all and Mum is excited because she wants to go and live in Sydney with him. If you could just forget about it …' Deidre collapsed on the table and burst into loud sobs. 'I'm sorry I've had a dreadful day, I've been insulted by Millicent Wilton-Smith and I don't want to go home when everyone there is upset and fighting with each other.'

Ben bent over and put his arms around her. 'Alright Dee calm down. Look things are looking up here, we can carry on for a while longer until hopefully things improve. You can tell your Dad I won't be pressing charges — waste of time anyway and as you say, I did pull a gun on him. Come on dry your eyes, you can stay here for as long as you like.'

'Thanks Ben, I might stay here tonight if that's alright I need to think a few things through. I'll sleep in the back of the ute with Rusty.'

'Don't be silly, you're welcome to stay in the house, and I insist you do. Rusty can camp next to you, there's plenty of room. Now cheer up and come and help us put the feeds out.'

By the time they had finished tea that night and Deidre went to help wash up she twigged to the fact that Ben and Fee were mad about one another.

It was quite obvious really, she considered, they couldn't stop touching each other and when Fee bent down to put the scraps in the chook bucket, Ben had his hand up her skirt.

After listening to them banging away in the bedroom next door what seemed like all night. Deidre got up early and drove back into Damengin.

She walked into the bank house and found her mum in her bedroom with the blinds drawn and a wet washer over her eyes.

'You okay, Mum?' Deidre asked walking over to the bed.

'Oh Deidre, I've had a terrible headache worrying about things. Thank goodness you're back, where have you been?'

'Oh out and about, is Dad at work?'

'Yes he wants to talk to you, just let me get up and I'll telephone him to come home.'

Huw arrived from next door looking apprehensive. 'Deidre, where have you been, we've been worrying about you.'

That'll be a first, Dee thought to herself.

'Well I was out at Rangoon working and then I called in to see Ben Bangor.'

'What did he say?' Huw said anxiously.

'Well, he wasn't too keen about forgive and forget at first but I managed to convince him that it was a mistake on your part and he has agreed to do nothing.'

'Oh thank God,' Audrey sighed gratefully. 'Now all we have to do is pack up and leave this awful town.'

Huw didn't say anything. Just that morning he had been told of the impending annual visit of the bank's auditors and he had received another hysterical message from Shifty via Cyril to send off ten grand to the bikies.

Where the hell did he think he could find ten grand in a hurry without security, and as for those documents he was going to get witnessed by that rogue Cyril Rowe, just pie in the sky stuff? If there was any argument about the signature being Annabel's he would be in even more trouble. No, the thought of what Shifty would do to him paled into insignificance when he thought about Bomber. He would flay him alive.

'I'm sorry Aud, but there are a few more little things I have to attend to before we can go. Maybe you and Deidre could go on ahead, settle in and I'll follow you later.'

'I'm not going to live in the city. I'll get a job on a property, don't care what I do, fencing, anything as long as I can take Rusty and Knacker. I can go and stay with Teddy for a while until I find something.'

Audrey sniffed. 'You must do as you like, Deidre you always have. I'll go and stay with Grannie in Double Bay and they can help me to look for an apartment so that Timmy will have somewhere nice to live. You can join me when you have sorted out things here Huw. Deidre, you should come and spend some time with your grandparents, they are getting older and you won't always have them.'

'Good riddance,' Deidre thought. 'Mum, be serious for a moment, Grannie hates me, look what happened last time she came to stay?'

'That's nonsense, Grannie just wants the best for you.'

'No thanks Mum, I'll stay out at Redlands.'

Huw went back into the bank and received a blast from Shifty who screamed down the phone at him.

'I'm telling you, this is a matter of life and death, those bastards have already tried to kill me, there's half a dozen bullet holes in my office window. Now, send off the bloody money before I come over there and break your neck,' he said, slamming down the phone.

Huw sat down and considered. Shifty's bank balance was in the red and he didn't dare transfer money from Annabel's account into it because Bomber had told him to put a stop on it.

His hands started shaking and he reached into the cupboard for his flask. There was only one thing to do and, taking a swig, he wiped the top carefully and replaced it before picking up the phone.

'Claude Hewlett speaking,' said the voice on the other end.

'Good morning Claude, its Huw Hawtrey here. I wonder can I have a word with you?'

'Certainly Huw, and how is Audrey and my goddaughter?'

'They're well thank you Claude, but unfortunately I've got myself into a bit of bother and not to put too fine a point on it, I think I might have to get a good solicitor.'

Huw poured out the story of his involvement with Shifty, embellishing his side hugely so as to portray himself as the poor sod who is bamboozled by a smooth-talking bully. He decided to omit any reference to Ben's foreclosure. *It was really his fault anyway*, he told himself, and *Deidre sorted that out.*

When Huw finished speaking, there was deadly silence at the end of the line.

'Well, what do you think I ought to do?' Huw asked timidly.

'If it was up to me, I'd put a bullet in your brain but Audrey is my brother's only daughter and I'm fond of that daughter of yours so I suppose I'll have to see what I can do. Look I'll talk to a few legal pals of mine and I'll get back to you as soon as I can. Do nothing and I mean absolutely nothing until I speak to you,' Claude said hanging up.

He sat at his desk and looked at the photograph of Deidre winning the state's Polo crosse championship on her horse Knacker. She had been so excited and her bloody parents didn't even come to watch. He had been very proud of her that day and taken her out to tea afterwards. And he had roared with laughter when she told of the tricks she got up to at school and sent her off with $50 to spend. He was deeply touched by the note she sent him thanking him for coming to watch her ride and for the money, which she said she had used to buy Knacker a new lambskin halter.

Although he was initially reluctant when Audrey asked him to be Deidre's Godfather, he had enjoyed the role. Particularly as neither of her parents seemed to give a damn about her, they were so completely besotted with their first child Timothy.

As Chairman of the Provincial Bank, Claude had been aware for some time that Huw was a dubious character and when he was caught insider trading, he had only intervened to save him because of Audrey. *As far as I was concerned, he could have gone to hell,* he thought to himself.

Now, he thought, *the stupid bastard was in another fix and it was going to be one hell of a job to get him out of it.*

Claude had never married and was very rich. He knew that Huw and Audrey expected to inherit from his estate when he karked it, but after Huw's scandalous behaviour and Audrey's disgraceful neglect of Deidre he had no intention of leaving them anything.

Deidre was something else. He had always been fond of her and admired her honesty and sense of righteousness. 'Certainly didn't get that from her old man,' he mused.

When her parents had telephoned him to say she had run away from boarding school because she couldn't bear to leave Knacker and there had been a police search, he was surprised how upset he was. And when she was eventually found hiding in Knacker's stable, he was so relieved he initiated a search to find a school that would accommodate the horse. Despite her parents' opposition (which disappeared when he insisted on footing the bill), he had booked her in and while she wasn't much of a student, she did win glory for the school by starring at Polo crosse.

He chuckled when Audrey telephoned in an absolute fit to tell him about her shearing adventures and laughed even louder when he heard she had punched her dad in the nose.

Perhaps he should play a bigger role in her life; with parents like hers, she certainly needed a helping hand.

He sat down in his armchair that looked out across the beautiful Sydney harbour and took a sip from his glass of single malt. *That's it, I'll settle some money on Deidre, she at least will appreciate it. I'll draft something for the solicitors tomorrow. In the meantime, what the hell will I do about bloody Huw, the idiot?*

Back at the bank, Huw slumped in his chair and thought

about his options. Was it too late to do a runner? What was Shifty going to do when they found out about the drought money? Would the bikies carry out their threats and kill Shifty and maybe him? His head was reeling, he felt sick and he knew things could only get worse.

Next door in the bank house, Deidre too was feeling sick. Sick at the thought of leaving Damengin and sick of her parents and their problems but most of all she was sick with worry about Angus. She was hoping he would telephone her. But she supposed it had just been a fling to him, a bit of fun and she'd had plenty of that. Let's face it, he was the biggest catch in the district — good looking, property owner, the sort of person her mum always wanted for her. But he seemed to like her, he certainly liked making love to her and she certainly liked making love to him, just the thought of it gave her goosebumps all over.

She wanted to pick up the phone and ring him but was too scared he might think she was chasing him. It was only a fuck, let's face it, she told herself. But she knew deep down it was much more. She loved working alongside him, she liked listening to him talk about his plans for Rangoon and most of all she adored him making love to her.

'Come on Rusty, let's get out of this place,' she called. 'We're going for a ride.'

Over at Rangoon Angus was also in turmoil. After telling his mum off for insulting Dee, he had gone straight to the telephone and called her. Audrey had answered and said she had no idea where Deidre was and couldn't say when she would be home. After that he didn't know what to do or where to look for her and so he decided to leave things lie until the next day and then try again.

'I hope she won't go rushing off somewhere crazy like she did before she ended up at Rangoon,' he said to himself. 'Bloody Mum upsetting her.'

His mum, Millicent, although somewhat of a snob, wasn't a bad person and was feeling sorry about what she had said to Deidre. When she had seen them in bed together she had been shocked, mainly because she had high hopes of Angus marrying someone much more acceptable and attractive. Also over the years she had listened to Audrey complaining bitterly about Deidre's outlandish behaviour and she had to sympathise with her, especially over the most recent debacle when she ditched poor Angela at the airport and cashed in her ticket to Switzerland. That would take some beating in her book. And while she did sympathise with Audrey she also recognised that Deidre had been neglected dreadfully by both of her parents and she felt a bit sorry for her. But not sorry enough to welcome her as a daughter-in-law. 'God forbid,' she groaned.

CHAPTER 25

SHIT HITS THE FAN

Shifty Grey sat at his desk in the council chambers rifling through a massive file of documents and sweat poured down his face. 'Shit it's bloody hard,' he moaned, resting his head in his hands. He had spent the last week closeted with his gun lawyer Vauny Brilliant QC, who, in answer to his frantic phone calls and with the expectation of earning an outrageously high fee, left his opulent Sydney office and jumped on a fast plane to Damengin to sort things out.

Over the years Vauny had helped Shifty to shift millions of dollars into a network of tax avoidance schemes, property investment portfolios, currency crossovers and a web of trusts so complicated they needed a brilliance far superior to Vauny's to unravel them.

By the end of the week, tired and bleary eyed, Vauny took off his glasses and gave it to him straight. 'You silly bastard,' he said. 'You've stitched yourself up properly by putting everything in Annabel's name. If she divorces you, you're gone. The only option is to persuade her sign a release so we can shove some of the property over to you. There's really nothing more I can do,' he said ignoring the look of despair on his client's face.

'Look, 'he said trembling slightly at the vicious looks Shifty was shooting at him, 'my advice to you is to initiate a reconciliation, that's your only option,' he said, closing his briefcase and standing up.

It wasn't all bad, he thought to himself. His fee for the week's work had soared to incredible heights and he had already telephoned his boyfriend Cecil and promised him a first-class trip to Las Vegas on the strength of it.

Shifty jumped up and grabbed his arm. 'Just a minute you slimy shit, wait right there,' he shouted pushing him back in his seat. 'You were the one who told me to put everything in her name to avoid tax. And I paid you a bloody fortune for that advice, so don't you dare send me another bill because you've got sod all hope of getting any more money out of me.'

Vauny shrugged and pulled back his seat. 'Pay me or I'll see you in court,' he hissed, 'and it won't be pretty,' he said stalking out of the door without looking back.

Shifty slumped back into his seat. 'Bloody lawyers, crooks the lot of them,' he moaned then turned and looked out of the window to see Vauny's BMW hire car roaring off in a cloud of dust.

How the hell would he get out of this, he pondered, leaning his head on his hands. Last night he'd got home late and picked up the mail in the box outside to find a large parcel. When he opened it he let out a blood curdling scream. Inside was what looked like a charred lump of steak but which on closer inspection turned out to be a liver? The note attached said, 'ten grand or we're having yours next with bacon and onions.'

Shuddering he had telephoned Huw Hawtrey in hysterics and told him to send the money urgently or he would go over there personally and break his fucking neck.

'And I'll have those documents signed and sent to you this afternoon so get to it or you'll be so deep in shit you won't be able to move,' he hissed.

On the other end, Huw was strangely silent.

Shifty hung up the phone. That will put the fear of God in him and should hold them at bay for a couple of weeks, he thought but he knew he had to get Annabel back and the bloody cow was still refusing to speak to him.

He didn't go over to the pub to try to see her in case Paddy caught him. Last time he had begged Paddy to persuade her to come back to him and the bastard had grabbed him around the neck and threatened to 'cut your bloody balls off' if he went near her.

'Fuckers obviously got the hots for her himself,' Shifty muttered through gritted teeth. No matter, he'd just have to forge her bloody signature and get someone to witness it. Cyril would do it, he owed him big time.

'Dolly,' he called out, 'get Cyril in here, now.'

Dolly, who was sitting at her desk in the next office

painting her nails a new vibrant purple, sighed. She was sick to death of him telling her what to do. One minute he was screwing her rotten and promising her the moon, the next pretending she didn't exist. Well, she'd show him.

Picking up the phone she dialled the council yard and asked them to send the Shire Foreman Cyril Rowe over to see the Shire Clerk at council chambers 'immediately'.

After he got the message, Cyril Rowe stubbed out his cigarette and, drawing a ring with his pen around a certainty in the third race at Eagle Farm, put down the racing pages of the Brisbane paper and got up.

'Bloody Shifty,' he muttered climbing into his work car, 'what does the sod want now?'

Over the past twenty years, Cyril and Shifty had shared more than the delicious Dolly McIntyre. Together they had created some fiendishly clever money-making schemes. With state government funding, they had authorised council to buy dozens of gigantic machines for road building and construction works and then sold them to crooked operators in the city for millions of dollars. In collusion with Councillor Steve Dixon, Damengin's only real estate agent, who was so crooked he couldn't even lie straight in bed, they had sold off non-existent farmland complete with non-existent crops as tax avoidance certainties to vulnerable city slickers seeking tax havens.

The trio, under the auspices of the council's sister-city status, had travelled the world supposedly generating goodwill exchanges and developing profitable trade links. But the only profitable trade they generated was for themselves. They had used their lucrative sister-city contacts in Japan to sell a group of Japanese speculators a large tract of the Simpson Desert for the development of an abattoir and feed lot. And by the time the Japs had discovered the nearest surfaced road was 500 km away and it hadn't rained for forty years, it was too late; the money was already in their Cayman Island bank account.

Happy days, Cyril thought to himself as he parked his car and wandered through the Shire Chambers to Dolly's office.

'Righto Dolly love, what does the old buggar want now?' he asked staring hungrily down her generously displayed cleavage.

Dolly shrugged and walked to the filing cabinet. 'Don't tell me nothing, been screaming and yelling at me all morning and I'm sick of him.'

'Not sick of me are ya, lovie?' he said pushing her against the wall and pressing his growing desire into her softness. 'Got time for a quickie out the back?' he whispered, nuzzling her neck.

Dolly whimpered wriggling against him. 'Not now Cyril,' she said pushing him away. 'Tonight, that's if you can get away from your wife,' she said with a sneer. 'Men, you're all the same, your dick rules your head but your wives wear the pants.'

'Well if you feel like that, I'll leave you to it,' Cyril said huffily, hitching up his pants and striding into Shifty's office.

'What's the trouble mate,' he said, dropping into the chair

opposite the desk and taking his cigarettes out of his top pocket.

'Don't you light up in here,' Shifty snapped. 'I don't want bloody cancer.'

'Bout the only thing you don't want,' Cyril muttered to himself, shoving the packet back in his pocket and leaning forward.

'We've got trouble, 'Shifty said slapping some documents down in front of him, 'big trouble and I need you to witness these documents that have just been signed by Annabel.'

'Pull the other leg,' Cyril said with a sneer. 'Alright I'll witness them, give them here,' he said flinching under Shifty's glare.

When Cyril had finished, he called Dolly and told her to take them over to Huw at the bank and wait until he released the documents, then bring them back to the office.

'Tell him the matter is urgent.'

Dolly opened the front door to leave, heard a loud roar and saw a mob of at least a dozen motor bikes driven by fearsome tattooed bikies approaching the shire chambers.

They pulled up and parked their bikes and walked slowly towards her.

Giving a shriek of terror, she fled back inside just before the window shattered as a bullet went flying through.

Dolly started screaming and Cyril grabbed her and pushed her under Shifty's desk where he was already whimpering.

'That's just for starters,' a guttural voice yelled, 'cough up or you croak.'

There was an eerie silence and then a roar as all the bikes started up in unison and they heard them drive slowly off.

'What the fuck was that?' Cyril said crawling from under the desk and lighting a cigarette with shaking hands.

Shifty followed him and took a quick look out of the shattered window. 'Bloody bikies, they obviously haven't got the money I asked Hawtrey to send them this morning, I'll kill the buggar for this. And you can put that bloody cigarette out.'

Cyril took half a dozen puffs and then stubbed it out with his foot. 'Christ, any closer and I would have been a goner. You okay?' he asked Dolly, who was shaking.

'Get up for God's sake Dolly,' Shifty yelled, 'it was only a warning shot, it's not in their interest to kill us, we're the cash cow. Now give me back those papers, I'll front Hawtrey myself.'

But Huw had his own problems. For years Shifty had used him to squirrel money away into overseas bank accounts for which he had been richly rewarded. Now he realised the shit was about to hit the fan and he was desperate to find a way of avoiding being splattered by the residue. 'Things couldn't have come at a worse time' he shuddered. He picked up the phone. 'Shifty that you,' he said. 'We've got big trouble.'

'Handle it or else,' the voice on the end of the line threatened. 'And I'm bringing these documents over so you can give me those titles.'

Meanwhile out at Redlands, Bomber had spent the morning directing the family solicitors in Brisbane to prepare a separation order and a financial settlement for Annabel.

'They need a record of your assets and liabilities and I've made an appointment with Huw Hawtrey at the bank for 2 pm,' he told her. 'Bring everything you can find with you.'

Later that day Annabel and Bomber arrived at the bank and Huw's nosey secretary Helen ushered them into his office.

'Afternoon Annabel, Bomber,' he said waving them to sit down. 'What can I do for you?'

Bomber threw a bundle of papers across to him. 'Huw, you've always looked after the family banking. Annabel is divorcing Shifty and we need an up-to-date record of her assets and liabilities.'

Huw peered down at the papers in front of him and then looked up. 'We're awfully busy at present, Annabel, this is rather complicated and could take some time. Let me get back to you in say a fortnight.'

'That's bullshit, Huw,' Bomber said leaning forward and thrusting his large red face in front of Huw's. 'She needs to get this organised now so that sod Shifty can't get his sticky fingers on anything. I want you to put a stop payment on all their accounts and give me everything you have in safe deposit. NOW.'

Huw went white. 'I can't do that, not without Shifty's permission,' he squeaked.

'Yes you bloody can, don't give me that bullshit. I know what Annabel took to the marriage because I bloody gave it to her. Now,' he said, glaring at Huw, 'you can either give it to me or I'm going to ring my mate Simon Fisher at Head Office in Brisbane and tell him I'm not happy. If I know Simon, he'll have the auditors up here quicker than you can chase a rat up a drainpipe.'

Huw shuddered. 'I see where you're coming from Bomber,' he said, his small eyes blinking furiously. 'Look, I'll get you all that is in the safe, but can you give me until tomorrow and I promise I'll have everything else ready?'

Bomber got up. 'You've got twenty-four hours,' he said taking Annabel's arm. 'We'll be back this time tomorrow and it better be ready.'

When they had gone, Huw sat down and closed his eyes. His life was over. Bomber would destroy his career if he didn't do what he wanted. The bank auditors would discover he tried to foreclose on Ben Bangor for no reason and he would be sacked. Shifty would drop him in it big time if he didn't do what he was told. Yes, he shuddered, jail was a distinct possibility. And Audrey, who had only just forgiven him and was the only person he had ever felt the tiniest bit of affection for, would divorce him and he would lose everything. As if that wasn't enough his son and daughter loathed him and even the cat treated him with contempt.

He picked up the phone. 'Shifty, we need to talk again, ring me back urgently.'

Shifty arrived at the bank and was shown into Huw's office.

'It's no good. I can't give you those titles or securities,

Bomber and Annabel were just here and they took them with them. They've put a stop on all her accounts and credit cards and there's no money in your account, so I can't pay the bikies.'

Shifty leaned over and grabbed him by his shirt.

'Listen you little fucker, you take ten grand from your account or anyone's account and send it off now, or you won't live to see tomorrow. I've got a bloody mob of bikies out to kill me and before they do, if you don't give me that money, I'm going to do you first. Now that's my final warning. Get to it,' he shouted so loud that the staff who had their ears jammed against the door and heard every word, had to jump in order to get out of his way as he marched out.

Huw sat slumped at his desk and there was a knock at the door.

'You okay, Mr Hawtrey?' his secretary asked.

'Would you please call Bomber Reed and let him know that I have some information for him?'

Making sure the door was secure, Huw dialled a number in Sydney.

Chairman of the Provincial Bank, Claude Hewlett, was presiding over a meeting of his directors that he had called earlier in the day.

'I have called you together to discuss a serious matter concerning my nephew Huw Hawtrey,' he said. 'Unfortunately, he has been involved with a scurrilous character and as a result will face the full force of the law. I believe we need to seek his resignation immediately so that if he does end up incarcerated it will minimise the damage to the bank.

'Because he is a relative, I had thought of citing his incompetence and giving him another warning, but I'm afraid no one would believe it. Some of the schemes he initiated are so clever that if it wasn't for the idiot at council, he would have got away with it.

'Anyway,' he said adjusting his glasses, 'he hasn't touched any of the bank's money, in fact he has made quite a substantial amount of profit for us so we don't have a problem there. No point sending auditors in, I'm sure he has dotted the eyes and crossed the tees. As for as the other matters, I say let the courts deal with it.

'Now what does everyone have to say, do you all agree? Right then,' he said, standing up, 'I'll ring and tell him.'

Back in his office, Claude picked up the phone. 'Good afternoon Huw, I have to inform you that at a special meeting of the bank today, it was decided to ask you to resign. You are to vacate the office immediately, pack your things and be out of the residence by tomorrow. Is that clear?'

Huw sighed with relief. 'Thank you Claude, I am on my way,' he said, putting down the phone.

CHAPTER 26

REVELATIONS

When he walked next door to the bank residence Huw breathed a sigh of relief. Audrey had already packed her things and left, Deidre wasn't there and he walked into the bedroom and started throwing things into suitcases.

It didn't matter what happened next, at least he would be free from Shifty's clutches. And if the bank wasn't going to press charges or send in the auditors, the only problem he had was if Shifty opened his mouth and knowing Shifty that was the last thing he would do.

All the money he had salted away in the last ten years had been put into Audrey's name and they would have more than enough to live well on. Thank God she had forgiven him. Now there was just the matter of Deidre to sort out. If she didn't come back, he would have to leave her a note because sure as hell he was leaving the place as soon as he could pack the car. The staff could send on their furniture later.

Deidre had gone for a long ride on Knacker and with Rusty trotting along beside them they followed the old tracks behind the town's cattle yards out to the town's rapidly diminishing water supply, Damengin dam. When she got there, she removed Knacker's saddle and sat under a tree on the edge of what had turned into a large muddy puddle. 'Well Rusty, she said stroking his head, 'where to from here?'

As much as she disliked her parents, now that they were finally leaving, she was concerned. At least while they were there when the chips were down, she had somewhere to go back to. Now she was completely on her own. She knew Teddy or even Ben would give her a bed but what with the drought, neither was in a position to offer her a job. As for Angus she didn't even want to think about him after the drama with his mum.

Any hope of getting another job with the shearing gang was gone, they were flat out finding work for themselves. She had scoured the pages of the *Country Life* looking for any sort of job on the land but there was nothing. Everyone was in the same boat and many landowners were walking off their land the drought had hit so hard.

'Bloody drought, it's ruining everything,' she said throwing a stone into the middle of the dam. Rusty immediately dashed after it, plunging into the muddy quagmire, racing back to drop it at her feet and shaking almost pure mud over her.

'Get off,' she yelled laughing, 'look what you've done to me, oh what the hell, who cares. Come on let's go home,' she said saddling up.

She left Knacker chomping on some fresh lucerne hay in his paddock and walked slowly back to the bank house. When she got there she saw Huw's car was gone and on the kitchen table was a note addressed to her anchored with a bottle of sauce.

Dear Deidre,

Have resigned from the bank and gone to Sydney. We are staying at Grannie's until we buy an apartment. The furniture will be picked up some time next week. You can contact us on this number 02334970. You will have to get rid of your horse and dog before you come. I am leaving you this cheque for your expenses.

Dad.

Deidre picked up the note and cheque and sat down to gather her thoughts. So it was all over, they had gone. Well there was no way in hell she was ever going to part with Knacker and Rusty and she would live in a humpy before she would go to the bloody city. So what now and how long could she stay here in the house?

There was a knock at the door and Cyril Rowe stood there.

'Morning Dee,' he said politely, 'I'm looking for your dad. The staff said he's gone, do you know where?'

'Well, he sure has gone, he's resigned and gone to Sydney, if that's any help,' Deidre said ruefully.

'Do you have an address?' he asked hopefully.

'Sorry Cyril, I can't give you that. Is that everything?' she said, closing the door on him.

'Nah, it's okay, thanks anyway,' he said dreading what Shifty would say to him when he gave him the news.

Sure enough, Shifty went ballistic. 'I'll fix the fucker, just let me get my hands on him,' he said seething. 'For certain he hasn't paid off the bloody bikies.

'Dolly,' he yelled, 'get me Dickey Davis on the phone, move your arse, NOW.'

Annabel and Bomber who arrived at the pub to tell Paddy about Huw leaving the bank, were greeted by an excited Paddy.

'Wait until you hear this. Sam Spink just telephoned and said he had a call from the editor of the *Canberra Guardian*. They had followed up on the drought relief story and managed to tie down the Minister for Agriculture. Get this, he said the drought relief had been sent regularly, over $2 million in the past three years.

'Apparently our bloody useless local member, the Honourable Dudley Dunkers MP has been sitting on his hands and didn't bother to let us know. That lazy swine's too busy playing golf and jetting off on trade missions to bother himself with such trifles.

'But what I want to know is, if they have sent the money as they claim, where the bloody hell is it. I'm about to ring Dudley now.'

Paddy put the phone on conference mode and dialled Dudley's home number.

'Susie Dunkers speaking,' Doctor Dickie's ex-wife said in her high-pitched posh voice, 'how can I help yew?'

'No wonder she left old Dickie,' Paddy whispered to Annabel.

'Well she did say living with him was like watching paint dry,' she whispered back.

'Shush you two, she can hear you,' Paddy said holding his hand over the receiver.

'Paddy Murphy here Susie, I have the mayor with me and we would like to talk to Dudley, is he there?'

'Certainly Paddy, just one teeny moment and I'll get him for you.'

Dudley came to the phone. 'Afternoon Paddy, how can I help you?'

'Look Dudley mate, there's some confusion about Damengin's drought money, the government says it's paid us two million quid but we've had zero this end.'

'Paddy, I have a letter faxed through to me this morning from the Minister with the record of payments. It is in fact right in front of me, and I can confirm that the money was paid each year direct into an account at the Damengin Shire Council. I'm happy to fax this on to you so you can check the numbers with your official records.'

Paddy sighed. 'I hope this isn't the bloody government trying to fob us, that's about the only thing they're good at, passing the buck.'

'Look Paddy, before you go making assertions, I suggest that you contact your Shire Clerk and Shire Treasurer and get them to look into it. There is obviously some type of mistake somewhere and despite your snide remarks, it is certainly not at this end.'

'Is that right? Well if something has gone wrong this end, we'll get to the bottom of it. Anyway, thanks Dudley,' Paddy said, putting down the phone.

'Well, now we have it,' he said turning to the others, 'and if it turns out that slimy little bastard Shifty Grey has done something with the money, I'll string him up.

'Bomber, I want you to call an emergency meeting of the full Shire Council to convene tomorrow morning at 10 am sharp. In the meantime, I'm going over to talk to Shifty, you coming?'

The two men marched into the shire offices, walked straight past Dolly who was just recovering from a tirade of abuse from her boss and Bomber threw open the door of Shifty's office.

'Shifty, you bastard,' he said before noticing the office was empty. 'Alright Dolly, where's he gone?'

'I don't know Mayor, he left here in a hurry carrying his briefcase.'

'Well you tell him when he comes back that I've just been talking to Dudley Dunkers and he tells me that the government has sent over two million quid to this council in drought relief and I want to know where it is. Right, just tell him that.'

Dolly nodded. 'Certainly Mayor, I'll tell him.'

'And you can also tell him the mayor has convened an

emergency meeting of the full council tomorrow and we want him there, or else. Now I want you to telephone every councillor and make sure they know that it is on.'

'Certainly, I'll do that right away,' she said picking up the phone.

Paddy led the way back to the pub where the two men spent the next few hours working out a strategy for the special meeting.

Next morning at 10 am the meeting at the Shire Chambers convened and Shifty walked in carrying a huge package of files and sat down in his chair with his head held high, not saying a word.

When they were all seated Bomber stood up. 'I've called this special meeting because of information I received yesterday regarding the drought relief funds. Yesterday I had a fax from the Minister's office to the effect that over $2 million in funds has been sent to this council over the past three years. This was confirmed by our local Member Dudley Dunkers.

'Now I put it to you Shire Clerk to tell me whether or not you received this money and if the answer is yes, where the bloody hell is it?'

Shifty stood up and looked Bomber straight in the eyes. 'I can assure the mayor that I have never received any money from the government and that is all I have to say on the matter.'

'Is that right? Well how do you explain this?' Bomber said, throwing a faxed copy of a list of payments from the

Minister's office with the numbered bank accounts they were sent to.

'Obviously it is a mistake,' Shifty said dismissively, 'the money must have been sent to some other shire. Before we go any further I seek leave to investigate this matter and will bring it to next month's council meeting,' he said standing up, preparing to leave.

'Sit down Shire Clerk, you will investigate nothing. As we speak a government appointed forensic auditor is on his way to inspect the Shire's finances and we require all the accounting records to be delivered to my office. Councillor Murphy will accompany you now to your office to collect these documents.

'Until that audit is done, you are restricted to this town and if you even look like leaving, I will personally have you locked up.'

Shifty stood up and glared at him. 'Don't be ridiculous, there are no grounds for arresting me. I have done nothing wrong and I will sue you for defamation if you do any such thing.'

Bomber scowled at him. 'Listen matey, I am deadly serious, brother-in-law or not, if you leave town, you will be locked up, now is that quite clear, Shire Clerk?'

There was deadly silence and then Councillor Sid Luxton piped up, 'Yes you little creep, we've had enough of this mucking around. Sort this out or you're gone.'

'How dare you speak to me like that,' Shifty said furiously. He turned to Paddy. 'As the local magistrate and Justice of the

Peace, I ask you to intervene in this. It is impossible for me to get the information you are seeking without me leaving town.'

Bomber stood up. 'Rubbish. Councillor Murphy and Councillor Luxton, please accompany the Shire Clerk to his office, collect all his files and documents and deliver them to my office. Shire Clerk, I want you to hand in your office and safe keys as well as the keys to your council vehicle to Councillor Murphy.'

Paddy bent over and whispered to Bomber. Bomber straightened up. 'Right Shire Clerk, you are advised to be available for interview tomorrow by the Government appointed forensic auditor here at the council chambers at 10 am. Meeting closed.'

Shifty was in a state of shock as Paddy and Sid Luxton followed him to his office at the back of the chambers. He numbly handed over his keys and watched as Paddy unlocked the safe and took out its contents.

When they had gone he started rifling through the drawers of his desk until he found what he was looking for, a small key that would fit something the size of a wardrobe lock. He put it into his shirt pocket and looked out of the window. Council staff were standing in a huddle talking, the word was out and the sooner he left the better. But before he left he had some jobs to do.

He was just closing his briefcase when the door opened and Councillor Micky Davis marched in. After the council meeting he had gone back to his office and made a few phone calls before deciding to see how Shifty was getting on.

'That was a close one. Hey where the hell do you think you're going?' he said. 'Don't think you're leaving me to face the music while you buggar off.'

Shifty glared at him contemptuously. 'For Christ's sake, the game's up, our only chance is to hit the road. There's a few loose ends I need to tie up and then I'll ring you,' Shifty said, pushing past him.

When Shifty had been escorted from the council meeting that morning he had no intention of returning the next day. He had already retrieved the book with the numbers of his accounts in the Cayman Islands from the safe in his office before the meeting.

He went home and made a call to Cyril Rowe. The pair waited until dark and then armed with shovels and torches they started to dig up Annabel's rose garden searching for a hoard of cash he had buried there years ago. Unluckily for him, Annabel who had a passion for exotic blooms, had extended the garden so that it occupied almost an acre of their substantial holding and the search wasn't helped by the moonless night.

'Ouch,' Cyril yelled, pricking his hands on the merciless thorns as he lifted a rose bush and dug under its roots. 'Nothing under this one Shifty. Oh hell, yuck what's this slimy stuff?'

'Cow shit you fool, keep your voice down, 'Shifty hissed. 'The fucking gardener's been fertilising again. Bring your torch over here I think I've found it.'

Shifty lifted up a large plastic bag and dragged it over to

the house. He sent Cyril off to the shed to pack the tools away before lifting out its contents. Inside was a leather pouch containing neat rows of $100 notes.

'This should take us a fair way away,' Shifty said smiling to himself. 'You right over there, Cyril?' he called.

They spent the night packing and then drove out to the tiny airport on the edge of town where Micky Davis was waiting in his Cessna 121. As dawn broke, they flew north-west in a cloudless sky with a tail wind to help them.

At 10 am Bomber and Paddy arrived at the council chambers with Sammy Benton, the government appointed forensic auditor who had arrived from Brisbane the night before.

The chamber was empty and they went down the hall to Shifty's office and banged on the door.

Dolly came rushing out to meet them.

'It's no use, he's gone,' she wailed.

'What are you talking about,' Paddy said. 'Who's gone?'

'They've all gone — the Shire Clerk, Micky Davis, and Cyril has gone too. His wife has been on to me all morning moaning and crying. I hope I've still got a job,' she said, looking anxiously at Bomber.

'Right, we'll call the police, get Percy Plod on the line Dolly, he can put out a warrant for the arrest of the lot of them. I knew we should never have let the bastard out of our sight.'

CHAPTER 27

COURTS AND CASES

Shifty and Cyril closed their eyes and hugged their knees as Micky made his third attempt at landing the Cessna. He flew along a rutted track in a flat area between two stands of spindly trees and dropped down. The plane hit the ground with a bang and shuddered so much Cyril screamed and Shifty began shaking and broke out in a sweat. Micky stood on the brakes with the full force of his puny might as the plane bucked and bumped along the ground until finally it jerked to a stop on the edge of a hollow.

'Thank Christ for that,' Micky said heaving a sigh of relief. 'For a few minutes there I thought we were stuffed.'

For once in his life Shifty was too shocked to make a smart arse remark and Cyril was busy trying to stop his hands shaking as he lit a cigarette.

'What the hell do you think you're doing, you fucking idiot,' Micky roared. 'Put that thing out before you blow us to pieces. Move it right now before the fuel tanks explode,' he yelled. 'Grab your stuff, with a bump like that anything could happen.'

Micky flung open the cabin door and they all clambered out falling over one another in the rush.

'Where the hell are we?' Cyril complained, looking around.

'Who cares where we are, with the bloody pilot we've got we're lucky to be alive,' Shifty said.

Micky glared at him. 'You're a bloody ungrateful lot, and not many people could have landed on this stuff. Any rate, I figure we're about five km from Darwin so someone will have to start walking.'

'Well it's not me,' Shifty said. 'I'm stuffed. Cyril, off you go, get a hire car and bring back something cold to drink, it's hot as hell here.'

Cyril reluctantly started walking and while he was gone Shifty took out his notebook and began making plans.

'Right Micky, what's the best way to get to Bali? And keeping in mind the mayor took my passport, it'll have to be the back way.'

Micky sat down on his heels and with a stick started writing in the dirt. 'Well we can't fly there in the Cessna for a start, not without a flight plan. Those Indonesians would shoot us down,' he said. 'What we could do is when we get to Darwin, buy a boat and sail north-west across the Timor Sea until we reach the Indonesian coast. If we land on one of the smaller islands I reckon we can see how the land lies, pay off a few people and get into Bali without much trouble.'

Shifty nodded. 'Right, when we get to Darwin you get out there and start looking for a boat, don't get anything flash that would draw attention from the authorities, just something sturdy that'll do the job. I've got enough cash to buy us a boat and get us there but after that we'll have to get some passports forged. Bound to be someone who'll do the job. Then we head for the Caymans — that's where the big money is.'

'What about my plane?' Micky asked. 'I can't just leave it here — someone will find it and they'll twig, it's a dead giveaway.'

Shifty stared at him. 'You're right, we'll burn it.'

Micky was horrified. 'You've got to be kidding?'

'Look mate, what's the plane worth?' Shifty said, shaking his head. 'It's so bloody old it's held together with bits of fencing wire. Burn it or you might as well put up a sign and say we're here.'

By the time Cyril arrived back with the hire car, the plane was well alight and Micky was watching it burn with tears streaming down his face.

'I loved that plane, it's the only thing that's never let me down,' he said.

'Bloody nearly did this time, you're well shut of it,' Cyril said throwing his cigarette end into the flames.

They drove into Darwin and booked into the Crocodile Pool Motel that had views over Fanny Bay.

'Hope there's no bloody crocs in there,' Cyril said, watching some tourists splashing around in the swimming pool.

'Nah, you don't have to worry, all the crocs are out there in Fanny Bay knocking off the sharks,' Micky said. 'Here have a beer, this is the life,' he said, lying back on his bed.

Cyril shivered. 'Don't get too comfortable mate, they'll be after us soon enough. Pity we couldn't bring Dolly, brighten things up a bit.'

'Just shut it will you?' Shifty hissed. 'We're not out of the woods yet. The sooner we leave here the better. Micky, you go and see what's available down at the marina and Cyril, go and get us some gear, sneakers, t-shirts, that sort of thing and sunglasses. I'll stay here and sort things out.'

Cyril lit a cigarette and shrugged before leaving. 'I hope things improve when we reach Bali. It's a bloody miserable business now.'

Micky went down to the marina and wandered around looking at the boats with for sale signs on. He settled on a 12 m keel boat with a large diesel engine and a 40 hp outboard motor. The owner was living on the boat and after some argy-bargy was persuaded to part with her for $30 000 including a full tank of fuel and provisions.

When Micky went back to tell Shifty the good news he found Cyril on his own watching *Neighbours* and no Shifty.

'Where's he gone?' Micky asked.

'No idea, he wasn't here when I got back. I thought he'd gone with you.'

'Bastard made me burn me plane, what if he doesn't come back?' Micky moaned. 'We're bloody stuck here.'

'Shush, the ads over and it's on again, 'Cyril said turning

back to the telly. 'Stop worrying, he'll be back.'

But Shifty didn't come back. While they were gone, he had opened the door and been hustled down the stairs by two thugs who had taken him to a shed on the shore of Fanny Bay. A massive thug covered in tattoos and with metal hanging off every piece of flesh was ramming his right arm up his back while another was holding a knife to his throat.

'Where is it, where's the dough?' the thug hissed, shoving his arm further up his back.

'Don't know, arghh,' Shifty shrieked. 'Look I'm telling you the truth, I don't have the money.'

'Listen you lying little fucker,' the thug said, spraying Shifty with his foul-smelling breath. 'You have two choices, one I do you slowly with this,' he said pressing the knife into Shifty's throat, 'or two, he donates you to the crocs, which could be fast or slow depending on how hungry they are. You choose.'

Shifty eyes flickered right and left and he choked, 'Look, let me go and I'll do a deal. I'll give you all the money I have and sign the Tattoo Parlours over to you. Now release me first.'

The thugs relaxed their grip and Shifty fished around in his pants and came up with a roll of money.

'Here take it, you can have the lot.'

The largest thug grabbed the roll and inspected it. 'What's the catch?'

'No catch, you let me go and I'll give you the Tattoo Parlours. Is it a deal?' *No bloody good to me over in the Caymans anyway,* Shifty thought to himself.

The two thugs looked at each other and nodded. 'We'll have to check with the boss, you stay here and wait. Alright, tie the bastard up Archie,' the big fellow said lighting a fag.

Shifty was trussed up and propped against the far wall and they went out, locking the door behind them.

When they had gone Shifty manoeuvred himself into a sitting position and, using the wall to steady himself managed to stand up. How the hell would he get out of this before they came back, he thought, and then he heard a noise.

'Anyone there, help, help,' he shouted.

Someone was trying the door handle.

'It's locked, try the window,' he called out.

A face appeared at the dirty window.

'For God's sake help me,' Shifty cried. 'I've been attacked.'

'I'll get the police,' the voice said.

'No, no don't go,' Shifty screamed. 'Come back, look break the window, don't get the police, I'll give you $100 if you get me out.'

There was silence and then the window shattered as a rock flew through it and a scruffy looking old man appeared in the window frame.

'Where's the money?' he asked.

'Climb through and untie me and then I'll give it to you.'

Using an old piece of rag, the old man pulled out the broken window pane and with some difficulty managed to pull himself through. He landed with a bump on the floor, stood up and went over to Shifty to untie him.

'Thanks,' said Shifty. 'Now turn your back and I'll get

your money.' He bent over and pulled a roll of money from a pocket stitched into his underpants. 'Here's your money,' he said peeling off a note. 'Now, no going to the police, okay?'

The old man nodded and Shifty helped him climb back through the window and without a backward glance he raced back to the motel and burst through the door.

'Thank God you're back,' Micky said, getting up from his chair. 'Where've you been?'

'Never mind that,' Shifty said, frantically grabbing his bags. 'The bikies are after us, for fuck's sake, get your things we're out of here.'

'How did they find us?' Cyril said, reluctant to leave *Neighbours* before the end.

'How the hell do I know? Those bastards have got contacts everywhere, they're like the mafia. We've got to get out of here fast. They tied me up and left me while they went to consult their bloody boss. I gave them some money and told them I'd give them the Tattoo Parlours. That's a laugh, they're going to be bloody furious when they find out they're only leased.'

'You bloody fool, they'll kill us for that,' Micky yelled.

'Only if they find us — now let's get out of here.'

Ten minutes later they were down at the marina impatiently waiting while the owner of the boat slowly counted out the wad of money Shifty gave him.

They finally cruised out of the harbour, watching the lights of Darwin disappearing in the distance, sipping a beer and completely oblivious of the cyclone warnings that were jamming the airwaves.

Back in Damengin, Bomber had sparked a nation-wide police alert for the three crooks and the Government's Forensic Auditor Sammy Benton had arrived and taken over Shifty's old office.

As he inspected council's finances, he became increasingly exasperated until he finally exploded and summoned the Shire Treasurer Scrooge McKay.

'This is the most creative accounting I have ever seen in my life,' he said furiously. 'I can't make head nor tail of the rubbish. Sit down Mr McKay and start explaining,' he said, throwing the council's financial records down in front of him.

Scrooge sat in front of him with his head down and sighed. 'I'd like to speak to my solicitor before I say anything,' he mumbled.

For years he had done the bidding of the syndicate, syphoning off millions of dollars of the town's finances. He had flattered and charmed council's finance chair Councillor Maisie Matten disgracefully to ensure she had no bloody idea what he was up to and now, he realised the game was up. Shifty and Co had left him to face the music.

'You are very wise to want your solicitor,' Sammy said looking at him seriously. 'From what I have already gleaned, this matter could see you locked up for about twenty-five years.'

Scrooge slumped forward and put his head in his hands. In twenty-five years, he would be over seventy — too old to spend his share of the money, if there was any left.

'But,' Sammy said persuasively, 'there is another option. With your complete cooperation we could perhaps come to an agreement.'

Scrooge lifted his head and looked at him. 'What do you mean?' he asked hopefully.

'Well, as you would understand, our main purpose is to retrieve the government's money. If you were to help us with this, then I could, in the circumstances, put in a good word for you with the Crown Prosecutor.'

Scrooge thought about it. What choice did he have, years in jail or maybe a suspended sentence?

'I'd need some sort of written assurances,' he said.

'Look Mr McKay, I'll lay my cards on the table. We need to know immediately where the money is before those thieves get their hands on it. That being as it is, I would be willing to commit to you that if you help us to access the funds, I will see that you get some sort of leniency in sentencing.'

Scrooge hesitated. 'I still need to speak to my solicitor so that this can be formally recorded,' he said.

Sammy straightened up. 'Alright, I agree, but you need to do this immediately. As I have said, speed is the essence.'

Scrooge went back to his office and telephoned his solicitor who, after listening to him for over an hour, agreed to draft a plea bargain and fax it up for signatures.

'Will this be enough to keep me out of jail?' Scrooge asked him.

'I have no idea, but you don't have any other option as far as I can see,' his solicitor told him. 'You've been a bloody fool, the only thing we can hope is that by giving Queen's evidence they go easy on you.'

When the plea bargain was signed, Scrooge spilled the beans and gave names, places and bank details to Sammy. Armed with the information, Sammy and a Federal Officer flew immediately to the Cayman Islands where they managed to retrieve just over $750000, all that was left of the $2 million flood relief money.

When they got back it was lodged in a special account to be overseen by Sammy, who was staying on as Council Administrator until a new Shire Clerk and Treasurer could be recruited.

Sammy took over the Shire Clerk's office and Dolly McIntyre used her obvious charms effectively and was retained as his secretary. To her delight she found he wasn't married and was even better endowed than Cyril.

At the next council meeting it was decided that, while the funds were far less than they should have been, they would begin distributing them to the neediest properties.

'First thing to do is to organise a water delivery service from Longreach to keep the town supplied when we run out,' Bomber said. 'And the way things are looking this will be sooner than later. Then we'll start sending out the cheques and I think Ben Bangor can be first cab off the rank.'

There was more good news when the television film showing Ben Bangor receiving the hay and grain donated by city people was aired. It also showed Bomber in his hospital bed thanking everyone and there was a shot of Chloe looking so appealing bottle-feeding a tiny orphan lamb, it had everyone in tears.

As a result, a convoy of trucks, utes and even cars descended on Damengin and unloaded their cargoes at the showgrounds.

There were people everywhere. Maisie's 4 Square was overrun with people buying food, drinks and whatever else she had. Her daughter Chloe, looking striking in a scandalously short mini skirt and eye-catching top, dashed here and there talking to everyone and taking photographs. She had been commissioned by the *Brisbane Mail* to write an article about the food drops and was hoping for some follow up work or maybe a cadetship.

'This is amazing,' Paddy said to Rosie when he returned home after delivering a truck load of feed to Ben at Abington. He was exhausted but had agreed to do just one more delivery to a station west of Rangoon that was in dire straits. On the way back he intended to stay the night at Paddylea with Billy and Mary and if he had time in the morning, he thought he would pop in on Angus at Rangoon, see how he was managing. *He has never asked for anything,* Paddy thought, *but sometimes those who don't ask need it the most.*

Since Deidre had left after being insulted by his mum, Angus had been miserable and had accused his mum of ruining his life.

'Well if you're that keen on her, you can have her and on your own head be it,' his mum said, leaving in a cloud of dust. Apart from Charlie, he had been on his own since and had buried himself in work.

Early the next morning he heard the dogs barking and walked out onto the verandah to see Paddy drive into the yard.

'Morning, Angus,' he said getting out of the cab of the truck. 'Thought I'd call in for a cuppa, see how things are at Rangoon.'

'Come on in, good to see you,' Angus said, shaking his outstretched hand.

They sat down at the kitchen table and Paddy brought him up to date on the council happenings and told him about the outpouring of help arriving from the city.

'It's overwhelming, I can't keep up with the deliveries,' Paddy joked. 'Any chance you could do with some hay?'

Angus went red. He was down to the last of his feed and had already decided to cull his breeders.

'That's generous of you Paddy, as a matter of fact, I wouldn't say no, as long as everyone else has been looked after.'

'Plenty for everyone, might as well use it up before it goes stale. If the drought keeps up, nothing will save us but this will buy us time.'

'Any word about the Hawtreys?' Angus asked tentatively.

'As far as I know, they have gone to live in Sydney. It was all hushed up but between you and me, Huw was in big trouble for helping Shifty. Bomber knows more about it than I do because of Annabel but I think he got off with a warning. By the way, Annabel and Shifty are finished,' he said smiling. 'She's much too good for that bastard.'

'Any word of Deidre?' Angus asked hopefully. 'Did she go with them?'

'Haven't seen her around and her horse isn't in the paddock by the showgrounds. The bank house is empty and they've been cleaning it out. Apparently the Hawtreys left a lot of their stuff behind and there's a new bank manager coming in a couple of weeks.'

When Paddy left, Angus went over to the shearer's quarters and sat on the bed Deidre had slept in. He ached with misery and couldn't believe how much he missed her. He thought about telephoning her in Sydney but she probably hated him after the way his mum had behaved. Bloody parents, too selfish to help, there's no way I can carry on without destocking even if Paddy brings out a load of feed. It's not going to see me through. I'll start culling tomorrow, send them off for mutton.

HAWTREYS GO SOUTH

When they arrived in Sydney after their hasty exit from Damengin, Huw and Audrey Hawtrey and their son Timmy moved in with Audrey's mum Edith who lived by herself in a smart town house at Double Bay. Her husband Reg had left her years ago, driven mad by her nagging and was happily settled with his girlfriend Gina, a masseuse at Bondi.

From day one, Edith complained and by the end of the first week Huw was spending more time in the local pub than at the house to get away from her. This caused more trouble and as well as attacking him for losing his job, he was labelled an 'inebriated incompetent' by his mother-in-law.

Poor Audrey, who — ever since she had married Huw against her mum's wishes — had suffered her attacks in silence, finally let fly on Saturday night when the old bat slagged off at her darling Timmy.

Timmy had put on his favourite pink shirt and new blue floral pants to go to a gay bar with a new friend he had made when Edith unleashed a barrage of sarcasm.

'You can't possibly go out wearing that, you look like one of those dreadful homosexuals,' she sneered.

'That's because I am one,' Timmy replied, walking out the room and slamming the door behind him.

'What did he say to me, how dare he?' Edith screamed. 'It's all your fault,' she said pointing at Audrey. 'You have spoilt him, turned him into a pansy. Send him into the army, they'll sort him out, make a man out of him.'

'Don't you dare talk about my Timmy like that, you're not fit to tie his shoelaces,' Audrey sobbed, running up to her bedroom.

Huw followed her and they sat huddled together on the bed. 'The sooner we get out of here the better,' he said, stroking her hair.

In fact, it was sooner than he expected because when Scrooge McKay dumped on the council syndicate to Forensic Auditor Sammy Benton and he named Huw as a 'person of interest' in the matter, the federal police swooped and Huw was summonsed to appear in the District Court for his part in the embezzlement of government funds.

When the court-appointed bailiff arrived on Edith's doorstep and served him with his notice to appear, much to the amusement of the neighbours who were watching through their upmarket timber blinds, his ma-in-law went ballistic and threw him out.

Timmy tried to intervene. 'You're just a stuck-up old cow. If he goes I go too,' he said, following him out the door. And Audrey, frightened of losing her darling son and terrified Timmy might prefer Huw to her, threw a look of pure hatred at her mum and went racing after them.

With all their money frozen by the Court, the family were stuck in a dingy hotel for a fortnight living on take-aways before Audrey, worried about Timmy's spots, decided to tap Uncle Claude for help. He arrived in his Rolls Royce Silver Cloud, packed them all in and took them home to his magnificent apartment on the harbour, where they settled comfortably.

A little too comfortable for Claude, who went white thinking that if Huw was put in the slammer, he would be stuck with Audrey and Timmy for possibly years. While he did have a soft spot for Timmy, the thought of Audrey living with him gave him the horrors and he immediately instructed a leading member of Sydney's legal fraternity, one Donald Trust QC.

Closeted with Huw in his palatial chambers close to Sydney's courts, the Queen's Counsel rested his head on his hand and kept one eye on the clock as he listened to his incoherent ramblings. The timer on his desk went off signalling two hours and several thousand dollars in fees so far as he gleaned from Huw that Audrey had driven him to cook the books.

'She was at it all the time,' Huw wailed. 'Wanted money for a sheep station, money for a BMW, money for a Swiss finishing school for Deidre, it was want, want, want. I can't even describe the pressure I was under, I couldn't sleep, couldn't eat (not that Audrey bothered to cook much she was always out) I was a nervous wreck. And my staff laughed at me behind my back,' he said breaking down and sobbing.

Donald Trust QC handed him a strong whisky and poured one for himself. 'I know what you mean, my bloody wife is just as bad,' he said sadly.

'Look, I think we can justifiably plead you did what you did because you were under tremendous pressure, which destroyed your reason to differentiate between right and wrong, or in layman's terms, you were off your head.'

Huw shook his head. 'Are you saying I'm nuts?' he asked crossly.

'Well I suppose if you want to put it that way, you could say that but if you want to avoid incarceration, the only option is to plead insanity,' he said. 'My wife drives me to drink, insanity sounds like a reasonable option to me.'

He wrote a telephone number on a piece of paper and handed it to Huw. 'Give this fellow a call, he will do the right thing and give us the report we need.'

Benny Epstein, the psychiatrist he recommended, was quite outrageously insane and fiendishly expensive. He sat beside Huw and listened to him for hours with such a caring look on his face (helped no doubt by reflecting on the massive bill he would send Uncle Claude) that Huw confessed everything from the time he pinched his sister's tuckshop money to his insider trading jaunt at the bank and his banishment to Damengin and finally his work with Shifty and the syndicate. 'I couldn't resist,' he said brokenly, 'I'm a crook and Aud always put so much pressure on me.'

Benny, who was driven mad by his wife to buy a holiday home at Noosa, was overwhelmed with sympathy and provided Donald Trust QC with a certificate stating that at the time of the felony, Huw was insane and not responsible for his actions. He included a massive bill to send on to Uncle Claude.

When Donald Trust QC presented the evidence to the Court stating that Huw was not in a fit state to face a trial, the Court agreed and he was returned to his family feeling much better and even optimistic about the future.

Unfortunately, Huw had to refund the money he had earned for his part in the syndicate and salted away in Audrey's name, which left the family broke. But Uncle Claude, as Chairman of the Bank, was able to persuade his fellow directors to allow Huw to receive his generous bank pension.

'Let's face it,' he told them, 'he has been certified insane and could quite easily sue the bank for compensation.'

Sick of having the family under his roof, Uncle Claude also gave Audrey a generous financial settlement to buy them a home and she found a comfortable unit close to Uncle Claude's with a glimpse of the harbour.

After they settled into their new home, Audrey decided to celebrate by having her hair done and a full beauty treatment at an upmarket salon and persuaded Timmy to come too. Poor Tim had been feeling lost since arriving in Sydney so

Audrey booked him in for blonde streaks and a leg wax to cheer him up.

Things went so well that by the time Audrey came to pay the hefty bill, Timmy was also booked in for dinner with Giorgio, the salon's owner, a gorgeous Italian with flashing black eyes. And dinner worked out so well that Timmy scored an apprenticeship and a new boyfriend.

One morning a few weeks later when Huw had left with a huge smile on his face for his weekly session with his psychiatrist Benny (the two had become great mates), Audrey decided to write Deidre a long letter and bring her up to date. In fact she was feeling a bit guilty as they hadn't been in touch since leaving the bank in such a hurry.

Not that she can't look after herself, she thought. But when the letter was finished and sealed there was a problem — where should she send it?

When Huw came home and she asked him, he looked at her in surprise and told her he had no idea where she was.

Audrey was very fed up that after writing such a long letter she couldn't post it. 'I'll ring Uncle Claude,' she told Huw, 'he'll know what to do.'

Claude was shocked when she asked him. 'Do you mean you have no idea where your only daughter is, or how she is surviving? Right, leave it with me,' he said curtly and hung up.

After he got off the phone, Claude had a brief conversation with Damengin Bank's teller who immediately started making enquiries on his behalf.

As is turned out, when Deidre returned from her ride on Knacker and found her dad's note on the kitchen table of the bank house telling her he had gone, she felt deserted by her family and had no idea where to go. She packed up her things and telephoned Teddy at Abington Station to ask if she could stay for a few days.

'Mum and Dad have gone, they've told me to get rid of Knacker and Rusty and left me money for my ticket to Sydney but I'd rather die first,' she said pitifully. 'Can I bed down in the shearer's quarters at your place for a few days until I can find some work?'

Teddy told her to stay as long as she liked. 'Dad's home and you don't need to stay in the quarters, stay in the house, there's plenty of room.'

But when she arrived at Redlands, Deidre was adamant that she would stay in the quarters.

'I don't want to be a burden,' she said. 'I like being by myself.' She was also embarrassed that the last time she had stayed in the house had been in his bed and they had spent the night bonking. And while her sex drive was usually well tuned, she just didn't fancy him anymore.

Teddy, who by this time was half in love with Phoebe and had invited her out for a meal that night, was also reluctant for a repeat and gave in. 'But you've got to come over here for your meals,' he said. 'I know what a bloody awful cook you are and Aunt Annabel's here looking after Dad and she's a fantastic cook.'

Deidre settled Rusty and her gear into the shearer's

quarters and sent a delighted Knacker out to run with the Abington horses. But she had no idea what she would do next or where she would go to get work. She had still got the cheque Huw had left for her and some money from her work at Rangoon but it wouldn't last long. She wandered over to the homestead at dusk for dinner and was surprised to find Phoebe sitting on the verandah with Teddy and Bomber.

'Come in and sit down next to me,' Bomber said, making a place for her next to him. 'Have you met the gorgeous Phoebe? She looked after me in hospital.'

Deidre smiled hello at Phoebe and sat down. 'You must have done a good job, Phoebe — he looks great,' she said. 'All better now?' she asked Bomber.

'Just about right and as soon as I get this arm out of plaster, I'll be dangerous. Ah here's Paddy,' he said as the ute drove into the yard. 'I'll just give Annabel a call and tell her he's here,' he said, going into the house.

Deidre raised an eyebrow and looked at Teddy. 'What's going on there?' she asked.

'Aha, love's old dream,' he said grinning. 'It all started when she left Shifty, true love or something like that. Watch out, here he comes.'

Paddy strode onto the verandah and stood looking around. 'Well who have we here?' he said smiling. 'It's Deidre, the shearer's favourite cook. How are you Dee, haven't seen you for ages,' he said bending down to give her a smacking kiss on the cheek. 'And how is the lovely Phoebe?' he said giving her a chaste peck.

'Teddy, working hard at last I hear,' he said shaking his hand.

At that moment Annabel arrived on the verandah looking very flushed.

'Bella,' Paddy said walking over and giving her a big hug, 'you look wonderful and something smells really good.'

Bomber walked over with a beer in his hand. 'Will you put my sister down,' he said smiling. 'Here, what's everyone having to drink, we've got iced beer, champagne or perhaps a gin and tonic. What will you have Phoebe?'

After drinks on the cool verandah Bomber led the way into the dining room where candles glowed softly lighting up the old cedar table which was decorated with beautiful lilac mats and moss green napkins. Old family silver gleamed complementing heavy crystal goblets and the fine china that had been brought over from England by Bomber's grandparents.

Annabel had enlisted Teddy's help to knock off two geriatric chooks and had turned them into a delicious chicken pie which she served with baked potatoes and green beans. There were moans of appreciation for her offering and even more compliments for the chocolate mousse dessert.

After dinner, they moved back to the verandah for coffee and Bomber brought out some seriously good port.

'That was a really great meal, Aunt Annabel,' Teddy said, sipping his port. 'Now, if it would only rain.'

Deidre sat back in her chair and looked out into the distance. *If only,* she thought, *I wonder how Angus is managing at Rangoon.* She longed to ring him but was still angry at the way his mum had spoken to her.

'Think I'll turn in now,' she said getting up and calling Rusty who was sitting in the kitchen hoping for scraps. 'Thanks for a top evening, I really enjoyed it.'

Paddy watched her go. 'Dee's very quiet, Teddy, anything upsetting her?

'Well you could say that, her old man's left town in a hurry without even saying goodbye, just left her a note, her mum cleared off and didn't even do that, can you blame her for being upset? As far as I'm concerned they both need shooting. Dee's worth ten of both of them. She doesn't want to leave the west but can't find work. If you hear of anything Paddy, give her a call.'

'Will do,' he said. 'Well I suppose I might as well head back to town.'

'Plenty of room here,' Bomber said. 'Annabel will make you up a bed won't you, Bella?'

Annabel blushed. 'Please stay Paddy, you've had a bit to drink.'

Paddy grinned. 'Sounds good to me. I'll give Rosie a ring first and let her know, she worries if I don't come home.'

Phoebe had been very quiet during dinner; the truth was she was overwhelmed with the magnificence of the homestead and the meal. It was a far cry from the dingy little housing commission flat she had called home and the sausages and chips they had regularly for tea.

How could she possibly fit in, she worried. With his

background, Teddy would want someone who could take all of this in their stride.

But Teddy, who had spent most of the meal trying to keep his eyes and hands off her, was totally unaware of her concerns. All he wanted to do was get her into bed as quickly as possible.

He moved closer to her on the verandah couch and whispered, 'I think I might have had too much to drink to take you home, Phoebe. Stay here and I'll drop you back early in the morning.'

Phoebe nodded, 'If it's not too much trouble.'

'No trouble at all.'

CHAPTER 29

LAMBS AND EWES

The day after the dinner party at Redlands, Paddy pulled up outside the Damengin Bank and walked into a blast of cold air. 'Whew, that's marvellous,' he said. 'Cash this will you, John?' he said, handing over a cheque to the teller.

'Certainly Paddy, how are things out at Paddylea?'

'Same as everywhere else I guess, dry. Thanks for that, John,' he said pocketing a wad of notes.

John leaned over the counter. 'Paddy, have you heard where Deidre Hawtrey is? I had her uncle on the phone a while back looking for her,' he said.

Paddy smiled. 'She's staying out at Redlands, bunking down in the shearer's quarters and looking for work, by the way, if you hear of any let her know. Gutsy person Dee, not like her bloody parents clearing out and leaving her to rot without so much as a word.'

As soon as Paddy left, John telephoned Uncle Claude with

the news.

'Good man,' he said, 'I'll get right onto it.' He telephoned Audrey and told her where Deidre was living and then sat down to consider what to do next.

For years he had watched Deidre change from an independent minded toddler to an obstinate teenager and become a strong free-thinking woman that he admired and liked. He always empathised with her love of animals and the land. Now Deidre was in strife and his heart went out to her. He was a wealthy man, he could give her a large financial settlement, after all, he had never married and she was his godchild but that wasn't Deidre. *No, he thought, I'll go out and see her, talk to her and find out what she wants to do with her life and then see what I can come up with.*

Deidre had just come back to the homestead after helping Teddy mark the new lambs and Bomber handed her a letter.

'Came this morning for you,' he said, watching her as she opened it. 'Come inside and have a cold drink, you look like you need one.'

Dee sat at the kitchen table and read the letter from her mum telling her all the news.

'It's from Mum,' she told Bomber. 'They've bought a unit at Double Bay and Timmy is working as an apprentice hairdresser for a top salon. And get this, they are all going to the gay Mardi Gras. Mum says Uncle Claude is coming to see me on the 29th, that's next week. I'll go over and pick him up. Anyway, she says he's going to ring me here. I wonder how they found out where I was?'

'Bush telegraph,' Bomber said smiling, 'it never fails. Well that's good news for you.'

Deidre was waiting on the tarmac for Claude when he arrived in Longreach and drove him back to Damengin where he had booked them both into the pub. That night after dinner he asked her what she intended to do with her life.

'I don't know, all I ever wanted was to work on the land but with the drought, there's no work anywhere. It's not much use going to ag college either because half the people are having to leave and there's no work at the end of it. I guess the only other job I could think of doing is engineering but I didn't get the marks to get into the course.'

Claude nodded. 'This drought won't last forever and when it's over everyone will be restocking and fertilising like mad. I believe there still is a future in agriculture, everyone needs food and clothing. What about if I set you up in an allied business — can you think of anything?'

'Well if I had some land and feed I could rear lambs and maybe save some ewes,' she said excitedly. 'There will be a market for breeders after the drought, most people are shooting their lambs because the ewes are too weak to rear them. If we could carry them through the drought, it would be an investment in the future. We would need plenty of grain and hay and milk powder and bottles. Once the drought breaks and people restock, there would be a profit at the end.

'I know Mary, Paddy's sister, is doing it out at Paddylea and I think Annabel was thinking about saving some of the lambs at Redlands but she's become too busy looking after Bomber. The truth of it is, she's running back and forth between town and home because there's an attraction here at the pub and it's not beer.'

Claude grinned, 'Are you referring to our good host Paddy?'

'That's the one,' Deidre said, winking.

'Any idea where we could buy or rent a suitable place?'

Deidre thought for a moment and then her face lit up. 'Sid Luxton's place, he's already destocked so it's empty. Fee Fluke used to live there but now she's living with Ben Bangor, I've been told they're madly in love,' she said laughing. 'It's amazing, two more different people you couldn't find, one greenie and one kangaroo shooter.

'If we could rent Sid's place, we could house them in the large shed and grow them out. Uncle Claude,' she said, her face bright with excitement, 'are you really serious? Would you help me do this?'

Claude looked at her. 'Deidre, I am disgusted with the way your parents have treated you and I'm also impressed with the way you have looked after yourself and never asked for anything. This is your chance to prove yourself and I will give you all the help you need.

'Come on we'll talk to Sid Luxton and see if we can come to an agreement.'

Sid, who was living at the pub, was more than keen to rent them the property. 'You can live in the homestead and use whatever you like,' he said handing over the keys. 'I won't be back there, me back's gone and I'll put it on the market when things pick up again.'

Claude and Deidre drove out and inspected the abandoned property and decided the large shed would be perfect for their plans. 'I'll give it a good clean and make some pens,' Deidre said, already planning where to attach calf feeding units and store the feed. 'There's still plenty of bore water coming into the shed tank but I'll mix the milk over at the house tank and then bail it out into jugs to pour into the feeding units. I can build another holding pen outside for when they grow.'

Claude nodded his approval and after a quick look at the homestead, which was in a dreadful state after the years of neglect, they went back to town and he arranged an account at Fitzgerald's Produce Store and Deidre handed over her order for the project. She was growing more and more excited about the project and enjoying Claude's company.

When he told her he had to get back to Sydney, she was visibly upset. 'I was hoping you could stay a bit longer and come to the sales with me,' she said.

'Not this time, this is to get you started buying lambs and for living expenses,' he said handing over a large cheque.

Deidre hugged him. 'This is more than enough, thanks Uncle Claude, and I won't need much to live on.'

'Yes you will, there'll be all sorts of things, now look after yourself and I'll be back up here to see you in a month or so. Have to keep an eye on my investment,' he said, winking at her.

Deidre dropped him at the Longreach airport and then

drove back to Sid's full of excitement and enthusiasm. Later that day Tom Fitzgerald arrived with a truckload of goods and she showed him the feeding shed.

'I'm off to the sheep sales next week to buy lambs and then it'll be full on,' she said. 'I can't believe my luck.'

The following Tuesday, Deidre and Rusty got up early and drove to the lamb sales at Longreach where hundreds of tiny lambs bleating pathetically were penned in groups of fifty.

Deidre began an inspection and picked out three pens of slightly older and sturdy looking lambs. She waited near the pens until the auctioneer made his way along the aisles to them and the lamb buyer from the local abattoir walked up. They were the only bidders and she picked them up for $200 a pen. Only the thought of feeding more stopped her from buying a lot more.

Afterwards, while she was standing at the tea stand to buy a cuppa and some corned beef sandwiches, she saw Angus arriving with a truck load of ewes and her heart stopped.

It was a bad day for Angus, with no relief in sight for the drought, he had decided to sell off 500 of his prize breeding ewes. The fodder deliveries by Paddy had helped but he knew that even if the drought did break soon, there would still not be enough feed to carry the rest of the flock through. The only solution was to cull the oldest and hope he could carry the young through.

After he had unloaded, he wandered around the pens looking at the huge numbers of sheep and then went into the office to sign some papers.

Deidre saw him unload the truck and went over to the sheep pens. She immediately recognised his breeders by their unusual fine wool. *How could he sell off his pedigree flock, surely things weren't that bad,* she thought to herself. She had almost decided to go over and talk to him when she saw him get into his truck and drive off.

The truth was, he couldn't stick around and watch the pride of Rangoon be sold for mutton.

Deidre stayed until the ewes went under the hammer and bought them for less than she paid for the lambs. She couldn't lose, she reasoned. Although they were a bit poor, they would pick up after some good food and with all the fodder Uncle Claude had bought, she could easily carry them through the next six months when many of them would lamb, giving her a bonus. Then she could perhaps buy some rams and breed from them.

On his way back to Rangoon Angus decided to call in to see how Ben Bangor was going and found him in a quandary.

Although things had picked up since the fodder drops had started, he still didn't have an income and couldn't make any payments to the bank.

'I don't want to go back to culling roos because I know how much it upsets Fee but Paddy doesn't have any work driving and I don't have any income,' he told Angus.

'Fee's got nothing and has gone into town to pick up the mail. Out of the blue, she had a letter from her parents, she hadn't heard cooee from them for years. They've moved to a retirement village in Queensland and wanted to hear how she was. Anyway, she wrote back and told them how things were with the drought and asked if she could borrow some money.

'Come back to the house and we'll have a beer, it's hot as hell out here.'

They were sitting on the verandah commiserating with each other over a few beers when Fee drove in with a huge smile on her face.

She almost ran up the front steps to Ben and threw her arms around his neck. 'Guess what,' she said. 'We're rich, look at this,' she said waving a wad of notes at him.

'I got a letter from Mum and Dad and they said they had been putting money into an account for me since I left school, and there was a trust they set up when I was born. I never got the advice the bank sent because they didn't know where to contact me.

'I went to the bank and there was thousands and thousands just sitting there. We're rich. I paid off your mortgage and overdraft and there's a big order coming from Fitzgerald's and I've bought champagne. And,' she said looking at him shyly, 'there's something else. When I got to the bank I felt something move in here,' she said pointing to her tummy. 'I popped in to see Dr Davis and I'm pregnant.'

Ben was so overwhelmed he couldn't speak, tears were coursing down his cheeks. 'I thought you were getting a bit fatter,' he choked. 'This is wonderful,' he said hugging her and smothering her face with kisses.

Angus decided it was time to leave and got up. 'Absolutely

great, I'm stoked for both of you,' he said. 'Got to go, sheep waiting.'

'No stay, help us celebrate,' Ben said grabbing his arm. 'Share our luck.'

But Angus was feeling too depressed. It was going to take him a long time to get over the sale of his ewes and after listening to Fee's good news he was furious with his parents who refused all his appeals for help.

'They've got more money than God tied up in assets and investment,' he raved to himself as he drove along and away from Rangoon. 'For years they've bled the place dry and now it's haemorrhaging and needs a transfusion they won't lift a finger to help.

'To hell with them, I'll get through and when things improve there'll be no way they'll tell me how to run the show or lob up with their bloody friends in tow and expect to be entertained. Those days are long gone.'

As he drove along he got even angrier remembering the way his mum had treated Deidre. 'She was the best thing to ever happen to me and Mum ruined it, bloody ruined it,' he shouted, banging his fist on the wheel.

Late that same afternoon, the carter arrived at Sid's place with the lambs and sheep and unloaded them into the newly constructed holding paddock. After he left, Deidre and Rusty moved the ewes out into the home paddock and distributed a large stack of feed for them. Then she moved the madly bleating lambs into the pens inside the shed. While she had waited for them to arrive she had filled the feeding units that were attached to the pens with milk. But it was a nightmare trying to get the frantically hungry lambs to suck.

'Get your silly little mouth around that teat,' she said, shoving a protesting lamb onto the feeder.

Almost dead on her feet, she finally crashed and she woke up to Rusty licking her face and wondered where she was, until she realised she had fallen asleep in one of the pens.

All around her lambs were bleating frantically for food and she staggered out to the tank and began making up bottles again. By the time she had finished she was gasping for a drink and realised she hadn't eaten since the corn beef sandwiches the day before. She walked over to the homestead, made herself some tea and ate one of the cold sausage rolls she had bought at the sheep sale the day before.

'Lucky we're not fussy, Rusty,' she said, sharing one of the congealed bits with him. 'Tonight we'll cook a few chops or something I promise. Come on back to the pens.'

Deidre had never been happier. Knacker was in the paddock outside and whinnied whenever he caught sight of her, she adored feeding the tiny lambs and got a kick out of seeing the ewes with enough to eat.

Each day she worked to a routine of feeding the lambs, cleaning their pens, distributing feed to the ewes, checking their water and building new pens. And by the time she had done her jobs she was whacked and much too tired to cook. 'It's only fuel,' she told Rusty sharing a tin of cold baked beans with him.

Before he left, Claude had made sure the place was well

provisioned. Although the fridge in the kitchen was ancient it still worked in a fashion and he had stocked it with a variety of food and there was plenty of tinned food in the pantry.

Dee was generally too tired to make anything and dined out on stale bread and peanut butter. Rusty dined well on the chops and steak she couldn't be bothered cooking.

At night she slept exhausted, cocooned in her sleeping bag in a small room at the front of the house with Rusty snoring beside her.

Down in Sydney after a blistering attack from Uncle Claude about their treatment of Deidre, Audrey and Huw Hawtrey were feeling rather ashamed of themselves.

Claude told them he had set Deidre up in the lamb rearing industry and was going to make her the beneficiary of his will. Audrey was devastated. 'What about Timmy?' she asked him.

'I haven't forgotten Timmy and I will happily help him when he needs help. Timmy has enjoyed every advantage while you have all but ignored Deidre, now it is her turn and she is my goddaughter,' he said firmly.

CHAPTER 30

CITY COUNTRY MEET

Back in Damengin, truckloads of hay and grain were arriving almost daily from the city, and Paddy, who had distributed what remained of the drought relief money, was busy ringing graziers to pick up food, and when he had time, dropping off fodder to people.

The biggest problem facing the small community now was water, or lack of it. While the properties and stations were still able to tap into the Great Artesian Basin using windmills to lift the water into tanks, the town itself was in dire straits relying wholly on a muddy water hole, all that remained of its reservoir.

House tanks had dried up months ago and now the town's only water supply was trucked each week from Longreach, 200 km away.

Paddy walked into the pub kitchen where Annabel was sitting at the kitchen table talking to Rosie. 'Just spoke to

Jeff Parks over at Longreach and he said their reservoir is dropping at a fast rate. We'll be in a bloody awful mess if Longreach dries up.'

Rosie shook her head. 'I've put signs in the bathrooms, two-minute showers and no flushing for peeing.'

'That's a bit rough isn't it,' Annabel said, laughing at her.

'Well I could have told the blokes to pee out the back but I know you do anyway,' she said, nodding at Paddy.

'Better than using our valuable water and anyway it's watering the trees,' he said wryly.

'Bella, I'm off to deliver a truckload of food out past Paddylea, want to come with me and we can call in on Mary and Billy on the way back?'

Annabel, who had abandoned Bomber to Teddy's care (do him good to look after his dad for a change, she told Rosie) had been spending most of her time at the pub with Paddy. Anyway, she thought, after all those wasted years with that bastard Shifty, to hell with it, Paddy was addictive. He knew how to treat a woman and just looking at him made her weak at the knees.

As soon as it rained she intended to move back into her once magnificent home, now sadly dehydrated with taps that discharged dust, and drag Paddy in with her. Shifty had stupidly put the house in her name to avoid paying tax and it was the only thing she had salvaged from his dastardly deeds.

'Buggar this bloody drought, give a man an ulcer,' Paddy said as they drove along the western road.

Annabel reached over and grabbed his large rough hand. 'You know if it wasn't for this 'bloody' drought, we wouldn't be together so we can't be too 'bloody' about it,' she said, smiling up at him. 'Shifty would still be stuffing Dolly and I would be stuck without a man to love.'

Paddy turned to look at her. 'Do you love me, Bella?' he asked with a twinkle in his eyes. 'And here's me thinking it's just lust you felt for me.'

'Lust is lovely,' she said moving her hand to his crotch which stirred it into life, 'but yes I do love you as well when I think about it.'

'Well in that case I suppose I better make an honest woman of you. How about it? Will you marry me?' he said, looking at her quizzically.

Annabel stared at him. 'Paddy, are you serious?' she asked.

The truck veered off the road and skidded to a halt in a drain terrifying a passing car whose driver was temporarily blinded by flying gravel.

Paddy leaned over and pulled her towards him. 'Bella, I love you, will you marry me,' he asked kissing her. 'I was crazy about you thirty years ago and then you up and left town and while I cooled my heels waiting for you, what did you do but come back married to that loser,' he said nuzzling her neck. 'Now we're going to make up for lost time.'

After dropping off several loads of hay and grain at properties to the west, they arrived at Paddylea late in the afternoon and shared their news with Mary and Billy.

'That's fantastic, Dad,' Billy said pumping his hand. 'Aunt

Mary and I wondered about you two, you were becoming a bit obvious.'

'What do you mean,' Paddy said feigning annoyance, 'our behaviour was exemplary.'

'Oh get over yourself,' Mary said, hugging them both.

'Come on, Annabel, let's go and visit the lambs and leave these two to themselves,' she said.

'I've got over 200 now and most of them are thriving,' she said proudly leading the way to the shed. 'I've got the feeding down to a fine art, Billy helps me with the mixing and carrying and then it's just a matter of filling up the feeding units. They're all such greedy little things, they shove and hustle one another and I have to watch out that the weak ones get a feed.'

Billy had just finished marking some lambs and Paddy followed him to the yards to help him tidy up.

'Things going okay with Mary?' Paddy asked quietly.

'She's a changed person,' Teddy said shaking his head. 'You wouldn't believe the difference in her. Gets up each morning and does the feeds, plays the piano, reads, not much of a cook but tries hard. I'd kill for a beer but I haven't dared bring one to the house in case she has a relapse.'

'No, don't risk it yet, not until she proves she can resist. She's had a terrible time but I think in a few more weeks she'll be more stable, anyway we'll take it little by little.'

Annabel cooked tea that night, a delicious shepherd's pie made from some cold mutton and topped with cheese. After baked custard and some tinned fruit, they sat at the kitchen table talking and drinking tea.

'I don't know what this region would have done without the help we are getting from down south,' Paddy said quietly. 'If we really think about it, we owe them our survival.'

'If it ever rains, we should do something to show our appreciation,' Annabel suggested. 'Perhaps have a big party, invite them to the town for a celebration?'

Mary stood up and began clearing the table. 'I'm off to bed, have to get up to my babies in the morning — are you two staying?'

Paddy looked at Annabel. 'What do you say, stay here for the night?'

Annabel nodded. 'I'm tired too, and it's been an exciting day,' she said her eyes sparkling. 'Not every day I get a marriage proposal.'

Paddy and Annabel were lying entwined in his big bed replete after making love when a flash of lightning lit up the room.

'Another of those bloody lightning storms, all wind and no piss,' Paddy said cushioning her head in his shoulder.

Suddenly there was a huge bang and a gust of wind rushed through the French windows. Paddy got up to close them and then called Annabel to him. 'Listen,' he said, 'hear that?'

Annabel held her breath and heard a tiny patter on the old tin roof. 'Is that rain or just dust,' she asked. They both stood like statues listening, their ears strained. Again there was a tiny patter and then — nothing. 'That's it, just another sparrow fart,' Paddy said ruefully. 'Come on back to bed.'

'Listen,' Annabel said. Then they both heard it, a steady patter on the roof followed by a rush of wind. They walked onto the verandah and looked out into the black night. A gentle patter of rain was coming down sending up wisps of dust as it hit the ground.

'I think it's getting heavier,' Annabel whispered.

'Shush,' Paddy said, holding his finger up, 'don't put the mockers on it.'

A bolt of lightning ricocheted in the distance lighting up the sky and revealing black angry clouds. A loud crash of thunder exploded from the sky, there was a great roar and down came the rain.

It fell from the sky in huge sheets, hammering the old tin roof and flooding the gutters. The noise was deafening.

Paddy stood with his arm around Annabel watching as the heavy curtain of rain hit the hard dusty ground creating rivulets of mud and water spouts.

It was too much for Paddy and he rushed outside.

'You bloody beauty,' he yelled with his arms outstretched. 'You absolute bloody beauty.'

Annabel wrapped herself in a bath towel and stood watching him with tears running down her cheeks.

Billy came and joined her on the verandah and put his arms around her. And Mary, who had heard the bang and dived under the sheets terrified, heard the shouts and joined them.

They hugged one another shouting and laughing and watched fascinated as the rain continued.

It rained all night and was still pouring down the next morning when they gathered in the kitchen.

'Just checked the rain gauge and we've had 200 ml so far, that's ten inches on the old scale,' Billy said, shaking his wet raincoat out and hanging it on the verandah. 'If this keeps up we're set, the house dam is already running over and the paddocks are a quagmire.'

'Doesn't take much to fill that buggar,' Paddy said. 'After breakfast we'll go out to the creek and see if she's running again. I'll give Bomber a ring and see how they're going at Redlands.'

Bomber reported 250 ml and said he'd been talking to Abington and Rangoon stations and they'd received the same.

'Looks like the rains have finally got here,' he said jubilantly, 'and thank Christ for that.'

'Got some other news for you mate, another celebration,' Paddy said. 'I asked your sister to marry me yesterday, she told me to piss off at first but I finally persuaded her.'

Annabel stood shaking her head at him with a big smile on her face.

'That's bloody marvellous, put her on,' Bomber said.

'Congratulations, Bella, couldn't think of a better excuse for a party. I'll give you the wedding you should have had the first time, biggest in the district.'

Paddy and Billy went to check the sheep and Annabel threw some chops on the range to cook for breakfast. Mary had gone to see to the lambs and returned an hour later soaked through.

'It's still pouring down and there's leaks everywhere in the lambing shed,' she said laughing. 'The poor little lambs don't know what's happening to them.'

Annabel poured her a cup of tea. 'It's just so wonderful, now we can make plans.'

'I was thinking about what we said last night about thanking the people who donated fodder,' Mary said. 'What about we resurrect the Damengin Picnics and hold a ball that night at the showgrounds, it would be like the old days.'

'What a fabulous idea. I think I'm still chair of the Ball committee although we haven't held one for years and Paddy is president of the Picnic Races. We'll see what everyone else thinks and if they agree.'

Over at Abington Station, which was built on a ridge overlooking the Abington River, Ben Bangor was standing looking down at the rapidly rising waters. If it kept raining, he would have to move what was left of his sheep to higher ground. At least he had that option unlike Sid Luxton next door, whose property was downstream and copped the brunt of any flooding right up to the home paddocks.

Which reminded him, Deidre was living there, and he'd better go over and warn her to keep an eye on the rising waters.

But Deidre was well aware of the flooding danger. She had been up all night splashing around fixing leaks and had trudged through the mud to the river bank. She had watched the rain come down, saturating the parched ground until it could take no more.

Now she was watching as a tiny trickle of water dribbled

its way along the dry dusty gulley that was all that remained of the Abington River. It was gobbling up the soil as it went and the tiny trickle was becoming stronger and faster. The mud was becoming a puddle and the puddle a pool, the trickle became a flow and the pool became a river ever widening until it reached the edge of the bank. As she watched fascinated, the water ran faster and then changed into a powerful torrent that rushed frantically between riverbanks dislodging small trees and obstacles in its path.

Deidre looked on, thrilled and excited to be part of it all.

As she trudged back to the homestead through the torrential rain, Rusty raced ahead of her jumping and splashing in puddles, snuffling his head deep in the water and then running round in circles.

'Come on you crazy mutt,' she said laughing at him. 'Let's give these hungry lambs some tucker.'

She fed the lambs and went back into the rain. Opening her arms, she put her head back and let the rain wash her face.

It had all been worthwhile, she thought to herself. In a matter of days, green fuzz would push its way through the mud and then tiny fingers of green would appear waiting for the first rays of the sun.

Finally, in only a blink of time, there would once again be those beautiful waving fields of Mitchell Grass as far as the eye could see.

Deidre was suddenly overwhelmed with sadness and began to weep realising that the lamb rearing would be finished. What would she do next?

Over at Rangoon, Angus had been out all night moving his flocks to higher ground and he returned to the homestead soaked and wondering how Deidre was getting on. He had telephoned the bank house but there was no reply and he didn't know where else to contact her.

'Ben Bangor telephoned,' Charlie said, pouring him a cup of tea.

'What did he want,' Angus said, shaking his wet coat out.

'I dunno, you ring.'

Ben told him they had 250 ml of rain the night before and another 100 that morning.

'It's fantastic,' he said. 'I've just moved the ewes to higher ground. Went over to warn Deidre about the river rising but she already knew.'

'What do you mean, where is Dee?' Angus asked impatiently.

'She's at Sid's place, been renting it from him and rearing lambs, she buys them at the markets and has set up a feeding unit. Her mum's uncle lent her the money or something.'

'Have you got her number?' Angus asked. 'I'll give her a ring.'

'Sorry mate, she hasn't got the phone on, that's why I went over.'

Angus hung up the phone and decided to drive over to see her. But by the time he got to the first gate about a kilometre from the homestead, the creek was over the road. He drove slowly through the water until it came up to his window and then reversed. It was hopeless, he couldn't get out. He drove back to the homestead and almost wept. Buggar, buggar, buggar. He knew it could be days before the rain stopped enough for the creek that flowed into the Abington River to drop. And until it did, he couldn't get to see or speak to Dee.

'I never thought I'd wish for the rain to stop,' he groaned, 'but I do now.'

All around the district properties were cut off, creeks burst their banks and flooded roads and crossings. The Abington River that had been a dust bowl for years was almost a kilometre wide and powering downstream taking anything in its way along with it. Roofs sprung leaks and mould covered walls and furniture with veils of grey. At night, sleep was impossible because of the loud croaking of frogs frolicking deliriously in drainpipes and sheep staggered drunkenly under coats weighed down with rain.

The heavy rain continued for days drenching the parched land as far west as the border, roads were cut, properties isolated but no one complained. Planes dropping off fresh food and medical supplies flew across an inland sea covering thousands of hectares.

Finally after fifteen days, the rain stopped and life began in earnest. Council graders worked nonstop to get the roads open and graziers repaired fences washed away by the floods.

Within two days, the raging torrent that had been the Abington River, which had cut off the town, had dropped below the bridge allowing access to the town again. Trucks delivered fresh supplies and most importantly, beer, to the pub.

CHAPTER 31

DAMENGIN RACES

Determined to get back to town before they were flooded in, Paddy and Annabel left Paddylea early the next morning with rain still bucketing down. Mary and Billy waved them off with huge smiles on their faces and for good reason. Tanks were spilling over; the house dam had overflowed and was pouring over the spillway and the once dry gulley below had turned into a raging torrent and was hell bent on forging a wide path down to the already swollen creek.

Driving carefully along the lane which was already knee deep in mud, Paddy stopped and got out of the ute to gauge the depth of water flowing over the timber bridge at the property's entrance.

'I think we'll just make it' he called to Annabel, getting back into the cabin dripping wet.

Slipping the ute into low gear he drove steadily through

water that was almost up to the windows and which poured in through the doors sloshing around on the floor and soaking their feet. They reached the main road and just made it across the One Mile Bridge before it went under. This meant the road west to Longreach was cut and the only way out was south, if the bridge at Findon was still open.

Rain was still pelting down when they drove into town where the main street resembled a river. The Shire's council chambers were already an island but fortunately when the town fathers had planned the town they'd had the foresight to raise the plots above the level of the 1905 flood and only a few sheds and barns were affected. The good news was the town dam was already half full of water, house tanks were brimming over and the local swimming pool had its first taste of water for years.

Everyone was celebrating and the Damengin Pub was full of people when Paddy and Annabel walked in.

'What's the news out there?' Sid Luxton called out loudly, competing with the rain pelting down on the pub's old tin roof.

'All good,' Paddy yelled back smiling. 'Roads are cut, creeks are flooded, the river's rising but it's all bloody good stuff. Drinks on me, Annie fill em up,' he said walking over to the bar and accepting a drink.

'Here's to the rain,' he shouted, downing his beer and putting the empty glass on the counter.

He put his arm around Annabel and gave her a hug, 'No matter what happens now, we'll be okay. In a couple of months there'll be grass so high you won't be able to walk through it.'

'Yep,' said Sid, gazing out through the curtain of rain. 'It'll be good times from now on and about bloody time.'

'Well Paddy, I hear we're getting a new bank manager,' Sid said. 'Hope he's an improvement on the last one.'

'Fellow by the name of Roberts, Rosie says he's due here next week, going to stay in the pub for a couple of nights until his stuff arrives.'

'Way things are going, he won't get across the Findon. They'll have to fly him in.'

'How are things out at your place?' Annabel asked Sid.

'Deidre Hawtrey's out there on her own, she rented the place from me to rear lambs.'

'Will she be alright?' Annabel asked, looking concerned.

'Well there's no phone but Ben called over to see her and he says she's happy as a pig in mud. You don't have to worry about Dee, she's a tough bird.'

'She'll make someone a good wife, should line her up with Billy,' Sid said, winking at Annabel.

'Not his type,' Paddy said dismissively. 'More Teddy Reed's.'

'Ah if I'm not mistaken I think he has his eye on a little nurse at the hospital,' Sid said. 'His car's been doing the circuit from Redlands to the nurses' quarters fairly regularly, got to be something attracting him.

'Any rate,' he said finishing his beer, 'unless it whinnied or barked I don't think Dee would be interested.'

Paddy laughed. 'Well the next big event will be a

celebration. Bella and I are getting married and as soon as this rain stops we'll start making plans.'

'Congratulations,' Sid said leaning over to shake Paddy's hand and giving Annabel a peck on the cheek. 'That's something I will look forward to. Are you having it at Redlands?' he asked Annabel.

'It's too early to make plans yet. Paddy has forgotten that I have to get the divorce done and dusted but we are thinking of organising something to show our appreciation to the city people who supported us during the drought.'

'That's a great idea,' Sid said. 'What are you thinking about?

'Maybe resurrecting the Picnic Races and having a ball,' Annabel said.

Paddy nodded. 'That's something we can start planning to coincide with the Easter public holiday. We could make it a four-day weekend with the Races on Saturday afternoon and ball that night. That means people could have Friday to travel out here and Sunday to recover before leaving on Monday. We could charter a few buses and put up tents in the showgrounds. We'd need to know how many would be interested.'

'We'll get a committee organised, Mary wants to help and I'll ask Chloe Mattens to do the publicity, she's a great operator,' Annabel said excitedly.

As soon as the rains stopped out at Rangoon, Angus couldn't wait to head over to Sid's place and see if Deidre was alright. He had been depressed and worried about her and wanted to apologise for what his mother had said.

'Bloody old cow, treating Dee that way,' he said to himself.

Deidre was the only girl he had ever been interested in. Sure he'd had a few girlfriends, mostly those he had met at ag school and he'd enjoyed some pretty hectic sex with many of them. But they were nothing compared with Dee. He enjoyed every minute spent in her company.

When they were working together, she instinctively knew what he wanted, whether it was fixing a broken pump or straining a fence. In bed, he adored her deep sexy chuckles and her body was a joy, strong, energetic and sensationally responsive. Just thinking about her drove him crazy and he ached with longing for her.

Deidre was trudging in mud, repairing the fence around the paddock closest to the river that had been washed away with the flood. Rusty had become addicted to water and was having a wonderful time diving and splashing in the rising waters and neither of them heard Angus' ute when it drove into the homestead.

He poked his head through the open front door and knocked. When no one came he went over to the shed to look for Dee's red ute. Finding it gone he followed the muddy tyre tracks until he found her.

'Gidday Dee,' he called getting out of his ute and walking towards her. 'You okay? How did the flood treat you?'

Deidre looked up in surprise and walked towards him. 'Pretty good, thanks mate, how did you know I was here?'

'I was talking to Sid and he told me. I wish you had let me know. I was frantic when you ran off. I've been looking for you everywhere since that night my mum was so foul. Dee,' he said taking her arm. 'I'm really sorry for the way Mum behaved. If you want to know I told her to clear out and she did. She had no right to speak to you like that. You shouldn't have run off, I didn't know where you'd gone and I've been worried sick about you.'

Deidre looked at him in amazement. 'I didn't know anyone was looking for me, certainly my parents didn't give a hoot. Anyway, it was all so bloody embarrassing, Angus, and I just wanted to get away. Look, you don't have to be sorry, I know it wasn't your fault. And, well I guess your mum got a shock finding us together like that,' she said with a grin. 'I know my mum would have had heart failure.'

Angus turned her towards him and took her hands in his. 'Dee,' he said looking into her eyes, 'I honestly don't care what my parents think of you. Will you come back with me to Rangoon? I really enjoyed having you there, we worked well together. The truth is, I miss you,' he said shyly.

Deidre turned away and bent down to pick up her fencing pliers. 'I don't know, Angus. When I left your place and found my parents had left, I was in a real mess and didn't know what to do, it was one hell of a shock. Then I had a visit from my Uncle Claude, would you believe, he was the only one who bothered to come looking for me. Anyway, he actually asked me what I wanted to do and offered to help me and I got the idea of buying orphan lambs and rearing them so he bankrolled me.

'We rented Sid's place and got me set up and I'm really enjoying it and now that the rains have come, I should be able to sell them for a good price and maybe move on to something else. It's my one chance of being independent because there's nothing out there for me. I only want to live on and work on the land, that's it.'

Angus sighed, he knew that financially he was still in such a mess and that he couldn't really afford to offer her anything. And he was put off by the fact that she really seemed to be content and happy without him. Seeing her again made him want to grab her and take her away with him. Just looking at her was agony, he wanted to tell her he loved her (yes, he really did, he admitted to himself in surprise) and how he longed to have her with him, especially in his bed.

Deidre waited for his reply. She knew she was hugely attracted to him but she also knew his parents didn't approve of her and there was no future for her at Rangoon.

'Angus, I don't want to seem ungrateful and I'm really touched that you came looking for me but I want to have something of my own and this is my big chance. Uncle Claude has leased Sid's place for a couple of years to give me a start and if things work out, he says he will look at buying me something.'

'I see,' Angus said quietly. 'Well perhaps I can come and visit, take you out sometime,' he suggested tentatively.

'Sure, I'll look forward to that,' she said, shoving her fencing plyers in her jeans.

'Right, well I'd better leave you to get on with it,' he said turning to walk back to his ute.

Deidre couldn't believe how miserable she felt as he drove away. 'There goes the only man I will ever care for,' she told

Rusty sadly.

Over at Redlands, Teddy and Bomber had been out repairing fences and had just come in for smoko when Annabel telephoned.

'I want to let you know we've slotted the Easter long weekend next month for the big celebration party,' she said. 'We'll need to get organised and I've called a meeting tomorrow night at the pub, Paddy as President of the Picnic Race Committee will chair it but I want you there, Bomber, Teddy too if he's interested.'

'Fine we'll be there, what time, 7 pm? Righto.'

Bomber turned to Teddy. 'Bella's organising a big party to say thanks to the city people, wants us both there tomorrow, okay?'

'Sure Dad, I'll see if I can get Phoebe to come along, maybe Maggie too,' he said, watching Bomber go red.

Annabel put down the phone at the pub. 'I've got Bomber and Teddy coming and Ben and Fee, can you believe the difference in her, then there's Mary and Billy, Maisie and Chloe of course and Sid and Sam Spink, Tom Fitzgerald and the new bank manager — what's his name, Roberts, isn't it?'

'Yes, John Roberts, seems a nice sort of a fellow, and what about Dickey Davis and Maggie?'

'Right I'll give them a ring, we'll need all the help we can get. Can you ask Rosie to organise some food and drinks for later?'

At 7 pm the next night the group assembled in the large saloon behind the main bar of the pub and Paddy stood up to welcome them.

'Right everyone, thanks for coming. I think we all know why we're here, it's to say thank you to those generous-hearted people who helped us during the drought. Bella has suggested that we hold a race meeting on Easter Saturday with a ball that night and invite everyone who had anything to do with the flood relief to come. What does everyone think of that idea?'

'Sounds good to me,' said Bomber. 'I think everyone here agrees with the proposal so I say, let's get on with it.

'Paddy, how about you continue as chair and Bella as secretary, I'll take on race organiser, Teddy can help me and I suggest Chloe does the publicity. Maisie, how about you organise the food with help from Mary and a few others, and Maggie, could you help with first aid for the races.'

'Sure, Bomber,' Maggie said smiling at him. 'I'll get the rest of the staff to give a hand and I'll organise a few volunteers for the first aid station.'

By the time the meeting ended everyone was full of enthusiasm and it was full steam ahead for the celebrations. Chloe went back to Sam's and fired off press releases to media outlets, Sam contacted some racing mates in Sydney who promised horses and bookies and Otto, bursting with leftovers from the pub, snored happily at his feet.

During the next few weeks there was a frenzy of activity leading up to the celebrations with plenty of hot tongues and cold shoulders. Maisie and Mary were not speaking to each other, something about a cake decoration; Chloe was devastated because she had been hoping Billy would ask her to the ball but he didn't; Bella was sick of Millicent Wilton-Smith (who had dropped in unexpectantly after hearing about the party from a friend) and was determined to take over, and Dr Dickey Davis refused to help with the First Aid station when he heard that Maggie had agreed to act as Bomber's hostess at the pre-ball party at Redlands. Phoebe was depressed because Teddy hadn't invited her to the ball and Angus was furious because his parents had flown in.

'Now they're here, I can't ask Deidre back after the ball,' he said furiously.

Deidre meanwhile was fed up because Angus hadn't bothered to ask her to the races or the ball and decided she'd take off for the day instead.

The sun shone brightly on Easter Friday heralding the start of the Big Bush Bash at Damengin and the road into town was jammed with buses and cars arriving for the weekend. The showground had been turned into a tent city with a large army-style kitchen and dozens of cold boxes for beer and wine. The remains of the council work force had dug dozens of long drop toilets on the perimeter of the grounds but when Paddy saw the crowds of people he roared off to Longreach and returned with a truckload of porta-loos.

Bomber, Teddy and a group of mates were helping people pitch tents and Billy and Tom Fitzgerald were organising the car and bus parking.

By 5 pm everyone was settled in, barbecues were lit and people were sitting or standing around enjoying a beer or just talking.

'It's really beautiful out here,' a pretty looking girl said, sipping her drink and looking out over the lush green to the horizon.

'You should have seen it a few months ago,' a local told her. 'It was just a desert.'

Someone strummed a guitar and a group gathered round for a sing-a-long. Children clutched sausages and parents tucked into huge steaks provided by the grateful graziers.

Paddy and Bella wandered around chatting to the visitors and seeing that everyone was fed and comfortably settled.

'Just look at the place, Bella,' Paddy said turning her round to face the west. 'Just a few weeks ago and it was bone dry desert, and now, it's hard to believe.'

'It's amazing how such a terrible event like the drought can bring out the best in people,' Annabel said linking arms with him as they walked along.

'Or the worst,' Paddy said.

'I wonder where Shifty is now.'

'God knows. But never fear, I'll find him if it's the last thing I do and make him pay for his rotten tricks.'

Annabel shrugged. 'The thing that worries me is that unless we can find him, I can't divorce him.'

'Yes you can, it may take a bit longer but you can get him on desertion. Now stop worrying,' he said putting his arm around her, 'we'll sort it out. In the meantime you'll just have to continue to live in sin with me.'

'Sounds like fun,' she said giggling.

CHAPTER 32

THEY'RE OFF AND RACING

Damengin Race Course was bursting at the seams as hundreds of people descended on it for the inaugural Damengin Cup sponsored by an anonymous donor to the tune of $50,000. And with the temperature hitting thirty and rising, people desperate for anything to quench their thirst were queuing ten-deep at the makeshift bar that ran along the side of the grandstand.

Paddy was frantically ferrying kegs over from the pub and the bar-workers were frazzled, dashing here and there, pouring drinks and squashing fights as people pushed and shoved in the long lines. Cash tins filled over and the dirt floor was a sea of mud from the spills.

'They'll all be plastered by the time the races start,' Annie the barmaid from the pub said to Sid, who was tapping one of the kegs Paddy had just dropped off. 'Soon as I get this bastard plugged, I'll be joining em,' Sid said, struggling with

349

a keg. 'If I don't get a drink soon I'll kark it.'

'Here, get this down you,' Annie said, handing him a stubby.

Over in the stalls thoroughbred horses shook their heads and stamped impatiently at the strappers who brushed and plaited manes and tails. Next door in the jockey's changing room the old adage 'small bloke big dick' was proven when jockeys stripped naked to struggle into skin-tight jodhpurs and colours.

Owners stood around whispering and watching, waiting for the call up.

Sam Spink's call to arms to his Sydney racing mates and the prize money of a hefty $50,000 had worked a treat. The racing fraternity had taken the bait and rolled up with some of their best stayers for the race and the few bookies who made the long trip west had huge smiles on their faces as they spotted the size of the crowds.

Sam, who was closeted with several owners in the press box enjoying a quiet beer, was in his element. An avid punter and lover of horse flesh, he was also a talented spruiker and looked forward to calling the races, telling everyone the freshly raked sand track would be fast and favour the sprinters.

Life-giving rains had transformed the former paddock of dirt into a carpet of lush green and even the grandstand had been given a bright green facelift.

'Bit over the top,' Bomber had grumbled to the groundsman and insisted he slap plenty of white on the railings.

Autumn sunshine blazed down and people gathered under the shady awnings and tents set up around the perimeter of the course. Country and city collided in a cacophony of sound, drinking, laughing, gossiping and arguing, but the question everyone asked was 'who's gonna take out the bloody Damengin Cup?'

The Race Committee had arranged prizes for the best dressed lady, the best hat and the best couple. These were to be judged by Millicent Wilton-Smith who, after getting a tip-off on the grazier's grapevine about the races, had dragged Malcolm off the Gold Coast golf course and told him to fly her straight to Rangoon.

She arrived back two weeks before the races, swanned into the Race Committee's final meeting and snatched Fashions on the Field from Maisie Matten by offering to donate the first prize, an all-expenses trip to the Gold Coast.

Maisie, who had been lumbered with the job by Annabel, had arrived at the meeting wearing one of Chloe's disgracefully short shirts and a skimpy top because everything else was in the wash.

Millicent looked her up and down and said, 'Let's face it darling, your style is more nightclub than vogue.'

Maisie went bright red and would have given Millicent a mouthful of abuse if Mary Murphy hadn't distracted her by wailing she had nothing to wear.

Instead she shrugged, and told Millicent she was welcome to the bloody job. Anyway she'd been working her arse off at the shop and was stuffed.

'I'm much too busy for that sort of crap,' she said, turning her back on a red-faced Millicent. 'Now, for God's sake Mary, stop complaining, I'll drive you to bloody Longreach and get you a frock.'

True to her word she took Mary shopping and talked her into a smart black and white dress teamed with a matching straw hat with a large red poppy at the front.

'There you are Mary,' she said twirling her round. 'You're a knockout.'

Mary blinked at herself in the mirror and went pink. 'Well,' she said, 'it is a nice frock.'

'You look lovely, all the fellows will be chasing you,' Maisie said, grabbing her arm. 'Now come on I'm going to get something for myself.'

Mary turned round. 'Maisie, I just want to thank you for everything, you and darling Chloe have been so kind to me,' she said, blinking back tears. 'I haven't been this happy for years.'

'Come on, don't be silly,' Maisie said slipping her arm through Mary's. 'Let's see what we can find for me.'

Maisie bought herself a pretty pale blue and white floral silk dress with matching blue shoes and a pretty daisy covered cloche hat. 'Let's see what that old cow Millicent thinks about this classy little number,' she said winking at Mary. 'I'll give her "night clubby"'.

'Now let's find something for Chloe. She's been working so hard, she deserves something nice.' Maisie found a slinky khaki dress that buttoned up the front and had a wide plaited yellow belt and Mary insisted on buying her a madly expense dinky miniature Stetson to wear with it.

Chloe was over the moon when she tried it on and offered to do Mary's hair and face for the races.

'There you are,' she said dabbing some Eau de Lancôme behind Mary's ears. 'You look a million dollars.'

The three friends had driven to the racetrack together and paraded around the course chatting to all and sundry and showing off their finery. 'What a laugh if one of us wins Fashions of the Field,' Chloe giggled.

'Not a chance with that bitch in charge,' Maisie said, looking around the course.

'Look there's Billy Murphy,' Chloe said waving. 'Come on, let's see what the gossip is.'

Billy Murphy almost dropped the keg of beer he was carrying to the bar when he saw them.

'Wow, don't you all look gorgeous. Just look at you, Aunt Mary, you're beautiful.'

Mary blushed. 'Thank you, Billy — Maisie and Chloe are so clever they gave me a going over.'

'You mean makeover, Mary love,' Maisie said laughing.

'Well you look great, all of you,' Bill said. 'Chloe, you've really scrubbed up well, all grown up,' Billy said, winking at her.

'I am seventeen you know, not a kid,' she said grumpily.

Billy laughed. 'Are you going to the ball tonight?'

'Course I am, wouldn't miss it.'

'Well save me a dance,' he said lifting the keg onto his shoulder and disappearing behind the bar ...

Ben and Fee drove into the course and parked their car under the shade of an ancient fig tree close to the finishing post. They had cleverly brought their own chairs and Fee had packed a picnic. She was wearing a long loose-fitting dress of crimson paisley cotton that she had made herself and a wide-brimmed straw hat decorated with ribbons.

Fee's now short black hair fell in soft curls around her face accentuating her huge brown eyes and sensual mouth. Ben thought she had never looked more beautiful and he settled her comfortably with a cold drink and went off to have a bet.

He arrived back carrying a stubby, accompanied by Maggie Spink and Phoebe, who had been parading in their new frocks and hats hoping to catch the judge's eye but didn't attract so much as a glance from her.

'She's not going to choose us,' Maggie said flopping down next to Fee. 'It'll be some la-de-dah type from the city so we might as well relax and enjoy ourselves. Yes, I'll have a glass of champers,' she said taking the glass Ben was offering her.

'Fee, you are looking, dare I say, blooming — pregnancy giving you any trouble?'

Fee's eyes sparkled and she patted her round tummy. 'No, not at bit, I still can't believe it.'

Ben bent down and stroked her head lovingly. 'As soon as we can arrange it we're getting married. Fee wants to see if her parents can come, they're in a retirement village and we're going to see them next week. My parents are over the moon, Dad had given up on me producing anything except sheep and Mum's desperate for another grandchild.'

Phoebe sat down next to Ben and sipped her champagne slowly. Her eyes kept darting around scanning the crowds. She hadn't seen or heard from Teddy for weeks and was worried he might have gone off her. Egged on by Joyce and Vi she had spent a small fortune on a lilac and cream gown for the ball that night and was terrified she'd wasted her money.

Back at Rangoon, Angus Wilton-Smith had been pissed off when his parents had flown in for the race meeting because he knew if Deidre saw his mum she would give him a wide berth.

He had decided not to go and was in his office sorting out his lambing book when Charlie yelled that Teddy wanted him on the phone.

'Morning mate, how are things?' Angus asked.

'Look Angus, I don't know what your plans are but we desperately need another steward. Old George has fallen down the steps and hurt his back, can you give us a hand?'

Angus sighed, the last thing he wanted was to parade around in a red jacket. 'I've got a few things on here,' he said. 'Can't you get someone else?'

'Everyone's working, it's for a good cause mate, but I don't have to tell you that.'

'Sorry Teddy, of course I'll come, how could I not? See you in an hour?'

When he drove into the racetrack just over an hour later he kept his eyes skinned looking for Deidre, hoping she would be there.

But Deidre had gone for a ride on Knacker early that

morning and decided not to go to the races even if Angus asked her, which he hadn't.

On the way home from her ride to the river, she was hot and thirsty and called in at Abington, where Fee and Ben were just about to leave.

'Come with us,' they begged. 'Go home and we'll wait for you, save you driving in by yourself.'

'No, you go on don't wait, but I'll think about it,' she said jumping on to Knacker's back. 'Thanks for the drink.'

When she got home, she gave Knacker a rub down, released him in the paddock and then fed the lambs. They were almost ready to be put out to pasture and had grown into sturdy little things. She walked back to the homestead, sat down on the verandah and suddenly huge waves of loneliness washed over her.

'Buggar it,' she said standing up, 'I'll go to the races and if Angus is there, so what, I'll just be myself.'

By the time Deidre had showered and washed her hair it was almost midday and the awful truth hit her, she had nothing to wear.

'At least bloody Cinderella had a rag frock,' she moaned, scrabbling through the bags she had taken from the bank house. She pulled out a clean pair of jeans, found a shirt that wasn't too crushed and rubbed a cloth over her best boots before putting them on.

'Right Rusty, that will have to do,' she said, ramming her Akubra hat on her head and roaring off.

Deidre arrived at the course and had just got out of the car when the loudspeakers announced, 'Mayor Bomber Reed will welcome everyone before the start of the first race.'

Bomber stood on the podium and beamed out at the crowds.

'Welcome everyone to the Damengin Picnic Races,' he said.

'Today on behalf of the people of Damengin and district I want to thank all our city cousins for helping us so magnificently during our recent drought.'

'You answered a call for help, you gave unstintingly and without your generosity many properties would have gone to the wall and hundreds of livestock would have been shot or died of starvation.

'This district owes you a huge debt of gratitude and we offer you our hands in friendship and tell you that you will always be welcome here at Damengin,' he said, his voice cracking.

'Hear, hear,' someone shouted and people began to cheer and clap.

Paddy stepped onto the podium and called for quiet.

'I want to say that I support everything the mayor has said and I also want to thank the anonymous person who donated the generous prize money for the winner of the Damengin Cup. Now I think we can start the races, what do you reckon?' he asked.

Deidre parked her car and wandered over to the course to see if she could spot Fee and Ben and bumped into Tom Fitzgerald, who was talking to Chloe Mattens.

'Hi Dee, how are things with the lambs?' Tom asked.

'Great now that it's rained. You look nice Chloe, new frock?'

Chloe grinned. 'Mum bought it and Mary bought the hat, she's hoping I'll win the Fashions on the Field but with Millicent Wilton-Smith judging not much chance.'

Deidre frowned. So that was why Angus hadn't telephoned.

'Have you seen Fee and Ben?' she asked.

'Sure, they're over by the finishing post, next to the Red Cross tent.'

Deidre waved her thanks and made her way through the crowds feeling like a frump. Why hadn't she made more of an effort, there were clothes in some of the bags she had rescued from the bank house that her mum had bought for her to go to Switzerland. She wished she'd worn something nice.

'Over here,' Ben called, when he spotted Deidre through the crowds.

Deidre waved and made her way over to them just before Sam announced the start of the main race, the Damengin Cup.

'Glad to see you got here,' Ben said, offering her a seat and a drink.

'Thanks Ben,' she said accepting a beer. 'It was a bit of a rush. I think I'll stand at the rail, see more.'

She could just see Angus and Teddy looking gorgeous in their red Stewards jackets over at the starting gates helping jockeys settle nervous mounts and pushing obstinate horses behind the barrier gates. Race favourite, a massive chestnut four-year old stallion named Claude with a dozen wins to his name, was tipped to win. Up against him were several first-class country winners and a few untried novices brought on for a run.

The bugle sounded, Paddy fired the starting gun and they were off.

Down the straight they charged with a flurry of hooves and a tangle of horses, riders shouting and jostling for positions. Yelling crowds cheered them on as they surged round the first bend still in a tight pack. Coming into the straight, the solid mass started to spread out and a leader's pack of nine spearheaded the charge leading into the second bend. Around they went, then suddenly there was a roar from the crowd as from way back at the rear, a small bitsy grey mare moved like lightning, sprinting ahead eating up runners on her way. Finally she made it to the front five but big Claude's jockey saw her out of the corner of his eyes and moved sideways to block her on the rails, but the feisty little mare dodged and darted wide. They powered down the course fast and hard and by the time they moved into the final stretch there were only two far in front leading the pack. The crowd were on their feet cheering as they watched the David and Goliath contest between a gutsy grey and the giant chestnut. Neck and neck they raced, jockeys crouched low, arms like pistons plying the crop. The flag was in sight and the pair were still battling it out the chestnut charged to the front, the crowd went wild willing the mare on. Her jockey dropped low on her neck seemingly begging her for more and the gutsy mare seemed to sprout wings and flew past to win by a nose.

The crowd went ballistic, people hugged one another, cheered and waved. On the rails, close to the winners' circle, the mare's owner, Col Ryan, who ran a small cattle property west of Longreach, was speechless with shock.

His hands were shaking as he accepted the cup from Bomber.

'She's the best bloody mare in Australia,' he said, tears coursing down his cheeks. 'A real little champion with a heart as big as a bloody house.'

After the presentation, the crowd wandered off to the front of the grandstand to check out the Fashions on the Field, which were being judged by Millicent Wilton-Smith.

By this time, there were few fashionable ladies to choose from as most had ditched their heels, stashed their hats and were slurping champers out of paper cups and tottering around clutching each other.

'Who gives a rat's anyway?' Maisie said sitting down to watch proceedings under a shady tree. She poured herself a champagne from a bottle she had bought, was about to offer one to Mary and stopped just in time

'Sorry Mary darl, didn't mean to tempt you,' she said, putting the bottle down.

'S'okay Maisie, you didn't tempt me,' she said, attempting to smile. 'I learnt my lesson well.'

Poor Mary, who was sick of being plied with drinks and was fighting a heroic battle to stay sober, was relieved to see Billy walk up.

'Need a hand anywhere?' she asked.

Billy, who knew the battles his aunt had been having staying off the grog, twigged immediately.

'Sure do, come with me Aunt Mary,' he said taking her hand and dragging her away. 'They're desperate for another pair of hands in the food tent.'

On her own Maisie leaned back against the tree, kicked off her shoes and thought about Simon 'Scrooge' McKay. He would probably end up in jail over his part in the council debacle, she thought. But he had always been nice to her and she missed his company.

'Not much pickings in town,' she mused to herself, taking another slug of her drink.

'You're the lady who owns the 4 Square in town,' a rather nice voice said. 'John Roberts, I've just taken over the bank in town, and can I join you?'

Maisie looked up at the rather attractive middle-aged man smiling down at her and was impressed.

'Sure you can,' Maisie said smiling offering her hand. 'I'm Maisie Matten, won't you join me?'

At that moment the loudspeakers blared that the winner of the Fashions of the Field was about to be announced. Lined up on the stage, preening and posing, were the ladies chosen by Millicent's spotters (mostly her snooty friends from the city), who had wandered among the crowd choosing the most 'fashionably attired'.

Wearing a simple cream suit with a wide-brimmed black hat, Millicent mounted the podium as regally as her killer heels would allow to announce the winner.

Flashing a brilliant smile at the cameraman from the *Country Chronicle*, she tapped the microphone and coughed.

'Ladies and Gentlemen, honoured guests, choosing the winner of this year's Fashions of the Field was an extremely difficult task,' she said frowning to emphasise just how awful the job was. 'And after much deliberation I have finally chosen Valerie Vanders (a filthy rich old crony of hers from the city) who is wearing a delightful little Chanel suit bought at this season's Paris collections.'

'The only place that suit would be suitable is at a bloody funeral,' some old fart in the audience yelled out, and the crowd dissolved into laughter.

Just then Chloe Mattens sauntered past looking outrageously sexy and stunning in her new khaki frock and dinky hat.

'Wowie, look at that,' the old fart cried out. 'Now there's a bloody good-looking outfit, good onya Chloe, she's the one should've won,' he yelled and the crowd cheered their support.

'Philistines,' Millicent muttered and, throwing them a filthy look, stumbled down the steps of the podium in her rush to leave. She went in search of Malcolm and found him drinking with Teddy and Angus at the member's bar.

Angus had been told by Teddy that Deidre was miserable he hadn't asked her to the ball. How could he, he thought to himself, when his bloody parents had arrived and his mum had snatched the arrangements from Annabel. He knew if he had asked her, it would all end in tears.

To hell with them, he thought, *I'm sick of them ruining my life.*

He sat at the bar simmering with rage and hardly spoke to his mum. He kept looking around in the hope of seeing Dee and when he spotted her by the grandstand talking to Col Ryan, the owner of the grey mare, he quickly downed his beer got up and left.

'Was it something I said?' his mum said sarcastically to his back.

'Dee,' he called out, striding towards her, 'I've been hoping to catch up with you.'

Deidre stood still and waited until he stopped.

'How are you and are you going to the ball tonight?' he asked.

'Haven't been asked.'

'Please come with me,' he said. 'I'm sorry I didn't ring earlier, it's a long story but my folks arrived, curse them, and I've been flat out.

'I'll pick you up if you like, say around 7 pm?' he pleaded.

Deidre smiled. 'That sounds okay, well I better get home and find something to wear.'

'You'll look great in anything,' Angus said wistfully, watching her go and thinking how lovely she had looked in nothing at all.

THE BALL

Deidre arrived home thrilled at the prospect of going to the ball with Angus. She rushed through her chores sloshing milk into the feeders for the lambs and measuring out grain for the breeders she had bought at the recent sales.

Back at the house, she fed Rusty and headed for the showers.

'Buggar,' she said dabbing soap on her leg to stem the blood pouring from a razor cut. 'Have to be more careful,' she said lathering herself under her arms. 'Tonight could be the night, Rusty, need to be fuzz free and squeaky clean.'

Rusty who was sitting on the bathmat watching her put his head on the side as if to say, 'go girl'.

Shampooed and scoured she stepped from the shower and rubbed herself vigorously with the towel. She slathered some body lotion over herself and put a band-aid on her leg, which refused to stop bleeding.

'Now,' she said to Rusty, who had followed her into the bedroom and was lying sprawled across her bed. 'What will we wear, let's see what we can find.'

She dragged out the bags she had rescued from the bank house and started throwing clothes everywhere.

'Ye Gods, Mum went to town with these,' she said, throwing an armful of clothes on the bed just missing Rusty, who lifted his head and gave her a sour look. She held up a long pale green silk organza frothy thing. 'Look like the fairy on the Christmas tree in this,' she said pulling it over her head.

But when she put it on she gasped. The silk cascaded downwards from tiny shoulder straps to caress the lovely curve of her breast before sliding down her hips and flowing joyfully over gorgeous long legs to just skim the floor. As it went, it radiated a soft glow that lit up her face and bathed her bare skin with colour.

'Wow,' she said looking at herself in the mirror. 'This should do the trick.' Digging through another bag she found a pair of silver sandals and a matching purse.

'I'm Cinderella and I'm off to the ball,' she said fluffing her still wet hair up and searching in the bag for a brush.

Angus was busy in the shed when his parents arrived home from the races and by the time he got back to the homestead he could hear them talking in their room getting ready for the ball. There was no way in hell he was going to tell them he was taking Deidre. He showered and dressed in a flash and called out to them he was off before they could ask him any questions.

Deidre was standing on the front verandah waiting for him when he arrived and he was so shocked to see her all tarted up he was lost for words.

'Where's my knockabout farm worker?' he quipped, walking up and planting a smacking kiss on her mouth.

'Watch it, I've spent hours slapping this stuff on,' she said pushing him away.

Angus laughed. 'Let me have a look at you,' he said, turning her around. 'Yes, your mum and mine would be very surprised to see the new Miss Hawtrey going to the ball.'

Dee grinned at him. 'It's so not me but what the hell,' she said, twirling round in front of him.

Angus laughed with her. 'Well, it's not your usual gear but it is really nice, honestly,' he said.

'You look pretty good yourself, young fellow,' she said taking in the tall dark and very handsome escort looking stunning in his formal dinner suit.

'Come on then, let's go,' she said taking his arm. 'Let's give em heaps.'

One hell of a racket was coming from the Damengin Hall when they entered the car park.

'Christ almighty,' Deidre shouted, 'listen to that.'

'Whaddya say, I can't hear a thing,' Angus yelled.

The Whacky Whacko County Bumpkins were having a ball, lead singer Rex Egmolise was blasting out country and western favourites at a thousand decibels and what looked like the entire population of Damengin and half of Queensland were singing and bopping along with him.

Angus tried to push their way through the crowd to the bar but was forced back by the crush of people.

'To hell with this, come on, let's go through the back to the kitchen, there's got to be some grog somewhere,' he said, leading the way to the supper room at the back of the hall where they found the bastions of the committee putting the finishing touches to a huge supper.

Deidre shook her head. 'Waste of time, come with me to the car park, there's bound to be some smart arse with grog in their car.'

Sure enough they found Teddy and Tom Fitzgerald guarding a cache of beer in the boot of Tom's car surrounded by a group of dedicated drinkers.

'Spare us a drink mate,' Angus asked, walking over.

'Bloody hell,' Teddy said throwing his arms out wide. 'It's our Dee looking like Miss Australia. Where did you get that dress?'

Deidre grinned. 'What about you, you're looking bloody good tonight, and where did you find that getup?'

'Now shut up Teddy,' she said taking a beer off him. 'Or you might get this over you instead of into you. How's your old man?'

'Last I saw the old buggar, he and Maggie were livening the punch up with a few bottles of vodka, should really sort out the wowsers.'

Deidre laughed. 'Better go back inside later and watch the fun.'

'How are things out at Rangoon?' Teddy asked Angus.

'Fine, who did you come with?' he asked, worried that Teddy might latch on to Deidre.

'No one — thought I'd come and check out the talent.'

'Thought you were sweet on that little nurse?'

Teddy shrugged. 'She was coming on a bit strong, thought I'd lay off for a bit.'

Pity, Teddy thought to himself, she was bloody fantastic in the cot but he was scared shitless of commitment. Last time they were in the cot together she was sloshed and told him about her terrible family, two crims of brothers both in the slammer. Christ what a life she'd had. Then again, at least she and the eldest brother had lifted themselves out of the mire and done something with their lives.

When he thought about it, he felt desperately sorry for her and he wanted her like hell. Not only was she gorgeous to look at, but she was also sweet-natured and his old man was besotted with her, said she was a wonderful nurse.

At the races when he was doing his stint as a steward, Teddy had carefully avoided contact with her so that he wouldn't have to ask her to the ball. Phoebe, who had spotted him, had been devastated that he hadn't bothered to speak to her and collapsed in floods of tears when she got home. Her fans Joyce and Vi didn't know how to comfort her. 'We all love ya, darl, all the patients even old Jacob in Ward 3 and he hates everyone,' Flo said, stroking her heaving frame.

'But Teddy doesn't care about me,' she sobbed. 'I haven't seen or heard from him since that night at Redlands. I've stuffed it,' she moaned, 'I stupidly told him about my family and my rotten brothers and now he thinks I'm not good enough for him. It's not my fault they're so foul, if you could choose your family, I'd put mine at the bottom of the list,' she said, sobbing as if her heart would break. 'And I've spent a fortune on my new dress, all my wages and now he's gone off me,' she wailed. 'Wonder if I can take it back?'

'Don't be silly,' Vi said stroking her heaving back. 'I don't think Teddy Reed is the sort of person who cares about where you come from, it's what you are is the important thing.'

'Look lovie,' she said, shaking Phoebe gently, 'get dressed, go to the ball and knock him dead, that's what I'd do.'

'Yes love,' Joyce said nodding agreement. 'Play hard to get, he'll come running back, he won't want anyone else moving in on his girl.'

'That's the trouble,' Phoebe sobbed, 'I'm not his girl.'

'Now come on darl, dry your eyes. You bought that lovely frock especially. Pop in the shower and we will help you get dressed.'

Still sobbing Phoebe shuffled off down the hall to the shower and Joyce and Vi began sorting out her clothes.

There was a knock on the door and Matron Maggie walked in.

'Just thought I'd come and see what Phoebe is wearing tonight,' she said. 'Where is she?'

'Gone to the shower, the poor love is heartbroken,' Flo said. 'It's that Teddy Reed, he's let her down, didn't even ask her to the ball and ignored her at the races.'

'No, that's awful of Teddy, the poor thing,' Maggie said

shaking her head. 'Look I've got an idea, don't say anything to her and leave it with me.'

Maggie went back to her room and telephoned Bomber.

'How would you like to take two of the best-looking birds in the district to the ball?' Maggie asked.

Bomber laughed into the phone. 'Good grief Maggie, I don't know if I could cope with two of you but then again, I'd have every buck in the district green with envy,' Bomber said. 'Who's the other stunner?'

'It's Phoebe, she's been let down by your rotten son and the poor girl's devastated.'

'Right, I'll fix the bastard,' Bomber said angrily. 'How dare he treat that lovely little nurse like that!'

'No way, don't say anything to him, we'll sort him out. Leave it to me.'

Bomber, looking mayoral and majestic in his black tie and dinner suit, entered the Damengin Hall with his partners and every red-blooded male in the hall turned to gaze in wonder at the enchantingly lovely Phoebe in a slim fitting black dress that emphasised her fragility and with her blonde hair cascading over her shoulders. When Rex called the next dance, the trio was almost flattened by the rush of males wanting to dance with her.

'Wow, look at that,' Chloe complained bitterly to her girlfriend Sal, 'Phoebe's got every eligible bachelor in the district after her.'

'What are you whingeing about?' Billy Murphy whispered into her ear as he turned her to face him. 'How about that dance you promised me?'

Chloe grinned and grabbed his arm. 'What's the matter, did you miss your chance with the beautiful nurse?' she sneered.

'Oh keep quiet and just be grateful I'm rescuing you from the wallflowers,' Billy said, pulling her onto the dance floor.

Teddy, who had spent several hours getting tanked up in the car park, wandered into the hall to check the talent and saw Phoebe being whirled around the dance floor looking like a dream. He leaned against the wall and watched, getting increasingly agitated as her escort, a cattle grower he knew from further west, crushed her to him brushing her hair with kisses and whispering in her ear.

Finally, Teddy cracked. It was just too much, and he strode over and cut in.

'Excuse me, this one is mine,' he said to her partner.

'Like hell, this is my dance,' he said, pulling Phoebe towards him.

'I told you, buggar off, she's my girlfriend,' Teddy said, pushing the other fellow away.

Crash, a hard left landed on Teddy's chin and he fell to the floor.

Phoebe screamed and bent over him.

'Fight, fight,' someone called, and the floor was crowded with excited blokes raring to go.

Bomber spotted the trouble and pushed his way through the crowd. 'Right, you, Teddy get up and get out. There'll be no fighting in here. You've had a skinful, get outside, and don't even think of driving your car. And before you go, you can apologise.'

Teddy got up stroking his chin. He suddenly grinned. 'Sorry mate,' he said offering his hand. 'Got a bit stirred up. Sorry Phoebe,' he said, walking towards the door with Bomber.

Bomber escorted him out of the hall and helped him into the back of his ute. 'You stay there and sober up, I'll take you home later. I don't know what you think you were doing, first you treat the girl like dirt and then you embarrass her. Everyone loves her, she's an angel. You don't bloody deserve her.'

Teddy slipped into alcoholic stupor and Bomber went back to the dance. Maggie had shepherded Phoebe into the kitchen and was giving her a drink.

'Once everything has settled down, we'll take you home,' Bomber said, really pissed off. He was fond of Phoebe, who had looked after him while he was in hospital, but he had been looking forward to getting Maggie in the cot after the ball and now all his plans were stuffed.

Millicent and Malcolm Wilton-Smith arrived at the ball too late to see the fight but just in time to see their beloved Angus with his arms around Deidre Hawtrey laughing at something she had said.

'He might have told us he was taking that girl to the ball. We give him the best of everything, and he ends up with the dregs of society,' she said huffily. 'And he hasn't got the decency to tell us he's taking her.'

Malcolm sighed. 'Well after your reaction last time you saw her, why would he?'

'You don't think he's serious do you?'

'Very serious and you better get used to it if you don't want to lose him,' Malcolm said sharply. 'We're going over to speak to them and try to be pleasant.'

But as they were approaching, supper was called and Deidre went off to help.

'Want a hand?' Deidre called out to Mary, who was juggling trays of food and dishes between the kitchen and supper room.

'Could you,' Mary said gratefully. 'Here take these and put them out on the far table, and could you get some more hot water?'

While Dee was helping, Millicent cornered Angus, who was leaning against the wall eating a sausage roll.

'We saw you dancing with that Hawtrey girl, are you serious about her?' she asked bossily.

Angus stared at her, his lips in a grim line. 'If you really want to know, I'm bloody serious. In fact I'd marry her tomorrow if I could but I've nothing to offer her.'

Millicent glared at him. 'What do you mean, you've got the finest property in the district.'

'That's all you know,' Angus said.

Malcolm, who had stood back reluctant to get involved, pricked up his ears. 'What do you mean? Things are fine now, the drought's over,' he said.

'For Christ's sake, Dad, where have you been hiding yourself, the drought may be over but it's taken one hell of a toll on us. I had to sell off my breeders and there's bloody nothing to restock with, the bastards at the bank won't give me a cent, and it'll take me years, if ever, to get the place back to what it was.'

Malcolm looked at him in horror. 'What are you talking about, you didn't say.'

'Yes I did, I told you and told you but you didn't want to know, too busy sodding off to the Gold Coast. Anyway, this isn't the time or place.'

Millicent was shocked at the thought of losing Rangoon and while Deidre wasn't the type of girl she wanted for her son, she didn't want to lose him.

'There is no way your father and I will allow anything to happen to Rangoon,' she said. 'We will discuss this later.'

'Look son, perhaps I've been too hard on Deidre, if you really care for her, then I'm happy for you,' she said, going over and giving him a kiss on the cheek.

'You were wrong, Mum, she's one in a million,' he said, overwhelmed with relief.

After supper, Deidre saw Angus having what seemed like a deep and meaningful talk with his parents and hoped it wasn't about her. She knew his mum couldn't stand her and the feeling, if she was honest, was mutual.

What the hell, she decided, she'd go over and join them. After all, Angus did ask her to the ball.

'Lovely dress dear, did your mother choose it for you?' Millicent said, giving her a peck on the cheek.

'Yes, it's not really my style,' Dee said, smiling through gritted teeth.

'Well, I think you look lovely,' Malcolm said kindly. 'I hear you have been a great help to Angus at Rangoon.'

Deidre smiled. 'It's a beautiful place, I really enjoy working there.'

'Come on Dee, let's dance,' Angus said steering her away. 'Let's get out of this place, it's hellish crowded and I've just about had enough, how about you?'

Deidre nodded. 'Yes, let's go, there's a few beers in the fridge at home, it's a lot quieter and more comfortable.'

When they got back to Sid's, they sat on the verandah drinking stubbies and watching the stars twinkle in the dark blue sky.

'Come to bed with me?' Angus asked pulled her to him. 'I've really missed you, Dee,' he said dropping soft kisses on her face.

'Me too,' Dee said nuzzling into his neck.

'Dee, I haven't much to offer you, in fact pretty much nothing, but when things get better, would you marry me?'

'Are you serious, Angus Wilton-Smith?' she asked, looking at him with a huge grin on her face.

'Bloody oath I'm serious. Will you?'

Deidre laughed, 'Of course I will — I thought you'd never ask. But what about your folks, they're not going to be pleased.'

'Buggar them, it's my life and I want you and only you. Now come to bed, you're on a promise and a bloody big one.'

'I hope you've got a big one?'

'That's one thing you can count on,' he said pulling

her towards him. 'Now do as you're told and get into that bedroom before I take you here on the floor.'

'You wouldn't dare,' Deidre said, pulling away from him.

'Don't push your luck,' he said, marching her into the bedroom.

The next morning, exhausted from a hectic night of sex, they were woken by Rusty's furious barking and watched as Teddy drove into the yard.

'Anyone there?' he called out and then spotting Angus's ute stepped gingerly onto the verandah and poked his head around the door.

'I hope I haven't interrupted anything,' he said to Deidre who was coming towards him wrapped in a towel.

'No, we were just getting up, put the kettle on and we'll be with you in a sec, what's the problem?'

'Tell you in a minute,' Teddy said, walking into the kitchen.

Angus got dressed and Dee had a quick shower and joined them at the kitchen table where Teddy had poured three mugs of tea.

'Got a problem,' he said mournfully. 'Dad's ropable with me, Phoebe's not speaking to me, Maggie's furious and I'm in a bloody mess.'

Deidre laughed. 'Well I have to say it's your own fault. You did pick a fight, you were drunk, you treated poor Phoebe like dirt, that about sums it up. What did you expect?'

'I know, but what do I bloody do, how do I sort things out.'

Angus shook his head. 'Got no idea, but the first thing I'd do is apologise to everyone.'

'I did it last night.'

'Yes, but were you sober? I don't think so. Maybe you need to start again and send Phoebe some flowers or something.'

'Hey that's a great idea. I tried ringing but she won't come to the phone and those two old tarts Joyce and Vi are bloody savage at me.'

'Well I suppose they're fed up with the way you've been treating her. Can't really blame them. Anyway, are you messing around with her or serious?'

'I was having cold feet, she told me she wanted to settle down, have kids and I freaked. Then when I saw that fellow all over her like a bloody rash, something cracked and I couldn't stand it. Made me realise that I do want her, I'm mad about her. Now the irony is she doesn't want me.'

'Look write her a note, tell her you're sorry, go round there, keep trying. I know she was really keen on you, Maggie told me.'

Teddy finished his tea and got up. 'Ah well I'll go and see what I can do, get some flowers and go round again, I can only try,' he said. 'Thanks for the advice.'

After he'd gone, Angus took Dee's hands. 'I think it's time I asked your dad for his daughter's hand in marriage.'

'You're not going through that old fashioned stuff are you?' she said, with a grin.

'I most certainly am, have to do this properly.'

Down in Sydney Huw Hawtrey was just sitting down to breakfast in the sunroom of his new luxurious town house with Audrey when Angus rang with his important question.

Huw's eyes lit up and he smiled. 'You have my permission and my congratulations,' he said. 'I couldn't think of a better person for a son-in-law.'

'What's that?' Audrey asked, shaking him impatiently.

'It's Angus, he wants to marry Deidre,' Huw said, holding the phone away.

'Oh my God,' Audrey shrieked. 'Angus Wilton-Smith, that's wonderful, give me the phone. Oh Angus, we are so happy,' she gushed. 'Is Deidre there?'

'Hi Mum,' Deidre yelled down the phone, 'isn't it exciting, better get yourself a new frock.'

Audrey was so excited she could hardly breathe. Her dreams had come true, Deidre was marrying into the landed gentry and she, as mother of the bride, could hardly wait. She would tap Deidre's doting godfather Uncle Claude to help with the finances and organise the most spectacular wedding the district had ever known.

When Angus told his parents, they sounded relieved and Millicent even sounded excited.

'We'll have a magnificent wedding here at Rangoon, I'll handle everything, just leave it to me,' she said.

'Mum will help,' Dee said interrupting, 'She loves organising things like that.'

That night Angus and Deidre clung together, legs and bodies entwined, and discussed their future.

'It will take years to get the place back to what it was,' Angus said. 'The first thing we have to do is go and flush out some good breeders and rams.'

'Well, there's a funny thing' Deidre smiled up at him. 'If you are extra nice to me, I could set you up with several hundred prime breeding ewes from one of the best fine wool properties in the west,' she said, tracing the lines of his face with her finger. 'Fellow had to cull them and I picked them up for a song.'

Angus looked at her in amazement. 'Did you buy my ewes, you canny little thing?' he asked, shaking her. 'Well I'm going to reward you for that, and it could take all night.'

Teddy, meanwhile, was carving a track between Redlands and the Damengin Hospital and his florist bill was into three figures as he battled to win back Phoebe.

Maggie was sick to death of him ringing the hospital and Vi and Joyce were at last feeling sorry for him.

'Give in, Phoebe,' Vi begged her, but Phoebe was still feeling mortified. 'I can't bear to see him. I know he is ashamed of me because of my family and it'll never work. I'm going to leave and go back to the city.'

When Maggie heard the news she decided enough was enough and telephoned Teddy.

'If you want to get her back, I'll tell you what to do,' she said.

That night Teddy arrived at the hospital and Maggie led him through to the nurse's quarters where Phoebe was watching television.

'Got a visitor,' she said.

Teddy walked in behind her carrying a bunch of red roses and a bottle of champagne.

'I've come to ask you a question and I'm not leaving here

until you answer it,' he said going down on one knee in front of her.

'Phoebe, I'm sorry I'm such a shit and I promise to never do anything to embarrass you again if you will marry me,' he said, offering her a small velvet box.

Phoebe looked at him in astonishment.

'Phoebe, stop looking at me like that and say something,' Teddy said impatiently. 'Will you marry me?'

Phoebe took a deep breath and said softly, 'Do you love me?'

'For crying out loud, I'm not kneeling here like a fool asking you to marry me if I don't love you — of course I love you, I'm mad about you, now will you marry me and that's the third time I've asked.'

'Third time lucky,' she said smiling, 'and yes, I will marry you.'

The entire district turned out for the Hawtrey-Wilton-Smith nuptials which were held in July in the grounds of Rangoon. Millicent and Audrey had spent the preceding weeks screaming at each other about everything from the choice of menus to the number of guests.

Dee and Angus were sick of the fights and threatened to elope if the pair didn't stop fighting and they finally called a truce a week before the wedding.

Under a canopy of white gardenias the couple promised to love, honour and cherish each other (Deidre struck out the obey bit) and a riotous party that included almost the entire district followed.

During the cutting of the magnificent three tier cake, a blooming Fee Fluke was rushed to hospital and delivered of a healthy baby boy by Maggie and Phoebe. Ben was beside himself with joy and Sid Luxton was so thrilled when Ben told him they'd decided to call the lad Sidney Aaron, that he choked on his false teeth and sent them flying.

A feast of weddings followed with Bella and Paddy leading the charge. Bella, as it turned out, didn't need to get a divorce to marry Paddy because Shifty Grey hadn't bothered to divorce his first wife who was still living in New Zealand and had been looking for him for years.

Next was Teddy, who was so keen to tie Phoebe down, that he booked the priest for the week after Deidre and Angus and the newlyweds raced back from their honeymoon to attend. Her brother the judge gave her away and Phoebe had never looked lovelier.

The rains kept coming and the town had the wettest August on record, dams were spilling over, creeks were running and the river had turned brown with all the silt from upstream. Once again, the tall Mitchell grass stretched for as far as the eye could see across the western plains.

And somewhere on the Indonesian Coast, three Aussie reprobates had opened a sleazy bar after surviving a cyclone in the Timor Sea.